BUSTED

By Diane Kelly

Cover Design by Lyndsey Lewellen

D1508897

Acknowledgements

So many people helped make this book happen, and my undying gratitude goes out to all of them. To Angela Cavener, Jaci Kenney, Urania Fung, Gay Downs, Charles McMillen, Simon Rex-Lear, and Michella Chapell. Y'all are the best critique partners a writer could ever ask for. Thanks for your input on my work!

And special BIG thanks to biker chick Colene Drace (pictured below) for giving me the inside scoop on motorcycles and the best funny line in the entire book. (I won't repeat it here to avoid spoilers.) You rock!

CHAPTER ONE

READY, AIM, FIRE

He's coming.

The far-off drone of a high-performance motorcycle engine drifted up the two-lane highway on the warm, early September north Texas breeze, the volume and pitch escalating as the bike grew closer. I had no idea who rode the Ninja, but I'd had my eye on him for weeks.

Today I'm going to nail him.

Sitting on my Harley-Davidson, I dug the heels of my knee-high black leather boots into the loose mix of dirt, gravel, and cigarette butts edging the highway. I eased the machine back from the shoulder until I was fully obscured by the faded yellow sign that read "Welcome to Jacksburg—Population 8,476 Friendly People," under which "and a couple of assholes" had been added in thick red marker, probably by last year's senior class from the rival high school in Hockerville.

Dressed head-to-toe in dark colors, I'd be difficult to spot. A couple of overgrown oleander bushes with pink flowers flanked the sign, providing extra cover. The guy would never see me lying in wait, gun in hand. He wouldn't know what hit him until it was too late.

Heh-heh.

I grasped the gun tightly, resting the grip across my right thigh, grown noticeably thicker over the last few months. *Gah. Time to hit the treadmill.* Craning my neck, I peeked between the swaying limbs of the bush, my gaze locked on the small rise a half mile up the road. A few strands of my dark hair pulled free from my long braid and blew in the breeze, tickling my freckled cheeks. Some might refer to the reddish streaks in my hair as highlights, but the coppery tones were unintentional, the result of wind and sun damage. Mother Nature was my hairdresser now. She was much less expensive than the stylist who'd coiffed my hair when I'd lived in Dallas.

The motor grew louder and my breathing ceased, every muscle in my body locked in place. I was a sniper, waiting for my target.

Waiting . . .

Waiting . . .

And there he was.

The golden-yellow and black Ninja ZX-14R popped up over the hill, the noise from its powerful engine now a full-blown primal scream, its rider hunched forward over the sport bike like a jockey over a racehorse to maximize aerodynamics. I raised the gun with two shaky hands, resting my forearms on the platform of my double-D breasts. Leveling the barrel, I sighted, squinting through my tinted goggles, and whispered, "One . . . two . . . three."

I pulled the trigger.

Crud. The display on the ancient radar gun read 729 miles per hour. A Ninja can haul ass, but it wasn't a frickin' rocket. I yanked the gun's power plug out of the bike's cigarette lighter, reinserted it, and tried again. By this time, the Ninja was right on me. I took aim, squeezed the trigger a second time, and checked the readout. 56 mph. Nine miles under the speed limit. *Damn.* Looked like I'd never find out who rode that kick-ass bike.

The motorcycle roared past, kicking up a dusty, warm wind, its rider decked out in a sporty jumpsuit of yellow and black coordinated to match the bike. A quarter mile down the road, the bike turned left onto Main Street, disappearing into the distance and into my dreams.

I sighed and shoved the radar gun back into the plastic sheath mounted on my patrol bike. Maybe I'd be luckier tomorrow and catch the Ninja performing an illegal lane change. I'd pull the rider over, pat the guy down, maybe perform a strip search. One thing would lead to another and—

What the hell am I thinking? Lusting after a guy I'd never met made no sense, but I felt as though I knew him. The bike he rode told me he was cool and adventurous, the fact that he obeyed the speed limit told me he wasn't crazy, and the fact that he passed this way at eight o'clock every weekday morning and again at five o'clock every evening told me he was gainfully employed and responsible. Not to mention that his form-fitting jumpsuit told me he had a tight, lean bod. All points in his favor. *What more could a woman ask for?*

I pulled my phone from the clip on my belt. Might as well listen to some tunes while I was stuck out here on traffic duty. My musical tastes leaned toward classic rock from the 70's and 80's, the songs my parents had grown up with, the ones my mother used to sing along with on the radio during my childhood, the songs my father still listened to today. I dialed up some Bachman Turner Overdrive to keep me company while I waited to catch some unlucky speeder. Yup, I was "Takin' Care of Business". My business was keeping the world, or at least the citizens of Jacksburg, safe.

Yeah, you guessed it. I'm a cop. Knew I'd become one ever since I was a little girl. Back then I'd fixated on Wonder Woman, the only female among the Super Friends, the cartoon airing just after school let out each afternoon. I'd run from the bus stop as fast as my sneakers would take me, charge through the front door, and hurl my backpack aside, jumping onto the couch and sitting enraptured for the next half hour while Wonder Woman and her friends brought hardened criminals to their knees. Mom would bring me a tray loaded with my favorite after-school snack, a root beer float and fresh popcorn she popped the old-fashioned way, in a covered pot on the stove. Wonder Woman was strong, smart, and sexy. She had whatever it took to save the day, no matter what the situation. When I grew up I wanted to be just like her, not like the doctors who lacked the skills and tools to save my mother's life.

Even at six years old I knew superheroes weren't real and I figured becoming a police officer was as close as I could hope to get. Twenty-five years later, I'd long since forgiven the doctors—and my mother—for her early death, and after nearly a decade patrolling the streets of Dallas, I'd experienced enough dangerous situations to last a lifetime. Actually, I'd experienced one dangerous situation too many. It didn't end well. But I'm trying my best to put that behind me. *Easier said than done.*

Traffic detail isn't the most exciting task in small-town law enforcement, but I'm okay with that. It's not like there's much threat in Jacksburg anyway. The worst crime to hit town lately was a couple of ten-year-olds who dared each other to steal Tootsie Rolls from the Grab-N-Go. Besides, what other job would pay a woman to ride around all day on what was essentially a 140-horsepower vibrator?

An older Dodge pickup came over the hill at fifty-two miles per hour, its left turn signal flashing like a Las Vegas casino marquee. *Blink-blink. Blink-blink.* How could the driver fail to notice a flashing indicator light on the dash right in front of him? How could he not hear the sound? *Blink-blink. Blink-blink.* Anyone that oblivious shouldn't be entitled to a driver's license. Unfortunately, there was no point in pursuing the driver. Stupidity wasn't a crime. *But maybe it ought to be.*

Bruce Springsteen's "Born to Run" cued up just as a late-model maroon Ford Taurus came up the road. I raised the radar gun and pulled the trigger.

Busted.

The readout showed the vehicle was doing sixty-nine. Only four miles over the speed limit but that was good enough for me. I hadn't written a single ticket all morning and it was time for me to head back to the office to finish some long-neglected paperwork. Returning to the office without writing at least one ticket would be downright shameful. *Sorry, dude. Over the limit is over the limit.*

I slipped the radar gun back into the sheath, slid my goggles into place, and switched on my flashing lights, pulling onto the highway just after the car drove by. A half mile down the highway, I caught up to it. Red brake lights lit up as the driver spotted me in pursuit. The car slowed, pulled onto the shoulder, and stopped. I rolled to a stop behind it.

I turned down the volume on my phone and squeezed the button on the shoulder-mounted radio that connected me to dispatch. "Hey, Selena. Run a plate for me."

"Sure thing, Marnie," Selena's voice called back over the airwaves. "Whatcha got?"

I lifted my goggles and rattled off the numbers and letters from the license plate. Five seconds later Selena's voice squawked back. "It's a rental."

A rental generally meant one thing. A lost tourist. The few tourists who ventured through Jacksburg had usually set out from the Dallas-Fort Worth metroplex for Southfork Ranch, the setting for the popular 80's television show "Dallas," and had missed a turn somewhere. Jacksburg was situated sixty-three miles northeast of Dallas, between the Big D and nowhere. We weren't near a major interstate and there was nothing in town to draw outsiders in. We had no bed and breakfast, no quaint antique shops, and no historical sites unless you believed the legend that Jesse James had once stopped in town to relieve himself in the outhouse behind the city hall. Being as neither the old city hall nor the outhouse were still in existence, there was no place to hang a plaque.

I steeled myself for the bullshit arguments the driver was sure to make, the same ones I'd heard hundreds of times before from other misdirected tourists, and I had my well-rehearsed, pat responses at the ready:

Driver: "I'm not from around here, so I'm not familiar with these roads."
Me: "All the more reason to slow it down."

— Driver: "I'm not used to driving this rental car."
Me: "All the more reason to take it easy."

Driver: "This is a rental car. It ain't my fault if the speedometer's screwed up."
Me: "Tell it to the judge."

I cut the engine, climbed off my bike, and retrieved my ticket book from the white fiberglass saddle bag on the side of my bike. As I stepped up to the car, I pulled off my right glove and touched my fingertips to the trunk, a standard police procedure that served two purposes. Checking the trunk not only ensured the driver hadn't popped it open to access a hidden stash of weapons, but it also provided physical evidence of the traffic stop, the cop's fingerprints, in the event the driver tried to make a run for it. In many jurisdictions, body and dashboard cameras had rendered the procedure moot, but here in Jacksburg, where the department's budget was too small to provide for modern technologies, we did things old-school style.

An inch of gray fabric stuck out from the closed trunk of the rental car. I reached out and fingered the material. From the look and feel it appeared to be the hem of a pair of men's dress pants. The driver must've been in a hurry when he'd packed his trunk.

The window came down as I stepped up next to the car. The enticing hint of Hugo Boss cologne, the same scent my ex-husband used to wear, wafted from the car. In the window appeared the face of a guy in his early thirties, his light brown hair close cropped, his blue button-down shirt starched and neat. *Not bad. Not bad at all.*

His eyes locked on my chest. *Typical.* There weren't many female motorcycle cops, even fewer with both a .38 on her hip and a couple of 38DD's pulling her uniform tight across her chest. I was built like a cement mixer. Large and round on top, squat and sturdy on the bottom.

I put my hand in front of my breasts and raised my index finger to point at my face. "Up here, buddy."

The guy's deep green eyes, a shade darker than mine, snapped to my face. "Sorry." A pink flush spread up his tensed jaw. "I wasn't expecting a woman."

Ticket book at the ready, I hesitated. This guy was cute and had the decency to blush and apologize for ogling me. He wasn't feeding me some lame excuse. Besides, he smelled good. And the way he was looking at me with those sexy, emerald-colored eyes . . . Maybe I'd let him off with a warning. He was only four miles over the limit, after all. No sense giving Jacksburg the reputation for being a speed trap. With any luck, I could score a date.

It was a desperate move, sure. But, hell, I *was* desperate. It's not that there aren't eligible men in Jacksburg. The problem is they're eligible for social security, food stamps, or parole. It wasn't my fault I had to troll for potential dates among the traffic violators I pulled over on the highway.

Time to find out who this attractive man is. "License, please."

He pulled his wallet from his back pocket, removed his license, and held it out to me with his left hand. He wore no wedding ring. My own ring had been cut in half and refashioned into a pair of hoop earrings last year after my divorce from Chet. I was single again. A free woman. Unattached and available. Of course, those were only fancy ways of saying I'm all alone.

As I took the license from him, he gave me a soft smile that drew my eyes to his equally soft lips. How long had it been since I'd been kissed? It felt like forever. I glanced down at the card in my hand, an Illinois license with a Chicago address. This guy and his green eyes and kissable lips were a long way from home. The name on the license was John William Fulton.

"Stay put, Mr. Fulton. I'll be right back."

I stepped to the safety of the highway shoulder while I called his driver's license in. Through the speakers built into my helmet, I heard Selena mutter a curse in Spanish followed by a banging sound, no doubt her beating on the computer.

"The stupid system's crashed again," she said. "I can't access anything."

First the radar gun and now the computer. The indignities of working for an underfunded police force. Oh, well. The guy was clean cut and didn't give off any strange vibes. Should be safe to send him on his way.

I stepped back up to the window. "It's your lucky day." I shot him a flirtatious wink. "I've decided to let you off with a warning." I handed Fulton's license back to him and his face relaxed into a smile. "Slow down a bit, okay? Speed limit's sixty-five on this stretch of highway."

"Will do. Thanks." He slid the card back into his wallet.

"Where you headed?" I couldn't help but wonder what someone from an exciting place like Chicago would be doing out here in the boonies.

The guy paused for a moment, staring straight through the windshield for a few seconds before turning to look up at me. "Rocky River," he said, naming a town forty miles up the road. "Visiting my aunt."

How sweet. A family man. But I let it drop. As lonely as I was, a long-distance relationship wasn't what I was looking for. "Enjoy your visit."

"Thanks for letting me slide." He flashed another smile.

I grinned back, shamelessly flirting now. "Just this once. Next time you'll be in big trouble, mister."

Fulton waved as he pulled back onto the road. Sighing, I slid my goggles down into place and climbed onto my motorcycle. I made a U-turn, heading back into Jacksburg, scanning the roadways and parking lots for any sign of the Ninja.

Nothing. My mystery man and his bike had vanished.

CHAPTER TWO

CUT TO THE CHASE

As the department's captain, I was a Jill-of-all-trades, serving the dual roles of part-time peace officer, part-time office manager. While I rode back to the office, I mentally ran through my to-do list for the afternoon.

Item one: prepare a memo reminding the officers of the annual Jacksburg Jackrabbit Jamboree scheduled for the end of next month, the weekend before Halloween.

Item two: pay the department's light bill.

Item three: type up my notes from yesterday's investigation of a domestic violence call reported by a neighbor who'd heard squealing and banging coming from the trailer next door. Turned out to be nothing more than a raucous nooner between two consenting septuagenarians lacking the forethought to close the bedroom window.

Through the radio, I heard my fellow officer Andre call in a "ten one-hundred," code for a bladder in distress, meaning he'd be out of pocket for a few minutes. "On second thought," he came back, "make that a ten *two*-hundred."

"Ewww," Selena radioed in reply. "Too much information."

Andre and his identical twin brother, Dante, worked the day

shift with me. Both were relative rookies, having been on the force only three years, but what they lacked in experience they made up for in sheer bulk. They were enormous African-American men with shaved heads and skin the color of coffee with cream. They stood six-foot-three and weighed in at two-sixty apiece. Needless to say, nobody gave them any crap.

I was approaching Easy Eddie's Used Tires, the business marking the outer perimeter of the town's commercial district, when Selena's frantic voice shrieked through the radio. I tweaked the volume button on my phone, Pat Benatar's voice now a mere whisper as she begged her man to *treat her right*.

"Marnie! The computer's back up. I ran Fulton's license. An arrest warrant's been issued for him in Illinois."

"What's the charge?"

"Homicide!"

Whoa. And to think I'd flirted with the guy.

My phone began to play Poison's "Every Rose has its Thorn", one of my all-time favorite love songs but far too mellow for the moment. I slid the device from my belt, held it up so I could read the screen, and quickly scrolled through the songs until I found a more appropriate choice for pursuing a murderer—Blue Oyster Cult's classic "Don't Fear the Reaper". *That's the ticket.*

I returned the phone to my belt and braked fast, leaving a trail of rubber on the asphalt and skidding into a one-eighty, my long braid whipping around to smack me in the face. I cranked my wrist back on the accelerator until it hurt, the front tire of my bike leaving the ground momentarily before gravity took hold and brought it back to earth. The pavement was a gray blur under me as I switched on my lights and siren and sped after Fulton. *I'm only supposed to be writing traffic tickets, dammit, not chasing down killers!*

Selena's voice came through the radio again, calling Dante

and Andre for backup. Only Dante responded, Andre having yet to finish his business in the Tasty Freeze men's room.

I took the short cut that ran behind the library and nursing home. There'd be fewer signal lights, less cross traffic to get in my way and slow me down. I turned down a side street and barreled past the Grab-N-Go. The Ninja was parked at the convenience store's single pump, the rider filling it with gas, his head turning as I sped past. I didn't have time to get a good look at him, noting only that he had dark hair. He, on the other hand, would have a full view of my backside as I drove by. I hoped the navy-blue police-issue trousers didn't make my butt look big. *Oh, who am I kidding?* I only hoped they didn't make my butt look any bigger than it actually was.

As I sped past the buildings and turned onto the highway, I tried to determine how far ahead Fulton would be, concocting an elaborate word problem in my head: *If a murderer with a sexy smile heads northeast for four minutes at sixty-nine miles per hour while a desperately lonely motorcycle cop with thick thighs pursues the creep at one-hundred and sixteen miles per hour, when will the officer overtake the killer?*

Let's see. Sixty-nine times four is . . . hell, who knows? I always stunk at math.

My heart raced as fast as my bike. I passed a highway mile marker and hollered my location into the mic, my voice barely audible over the wail of my siren. "Dante! Where you at?"

"Turning from Main onto the highway."

Dante was three miles, and at least two minutes, behind me. In a situation like this, two minutes could be critical. *Deadly* critical.

Seconds later I rounded a bend and spotted the sedan a half mile ahead. I gained on Fulton for several seconds, then the distance between us stabilized as Fulton noticed me in pursuit and floored the gas pedal.

"We've got a runner!" I shouted into the mic. "Call the county!"

Another mile and this guy would leave the city limits of Jacksburg. Though an officer in hot pursuit could continue a chase into another jurisdiction, this situation clearly called for backup. Ruger County Sheriff Donald Dooley would be thrilled to have us chase a wanted murderer into his hands. An easy catch, an easy way to increase his department's arrest statistics.

The rental car topped out. My bike was faster and more maneuverable and in seconds I was on his tail. *Heh-heh.* Okay, I admit it. A small part of me still enjoyed taking risks, the thrill of the chase, a good bust.

Dante's voice came through the helmet's speakers. "Got you in sight, Captain."

I checked my side mirror and saw Dante's lights flashing in the distance behind me. The 2002 Crown Victoria had logged over nine-hundred thousand miles on patrol and was on its third engine, but it could still haul ass. In front of me, the sedan suddenly braked and pulled a hard left down a narrow county road flanked by cow pastures and hayfields. Fulton must've known we'd radio backup and probably figured a roadblock was set for him on the highway ahead. This guy was thinking like a professional criminal. *I hate it when they do that.*

I took the corner behind Fulton. Dante lost ground at the turn, but the black and white cruiser soon caught up, too. A half mile down the road we passed a metal sign marking the end of the Jacksburg city limits, the end of our jurisdiction.

The poorly maintained road was pocked with potholes and bisected by cattle guards that caused my bike to shake roughly between my legs when I crossed them. Not an entirely unpleasant feeling, truth be told. If I didn't get a date soon, I might have to come back and drive the road again.

Given the unfavorable driving conditions, the sedan was forced to slow down. Fulton had no idea what lay ahead of him. But I did. I chuckled into my headset as the road narrowed and the asphalt gave way to dirt. *Welcome to the country, city boy.*

An instant later, Fulton found himself hood-deep in hay in the middle of an open field. I stopped at the edge of the tall grass and watched as he careened and bounced across the uneven ground, leaving a wake of flattened hay, failing to notice the barbed wire fence looming ahead of him.

CRACK! Several of the weathered wooden fence supports splintered in two as the car plowed through the barbed wire. The strands of rusty metal closed around the car like a spiked net, the barbs scratching the paint and cutting into the tires. In seconds, all four tires were hopelessly flat. Fulton rolled another hundred feet on his rims before the car came to a stop.

I cut my engine and quickly climbed off my bike, crouching down next to it, keeping an eye trained on the sedan in the distance. I was out of range for most handguns, thankfully, but it couldn't hurt to play it safe. I pulled off my glove and removed my gun from the holster, hoping like hell I wouldn't have to use the thing. I'd had to fire my weapon only once in my nine years as a cop, but that one time had put an end to a life. It had nearly put an end to my career and my sanity, too.

Dante pulled his squad car up next to my bike, the Billy Graham bobble-head doll on his dash nodding frantically as the car lurched to a stop. He climbed out and crouched down next to me. With his brown head shaved bald, large round eyes, and full cheeks, he resembled a macho version of Mr. Potato Head. He eyed Fulton's vehicle, hopelessly stuck in the field, entangled in barbed wire. "What a dumb ass."

"Hertz will be none too happy with what he's done to their rental car." Holding my gun down at my side, I reached up with my free hand and grabbed the microphone for the public address system mounted on my bike. I squeezed the talk button. "Fulton! Come out of the car with your hands in the air."

Dante took the mic from me. "Yo-yo-yo. Wave your hands in the air like you just don't care." Dante had aspired to be a rap artist, but having grown up a hundred miles north in rural Oklahoma had failed to provide the proper environment to produce a successful hip-hop singer. Nobody wanted to hear bass thumping to a rhyme about baling hay or tipping cows. He'd had to settle for leading the choir at First Baptist Church.

"Cut the crap." I grabbed the mic back out of Dante's hand.

KAPOW! The retort of a high-powered rifle reached our ears as a bullet sliced through the air mere inches above us. We dived to the ground, scrambling frantically on our elbows and knees until we were behind the squad car.

"We're taking fire!" I hollered into my shoulder radio. I looked down at the wide metal bracelets surrounding my wrists, cheap replicas of those worn by Wonder Woman. What I wouldn't have given for a real pair of bullet-repelling bracelets about then. The only thing these were good for was hiding the deep, jagged scars on my wrist.

Selena said something back but we were nearly out of radio range so all we heard was "--opter . . . should be . . . county . . ."

"What?" I yelled back. Static was my only reply. *Dammit!*

I really wished Fulton hadn't shot at us because that meant we'd likely have to shoot back. I wasn't sure I could do that. Horrifying memories threatened to rush into my head, but I fought them back, forcing myself to focus on the sedan in the field. *Wonder Woman never let anything fluster her. Neither would I.*

A couple of bullets pinged off the hood of the cruiser. A third took out the plastic covering on the roof-mounted light bar, shards of red and blue plastic raining down on us.

"Aw, hell." To save money, I'd upped the deductible on the department's automobile insurance. The budget was already stretched thin and now, thanks to Fulton, I'd have to find room in it for a new light bar.

Dante curled up by the back tire. "Boy howdy, he's a good shot." His voice was calm, but the thick mustache of sweat he wore told me he was as freaked out as I was. We'd both assumed Fulton could be armed, but neither of us had expected such accuracy at this distance.

We continued to cower for a couple of long minutes when finally, from off to our right, came the *whup-whup-whup* of the county helicopter.

"It's about time you got here!" Dante shouted to the sky.

Seconds later, the sheriff's department S.W.A.T. team pulled up next to our cruiser in their boxy armored truck. The double doors on the back flew open and out leapt four male officers dressed in full riot gear, helmets on their heads and shields and guns at the ready. They bent low and took off running into the tall grass, two going in one direction, two in the other, surrounding the field. A fifth remained in the truck, crouched next to the small bulletproof glass window with the latest high-tech radio in his hand to coordinate their tactical operations. I've never had penis envy, but I'd kill for their equipment.

Tentatively, Dante and I peeked over the trunk of his cruiser. The sheriff's department chopper came in low, hovering at the far edge of the hayfield, the swift air from the blades kicking the hay into a swaying frenzy and sending up a spray of dirt and bugs. A marksman with a rifle leaned out the passenger side, testing the limits of his seat belt, taking aim at Fulton's car. Fulton opened the door and climbed out, throwing his hands in the air in surrender. I heaved a breath of relief. Looked like there'd be a quick end to this standoff, thank goodness.

Sheriff Dooley's voice came from the chopper's speaker.

"Turn around and put your hands on the roof of the car."

Fulton began to turn toward the car, hands still in the air, when all of the sudden he vanished from view, dropping out of sight into the tall grass.

"Shit." Dante exhaled sharply. "That can't be good."

The chopper flew in ever-widening circles over the field, the sharpshooter leaning forward in his seat, scanning the field, trying to get a fix on his target hidden somewhere in the tall, swaying grass. As the helicopter edged closer in the sky, we saw Sheriff Dooley's pasty face peek out timidly between the sniper and the pilot, his eyes wide. All three heads swiveled left and right, surveying the field, searching for Fulton.

I edged forward in a crouch and looked around the front bumper of the cruiser. "Fulton could be anywhere."

Dante looked at me. "What should we do?"

Chances were the guy was making a run for it and had headed farther out into the field. "Let's go. The sheriff's department can take it from here."

As the chopper swung out across the countryside to search for Fulton, Dante and I edged along the cruiser to the passenger side door, keeping our heads low, just in case. I stuck my gun back in the holster, yanked the door open and crawled onto the front seat.

"Gah!" I found myself face to face with Fulton, who was sneaking in the driver's side. There was no time to think. In my position I couldn't reach my weapons, so I did the only thing I could—use myself as a human battering ram. Face down, I lunged forward with all my might, head butting him full force with the top of my hard, white helmet. There was a sick *crunch* followed by a yowl of pain. Fulton fell backwards out the open driver's door, covering his nose with both hands, blood gushing between his fingers.

Dante may be big but he was also fast. In a heartbeat he ran around the car, tackled Fulton, and rolled him onto his stomach on the ground. Dante attempted to cuff the man's wrists, but Fulton writhed wildly under the former high school linebacker, trying to break free from the officer's grip. Dante shoved Fulton's bloody face into the dirt. "Don't move, cracker!"

Dante's language didn't exactly comply with police protocol, but I let it slide. I'd been known to say inappropriate things in the heat of the moment, too, once calling an obese drug-dealing pimp an "inbred lard ass" when he spat a gooey loogie onto the floor of my squad car. He'd retorted with "It takes one to know one, fatty-fatty two-by-four." *Real mature, both of us.* None of that exchange went into my written report.

Dante put a knee on Fulton's spine and yanked his arms up behind him. Immobilized, the man finally gave up the fight. I edged backwards off the seat and stood next to the cruiser, waving both arms over my head to signal the sheriff and hollering to the S.W.A.T. officer in the nearby truck that we'd nabbed Fulton.

The chopper soared in and set down in the field nearby. Sheriff Dooley jumped from the helicopter, stomping through the hay toward us, his face purple with rage under his gray military-style buzz cut. Dooley waved his nightstick at me and Dante. "What the hell do you two think you're doing? You're out of your jurisdiction. I told your girl we'd handle this."

"We didn't get the message," I said. "We're out of radio range."

I could've argued with the sheriff. After all, we'd been in pursuit and had every right to chase the guy down and haul him in. But given that our department lacked the funds to have Fulton's broken nose seen to or to provide him room and board until the state of Illinois could prepare extradition papers, we'd have to let the sheriff's department have him. They'd get the glory, but they'd also get the paperwork and the bills.

The S.W.A.T. officers tromped back through the hay, shoulders slumped, dragging their shields, disappointed they hadn't gotten to kick some ass. Dooley stepped over to Fulton and hauled him up by one arm. Dirt was stuck to the blood on Fulton's face, a dazed ant ambling across his chin. *Yuck.* I had no thoughts of kissing him now.

Dooley shoved Fulton forward across the hood of Dante's cruiser, playing tough guy now that Fulton was in cuffs. A brown and tan sheriff's department patrol car pulled up behind Dante's cruiser, followed by a county crime scene van. A deputy stepped out of the cruiser and helped Dooley wrangle Fulton into the backseat. A man and a woman dressed in matching khaki pants and brown knit shirts climbed out of the van. The male tech set off trotting in a wide circle around the field, stringing a perimeter of yellow crime scene tape between the remaining fence posts. The female tech pulled an orange plastic toolbox from the back of the van, ducked under the tape, and headed into the field toward Fulton's rental car. *Good luck finding bullet casings in all that hay.*

Without another word to us, the sheriff shoved Fulton into the back seat of the county cruiser and climbed into the front passenger seat. The deputy drove them away. The S.W.A.T. truck followed behind them.

Dante brushed shards of red and blue plastic off the roof of his car. "That son-of-a-bitch did a number on my light bar."

I reached up and put a sympathetic hand on Dante's beefy shoulder. "Hate to tell you, but there's no money in this month's budget to cover the deductible. We'll have to sit on the repairs for a bit."

Dante sighed.

I gave his shoulder a squeeze. "Look on the bright side. You've still got one working light and at least he didn't shoot out your siren. You would've had to stick your head out the window and yell 'woo-woo-woo.'"

Dante leaned in through the open passenger door and grabbed an individually wrapped wet wipe from the glove box, holding it out to me. He pointed to my helmet. "Clean up on aisle five."

I removed my helmet and took a look. The top bore a smear of Fulton's blood. *Ick.* I swiped at the blood with the cloth and dropped the soiled wipe into a trash bag in the cruiser. Dante climbed back into the patrol car while I snapped my helmet on, climbed onto my bike, and eased myself around to return to Jacksburg.

Holy crap. There he is!

The Ninja sat fifty yards away at the edge of the dirt road, its rider watching us. My heart rate, which had only just returned to normal, skyrocketed again. I wondered how long he'd been there, what he'd seen, what he'd heard. The world stood still as I stared back at him.

His tinted faceplate was down so I couldn't make out his features. He raised a black-gloved hand and gave me a thumbs-up sign followed by a clenched fist in the air, the universal sign of victory. I sat there, dumbstruck, as he started his engine, maneuvered in a half-circle, and took off down the road.

"Who's that?" Dante called from the open window of his car.

"I have no idea." My eyes followed the bike for the second time that day as it disappeared out of sight. If I hadn't been caught off guard I could've taken down the license plate and run it through the Texas Crime Information Center system, better known as TCIC. The TCIC not only provided rap sheets and details on outstanding warrants, but the system also contained motor vehicle and driver's license records. *Mental note: Next time you see the guy, take down his plate.* Then I could determine the identity of my leather-clad man of mystery.

Dante drove past me and I followed him up the country road, passing a herd of humpbacked white Brahmas standing in a field. They mindlessly chewed their cuds, looking bored out of their skulls, as if waiting for something interesting to happen in their lives. I hadn't yet developed a hump, but I could definitely relate to their boredom. Other than chasing Fulton, there hadn't been much excitement in my life lately. On the bright side, it was highly unlikely I'd end up like the cows, slathered in barbecue sauce and devoured. Then again, with the right guy, being slathered in barbecue sauce and devoured could be fun.

CHAPTER THREE

JUST ANOTHER DAY AT THE OFFICE

Once we were back in town, Dante sounded his horn, stuck a hand out his window to wave goodbye to me, and turned east down Seventh Street to patrol. I beeped twice in reply and continued down Main.

As the excess adrenaline processed through my body, my teeth chattered so hard it felt as though they'd shatter and my body shook so violently I had to fight to keep my bike under control. *This is the payback for an exciting bust.* I pulled off the road and into the city park, stopping by a murky pond with a half dozen ducks and an empty Sunbeam Bread wrapper floating on top. In the middle of the pond gurgled an umbrella-shaped fountain. The effect was quaint and charming despite the fact that the actual purpose of the fountain was to keep the water circulating so it wouldn't stagnate.

I climbed off my motorcycle and sat down for a few minutes on the grass next to the pond. Wrapping my arms around my knees, I closed my eyes and listened to the soothing babble of the water, rocking involuntarily as if my inner mother were trying to comfort my inner child. I wished I had someone I could talk to, but I didn't. Dad would worry if he knew how my job got to me like this at times, and my best friend Savannah would tell me to quit trying to save the world and take a teller job with her at the credit union. I'd go nuts if I was stuck in a chair counting bills all day, a fake smile plastered on my face for the customers. But I wasn't sure I still had what it took to be an effective police officer, either. *What if things had gone worse back at the pasture? What if push had come to shove and I'd had to shoot Fulton? Could I do it?*

Wonder Woman's actions were always quick and decisive. She never second-guessed herself, never looked back. *I shouldn't either.*

I opened my eyes to discover the ducks standing at my feet, staring at me. "Sorry, guys. I don't have anything to feed you." One of them emitted an irritated *quack* before they waddled away and plunked back into the pond. After a few moments, my nerves had calmed a bit and I climbed back on my bike. Doubts or no doubts, there was paperwork to be done.

As I waited to pull out of the parking lot onto Main, a green John Deere tractor rattled slowly past. Mere inches behind the tractor followed a Mitsubishi Eclipse Spyder convertible, top down. The car was dark red. No, make that *blood* red. I'd never seen the car or the thin, twentyish blonde at the wheel before. *Definitely not a local.*

I pulled onto the road behind her. She blasted her horn impatiently and whipped twice into the left lane to try to pass the tractor, thwarted both times by oncoming traffic. The tractor eventually turned off the road and she barreled ahead, never once noticing the cop on her tail. I should have followed her and issued her a ticket, but after the morning's events I simply didn't have the energy. She'd be slowed soon enough by the stoplight ahead.

A deep male voice came over the radio. "Sounds like I missed all the fun." Andre and Dante were not only identical twins, but they also had identical voices. Since Dante had been with me at Fulton's bust, it had to be Andre speaking.

I squeezed the talk button on my shoulder mic. "You picked a fine time to take a potty break."

"A dude's gotta go when a dude's gotta go."

No smart-ass response from Dante. *Hmm.* I had a theory that

Dante and Andre might actually be one person cleverly posing as a set of identical twins in order to collect two paychecks. They were utterly indistinguishable, and in my year on the force I couldn't recall a single time in which I'd seen the two of them in the same place at the same time. Although they allegedly shared an apartment, they never rode to work or picked up their paychecks together. They claimed they'd been raised in Ardmore, Oklahoma, moving here after they'd interviewed—separately, of course—with Chief Moreno, so nobody in town could vouch for them, either. My theory would be put to the test next month. I'd scheduled both of them to work the same shift at the Jackrabbit Jamboree.

I turned into the station's parking lot, pulling my bike under the red metal overhang out front. Our headquarters were situated in a building that had once served as a Dairy Queen. The former police station burned down four years ago after an officer failed to search the pockets of a drunk driver he'd hauled in. Apparently a lit cigarette, an old mattress, and one-hundred-proof puke is all it takes to start a four-alarm fire. The building had been underinsured, and the only available piece of real estate in the department's price range was the rundown DQ building which had sat vacant for years after the building inspector closed it down for not meeting the safety code. Ironically, municipal government buildings were exempt from complying with local building ordinances. *Go figure.*

Surprisingly, the property functioned quite well as a police station. With a cheap metal-framed bunk bed, the freezer served just fine as a holding cell. The place had his and her bathrooms, plus a small office at the back of the kitchen for Chief Moreno. Each officer staked a claim to one of the ten scarred red Formica booths, which served as spacious desks. Selena sat on a stool behind the food service counter working dispatch on an outdated two-line phone, using the cash register to make change for those who came in to pay their traffic fines. We even fired up the grill occasionally to fry a bologna sandwich for ourselves or the rare prisoner we brought in. All in all, it wasn't a bad setup. The only downside was the occasional out-of-towner who pulled up to the drive-thru window hoping to score a dipped-top cone, driving away disappointed.

When I walked in, Selena looked up from the television set tuned to *The Price is Right*. Selena was nineteen and undeniably cute, with a round, brown-sugar face framed by dark hair cut in a short, sassy flip. A trio of tiny dark moles accented the curve of her left cheek like chips in a chocolate chip cookie and, like a home-baked cookie, she was sweet and wholesome.

She waved me over and patted the extra stool next to her. "You're just in time for the Showcase Showdown."

I stepped around the counter to watch the show with her. Without benefit of cable, the reception was fuzzy, but we could make out most of the details. By my best estimate, the ski boat, the trip to Acapulco, and the lifetime supply of suntan lotion should be worth at least thirty grand. The pimply-faced college kid on screen bid only ten thousand, having no clue how much things cost in the real world, his room and board no doubt provided by mom and dad. The granny who bid on the second showcase, which included a big-screen high-definition television and a five-piece living room set, won hands down and ran to give Drew Carey a kiss. He drew back in horror when the wrinkled woman tried to slip him some tongue.

"Way to go, granny." I stood and headed back into the kitchen, pouring myself a mug of coffee and adding hazelnut creamer from the industrial fridge. Gourmet coffee was the one aspect of big city life I missed. The city could keep its traffic, its crowds, its frantic pace—it could even keep my ex-husband—but I'd kill for a big-city coffee bar. Well, that and a good Italian restaurant. And somewhere to go for entertainment on a Friday night. *Okay, okay, so big-city life has some good points.* But still, I belonged here in Jacksburg.

I took a sip of warm, yummy coffee and headed to my booth. A cardboard copy paper box served as my inbox, its lid holding my outgoing documents. Around here, we made no pretense at keeping up appearances, opting instead for frugal functionality. I rifled through my inbox until I found the electric bill. Using a pocket calculator, I balanced the department's checkbook, pleased to find we could pay the bill and have a whopping eight dollars and thirty-two cents to spare until the city treasurer advanced our next allotment.

The remaining stack of papers consisted primarily of printouts sent by other police departments with photos of their most wanted. At the bottom was a flyer from the Chicago PD bearing Fulton's face and personal information, warning that he'd last been spotted heading south through Kansas and might be heading our way. *Mental note: From now on check the inbox each morning BEFORE heading out on patrol.*

Although the festival was still a full eight weeks away, the coordinator for the Jackrabbit Jamboree had already dropped off a copy of the parade route and lineup, a map of the festival grounds, and an event schedule. I scanned the listings. There I was. *Wonder Woman Performs Motorcycle Stunts.* My performance was scheduled for 7:00, the first in the night's entertainment lineup, right before Gretchen the Yodeling Doberman. *Good.* I'd seen Gretchen perform. She'd be a tough act to follow.

The deep rumble of an engine sounded out front as a truck pulled into the lot. A few seconds later, the bell on the front door tinkled and in walked Eric, the blond, broad-shouldered delivery guy who couriered packages from the distribution center in Dallas out to Jacksburg, Hockerville, and other neighboring towns. In one arm he carried a large box bearing the logo of an office supply store. Even with shipping charges tacked on it was cheaper to order our office supplies online and have them delivered rather than buy them at the overpriced store in Hockerville.

Selena looked up at Eric with long-lashed doe eyes. "Hey, Eric. Looks like you've got a big package for us today."

Eric cocked his head and raised a thick brow. "You should see my other package. It's *huge*."

Selena giggled as she took the box from him. "You're so naughty."

Oh, to be nineteen again. So full of hope. So full of dreams. So full of crap.

Eric handed Selena his handheld tracking device. Selena signed for the delivery, waving the stylus back and forth just out of reach when Eric attempted to retrieve it from her.

"Tease." Eric grabbed her wrist gently with one hand and the pen with the other. He gave me a quick nod, turned, and headed out the door.

"See ya later!" Selena called after him.

Eric climbed into his truck and rumbled off to continue his deliveries. Selena watched him go, then swiveled on her stool to face me. "Eric's been sending me signals for weeks but hasn't asked me out. Think I should invite him to the Jackrabbit Jamboree?"

I came from the traditional school of dating and held to the belief that the man should do the pursuing, the woman flirting just enough to keep the guy guessing, never letting on whether she was really interested. In other words, toying with him. "Guys like a conquest. Make him come after you."

Selena snorted. "How's that strategy working for you?"

Okay, so I hadn't had a single date since I'd moved back to my hometown after my divorce last year. I'd needed some time to sort out my feelings, get over Chet, work through some major issues that Fate—the sick, twisted bitch—had thrown at me. I wasn't sure whether I'd worked through them yet. *Hell, I'm not sure I'll ever work through them.*

I stuck out my tongue at Selena by way of answer. Before resuming my administrative work, I spent a few minutes perusing the accessories in the latest Harley-Davidson catalog that had come in yesterday's mail, admiring a shiny chrome exhaust pipe. Biker chick bling. I picked up a pen and circled the pipes. If I scrimped, I might be able to buy them for myself come Christmas.

Thinking about my motorcycle brought my thoughts back to the Ninja. I had to find out who rode that bike. *But how?* Then it dawned on me. I didn't need his license plate number. I could run a computer search by vehicle make and model and track down the Ninja and its owner. *Duh. Why hadn't I thought of this before?* Good thing I'd never gone for detective when I worked with Dallas PD. My investigation skills sucked. With Jacksburg's low crime rate, they also suffered from lack of use.

I maneuvered my computer mouse and clicked on the link to the vehicle registration records. I typed in the make and model. A number of Ninja ZX-14R's popped up, but none with an address in the area. *Hmm.* The bike appeared to be new, so maybe the registration paperwork was sitting on a desk at TXDOT waiting to be entered into the system. *Mental note: Run the search again in a couple of days.* Hopefully the records would be updated by then.

An hour later, the bell on the front door tinkled again and Chief Moreno walked into the station, a lit Marlboro dangling from his lips. *Uh-oh.* The chief was a small guy, only an inch taller than my five-feet-five-inches, but his sharp wit and quick reflexes had made him a force to be reckoned with when he'd been on patrol. Like Selena, Moreno had naturally brown skin. With deep lines crossing his forehead, a slight under-bite, and salt-and-pepper stubble, he resembled an aged pug. He still wore his uniform every day even though he no longer patrolled the city. Instead, he spent most of his time on what he called "public relations" but which basically amounted to hanging out at the mayor's office, reading the newspaper, playing chess, and debating politics with his buddy.

I took a deep breath, partly to ready myself for the dressing down Chief Moreno surely had in store for me, partly to avoid breathing in smoke.

"Marnie!" The chief stepped up to my booth and skewered me with a pointed look, his forehead furrowed into deep, angry lines. "What'n the hell were you thinking? You could've got yourself killed. I told you to let the men handle the dangerous work." Though he didn't actively engage in police work anymore, Chief Moreno carried a radio and no doubt had heard our exchange with Selena.

His words were unapologetically sexist, but his concern was completely sincere. "Sorry, Chief."

He took a drag and pointed his cigarette at me, snorting smoke out his nose. "Sorry's not good enough. I'd never forgive myself if something happened to you, Marnie. Next time you let Dante and Andre take care of things, hear me?"

"Yes, sir." I ducked my head and lowered my eyes in a disingenuous gesture of shame and submission, the same way I had back in high school when Dad caught me and Savannah sharing a screw-top bottle of Boone's Farm strawberry wine.

The chief's face softened. "All righty then." With no ashtray at hand, he ground his cigarette out on the bottom of his shoe, tossed the butt into the trash, and took a seat opposite me. He pulled a package of Red Vines out of his breast pocket and held it out to me.

I shook my head. "No, thanks."

"Suit yourself." He shook a stick out of the package and ripped a bite off with his teeth. Amazing the guy hadn't yet died from lung disease or diabetes given he subsisted on a diet of tobacco and processed sugar. "By the way, the deputies found a body in Fulton's trunk."

The gray dress pants sticking out of the trunk. Oh, God, I'd fingered the hem! I shuddered involuntarily.

"Fulton's not talking," the chief added, "but my guess is he was looking for an out-of-the-way place to dispose of the body."

Jacksburg didn't have much going for it, but the abundance of undeveloped land surrounding the town would make it a convenient place to unload a corpse. Maybe our Chamber of Commerce could seize on that as a marketing slogan--Jacksburg,

Texas: A Great Place to Dump a Body.

CHAPTER FOUR

PICKUPS AND DELIVERIES

The chief left and I set back to work. I'd hoped to get out on the highway again that afternoon to keep an eye out for the Ninja, but at four o'clock Andre radioed for help bringing in Lucas Glick on yet another drunk and disorderly. Dante was allegedly tied up directing traffic around a disabled car by the high school.

I grabbed my helmet and goggles and headed out to my Harley, mentally cursing Lucas for keeping me from my plans. Glick was a hard-core redneck who'd committed so many misdemeanors you'd think we were giving out green stamps with each arrest. Drunk and disorderly, destruction of property, public urination. You name it, he'd done it. Unfortunately, despite the fact that Texas led the nation in executions, the state's prisons were severely overcrowded and judges were hesitant to give hard time to those committing minor, non-violent crimes, even if they were repeat offenders. Lucas had spent many a night in our freezer sleeping off a six pack or two, entirely unaware he was being punished. Before we released him, we made him take out the trash, scrub the toilets, and mop the floor as a penance. That's justice in Jacksburg.

Truth be told, like most of the girls in our class, I'd had a huge crush on Lucas back in high school. I'd been intrigued by his shaggy hair, his rebellious swagger, and the mischievous glint in his eye. To a sixteen-year-old girl, those bad-boy traits were exciting. Now, fifteen years later, his hair looked stringy and unkempt, his swagger was more drunken than rebellious, and the mischievous glint in his eye had evolved into an enraged, hate-filled glare. Lucas was hardly a delight when he was sober and he was a mean, nasty drunk. I wasn't looking forward to facing him this afternoon, especially when I'd hoped to play hide-and-seek with the Ninja.

I climbed on the motorcycle and headed down Main, George Thorogood and the Destroyers' "Bad to the Bone" playing on my phone, the perfect song to accompany an arrest of Jacksburg's resident screw-up. As I turned onto Renfro Street, a curb-less road lined with cockeyed clapboard houses a half century old, I noticed Eric's delivery truck parked in front of the old Parker place. The once-white house had stood vacant since Roy Parker, the man who'd owned it, passed away in his sleep four years ago. He might still be lying dead in his bed if Chief Moreno hadn't noticed the newspapers accumulating in the yard and stopped by to check on him. There's something to be said for living in a place where people look out for each other.

Parker's kids had long since moved off and had no use for the rundown house, so they'd put the home up for sale. Given that the house needed tens of thousands of dollars of work to be habitable, there were no takers. Not even the county wanted the house, refusing to foreclose despite the fact that property taxes hadn't been paid on the shack in more than two decades. The rusty FOR SALE sign sat forlornly in the weedy yard, leaning back against a misshapen cedar as if it had given up all hope of attracting a buyer.

A yellow school bus came up Renfro from the opposite direction and stopped across the street from Eric's truck. The red stop sign swung out and the lights flashed. I slowed to a stop behind the truck, put my feet down on each side of my bike to balance myself, and waited.

A gaggle of teenaged girls climbed off the bus, giggling and gossiping as they started up the street. They glanced over at Eric, sitting in his truck, and broke into fresh giggles. But, heck, who could blame them? I'd have found him attractive, too, if I were still that age.

Eric hopped out of his truck in front of me, a box tucked under his arm, and made his way up to the house, taking the sagging steps up to the porch two at a time. Eric placed the box on the stoop, inputting data into his tracking device as he stepped back to his truck.

This is odd. Who would send a package to a vacant house? Surely either Eric or the person who sent the package had the wrong address. But with Andre holding Lucas Glick, there was no time to stop and ask questions. *Mental note: Stop back and check on the package once Glick's in the klink.*

The air brakes hissed as the bus driver released them and headed on past me to continue his rounds. I wove around Eric's truck and drove on to the Watering Hole, the town's only bar, a honky-tonk housed in a metal pre-fab building where local bands played classic country and rock standards in exchange for all the beer they could drink, sometimes forgetting the lyrics late in the evening when they'd paid themselves too generously.

Typical for this time of day, only a handful of cars were in the parking lot. I parked next to Andre's cruiser and pulled off my helmet, hooking it onto the clip on my bike. Next to the cruiser sat Glick's secondhand tank truck, the bright orange cab bearing a trim of rust and a fair share of marble-sized dings courtesy of some long-forgotten hailstorm. A 1,500-gallon hard plastic tank was mounted behind the cab. Both the tank and the back wheels bore splatters of dried mud. Lucas had made no attempt to keep the truck clean, but when your job was servicing septic systems it didn't much matter, I guess.

I walked into the bar and paused inside the double doors to let my eyes adjust from the bright sunshine to the dark haze inside the bar. The smoke of a dozen or so cigarettes clouded the low-ceilinged interior and mixed with the odors of beer, sweat, and disinfectant.

Andre had Lucas's lanky body bent over one of the bar's four pool tables, his stubbly cheek pressed to the green felt. Even from across the room it was obvious Lucas was shit-faced. His bloodshot eyes were at half mast, his face slack. His faded blue T-shirt was half-in, half-out of the waistband of his jeans, the legs of his jeans half-in, half-out of his scuffed brown boots.

The stocky bartender raised his meaty hands in innocence as I made my way past. "I only served him two beers, I swear."

"Don't doubt ya." The guy'd had more than his share of trouble with Lucas and tried to discourage Glick from frequenting the place by refusing to serve him more than a drink or two. But with no other bar in town, Lucas kept coming back. More than likely, Lucas had a flask of whiskey hidden in his boot and had snuck swallows when the bartender's back was turned.

I stepped up to the pool table, noticing a stocky, dark-haired man wearing boots, jeans, and a western shirt with rolled-up sleeves standing off to the side. He held a piece of broken pool cue in each hand as if it were his turn at show-and-tell. His weathered face bore a thoroughly pissed-off scowl, his bottom lip protruding with a tell-tale bulge of Skoal chewing tobacco.

"See what that dumb fuck did? This here was a custom cue stick. Cost me six hundred bucks." The man set one of the pieces down and picked up a clear plastic cup, using it as a spittoon. *Yuck.*

I took off my gloves and pulled a notepad and ballpoint pen out of my pocket to take notes for my report. "Did Glick assault you?"

The guy shook his head. "Nah, he didn't touch me. Just grabbed my cue stick and cracked it over his thigh after I beat him in a game of eight ball."

For all the times we'd dragged Lucas in on one charge or another, I couldn't recall a single incident where he'd hit someone, though he'd taken many punches himself. I jotted down the man's name and contact information on my pad. "You want to file charges?"

"I ain't interested in spending time in court. I just want my cue paid for."

I radioed Selena and instructed her to contact my best friend, Savannah, a teller at the credit union where everyone in town banked. Savannah could issue the man full payment from Glick's account. Sure, it violated banking regulations and exceeded my legal authority as a cop, but Glick would know better than to protest. He may be an asshole, but he wasn't a total idiot. It was for his own benefit.

Lucas squirmed on the table, trying to free himself from Andre's grasp. "Stinkin' pig." His whiskey-scented words were muffled by Andre's hand, held firmly to his face. Lucas continued to struggle, but with Andre's hulky body positioned across his back, he couldn't lift himself off the table. His brows drew together. He was probably trying to think up another insult for the officer restraining him. You might expect a redneck like him to come back with a racial slur, but we citizens of Jacksburg weren't so much divided by the color of our skin as we are united by the color of our collars—all blue.

Apparently unable to come up with further insults for Andre, Lucas turned his one visible bloodshot eye on me. "Fat sow."

Andre jerked Glick's arm up behind him. "That's no way to talk to a lady."

"Especially one with pepper spray on her belt." If I'd had a Taser, I would've given Glick a few volts to the balls about then. I crossed my arms over my chest, partly in indignation, partly because Glick was ogling my breasts even as he verbally abused me.

It wasn't the first time Lucas had talked nasty to me. The first time was a spring night our senior year of high school as we lay on a mildewed sleeping bag in the woods behind the baseball fields, Glick wrangling with the hooks on my industrial-strength bra strap, whispering naughty nothings in my ear. It had been our first and only date. He'd never asked me out again, even though I let him get to second base. The shame of it still smoldered inside me.

But for now, the shame was replaced with a flare of anger. *Fat sow.* How dare a loser like him talk to me that way? For some reason, Glick hurling insults at me was more offensive and hurtful than Fulton shooting bullets at me. But I wasn't about to let this jerk know he'd got to me.

I bent down to look Lucas in the eye. "I'm not fat. I'm sturdy." I stood and tossed my head defiantly.

Andre put his mouth close to Glick's ear. "Listen up, Glick. I'm going to get off you and you better walk straight to my car and get your ass in the backseat without causing any more problems or you may not live to regret it. Got that?"

Glick didn't answer, but at least he'd stopped squirming. Andre nodded to me and I pulled my cuffs off my belt, holding them at the ready. Andre warily eased himself off Lucas and yanked his hands up behind him. I quickly snapped my cuffs onto Glick's wrists.

Lucas raised himself from the pool table and stood, swaying. Andre took hold of Glick's upper arm to guide him, but Lucas twisted, wrenching out of the officer's grip. He dropped to his knees and fell onto his side on the wood floor, running with his legs in a circle like a crazed break dancer.

Andre and I stepped safely aside to wait until Glick wore himself out. Andre looked down at the spinning man at our feet. "Can you believe this moron?"

"Unfortunately, this behavior doesn't surprise me at all."

Lucas continued to spin until he grew dizzy and ended up kicking the leg of a small table and knocking it over onto himself. The hard edge of the table smacked him squarely across the bridge of his nose. "Shit!"

I cringed. "That had to hurt."

Andre and I pulled the table off Lucas and yanked him to his feet, dragging him out to the squad car and shoving him into the back. I climbed in the passenger side to ride back to the station with Andre. Glick had been known to pull stunts in the backseat of the cruiser, once pulling down his pants and mooning the mayor's wife, who'd stopped next to the patrol car at a traffic light. We'd always cuffed him after that. Today, my eyes would be on him, making sure he behaved himself.

Andre backed out of the parking spot and headed onto the highway. I glanced back at Lucas, noting a purple-black circle developing around his left eye. "Looks like you've earned yourself another shiner, Lucas. How many does that make?"

Lucas frowned at me through the metal mesh separating the back and front seats, refusing to answer my question. Before he'd unexpectedly dropped out of high school our senior year, just a few days after our date and with only two months to go before graduation, Glick had shown up with a fresh black eye every month or two, bragging about how he'd kicked some dude's ass over in Hockerville. He'd gained a reputation as a tough fighter even though nobody seemed to be able to locate any of his alleged victims and verify his version of the altercations.

When I turned my eyes to the road in front of us, Lucas gave the back of our seats a forceful, two-footed kick, jolting me and Andre forward. My seatbelt yanked tight across my bust, jerking me back against the seat. "Hey!"

Andre glanced at Glick in the rearview mirror. "Cool it, asswipe."

Glick let loose with a primitive, guttural growl and kicked the seats again. Andre shot me a discreet look and I gave a small nod. We cops had special methods of subduing uncooperative prisoners, none of which you'd find in any official procedures manual.

Andre glanced back at Lucas. "Yo, Glick. You ever thought about becoming an actor in Hollywood?"

Lucas glared at Andre with red-rimmed eyes. "What the fuck you talkin' about?"

"Marnie and I think you could be the next Brad Pitt. In fact, we've decided to give you a screen test."

Lucas turned to me, his expression confused. He may not have known what was coming, but I did. I put a hand on the dash to brace myself.

Andre checked the rearview mirror then floored the gas pedal, sending Lucas and me rocking back in our seats. Once the speedometer reached eighty, he hit the brakes. Hard. *Skreeeeeech!* The cruisers' tires squealed, leaving a black trail on the pavement behind us and sending up a stench of burnt rubber as we skidded to a stop. Momentum carried Lucas forward in the backseat. He slammed face-first into the metal screen. *Bam!*

"Shit!" Lucas flopped back in his seat, his forehead bearing red marks in the cross-hatched pattern of the screen. "'The hell you do that for?"

Andre stared straight ahead, a wry smile tugging at his lips. "Sorry. Dog in the road."

Andre and I exchanged sideways looks and chuckled. I turned and glanced back at Lucas, expecting to be met with his standard scowl. Instead, he stared out the side window with lifeless eyes, a look of utter and complete hopelessness on his face, the same look I'd seen on my dad's face when the doctors told us my mother had, at best, a month to live. A hot flush of shame rushed through me and I had to turn away.

CHAPTER FIVE

THE TRUTH HURTS

On our way into the station, we passed Jared Roddy, a squat, paunchy night officer, who was on his way out of the building to begin his shift. He took one glimpse at Glick and rolled his eyes. "Our best customer, back again."

We deposited Glick on the bottom bunk in the freezer cell and removed an almost-empty flask of whiskey from his right boot. I emptied the liquor into the kitchen sink and tossed the empty flask into the trash. Technically, we were supposed to hang on to an inmate's property, but I was sick and tired of this routine. Every few weeks Lucas would drink too much, raise some hell, and give us crap. I'd noticed his arrests were becoming more frequent, his attitude more reckless.

Lucas is on a dangerous path. This has to stop.

I stepped back into the freezer and held out my hand to Glick. "Empty your pockets."

He stood and rotated his hips, leering drunkenly at me and pointing at his groin with both index fingers. "Why don't you empty them for me?"

I wasn't about to stick my hand into the front pocket of his jeans. I turned to Andre, leaning on the door jamb, his meaty arms crossed over his enormous pecs. "You want the honors?"

"Hell, no."

I eyed Glick's crotch. Didn't look like there was anything in his pocket other than a set of keys. I'd let him slide this time.

After we locked Glick in the freezer, Andre drove me back to the Watering Hole to pick up my police motorcycle. By that time, it was a quarter after six, my shift was up, and it was too late to intercept the Ninja. Looked like my mystery man would remain a mystery for the time being. *Damn!*

I drove the police motorcycle back to the station. Through the front windows I saw the swing shift dispatcher, Bernie, on duty now, watching dinnertime reruns and assembling a model car, this one bright blue, what looked to be a '72 Barracuda. Bernie's spongy, once-red hair had faded with age and was now the color of a Creamsicle.

I parked the bike and headed through the glass door into the station. "Hey, Bernie. How's it going?"

Holding a tiny white tube, Bernie squeezed a dab of clear glue onto a miniature tire and grunted in reply.

"Glad to hear it." I retrieved my purse from my desk and walked back out to the parking lot to my personal vehicle, a vintage Harley Sportster. The bike had belonged to my mother before she passed away and Dad had hung onto it for me. On reaching driving age, I'd chromed it up a bit and added a pillowy touring seat to better accommodate my badonkydonk butt, but I think Mom would've approved. The small brass bell Dad had given Mom back when they were dating still hung from the foot peg, alongside the bell Dad had given me, protecting me from evil road spirits and general bad luck during my journeys. Catholics have Saint Christopher medallions. Bikers have bells.

I stowed my purse in the fringed leather saddle bag and slid my head into Mom's helmet, a pink model adorned with daisies. The engine kicked in right away, the motor's distinct and predictable rhythmic cadence having a calming effect on me, like a motor mantra. The burdens of the workday seemed to ease away as I motored out of the parking lot and pulled onto Main. I dialed up some end-of-the-workday music on my phone, Cyndi Lauper's "Girls Just Want to Have Fun". After all, that's all I really wanted. Some fun. *Know where I can find any?*

After making a quick stop at the Piggly Wiggly for a few grocery items, I turned down the rural road that marked the final stretch in my drive home. It was dusk and the June bugs flew aimlessly about, like Scud missiles searching for a target. A bug on a windshield is nothing, but hitting a bug at forty miles per hour with only a thin piece of clothing for protection could sting something fierce. I slowed in the hopes of avoiding any suicidal insects. I got lucky, arriving home free of bug shrapnel.

I turned into the dirt driveway of our yellow double-wide mobile home. Next to the house sat a group of haphazardly parked vehicles—dad's last-century green Jeep Cherokee SUV, four pickup trucks of various makes and models, and Uncle Angus's metallic blue Kawasaki. Looked like the whole gang had shown up for poker night.

I pulled my bike into the detached garage behind the house and parked between Dad's Harley, a touring model with high-arching gorilla handlebars, and his flat-bed trailer, loaded with an assortment of chainsaws and pruning tools he and Uncle Angus used in their tree-trimming business.

Bluebonnet, my furry white Great Pyrenees, was lying on the front porch as I came up the steps with the groceries. After Chet and I divorced, I'd adopted her from the pound to keep me company. Bluebonnet had been relinquished by a cattle rancher who'd gone bust and could no longer afford to feed the hundred-pound beast. My marriage to Chet hadn't lasted, but Bluebonnet and I had a true for-better-or-worse, 'til-death-do-us-part relationship.

Bluebonnet's tail thumped against the floor when she saw me. She raised her enormous head and looked at me with hopeful baby blue eyes.

"Hi, girl. Got something for you. Come inside with me."

The dog rolled to her feet to follow me in, her collar and tags jingling. I headed into the kitchen to unpack the groceries, Bluebonnet padding along behind me, her toenails clicking on the lime-green and brown checkered linoleum.

The six men sat at the round pine table, four of them in kitchen chairs, a couple in lawn chairs brought in from the backyard.

"Hey, Dad. Guys."

The men offered a variety of greetings—a nod, a two-finger salute, a lift of a beer bottle—but none took his eyes off his cards. If there was one thing these men took seriously, it was poker. It certainly wasn't grooming. There wasn't a properly shaved face or a decent haircut among them.

I set the bags on the counter, pulled a rawhide bone out of a bag, and held it out for Bluebonnet. She grabbed it between her teeth and trotted off into the living room where she could chew comfortably on the colorful braided rug.

Dad laid his hand face-down on the table and stood to help me unload the grocery bags. At one time, Dad had resembled a member of ZZ Top, with long brown hair and a wooly beard. As time passed, his hair had turned gray and he'd trimmed the beard. Like me, he'd taken to wearing his hair in a single, simple braid. These days he looked more like Willie Nelson, or a skinny, hippie version of Santa Claus.

I pulled a six-pack of Shiner Bock longnecks out of a bag and plunked it on the table in front of Uncle Angus, my mother's little brother. Angus had been born years after my mother, had the same sturdy build as Mom and me, and the same dark hair with hints of auburn, though he wore his shoulder length. I looked more like him than I did my own father, and Uncle Angus was like a second father to me. Or maybe a big brother. If he wasn't getting me out of trouble, he was getting me into it. On my eighteenth birthday, he'd taken me to Dallas to get a tattoo, a tiny yellow rose behind my left ankle. He'd then confiscated the bottle of Apple Blossom wine I'd hidden under the seat of Dad's Cherokee, telling me I was too young to drink. *Talk about mixed messages.*

Angus looked up with a smile. "That's my girl. Just in time, too." He handed me his empty beer bottle and grabbed a fresh one from the table, twisting off the cap and taking a sip. I bent over and gave him a kiss on his rough, weather-worn cheek. "Ouch. You need moisturizer."

He made a face. "I don't need soft skin. I need a woman."

I gave his shoulder a squeeze. Poor Angus. He'd never met the right woman, never married, had no family to go home to. Dad and I were all he had. Well, us, his silver Airstream trailer, and a three-foot tall phallic-shaped potted cactus he called Señor Pepè.

If Uncle Angus hadn't come around and dragged my father kicking and screaming out of the house after my mother died, Dad would probably still be sitting on the couch, staring at a blank television screen, tears streaming down his face, his young daughter on her Sit 'N Spin at his feet, whirling frantically in futile circles, pretending the plastic disc was a time machine that could take them all back to a point before her mother found the lump in her breast.

Gah.

I tossed the empty beer bottle in the trash, noting the toe of Angus's black boot tapping under the table, a sure sign he held a good hand. I stepped behind him. A quick glance at his cards confirmed my suspicions. Three Aces. Maybe things were finally looking up for him. God knows he deserved it.

The groceries now properly stashed, Dad reclaimed his seat at the table and picked up his hand. "How was work?"

No sense telling him about Fulton shooting at me and Dante. Dad had already lost his wife, he didn't need to worry about losing his only child, too. "Work was fine."

Dad discarded a couple of cards and gestured for replacements. "Chip Sweeney at the Grab-N-Go says Sheriff Dooley busted some killer from Chicago in a pasture outside of town."

Angus tossed a couple of quarters into the pile in the center of the table. "I heard the guy opened fire with a machine gun. Took ten deputies with nightsticks to subdue him."

Ten deputies, my ass. Try one hard-headed woman. I turned away so the men wouldn't see the look of disgust on my face. Once again, Sheriff Dooley would bask in the glory of a Jacksburg PD bust, refusing to share credit with the officers actually involved in the arrest. *What a jackass.*

I set about making dinner for myself and the men, pouring three cans of baked beans into a stock pot and adding a package of sliced hot dogs. I pulled out a loaf of white bread from the breadbox, as well as a tub of margarine and a jar of baby dill pickles from the fridge. Not exactly Wolfgang Puck, but nobody would starve to death, either.

When the beans had been bubbling for several minutes, I turned off the stove and spooned up servings onto plates. I didn't mind feeding the gang since I had to cook for myself anyway, but no way would these guys stick me with a sink full of dishes to wash. I whipped my nightstick from my belt and pointed it at the men. "Rinse your plates when you're done and put them in the dishwasher."

Uncle Angus gave me a salute. "Aye-aye, Captain."

I returned the baton to my belt and aimed for the fridge. The night before I'd had a rare moment of domestic inspiration and baked a cake, my mother's signature recipe, what she'd called her Thunder Thighs Fudge Cake—chocolate cake with a hint of Mexican vanilla, topped with fudge frosting, chocolate chips, and chopped pecans. I helped myself to a huge slab and carried it into the living room to eat on the couch, a velveteen floral number that was both hopelessly outdated and endlessly comfy. I'd seen the same couch advertised for sale on E-Bay, described as "retro chic." *Yeah, right.*

With my uniform stretched to capacity, I should have felt guilty eating the fudge cake, but I refused to. The older I got the slower my metabolism seemed to become, but with a pair of thirty-eight double-D's on my chest it wasn't like I'd ever look thin anyway. Besides, I'd risk toppling over if my butt didn't balance out my front. *That's my excuse and I'm sticking to it.*

When I was done, I held out the plate so Bluebonnet could lick the few crumbs I left behind. She finished licking the plate clean, and I carried it into the kitchen, rinsed it off, and stuck it in the machine. I searched through the cabinets and found my Wonder Woman thermos, ladled another serving of beans and wienies into it, and buttered a couple of slices of bread. I wrapped the bread in foil and stuck everything in a grocery bag along with a paper napkin and a warm can of root beer. I didn't bother with the cake. Glick wasn't worth it.

I gave Dad a kiss on the forehead and waved good-bye to the men. "Later, guys. 'Got a prisoner to feed."

Angus looked up from the table. "Lucas Glick do somethin' stupid again?"

Don't be too impressed by Angus's discerning skills. It didn't take a psychic to figure out who was cooling off in the department's freezer cell.

I nodded. "Got in a bit of trouble at the Watering Hole this afternoon. Broke a six-hundred-dollar custom pool cue."

Angus shook his head. "That poor kid didn't stand a chance. His mother beat all the sense out of him."

Dad and the other men murmured in agreement.

My grip on the bag tightened involuntarily and a sick feeling invaded my stomach. "What are you talking about?"

Angus's eyes met mine. "Frieda Glick used to knock her boys around something fierce. Child protective services must've been out to their place a dozen times. Called 'em three or four times myself."

When he wasn't crashing on our couch, Uncle Angus lived in his travel camper at the trailer park behind the post office. Before Frieda Glick left town, she and her five boys had lived there, too. Lucas, the youngest of the five, still lived in the same trailer he'd grown up in, though now he lived alone, his brothers scattered to parts unknown.

Angus rearranged the cards in his hand. "Government never done nothin' about the situation. Freida'd give the social worker some sob story about how hard it was to raise five boys without any help from their daddies. She'd cry and wail and promise she'd never lay a hand on them again, then she'd be back at it again before the social worker hit the highway." He took a swig of his beer. "Where'd you think Lucas got all them black eyes?"

So Glick's stories about kicking ass over in Hockerville had been nothing more than him blowing smoke, covering up a shameful secret, the embarrassment and stigma of domestic violence. The abuse had apparently been common knowledge among the adults of the town but never trickled down to us kids, kept quiet, probably out of our parents' desire to protect us as long as possible from life's harsh realities.

My heart wrenched, as if twisted by unseen hands. Despite everything I'd seen during my nine years in law enforcement, I'd never grown immune to the violence. I'd learned to put up a tough front, pretend it didn't get to me. *But it did.*

Angus plunked a stack of nickels down, placing his bet. "Frieda took off the day Lucas turned eighteen, just a few months before he would've graduated. Never seen such a selfish woman."

I turned and set the bag back on the counter. I cut an enormous slab of chocolate cake, put it on a paper plate, and covered it with cellophane. I added it to the bag and headed out, stepping over Bluebonnet, now settled on her blue Indian blanket in the front hallway.

"Bye, girl." I bent over to give her a kiss on the head. "You be good now. Hear?"

CHAPTER SIX

CELLMATES

Ten minutes later, I waited at the traffic light at Main and Renfro, the cool evening breeze carrying a faint scent of garlic and onions from the pink stucco taco stand on the corner. *Dang.* I'd forgotten all about the package delivered to the abandoned Parker house on Renfro that afternoon, the package I'd made a mental note to check on. That's the problem with mental notes. They tend to be misplaced among the mental clutter.

I detoured down Renfro, climbed off my bike, and checked the porch for the package. The white box was nowhere in sight. I made another mental note to ask Eric about the package the next time he stopped by the station. Hopefully, this mental note would stick.

A few minutes later, I pulled into the station. A confused woman in a mini-van bearing Arkansas license plates sat in the drive-thru, tapping on the closed glass window. Bernie ignored her, focused instead on putting a pinstripe on his model.

I nodded to Bernie as I came through the front door and held up the plastic bag in my hand. "Got dinner for Glick."

He glanced up at me, grunted again, and turned his attention back to his model.

Glick lay on his side on the bottom bunk, facing the stainless steel wall. On the wall next to the bunk, an intricately etched eagle soared across the stainless steel, carved into the metal by the open pocketknife lying on the floor next to the bunk. Next time we arrested Glick, we'd definitely have to empty his pockets.

Defacing public property was a class C misdemeanor, but Glick's etching was surprisingly intricate, well-proportioned and detailed, betraying a natural yet unrefined talent, even more impressive given he'd accomplished the task with such a rudimentary tool. Maybe Glick wasn't as worthless as everyone, including himself, thought.

I pocketed the knife, set the bag of food on the floor next to Glick, and nudged him in the butt with the toe of my boot. No response. Probably still sleeping off the whiskey. Might as well let him rest in peace.

I turned off the light in the freezer but left the door cracked, the pale light over the dispatch counter casting soft shadows in the room. I pulled the plaid blanket off the top bunk and folded it, making myself a cushion on the floor. I plopped down on it and leaned back against the steel wall, cool against my back through the shirt of my uniform.

If I was going to be stuck here a while, I might as well listen to some music. I slid my headphones into my ears and scrolled through the song list. What better to listen to in the dark than Billy Squier's "In the Dark"?

Closing my eyes, I listened to Billy's resonant voice sing about loneliness, illusions, and memories, guarded hopes and pocketed dreams. My mind wandered to my own loneliness, my own illusions and memories, my own guarded hopes and pocketed dreams.

It had been twenty-five years since the death of my mother, one since the death of my marriage. Both had been slow, draping out over time like a long shroud, beginning as a transparent covering, growing increasingly dark and opaque until becoming a final, smothering black. Fate was an evil bitch. First, she deprived me of a mother-child relationship with my mom, then she deprived me of a husband-wife relationship with Chet. You know that saying about how it was better to have loved and lost than never to have loved at all? *Pure bullshit.* Having known love, then having it ripped from you, was hell. If you'd never experienced love, you wouldn't know what you were missing.

Ignorance is bliss. Now that's wisdom.

Chet and I had been happily married for several years when our marital bonds began to loosen. I had fallen in love with a country boy and his snaggletooth smile, unassuming manner, and simple, family values. But that small-town boy disappeared. While I found big-city life to be stressful, hectic, and isolating, Chet thrived in Dallas, becoming a successful commercial mortgage broker. In the process, he changed all the things I'd loved about him. He wore a set of invisible braces to straighten his teeth, traded in his Nickelback CD's for Michael Bublè downloads, and became more interested in property values than family values, insisting we put off having children until he was established in his career. We grew apart and, though we'd once meant the world to each other, we were heading in different directions, living in different worlds, wanting different things out of life. Our marriage had not been a mistake, but the relationship had run its course. Our time had passed.

We cut our losses before things got ugly, making love one final time the night before our divorce hearing, hugging each other and weeping in front of a confused family court judge far more used to estranged couples using his courtroom to engage in verbal sparring. Neither of us argued over the property, both insisting the other take what mattered to them. He kept the contemporary three-bedroom house in Dallas, paying me half of the accrued equity. I took the Bundt pan and our collection of classic rock CDs, and came home to a lonely life in Jacksburg.

If I ever meet Fate, I'll give that bitch the slap she so desperately deserves.

Clenching my eyes closed could not hold back the big, angry tears welling in them. Several escaped and rolled down my cheeks. I heard the squeak of bedsprings and opened my eyes to find Lucas sitting up on his bunk, watching me. Purple-black rings underlined his eyes, courtesy of his earlier stunt on the floor of the Watering Hole.

He leaned forward to get a better look at me. "You crying?"

I wiped my tears away with the back of my hand. "No."

"Liar. I seen you crying." He paused a moment. "You all right?"

"It's just allergies. Mountain cedar."

"Bullshit." He stood, stepped over to the switch, and turned on the light in the freezer.

I blinked against the harsh light, wiped away the last of my tears, and pointed to the bag on the floor. "Shut up and eat your dinner."

Glick sat back down on the bunk, pulled the bag onto his lap, and unloaded the contents onto the rumpled blanket next to him. He peeked under the foil at the chocolate cake, then looked at me. "Dessert, too? You got a thing for me or something?"

His teasing smile told me he knew a romantic relationship was out of the question. Our time had passed, too. I realized now why he'd never called me for a second date all those years ago. After his mother had abandoned him, he'd had his hands full trying to survive, a mere kid all alone with no one to help him.

I gestured at his etching on the wall. "Nice eagle."

Lucas glanced over at the bird and shrugged. "Guess that'll be added to my charges."

"Nah. Too much paperwork involved. Besides, I kind of like it."

"Really?"

"Uh-huh."

He wolfed down the dinner in two minutes flat, not even complaining about the warm root beer. When he dug into the cake, he forked an enormous bite into his mouth and closed his eyes. "This tastes just as good as I remember."

I sat up straight on the blanket. "When did you have Mom's Thunder Thighs cake?"

He stabbed at the cake with his fork, separating another large bite. "First grade Christmas party. You and me was in the same class, remember?"

My memories contained only vague recollections of first grade. A pair of red Keds with white rubber toes. Calluses on my hands from hundreds of trips across the monkey bars. A skinny, elderly teacher with a bleach-blond bouffant. Uncle Angus dressing me in a ruffled floral dress for my mother's funeral in early summer, not long after school let out. But whether Lucas had been in my class that year I couldn't recall.

"We were in Mrs. Pelfrey's class," Glick said. "That woman was a royal bitch."

"She wasn't so bad."

He shoveled the dessert into his mouth, swallowed, and pointed at me with the fork. "Maybe she was nice to you, Miss Goody Two-Shoes. But she hated me. She sent me to the office if I so much as sneezed. That was back when the principal was still allowed to paddle." He put a hand on his butt and rubbed as if he could still feel the sting.

The icky feeling returned to my stomach. Lucas got the short end of the stick, both literally and figuratively, and what's more, he got it at home and school, too. It's a wonder he hadn't turned out worse.

Glick swallowed his second bite of cake. "Your mom showed up for the Christmas party wearing a red Santa hat with a bell on the tip and carrying a huge chocolate cake. Best cake I ever had. She snuck me seconds when the other kids weren't looking." Glick licked fudge frosting from the back of his fork.

Lucas Glick remembered Mom. Her hat. Her cake. Her kindness.

A rush of sweet memories flooded my mind, bringing fresh tears to my eyes. "I'd forgotten about the Santa hat." She'd worn it so her hair, bald in patches from the chemotherapy, wouldn't scare the kids. The hat was probably still around in one of the boxes in the attic. I'd have to look for it come Christmas time.

Glick took a swig from the can of root beer. "That spring we took a field trip to the Fort Worth zoo, remember? Your mom was one of the chaperones."

My memories contained a hazy recollection of a bumpy bus ride and a rogue monkey flinging poop at Mrs. Pelfrey, a blob of it sticking to her hair, much to the amusement of her students. Mom had to put a hand over her mouth to hide her grin. She'd had such a warm, sincere smile. I'd often been told my smile was just like Mom's. Not lately, though. Lately I hadn't had much call for a smile.

Lucas downed another chug of root beer and set the can on the floor. "I skinned my knee running to see the lions. Mrs. Pelfrey said it served me right for breaking the rule about no running, but your mother put a Band-Aid on my knee, gave me a kiss on the cheek, and carried me around piggy-back the rest of the day."

Giving a hurt kid a piggy-back ride was just the thing Mom

would have done, even if she'd been exhausted from the cancer eating away at her. A smile crept onto my face as I thought about Mom, how selfless and caring she'd been. Apparently she'd been a rare source of comfort to Lucas, a child in desperate need to know someone—*anyone*—cared.

When Lucas noticed me smiling, his expression turned uncomfortable. He crushed the aluminum can in his fist, as if that tough act could negate the intimate feelings he'd shared with me. *Too late.* But it was time to change the subject before I fell to pieces and started bawling like a baby.

"You spend a lot of time over in Hockerville, right?"

Glick nodded. "Service some septic tanks over there. Those snobs in Hockerville think their shit don't stink, but believe me, it does."

We laughed together and it felt good. I'd almost forgotten what my laugh sounded like.

"Know anybody who drives a yellow and black Ninja?"

Lucas cocked his head. "Know the bike. Seen it around Hockerville a few times. Around Jacksburg, too, but I got no idea who it belongs to." He squinted at me. "Why?"

"No reason." I shrugged. "Just curious. It's a cool bike."

He smirked at me. "Just curious, my ass. You got a thing for the guy who rides it."

I rolled my eyes. "You can't have a thing for someone you've never met."

"I'm in love with Pink and I've never met her."

Lucas had me chuckling again. *Holy crap, am I actually enjoying his company?* Maybe he wasn't so bad after all—when he wasn't liquored up, that is.

"Want to run over to Hockerville and bowl a few games?" I asked.

He raised a brow. "Like a date?"

"Like two old classmates desperate for some fun."

"So you won't be putting out, then?"

I stood. "Keep dreaming, buddy."

He cleaned himself up as best he could in the men's room and we stepped outside. I unclipped my white cop helmet off the police bike and handed it to Lucas. "You can ride bitch."

We stepped over to my Sportster. After I took a seat, he climbed on behind me, reaching his arms around me, his hands out in front of my chest, fingers splayed wide. "If I accidentally grab onto something I ain't supposed to touch, it ain't my fault."

"Don't even think about it." I seized his outstretched hands and positioned them down low around my waist.

He leaned forward and spoke into my ear. "What's everyone in town going to think if they see the police captain hanging out with the resident fuck-up?"

"If I catch anyone looking, I'll whack you with my nightstick."

"Works for me. I don't want nobody thinking I'm friends with the po-po."

CHAPTER SEVEN

GAMES PEOPLE PLAY

We set out on the road to Hockerville.

Hockerville was the antithesis to Jacksburg and the towns enjoyed a sometimes-healthy, sometimes-heated rivalry. But for better or worse, the citizens of Hockerville knew they couldn't survive without Jacksburg and we in Jacksburg knew we needed Hockerville. If your toilet was clogged, you called a plumber from Jacksburg. If your arteries were clogged, you saw a cardiologist in Hockerville. If your floors needed waxing, you called a housekeeper from Jacksburg. If your brows needed waxing, you went to a salon in Hockerville. And if you wanted the best chicken-fried steak in Ruger County, you ate at the Chuck Wagon, situated halfway between the two towns.

The manager at the bowling alley let us have the lanes at no charge, freebies being one of the perks of going out in uniform. Lucas sprang for the snacks. "It's the least I could do after calling you a pig earlier."

I shot him a pointed look. "You called me a fat sow, and I'll have both popcorn *and* nachos."

"Fair enough."

We bowled a couple of games with me winning the first by

just a hair, Lucas trouncing me in the second. We were gearing up for a third when Glick looked up from the ball return and asked, "How come you got divorced?"

I raised my brows at him. "That's a little personal, isn't it?"

"Well . . . yeah."

I paused for a moment. Guess there wasn't any harm in telling him. "My marriage was over the day I opened the bathroom cabinet and found a pumice stone, self-tanning cream, and a box of Clairol hair color in sable brown."

Lucas shrugged. "So?"

"They weren't mine."

"He cheated on you?"

I shook my head.

"He was gay, then?"

"No. Just very concerned with his looks." For right or wrong, it had bothered me that Chet spent twice as much time in the bathroom as I did. It didn't seem natural for a man to put so much effort into his appearance. He'd said image was critical in the real estate business, but still. I'd never marry a guy prettier than me again.

Glick was quiet for a moment. "You regret marrying him?"

Even though things hadn't worked out for Chet and me in the long run, I had no regrets. I shook my head. "Getting married to Chet and moving to Dallas helped me figure out what I really want out of life."

"What's that?"

"A house. A husband. A kid or two. The simple things." Unfortunately, I'd also learned that just because the things a person wanted from life were simple didn't mean they were easy to get.

On the fourth frame of our third game, the group of men who'd been playing in the lane next to us packed up and left, a lone guy slipping into the now-empty lane. Like me and Lucas, he appeared to be around thirty. He stood a lean five-foot ten and wore a short-sleeved red-and-white striped cotton shirt over a faded red tee, both un-tucked. A pair of khakis, slightly wrinkled from the day's wear, rested nicely on his trim hips. He had the light skin that came from working an office job, the fair tone in striking contrast with the shiny black hair that stuck up in short spikes as if he'd forsaken the comb and simply run his fingers through it. He wasn't sloppy, though, more like casual, as if he had much more important things to concern himself with than his appearance. I found myself wondering what those things might be.

A plastic badge was pinned above the breast pocket of his shirt. He must've forgotten to remove it at the end of the workday. The badge read "TreyTech." *Huh.* The guy must be some kind of computer geek. Geek or not, he was a hell of a bowler. The monitor overhead showing he'd outscored me and Glick by a hundred points.

Lucas addressed the guy as he stepped over to retrieve his custom blue swirl-patterned ball from the return. "Dude, where'd you learn to bowl like that?"

The guy glanced up at Glick. "Right here." His deep voice held a hint of a southern accent. "My father was the Hockerville league champion from eighty-five through ninety-three. Taught me everything he knew about the game."

Lucas looked away. Clearly, his father had taught him nothing. I wondered if he'd even known his dad.

As the guy set up to bowl another frame, his shirt pulled taut across his well-defined shoulders. His biceps flexed as he sent the ball spinning down the lane, and a warm flush rushed through my body. Wait, was I attracted to this guy? Sure, he had a nice body, but brainy nerds, even attractive ones like him, had never been my type. My type was tough, adventurous, and daring, like the guy who rode the Ninja was sure to be.

After sending his ball at warp speed down the lane, the man turned around and our eyes met for the first time.

Whoa.

My brain felt as if it had been hit full-force with a strike, all intelligible thoughts scattering. His gray eyes were intelligent and intense, yet hinted at something dark and dangerous, like rain-slick asphalt. Clearly, there was more to this guy than lean muscle and a sharp mind. Our gazes locked for a moment, then a flicker of recognition seemed to pass across his face. Odd, since we'd never met before. But I sure wouldn't mind meeting him now.

His lips drew into a cockeyed grin, confident, bordering on cocky. Apparently, my gaze had lingered on him just a bit too long. A blush crept up my cheeks, one that wouldn't be camouflaged by foundation or blush since I wore neither. Why bother? My motorcycle helmet would just smear any makeup. But this guy wouldn't get the satisfaction of thinking he'd caught me getting hot and bothered over him. My eyes moved to the monitor above him, which showed the remaining pins. "Seven-ten split. Tough break."

"I'm always up for a challenge."

Now his smile was definitely cocky. And now I was also definitely intrigued.

The guy retrieved his ball from the return, then glanced my way as if to make sure I was watching him. He ran his palm once over the ball like a quick caress, positioning it in his hands. As he plunged his fingers into the holes, my thighs clenched involuntarily. *Gah!* I was far more desperate than I'd realized if a bowling ball seemed erotic.

Lucas and I watched as the guy turned his back to us, stepped into position, and with both grace and athleticism sent his second ball down the lane at the speed of light. The ball slammed into the ten pin at just the right angle to send it crossways across the lane into the seven pin. The pin teetered for a moment before falling backward. A spare.

The guy turned back around, his steel gaze locking on mine. "Impressed?"

Hell, yeah, I thought. "Not bad," I said.

"Not bad? That's it? Damn." He shook his head as if disappointed in my nonchalant response, but I knew better.

He was flirting with me. And I was enjoying every second of it.

Lucas and I finished our game. I managed to hit only three pins and threw a couple of gutter balls, distracted by the guy in the lane next to us.

He glanced over at me as I slid out of the rental shoes, his eyes flitting to my own name badge before he pointed up at my pitiful score displayed on the ceiling-mounted screen for all the world to see. "Looks like I could teach you a thing or two about the game, Officer Muckleroy."

I fingered the .38 on my hip. "You're lucky I'm out of my jurisdiction, buddy."

His lips spread in a slow, sexy grin that turned my insides warm and gooey, like the cheese on my nachos.

After returning our rental shoes, Lucas and I headed over to the pool tables and were lucky enough to snag one right away. We stepped up to the rack on the wall, sizing up the cue sticks.

I chose one of the shorter ones and turned to Glick. "You're not going to break another cue, are you?"

His expression became remorseful. "No. I wouldn't have broken that one earlier today if that jerk hadn't called me a good-for-nothin' loser."

You know that saying about sticks and stones? It's pure BS, too. Words may not break bones, but they could definitely hurt, especially if you never heard any positive ones.

While Lucas racked the balls, I headed to the snack bar to refill our pitcher of Coke. He wanted a beer but I promised not to file a report on today's incident at the Watering Hole if he stuck with soda. When I returned to the table, the guy from the lanes stood next to Glick, both of them chalking up pool cues. Two twenty-dollar bills lay on the table.

Lucas pocketed the chalk cube. "We've decided to make it interesting."

Lucas and I exchanged knowing looks. I'd seen Lucas in action. He was a kick-ass shooter, absolutely unbeatable—when he was sober, of course. When he was drunk, he sucked. But he wasn't drunk now. In all fairness, I probably should've warned the guy that Lucas was hustling him, but then he might have walked away. Besides, he was wearing expensive Timberland hiking boots. He looked like he could afford to lose twenty bucks.

"I want in." I pulled a bill from my purse and laid it next to theirs on the green felt.

The guy gently took hold of my wrist as I pulled my hand back. His touch was warm and just rough enough to send a power surge up the nerves in my arm and into my chest, where it zipped in figure eights around my 38DDs, making my nipples harden. I hoped they weren't noticeable through my uniform. *Should've worn my Kevlar vest.* The vest worked both ways, stopping bullets from the outside and hiding nipple erections from the inside.

His eyes bored into mine. "Who're you putting your money on? Yourself, your boyfriend, or me?"

Beside me, Glick snorted. "I'm not her boyfriend, dude. I'm her prisoner."

The guy looked at Glick then back to me, a gleam in his eyes and grin playing about his lips. "Good to know."

I managed to maintain an aura of cool, but inside I quivered with excitement. If the night went well, maybe this guy would ask me out on a date, my first in a year. *Mental note: Add barbecue sauce to the grocery list.* Maybe I'd be slathered and devoured after all. "My money's on Lucas."

The guy released my wrist—*damn!*—and shook his head. "You've broken my heart."

Now that he was no longer touching me, I could breathe again. I chalked my cue. "How can I bet on you when I know nothing about you?"

"You got me there." He switched his cue to his left hand and stuck out his right. "My name's Trey Jones. I'm a Taurus. My turn-ons include high-speed internet, banana pudding topped with Nilla Wafers, and women in uniform."

Clearly, Trey was a flirt and a goofball. But hell, my life could use a little comic relief.

I shook his hand. "I'm Marnie."

"Marnie," he repeated slowly, savoring the word as if it tasted good on his tongue, like his favorite banana pudding. "And your turn-ons?"

I didn't miss a beat. "Motorcycles, mochas, and men with a sense of adventure."

"Hmm." Trey's expression turned thoughtful.

Lucas scooped up the bills from the table and handed them to me. "You can play bookie."

We decided on a three-player game of cutthroat. Lucas flipped a coin to see who would break and Trey won the toss. As Trey eased by me I caught a subtle whiff of soap, a clean, crisp smell, not fussy, the smell of a masculine man. I stepped aside, trying not to be obvious as I eyed Trey's firm, broad shoulders when he bent over the table to line up his shot.

The end of the cue stick edged in and out between his fingers, the motion oddly sensual. His shot landed with a sharp *clack*, sending balls rolling in all directions, none of them making it into a hole. He stood and stepped aside to make room for Glick. "What did Marnie arrest you for?"

Lucas stepped into place for his shot. "Drunk and disorderly. Marnie's arrested me at least a hundred times. I've got a rap sheet as long as my—"

"Lucas!" I put one hand on my hip, holding the pool cue upright in the other.

"Hair!" Glick threw a palm up in innocence. "I was going to say my rap sheet's as long as my hair." He chuckled and a grin spread across his scruffy face. It was nice to see him having a good time. Heck, it was nice to see him sober.

Lucas leaned over the table and took his first shot, landing the six ball expertly in the corner pocket.

"Nice," Trey said.

Lucas eased himself around the corner of the table. "You ain't seen nothing yet."

My shots, as usual, were haphazard and mediocre, but since

my money was on Glick, it didn't much matter how I played. Ten minutes later, Lucas and I were each ten bucks richer. Trey could bowl a mean game, but he stunk at pool.

"I should be better at shooting pool," Trey said. "After all, it's just physics." He shrugged, as if physics was simple. Maybe for him. I wasn't sure I could even spell physics.

Trey took my cue from me and slid it into the rack next to the one he'd been using. "You up for a game of Ocean Hunter?"

I wasn't sure what Ocean Hunter was, but if playing it meant spending more time with Trey, hell yeah, I was game. I nodded and followed him to the video games section, carpeted with blue industrial-grade carpeting and populated primarily by pimple-faced adolescent boys with a few pubescent girls lingering on the fringes, eyeing the boys and giggling. A cacophony of beeps, dings, gunfire, and other video game noises greeted us.

Trey slid a five-dollar bill into the automated bill changer and a handful of quarters clanged into the tray. After pocketing all but a dollar's worth of the coins, he led me to a game enclosed in a large white console with two seats inside. I slipped inside, taking the seat on the right while he slid into the one on the left. Lucas rested his hands on top of the console on my side, peeking in to watch.

Trey inserted four quarters and pushed the start button. The game began, ocean noises and voices blaring from speakers built into the seat behind us as our characters descended the sea to explore underwater ruins. We grabbed our white metal shooters, my silver bracelets glinting in the bright light from the screen.

Trey gestured at my wrists with his free hand. "Are those Wonder Woman bracelets?"

"Yup."

"I'm a Flash Gordon man myself." With his left hand, he pulled his striped shirt open to reveal a lightning bolt on the red tee underneath. Looked like me and this sexy techie might have something in common after all.

The game began and we fired at a never-ending assortment of enormous eels, sharks with oddly shaped heads, and a mutant octopus intent on pulverizing us into fish food. Despite the noise and light from the video screen, being in the small confined area with Trey felt intimate, and a thrill skittered through me when his knee bumped against mine.

Even with my extensive police training, I managed to shoot only a small number of the sea creatures, which writhed and twisted on the screen. My life ran out long before Trey's and I sat back to watch him finish the game. When a giant shark ripped him to shreds fifteen minutes later, he'd managed to rack up the high score.

I slid my shooter back into the holder. "You're good."

"I've got skilled fingers." He waggled his fingers and shot me another sexy grin that hinted at what other activities those fingers might be good at.

We made our way around the video game area, hopping onto the simulated disco floor for a game of Dance Revolution. Trey impressed me with his sense of rhythm and physical agility, improvising funky dance moves, adding a few strategic pops, bumps, and grinds while I hopped around on the lighted squares like a rabid kangaroo, simply trying to get my feet on the right squares at the right time and failing miserably.

We moved on, playing a simulated jet ski game, a martial arts game, Pac-Man, and an ancient Asteroids machine, its simple, colorless graphics hopelessly lo-tech compared to the newer games.

Luckily, all of the games were rated, at worst, the equivalent of PG-13 and contained only clearly fictionalized fighting. Being a cop, I despised the realistic, ultra-violent video games. I'd seen violence up close and personal, and there was nothing fun or entertaining about it. To me, violence was anything but a game.

Trey stepped up to the final machine, a newer game I'd never seen before, one in which the residents of a small town faced an alien invasion.

I pulled the shooter from the holder. This one was black, its size and weight closely approximating that of a real handgun. I narrowed my eyes at Trey and pointed the gun at him. "This feels more like the real thing. I'll beat you this time."

"You're a good shot?"

"Hell, yeah." *Too good.* A bolt of nausea raced through me as grisly memories threatened to invade my brain. But when Trey grinned that cockeyed grin at me they fled to the far recesses of my mind. This guy was proving to be a great distraction. He was funny, amusing, playful. Just what I needed, someone to take my mind off the real world.

Trey pulled his gun from the holder. "You'll like this game. It has phenomenal graphics."

Lucas stood off to the side, digging in the bottom of the red and white cardboard popcorn tub for the few remaining kernels.

The screen geared up, directing us to choose our characters. To represent himself, Trey picked an obscenely muscular bald man dressed in camouflage while I selected a blond bimbo in tight jeans, a teeny T-shirt that revealed an abundance of cleavage, and pink high-top sneakers.

The game began with our characters wandering innocently down the streets of a town, past a bakery, a gift shop, and a pub. Eerie music came from the machine as a fleet of silver saucer-shaped airships appeared on the horizon, heading straight for us. Our characters ran into a pawn shop, grabbed an arsenal of guns and ammo, and headed back into the streets among a flood of terrified people fleeing the scene, their faces incredibly lifelike.

Trey was right. The graphics on this game were realistic. Maybe *too* realistic.

A tiny map in the bottom corner of the screen lit up with lime green dots to indicate the relative positioning of the aliens. The game reminded me of the simulated training scenarios we'd run through in the police academy.

Trey positioned himself and raised his gun to prepare for the alien onslaught. "Be careful not to shoot any of the townspeople. You lose points for each human you kill."

"Thanks for the warning." I knew all too well how it felt to kill someone, the sense that I'd lost critical points, that my karmic score would always be negative, at least until I found a way to even the count.

Trey took a quick glimpse at the map. "Look out!"

A trio of green-faced men came around the corner at the end of the block with their ray guns pointed directly at me. *Blam-blam-blam!* All three dropped to the ground in quick succession. I raised my gun to my face, pretending to blow smoke from the barrel. "Martians are no match for the Jacksburg PD."

Blam-blam! Trey brought down an alien who'd popped out of a doorway with a ray gun aimed at his player. The town appeared to empty as the citizens went into hiding and the aliens ran for cover. But we knew better. Those little green men were preparing for an ambush.

I took a quick look at the buttons on the console. "Where's the hyper-space key that'll transport me to Maui?"

"No such luck. Hawaii will have to wait until we wipe out these suckers."

We snuck slowly and carefully down the street, my character reluctantly following Trey's, turning into a narrow alley lined with overflowing garbage dumpsters. My heart jerked like a machine gun in my chest, sending forth bursts of blood instead of gunfire. This was only a game, yet for some reason my adrenaline had kicked in. My uniform felt hot, the polyester sticking to my damp, prickly skin.

I looked over at Trey. "Let's turn around and run away like everyone else." A note of desperation had crept into my voice, but Trey didn't know me well enough to notice.

He held his gun at the ready, his finger poised on the trigger, his eyes scanning the screen. "We can't. The fate of the free world rests in our hands."

"That's a lot of responsibility." That sick feeling returned. I wanted to put my gun down and walk away. I wanted to stop playing. But how could I bow out now without looking like a party pooper?

It's only a game, I reminded myself, feeling ridiculous. Nothing but a stupid game. I shook my head to clear it and forced myself to breathe.

We crept slowly toward a dumpster, leery of aliens that might be hiding behind it. Suddenly, a green dot ignited on the map directly in front of my character and a green face appeared on the screen at point-blank range, his oversized black eyes looking directly into mine.

But that's not what I saw. Instead, the face of a homeless man with wild brown hair and a scruffy beard appeared, his few remaining teeth dark with decay, his hazel eyes crazed and disoriented, surrounded by jaundiced whites.

I knew those eyes. I'd seen those eyes. I'd seen them just as they appeared to me now, and I'd seen them flare with fury as the man slashed at me with a steak knife. I'd seen them roll back, as if trying to see the gaping, blood-pulsing wound in his shattered forehead as he fell backward onto the sidewalk. And I'd seen those eyes, lifeless yet accusing, just before I'd lost consciousness and ended up on the ground next to him, my blood pouring through the shredded skin on my wrist, forming a deep red pool around my limp hand.

An involuntary scream erupted from my throat, searing my vocal cords. I hurled the gun at the machine. It struck the screen with a resounding *crack* and clattered to the ground. I felt the burn of everyone's gaze on me as I backed away from the machine, panting and gasping, my chest heaving.

I grabbed the seat of a car race game to steady myself. The confused young boy in the chair looked up at me, not sure what to think of the police officer hovering over him, making odd, high-pitched noises as she hyperventilated. Tunnel vision set in, white dots swirling in my peripheral vision like the green dots on the game screen, mixing with the colors and flashes of light from nearby video games.

Trey grabbed a chair from a nearby table and he and Lucas eased me into it. I yanked the cardboard popcorn tub from Glick's hands and bent over, putting my head between my legs and breathing into the popcorn tub to try to slow my breathing.

It was only a game, I told myself over and over again. *Only a game. Only a game.*

Eventually, my heartbeat slowed and my respiration returned to normal. I sat back up, my cheeks warm with an embarrassed flush. I wiped a spot of popcorn grease from my jaw and handed the tub to Lucas. Thankfully, pre-teen boys have short attention spans and, once I'd stopped gasping and squealing like a stuck pig, they turned their attention back to their video games.

Trey bent down on one knee in front of me, his brow furrowed in concern. "Are you okay?"

I nodded, looking into his gray eyes, wanting to escape into them. I gathered enough breath to whisper, "It was only an asthma attack."

CHAPTER EIGHT

SO CLOSE BUT YET SO FAR

What a lie. I didn't suffer from asthma. I suffered from PTSD, Post-Traumatic Stress Disorder. At least that's what the headshrinker at Dallas PD had told me.

I glanced up at Lucas. The expression on his face told me he knew I was lying, but the threat in my eyes told him to keep his mouth shut if he knew what was good for him. Nothing like a guy thinking you're emotionally damaged to send him running in the opposite direction. I'd enjoyed Trey's company tonight and I didn't want to scare him off.

Trey put a warm hand on my knee, sending a tingle up my leg. "Should we get you to a doctor or something?"

Clearly he knew squat about asthma or he'd realize that breathing into a popcorn bucket is the last thing someone in need of more oxygen would do. But I was glad he'd bought my story. I shook my head. "I'll be fine." *Just as soon as some pharmaceutical company invents a drug that erases memory.*

Lucas and I finished off our pitcher of soda. Trey retrieved his bowling bag and followed us out to the parking lot.

The outside air was cool and moist, the moon hidden behind

dark clouds. Looked like a storm was in the works. I glanced at my watch. It was past eleven, late for a work night. I'd be dog tired tomorrow, but it had been worth it. Despite the flashback, I'd had a hell of a time.

We stopped beside my bike and I unclipped the helmets. Trey's focus shifted from me to my motorcycle. "That's one sweet ride."

"You know it." I slipped into the pink helmet and climbed onto the bike, easing it back out of the parking space.

Trey ran his gaze over the bike. "No bell?"

"You know about the bells?"

He shrugged. "Heard the legends."

The bells bikers attach to their motorcycles allegedly wield much stronger protective power if given to bikers by someone who loves them. Although my personal bike bore both the bell my father had given to my mother decades ago and the bell Dad had given me along with the title, my cop bike had no bell. I had only my wits and luck to protect me while out on patrol. So far, they'd been all I'd needed.

After donning his helmet, Lucas climbed on behind me and put his hands around my waist, addressing Trey over my shoulder. "Anytime you're up for a rematch at pool, let me know. I got a truck to pay off."

"Yeah, yeah." Trey waved him off good-naturedly.

I started the engine and turned on the headlight. Trey stood in the lot, watching us pull away. He hadn't asked me out, hadn't even asked for my phone number. But something told me I hadn't seen the last of Trey Jones.

When Lucas and I reached the main exit of the parking lot,

the roadway was completely blocked by two carloads of teenagers, one on the way out, the other on the way in, both at a complete stop. The kids in the two cars were carrying on a conversation, oblivious to anything but themselves. *Oh, well. Been a teenager once myself.* I circled around the back of the building to go out the side exit.

And there it was. The yellow and black Ninja, sitting next to the building.

I slammed on my brakes, the tires on my bike emitting a short, sharp *screech.*

Glick's chest smashed against my back and our helmets met with a *thunk* as momentum carried him forward. "You ain't giving me another screen test, are ya?"

"No." *He's here.* I mentally ran through the faces of the men in the bowling alley. The only ones I'd paid much attention to belonged to Glick, Trey, and the bored boy at the shoe return, wielding an extra-large can of antifungal spray. The place had been packed, was still packed. Short of sitting here until the guy came out to his bike, there would be no way of telling which one of the hundred or so men in the bowling alley was him.

I checked the plates. The bike still bore the temporary cardboard plates from a dealership in Dallas, confirming my earlier suspicion that the registration paperwork was still in process at the DMV. There was nothing I could do but wait for the records to be updated. *Damn!*

***

I motored back to Jacksburg, my mind in overdrive. Luckily for me, it's virtually impossible to make conversation on a moving motorcycle, so I had plenty of uninterrupted time to think.

Who is my mystery man? What does he look like? What does he do for a living? At least I knew he liked to bowl. Besides motorcycles, that was one thing we had in common. Maybe he was ready to settle down, too, and had just been waiting for the right woman—*me, of course*—to come along. I knew it was unlikely, but a girl can dream, can't she? Even if she's not a girl anymore?

God help me if he turned out to be some spoiled sixteen-year old from Hockerville High or a married guy with seven kids who was going through a mid-life crisis. Then again, if the Ninja guy turned out to be a bust, Trey might make an acceptable substitute. The lingering looks he'd given me and his quirky sense of humor had made me feel twenty pounds lighter, both in body and in soul. For the first time in forever, I had real romantic possibilities.

Take that, Fate.

When we arrived back in Jacksburg, I pulled into the lot at the Watering Hole, coming to a stop beside Glick's tank truck, physically and mentally shifting gears. Lucas was on a definite downward spiral and if he didn't get his drinking under control he'd end up injuring himself or someone else. Maybe even worse. I knew what it was like to live with the guilt of ending a person's life. I didn't want Lucas to go through that, too.

He climbed off my bike, removed the white helmet, and held it out to me. I took it with one hand, putting the other on his forearm to keep him from walking away. "You ever think maybe you got a drinking problem, Lucas?"

Scowling, he yanked his arm free from my grasp. *And they say women are the ones with mood swings.* "The only drinking problem I got is that the price of liquor keeps going up. Damn sin taxes. Every time the government needs some money, they raise the taxes on alcohol and tobacco."

I ignored his bullshit. "What about AA? There's a group that meets at the Methodist church. I'll go with you if you want me to."

He smirked. "You gonna give me a piggy back ride? Like your mother?"

I clipped the helmet on the bike and looked up at him. "Lucas, I'm serious."

He looked away, his eyes narrowed and jaw clamped tight, but after a few moments the tight set of his jaw slowly eased. He turned back to me with eyes full of pain. "Drinking's not my problem, Marnie. *My problems* are my problem." He exhaled sharply. "In case you ain't noticed, my life's a fucking Jeff Foxworthy joke. I live in a piece-of-shit trailer that's falling apart at the seams. I got no friends, no woman, and I suck other people's shit out of holes for a living. It don't get much worse than that."

He had a point. But, hell, I wasn't doing much better. Divorced, living with my dad, watching my ass grow bigger by the second. Haunted by an event I was powerless to change and couldn't seem to put behind me no matter how hard I tried.

Lucas's voice softened. "I saw what happened back there, at the bowling alley. You think maybe *you've* got a problem?"

I looked down at the wide shiny bracelet on my right wrist, the one covering the jagged pink scar. "I don't think I've got a problem, Lucas. I *know* I've got a problem."

Unfortunately, my problem seemed to have no solution. Months of counseling hadn't helped. Neither had antidepressants or a two-week vacation in Cozumel, though I had come back with a nice tan, a set of hand-painted maracas, and a ridiculously cheap bottle of tequila which, despite the warning labels on the prescription bottle, I'd used to wash down the anti-depressants. Fortunately, the pills had come right back up. Unfortunately, they'd come back up on the Persian rug Chet had just paid two grand for at Horchow's.

Lucas seemed to sense I'd said all I wanted to say on the subject. He climbed into his truck and cranked the window down, crooking his elbow on the sill. "See ya around, Marnie."

"Stay out of trouble."

"If I stay out of trouble," he said, shooting me a wink, "you'd go out of business."

He had a point there.

***

A loud clap of thunder woke me the following morning. I glanced at the clock. 6:23 AM. Dang. The alarm wasn't set to go off until 7:00. Lighting flashed outside, followed by a second thunderbolt.

I lay in my cozy canopy bed, pinned under the lavender polka-dot comforter by a hundred pounds of fluffy white dog draped over my legs. I closed my eyes to try to go back to sleep, but another loud thunderclap jarred my nerves seconds later.

Might as well get my butt out of bed. I won't be able to sleep in this storm without a set of earplugs.

Bluebonnet opened one eye as I wrangled my legs out from under her, but she made no move to get up. I wouldn't either if I were her. I ruffled the fur on her neck. "Lazy girl."

I padded to the kitchen in my bare feet, turned on the coffee pot, and stuck my head in the fridge. *Hazelnut? French Vanilla? Nah. Today is an Irish Cream kind of day.* When the coffee was ready, I poured a good dose into a large mug and topped it off with a healthy shot of flavored creamer.

Rain beat down on the roof as I ate breakfast, the pitter patter above me competing with the *snap, crackle,* and *pop* from my cereal bowl. No sense rousing Dad. Can't trim trees in the rain.

I slipped into my uniform, today wearing standard black loafers rather than my motorcycle boots since there'd be no patrolling on the bike in this monsoon. Grabbing an umbrella on my way out the door, I headed outside to Dad's Cherokee, careful to avoid the mud puddles forming on the drive. A few drops of rain tagged me as I closed the umbrella and opened the SUV's door, which was stenciled in day-glow orange paint with the words I GRIND STUMPS followed by Dad's phone number.

Minutes later, I pulled up to the station. Dante had a dentist appointment in Hockerville that morning, a long overdue root canal, so his patrol car was up for grabs. Driving a cruiser wasn't nearly as fun as patrolling on the bike, but at least I wouldn't be stuck in the office all day and the cruiser had a cup holder, a definite plus on a blustery day like today. After checking in with Selena and topping off my travel mug with fresh coffee, I hopped into the cruiser and set out on patrol.

No need for my phone today since the cruiser had a kick-ass stereo. Dante had installed it himself. As I pulled out of the lot onto Main, I punched the stereo on, my eardrums immediately treated to raunchy rap lyrics, my ass treated to the vibrations of a booming bass line. I cranked the volume down and jabbed the scan button with my knuckle, stopping the radio on a classic rock station playing the Byrds' "Jesus is Just Alright with Me." The Billy Graham bobble-head nodded as if agreeing with my choice of song.

I drove out to Jacksburg's welcome sign and parked the cruiser behind it. Given the blustery conditions, the Ninja wasn't likely to be out today. Riding a motorcycle in the rain was a bitch, the raindrops pelting your body like shotgun spray, the windy conditions requiring constant correction. Whoever rode the Ninja might come by in another vehicle, but there'd be no way of knowing. *Oh, well. Guess I can daydream about Trey instead.* Something about that high-tech hottie put a buzz in my circuits.

The wind howled as gusts rocked the squad car and heavy rain pelted the windows, like Mother Nature's automated car wash. I'd been sitting in the cruiser for a few minutes, drinking my coffee, reading the newspaper comics, and performing isometric exercises with my glutes—*left cheek, right cheek, left cheek, right*—when a white Econoline van passed by. The van wasn't speeding, but one of its taillights was out, a potential hazard, especially in dark, wet conditions like today's. *Might as well make myself useful and warn the driver before somebody rear-ends him.*

I started my engine, pulled onto the highway behind the van, and turned on my flashing lights. The van eased over onto the shoulder by an undeveloped stretch of land covered with scrubby mesquite and cedar trees. I pulled the cruiser to a stop behind it. I picked up the microphone and squeezed the talk button. "Selena, run a plate for me."

"What's the number?"

I rattled off the plate.

A few seconds of silence followed before Selena came back on the radio. "It's registered to an Ignacio Barrientes. Want me to run his driver's license?"

"Sure."

There was a five-second pause and Selena's voice came back. "*Limpia.* He's clean."

"Thanks." I slid the mic back into its holder and opened my door. Sticking my umbrella out the door, I forced it opened before stepping out of the cruiser. The wind was gusty and virtually blowing the rain sideways. I sloshed through the wet gravel and dirt on the shoulder of the road, ducking my head against the driving wind and rain until I reached the driver's window.

I'd expected to find a Latino man in the front seat. Instead, I looked in the window to discover the passenger door gaping wide open and rainwater pooling on the floorboard. Through the door, I could see a man running full-speed into the field that flanked the highway. A glance into the cargo bay told me why he was running. A dozen potted marijuana plants filled the space.

Ay carramba.

A burst of wind caught my umbrella, ripped it from my

hands, and carried it into the branches of a nearby mesquite tree. *Gah.* I stepped to the hood, cupped a hand around my mouth, and shouted "Stop!"

The man ignored me and kept right on running, putting distance between us at an impressive speed. *He'd give Olympian Usain Bolt a run for his money.* No way would I ever catch the guy. In mere seconds, he'd disappeared into the rain as if he'd never even existed. The only evidence he'd ever been on the highway was the van, which remained behind, rapidly filling with rain, and me, drenched to the bone.

I slammed the van's passenger door closed, wrestled my umbrella from the tree, and dashed back to the cruiser. My hair and uniform were soaked and dripping. I radioed Selena again. "Get a tow truck out here."

I might not have caught the guy, but if he showed up to claim the van, he'd face drug charges. If he didn't claim the van within the allotted time period, the city could sell it at auction. Either way, I'd call it a success.

Once the tow truck had hauled off the van, I decided to forego traffic detail and head into town, see if anything interesting was happening there. *Not likely.* If I were back in Dallas, I'd be facing an armed robbery, a high-speed chase, maybe even a hostage situation. In Jacksburg, I'd be lucky to catch a jaywalker.

CHAPTER NINE

HELL ON HEELS

I drove back to town with the heater cranked up full blast to dry out my uniform. In seconds, the car felt like a sauna, hot and humid as the rainwater evaporated from my clothing. The windshield fogged up and I had to switch on the defroster. When I rolled slowly past the elementary school, a red convertible Spyder in the parking lot caught my eye, partly because it was one sweet ride, partly because it was parked crosswise across the only two handicapped spaces directly in front of the school.

The car looked suspiciously like the vehicle that had zipped past me the day before. The car had no handicapped plates, no handicapped placard on the dash, no handicapped tag hanging from the rearview mirror.

Busted.

I turned the cruiser into the school parking lot just as the tardy bell buzzed. The crossing guards in their bright yellow rain slickers trotted inside with their hand-held stop signs tucked under their arms. After waiting for a skinny redheaded boy intent on jumping into every puddle in the parking lot before darting into the building, I pulled up behind the Spyder. A red and blue sticker for Southern Methodist University, an expensive private college in Dallas, graced the back window of the car, along with another bearing three consecutive triangles, the symbol for Tri-Delta sorority, the school's most exclusive social organization. The car's vanity plates read "TIFFY T."

Still sitting in the cruiser, I called Selena and she ran the plate. There was a crackle of static on the line, then Selena returned. "The car's registered to a Kent Tindall out of Dallas."

"Kent Tindall? Huh."

Kent Tindall was the king of real estate development in Dallas. The man had an incredible knack for identifying undervalued properties, purchasing entire neighborhoods in blighted urban areas lot by lot. He'd raze the old homes and replace them with oversized mansions, enclosing the entire area with brick walls, gates, and security guards, turning them into modern fortresses built to keep out the riff-raff. Tindall bestowed elegant, pretentious names on his developments, such as Rivercrest Estates and the Arbors of Glenwood, selling the homes therein at an incredible profit to professionals looking for a short commute to their jobs downtown. His corporation also built an untold number of commercial properties, including at least one of the downtown Dallas skyscrapers.

Kent Tindall was my ex's idol. The pinnacle of Chet's career to date was handling an eighteen-million-dollar mortgage loan for Tindall's development company, the largest loan Chet had ever brokered, though mere chump change to Tindall. After the closing, Chet and I had gone to dinner with Kent Tindall and his wife at the Mansion on Turtle Creek, the city's most hoity-toity hotel.

For the occasion I'd bought a gently-used silk Versace dress at a resale shop near Highland Park and a pair of matching four-inch heels, the kind some women refer to as fuck-me pumps but which in my case were more like pick-me-up-when-I-fall-on-my-fat-ass pumps. My hairdresser had streaked three shades of highlights through my hair and added some layers to update my simple hairstyle. The clerk at the Neiman Marcus Lancôme counter worked wonders on me, covering my freckles in a thick coat of foundation, making my green eyes appear large and dramatic and my thin lips look soft and pouty.

I'd looked classy, chic, and sophisticated—and I'd felt like a complete phony. But I'd rather be me than a pompous prick like Tindall. He'd been so condescending to the waiters that I'd been afraid to eat my dinner, fearing what extra ingredients might have been added to the Bernaise sauce. His wife was no better, leaning toward me as if to share womanly secrets or inspiration, but instead whispering that "perhaps such a full-figured woman should avoid clingy fabrics." *If only I'd been carrying my Taser. I'd have given the woman a volt or two.*

What would a car owned by Kent Tindall be doing in Jacksburg? *Time to find out.*

I pulled over to the curb and parked in the red fire zone, but hey, it's not like I was going to write myself a ticket. Besides with all this rain coming down, the school wouldn't be catching fire any time soon. Cowering under my umbrella, I trotted up the walk. By the time I reached the double front doors, both of which were smudged with tiny handprints, my legs were once again soaked from the knees down and an inch of water stood in my shoes. *Uck.* I propped my umbrella against the red brick wall outside the front door so it wouldn't drip on the floor inside and pose a risk to the kiddos.

Last month, I'd come to the school to speak to the young students about safety issues. The kids had been more interested in knowing whether it was true prisoners were fed only bread and water, whether smoke came out of a person's ears when they were fried in the electric chair, whether I'd ever killed someone. The answers were "no," "I have no idea," and a sharp "I'm not going to talk about that. Next question."

I pushed the glass door open and was greeted by the strong scent of lemon disinfectant, the kind that was supposed to smell fresh but instead made you wonder what yucky event the fragrance was attempting to mask. As I sloshed my way to the office, my wet shoes sucking at my feet, the morning announcements concluded with the titillating news that it was sloppy Joe day in the cafeteria.

The redheaded boy trotted out of the office with a pink tardy slip as I reached the glass door. Gwennie Culligan, the school's thin, elderly secretary, looked up from her rolling chair as I stepped into the office.

Gwennie, her silver pixie haircut, and her shapeless purple cardigan, had been around forever. The woman had worked at the school since before I entered kindergarten. Because virtually everyone in town had attended Jacksburg Elementary at one time or another, Gwennie knew everybody's business. Which kids suffered from head lice. Which kids took ADD medication. Which kids were in danger of being left behind, yet again. She knew which parents earned so little their children qualified for free lunch, which ones couldn't manage to get their kids to school on time due to a head-splitting hangover, which parents had gone their separate ways, revising their emergency information cards to provide two home phone numbers instead of one. But Gwennie was discreet, never breaching anyone's trust, never sharing any sordid tidbits of gossip. *Darn her.*

Gwennie stepped up to the counter, pushing up the sleeves of her sweater. "Good morning, Miss Muckleroy." She'd called me the same thing back in fourth grade when I'd been sent to the nurse for pink eye.

"'Morning, Gwennie." I stopped in front of the counter. "There's a red convertible out front taking up both of the handicapped spots. Any idea who parked it there?"

Gwennie's expression turned sour, her lips pursing into a tight sphincter of disapproval. "Sure do. That car belongs to Tiffany Tindall. She's interning in Mrs. Nelson's kindergarten class."

"Is she disabled?"

Gwennie snorted and rolled her eyes. "That girl? Not hardly."

"Mind calling her to the office for me?"

"No problem."

Gwennie pushed a button on a panel in front of her and bent over to speak into a microphone. "Mrs. Nelson?"

A young woman's voice came back. "She's not here. She's making copies in the workroom."

"All righty."

Gwennie released the button and looked at me. "That was Tiffany. She can't leave them kids alone. Little buggers'll tear the place apart. You want to go talk to her in the classroom?"

"Sure. What room number?"

"Eight." Gwennie hiked her thumb to the left. "That way."

"Thanks."

I left the office and headed down the hall. When I reached room eight I peeked through the glass panel in the closed door. A dark-haired boy sat at a desk with an orange-tipped bottle of Elmer's, gluing pencils and crayons to the top of the desk. Next to him was a small girl with a brown pony tail pulled back in a white ribbon, tears streaming down her face, her tiny shoulders jerking as she sobbed. A tow-headed boy near the door rested his head on his desk, fast asleep, his mouth hanging open to reveal a gap where he'd lost an upper tooth. I squinted through the glass. Sure enough, it was Zane Nichols, the youngest son of my best friend Savannah, my favorite of her three boys though I'd never admit that flat out.

A blonde sat in a rolling chair at the front of the room, yakking on her cell phone, her back to the children. I opened the door and walked in.

I grabbed the glue out of the boy's hand. "You know better than that. Get some paper towels from the bathroom and clean this mess up right now."

I bent down next to the crying girl, putting a hand on her back and rubbing it up and down a couple of times to calm her. "What's the matter, honey?"

She half-choked, half-gasped as she tried to catch her breath between sobs. "I f-f-forgot my," she sniffled, "l-l-lunch money."

I ruffled her hair. "That's nothing to worry about." I reached into my breast pocket where I kept a small, ready stash in case of an emergency Snickers craving. I pulled out a couple dollars. "Here you go. Enjoy that sloppy Joe."

Her face brightened and she wiped her nose with the back of her hand. "Thank you. My mommy will pay you back."

"Don't worry about it, sweetie." I stood and glanced over at Zane. No sense waking him. Didn't look like he was missing anything.

As I walked to the front of the room, Tiffany continued to chat on her cell, oblivious to my presence. *Good thing I'm not an axe murderer.* "This internship sucks," she said into the phone. "I have to spend an entire semester out here in east Bumfuck with a bunch of redneck booger-pickers. I was hoping to get assigned to a school in Highland Park."

A chubby boy sitting near Tiffany chanted under his breath. "Bumfuck. Bumfuck. Bumfuck."

I put a finger to my lips and shook my head at him. Stepping around the chair, I stood directly in front of Tiffany. "I need to speak with you, Miss Tindall. Now."

She glanced up at me with unnaturally vivid ocean-blue eyes. Her lids were streaked with plum-tone shadow and rimmed with a gallon of mascara and heavy blue eyeliner. The enormous diamond studs in her ears sparkled in the fluorescent lights. She wore a low-cut, sleeveless top, much more appropriate for a Saturday night on the town than a school day in a classroom. She was thin and long-limbed like her mother, and her expression bore the same air of superiority as her father, the same merciless set of the jaw.

She said, "I'll call you back," before jabbing a finger at the screen to end the call. She looked up at me, cocking her head. "Yeah?"

"That your car out front taking up both handicapped spots?"

Her eyes narrowed, an unmistakable challenge in them. "That was the only decent parking spot left when I got here." She lifted her skinny legs, clad in tight blue jeans, onto the desk, settling her black spike heels on a stack of papers waiting to be graded and knocking over a pencil cup, sending a cascade of yellow number twos to the floor. She pointed at her feet. "These shoes cost three hundred bucks. I couldn't walk through the rain in them."

She snapped her fingers at a tiny, pale-haired girl sitting in the front row. "You. Ashley. Pick those pencils up."

"I'm Meagan."

"Whatever," Tiffany snapped. "Pick up the pencils."

The girl climbed down from her desk and began picking up the pencils from the floor.

The radio clipped to my belt squelched and I turned the volume down. "You need to move your car, Miss Tindall. I'll watch the class for you."

"You've got to be kidding!" Tiffany gestured toward the rain splattering against the windows behind the desk and huffed. "I'm not going out there in this typhoon."

So that's how this spoiled little bitch wants to play it, huh? I shrugged. "Suit yourself. You can pick up your car later at the impound lot behind the police station. The fine shouldn't be more than a couple hundred bucks. That'll cost less than replacing your shoes." I turned and headed to the door.

"Wait!" Tiffany jumped up from the chair and teetered after me. "You can't tow my car."

I never broke stride. "Watch me." Out the door I went.

Tiffany click-clacked into the hall after me, surprisingly fast in her heels. "Don't get your granny panties in a bunch. I'll move it."

I stopped and she tottered past me, muttering under her breath. She'd forgotten to take an umbrella or raincoat, but I didn't extend her the courtesy of reminding her. I stepped back to the open classroom door to keep an eye on the kids.

A moment later, a hefty woman with cropped dark hair and a collection of chins overflowing the neck of her dress came up the hall clutching an armful of copies. When she saw me, her eyes grew wide and she scurried my way. "What's going on?"

I held up a hand. "Nothing to worry about, Mrs. Nelson. Your intern just went to move her car out of the disabled parking spots."

Mrs. Nelson frowned. "If Tiffany wasn't working for free, I'd fire that girl. She has no interest in being a teacher. She only went to college for the parties, and she majored in education because she somehow got the impression that teaching would be easy. There's nothing easy about this job." Mrs. Nelson shook her head before making her way past me and ambling to her desk.

I turned to go. "Bye kids." Several looked up and waved to me, the girl who'd forgotten her lunch money giving me a big smile. Zane's only response was a soft snore.

Tiffany passed me in the hall on her way back to the classroom. Her wet clothes clung to her body and her hair hung in soggy clumps around her face. She glanced at me, her eyes blazing with fury. "These shoes are ruined. I hope you're happy."

What do you know? I *was* happy.

CHAPTER TEN

A NOT-SO-FUNNY THING HAPPENED
ON THE WAY TO THE DINER

My umbrella wasn't where I'd left it. I finally found it in the bushes outside the front door, where Tiffany had tossed it after the wind had turned it inside-out. *That Tiffany better watch her step. She's on my shit list now.* Cops are allowed a lot of discretion and I planned to exercise every bit of my discretion where this arrogant bitch was concerned.

"Marnie?"

I looked up to find Trey coming up the walkway, a large black plastic tackle box in one hand. He wore navy slacks today, with a red and blue plaid shirt visible through the unzipped windbreaker. The TreyTech badge was clipped above his left breast pocket. He was every bit as sexy as he'd been last night, maybe even more so with beads of water in his shiny black hair, his gray eyes sparking like lightning in a stormy sky.

I willed my racing heart to slow down. "Hey, Trey." I eyed the tackle box. "Surely you're not going fishing in this weather?"

"Nope." He raised the box with one hand while running the other over his hair. "Carry my tools in here. I'm upgrading the school's computer system. It's hopelessly outdated."

Just like everything else in Jacksburg. "We've got the same problem over at police headquarters."

He pulled a business card out of his shirt pocket, holding it out to me. "I'd be glad to stop by and take a look."

I held up my palm. "Sorry, not enough money in the budget. We'll have to make do." Unless, of course, he'd let me pay him in sexual favors. Heck, I might even throw in a generous tip.

"Take it anyway," Trey said, still holding out the card. "You'll need my number if you get a sudden urge for a Pac-Man rematch."

I had some other sudden urges I'd like to call him about, other games I'd like to play with him, games in which we could push each other's buttons and both score. I took the card and slid it into the back pocket of my pants.

He cocked his head. "Got any lunch plans?"

"Nothing I can't change." I'd packed a peanut butter and jelly sandwich and some carrot sticks in my Wonder Woman lunch box, but they'd keep until tomorrow. And who was I fooling anyway? The carrot sticks were for show. I'd never eat them. But if Trey picked me up at the station, Selena would spend the rest of the afternoon bombarding me with questions about him. "I'll be out patrolling this morning. Why don't I swing by here at noon and pick you up?"

He looked over at the cruiser parked at the curb. "In the patrol car?"

I nodded. "Ever ridden in one?"

"Once."

I raised my eyebrows in question.

"When I was eight I ran away because my mom wouldn't let me have a brownie before dinner. The police picked me up a mile from home. My parents grounded me from video games for a month. Worst four weeks of my life. I went through major Super Mario withdrawal."

"I'm glad to see you've recovered." I shot him a smile. "See you at noon."

As I headed down the sidewalk, I had to restrain myself from hollering "Woo-hoo!" and hurdling the metal bike rack. I'd missed the Ninja rider today, but now I had a lunch date with Trey. *Things are looking up.*

***

I spent the rest of the morning dealing with a couple of fender benders, standard fare for a stormy day. By noon, the rain had slowed to a gray mist that might have depressed me had I not been excited about my lunch date.

Trey was waiting inside the glass doors of the school when I pulled up to the curb. He trotted through the drizzle and hopped into the front seat. "Hey, again."

"Hey yourself."

"Where's the best place to get lunch around here?"

I gestured at the school. "It's sloppy Joe day in the cafeteria. Can't hardly beat that."

Trey cringed. "I found a hair net in my chocolate pudding once in junior high. Sworn off school cafeterias ever since."

"Can't blame you there."

Food options were limited in Jacksburg. Other than a half dozen fast food places, the only restaurants were a barbecue joint out on the highway, an all-you-can-eat catfish place, or Lorene's diner on Main. I put the car in gear. "Lorene's, it is."

I radioed Selena to let her know where I'd be, then pulled out of the lot and headed into town.

"I'm glad I ran into you," Trey said. "I was planning on driving into a tree and calling 9-1-1 so I could see you again."

"You could've just called the station and asked to speak with me."

He slapped his forehead. "Right. Duh." He shot me that same mischievous grin from the bowling alley, the one that made me want to wear crotch-less panties and dance and bake cookies, all at the same time.

When we stopped at a red light at Dumont and Main, Trey looked over at me. "What's it like, being a cop?"

In a big city, a cop was part soldier, part psychologist, and part referee. In Jacksburg, I felt more like a glorified hall monitor. "Honestly? Being a cop has its moments, but for the most part it's pretty boring. You just drive around town, always on the lookout for—"

"Whoa!" Trey's eyes locked on something out the window behind me. "You see that?"

I turned to spot the back of a tall guy wearing baggy jeans and a Dallas Cowboys hoodie. He clutched a handgun in his fist. He yanked open the door of the Grab–N–Go and darted inside. *Gah! An armed robbery. What a way to start a date!*

I turned on my flashing lights, gunned the engine, and careened into the lot of the convenience store. "Stay in the car," I ordered as I shoved the gearshift into park. "Don't let anyone come inside the store."

I radioed for backup, jumped out of the cruiser, and pulled my gun from its holster. My shoes slid on the slick pavement as I rushed up to the glass windows at the front of the store, but I managed to keep my balance. Displays situated against the window inside blocked my view into the building. I crouched down and peeked in between a cardboard potato chip display and a metal rack filled with *Thrifty Nickel* magazines. The guy in the hooded sweatshirt stood at the front counter, his gun pointed at the bald, jowly face of Chip Sweeney, the middle-aged, beer-bellied clerk.

My heart sputtered in my chest like the Icee dispenser. I held my gun in both hands, took a deep breath, and leaped up, shoving the door open and rushing inside. "Police! Put your weapon down and your hands in the air!"

The guy in the sweatshirt shrieked and raised both hands in the air, his right hand still clutching the gun. His face was dark, but the hands raised above him were definitely Caucasian. I squinted. The robber wore black panty hose over his face. *What a dumb ass.* With his hands in the air, his baggy jeans slipped down a few inches, revealing a pair of striped boxer-briefs and a belly button. The guy sported an outie.

I pointed my gun at his head. The dark hose obscured his facial features and pulled his nose flat, giving his face a warped shape. With the dark hosiery over his head and the baggy clothes, his age and physical features were indeterminable. "I said put your weapon down! Now!"

The guy looked up at his hand as if surprised to see the gun there. He slowly began to lower his hands, then changed tactics, yanking his pants up with one hand, turning, and bolting past a rack of disposable diapers as he ran to the back of the store. He barreled through the swinging door of the stockroom, slamming the door against the wall. *BAM!*

Through the glass doors I saw Andre's cruiser blast into the parking lot. "Cover the back door!" I screamed into my shoulder mic.

I ran into the dimly lit stockroom after the robber. The guy dodged around stacked boxes of beer and motor oil, looking for an exit, having trouble seeing with the black hose still over his face. When he realized I was catching up to him, he grabbed a four-pack of toilet paper off a stack and hurled it at me. The package bounced off my shoulder and landed at my feet. I kicked the toilet paper aside and ran down the row of boxes.

He spied the back door and scrambled toward it, tripping over a case of powdered donuts, smashing the top of a box with his knee and sending up a sweetly-scented poof of white powder that coated the front of his jeans. He staggered to the wide gray metal door and shoved the bar to open it. It didn't budge. "Fuck!"

A thick sliding bolt held the door in place. The guy jerked on the bolt with his left hand, but only managed to move it a couple of inches.

I crouched behind a stack of Diet Pepsi twelve packs and peeked out, my gun pointed at his hood. "Drop your weapon now or I'll blow your head off!"

It would have been easy to take the guy out with a bullet right then. But I couldn't do it. *Not again.* He was armed, had not put down his weapon, and my training told me to shoot. My instincts, however, told me otherwise. Police work was one percent training, ninety-nine percent instinct. As a cop, I'd learned to trust my intuition, my gut. But every once in a while instincts went wrong and cops died. I hoped this wouldn't be one of those times. *Getting myself killed sure would put a damper on my lunch date with Trey.*

The guy turned to face me. His hood slipped backwards off his head and the legs of the panty hose, still attached, dropped down, one on each side of his face like long bunny ears. He dashed forward, hunched over, heading back through the stockroom doors and into the store, leaving a trail of powdered sugar in his wake, the legs of the black panty hose streaming behind him.

Ugh. Should've shot him in the nuts while I had the chance. The world was already full of idiots like him. No sense letting him create any more. He wasn't even smart enough to cut the legs off the hose. *Definitely an amateur.*

He dashed out the front door, past the cruiser where Trey stood, half-in and half-out of the open passenger door. Ignoring my earlier orders, Trey took off after the robber, leaping onto his back and bringing him down in an oily puddle next to the gas pumps where the two of them narrowly missed being run over by a bright yellow Volkswagen bug pulling up to refuel.

The guy put up a good fight, bucking like a bronco, trying to shake Trey loose, sending up splashes of murky rainwater. But Trey held on, keeping the bastard down on the ground. Gotta say, I hadn't expected a brainy guy like Trey to be so tough, so brave, so fearless. *Maybe a computer nerd could be my type after all.*

When Trey saw me approaching, he rolled sideways off the man's back. I yanked my pepper spray from my belt, turned my head and squeezed my eyes shut, shooting a steady stream directly at the robber's face.

Busted.

"Aaahhh!" The guy covered his eyes and nose with his hands, and rolled around on the ground, kicking up more dirty rainwater with his tennis shoes. His jeans had again worked their way down and the waistband was now bunched around his knees, his drenched boxers clinging to his pasty ass.

Andre came around the side of the building, hurried over, and snatched up the gun from the ground where the guy had dropped it when Trey pounced on him. Andre looked the thing over, frowned, and handed it to me.

The gun was unexpectedly light. I examined it closer. The damn thing was one of those toy Airsoft guns that shoots plastic BBs. *This idiot could have gotten himself killed for carrying a stupid toy!* What's worse, I would've been the one to kill him, the one who'd suffer the overwhelming guilt. At least my other kill had been self-defense, necessary and justified. Hell, I'd almost bled to death from knife wounds myself before the ambulance arrived.

Chip stepped up beside us, noting the white powder on the robber's jeans. "Cocaine?"

"Nah. Powdered donuts. He crushed a case in the stockroom."

"Darn it." Chip frowned. "Powdered donuts are one of our best sellers."

After a moment or two, the initial effects of the pepper spray wore off, and the idiot stopped wailing and rolling around, settling into a soggy, sobbing lump on the pavement. Using my foot, I nudged him onto his belly, knelt across his back, and cuffed him. I backed off to kneel beside him. "Sit up."

He rolled over onto his back and rocked forward a few times in a vain attempt to sit up. He lacked the abdominal strength needed, so I stood, grabbed the legs of the too-tight panty hose, and pulled on them, hauling him by his head to a sitting position. "You ought to think about doing some crunches, buddy."

I yanked again on the hose, trying to remove them. The darn things were so tight on the guy's face they pulled his eyelids, lips, and nose upwards, his nostrils flaring like a pig snout.

"That hurts!" he cried.

"Tough." I pulled on the panty hose with both hands. Six yanks later, they were off. I checked the tag. Control top, petite size A. *What a doofus.*

I looked down to find an ugly, greasy-haired kid with a silver hoop through his eyebrow, a forehead hosting a zit convention, and a few scraggly brown whiskers, a sorry excuse for a soul patch, under his bottom lip. "How old are you?"

The kid looked down at his lap, coated with wet, white powder and tiny gravel bits from the parking lot. "Sixteen."

Just young enough to still be considered a juvenile under Texas law. Lucky for him. Texans don't believe in coddling children. Under our criminal justice system, seventeen-year-olds were treated as adults, eligible for life terms and lethal injections, though we don't trust them with beer until they're twenty-one. *Go figure.*

"Shouldn't you be in school?" I asked.

Before he could answer, the Star Wars theme song rang out loudly from the back pocket of the kid's jeans. I reached my hand into the pocket and pulled out a cell phone. The caller ID readout said "Banger."

I tapped the button to accept the call and held the phone to my ear. "Yo, Banger."

"Dawg?"

"Dawg can't talk right now. His sorry ass is being hauled off to juvie."

There was a short pause as Banger processed the information. "No shit?"

"No shit."

I ended the call while Andre pulled the kid to his feet. "Get in the car," I said. "And if you know what's good for you, don't give us any more trouble."

"Yes, ma'am." Tears began to well up in the kid's eyes. If he was looking for sympathy, he'd have to look elsewhere. *What if I'd shot the kid and later found out he'd been armed with a mere toy?*

I'd have never recovered from that.

Once the kid was settled in the back seat, I radioed Selena. "Get someone from juvie over to the station."

"Okey-dokey."

The car was quiet while we drove back to headquarters, the only sound being the kid snuffling in the backseat. Trey glanced over at me a few times during the trip, his expression one of admiration and awe. Heck, I was just doing my job. And, truth be told, I'd been scared to death.

I pulled under the overhang at the DQHQ, parked next to my Dad's SUV, and turned to Trey. "This'll take a few minutes. Want to come inside?"

"Sure."

I led the boy into the station. Trey followed. Selena glanced up from the TV, which was tuned to Family Feud. "Juvie's on their way." She did a double take when she saw Trey behind me. A suspicious smile crept across her lips.

I shot her a death glare to keep her from saying anything embarrassing. "Selena, Trey. Trey, Selena."

The two nodded to each other.

Trey followed me and the kid back to the freezer, eyeing the eagle Glick had etched into the stainless steel wall the night before. "Wow. That's good. Who did it?"

"Lucas Glick, believe it or not."

Trey cocked his head. "He's a darn good artist. Does he do that for a living?"

"Nah. He runs a septic tank service."

"It's a crappy job," Trey said, "but somebody's got to do it."

I groaned at his pun.

Trey stepped into the cell to take a closer look at the eagle. "Seems like a waste of talent."

Lots of things were wasted were Lucas Glick was concerned, including, most often, himself.

After Trey left the cell, I removed the cuffs from the boy's wrists and backed out quickly, keeping my eyes on the kid and my hand on my nightstick. The kid looked as though he'd given up but I'd seen desperate people make desperate moves. I'd learned to be ready for anything.

Trey settled in on the opposite side of my booth, checking e-mail and playing games on his cell phone while I filled out paperwork and telephoned the boy's mother. *No father, no big surprise there.*

When I finished, I left Trey at my booth and spent a few minutes in the bathroom with the blower aimed at my uniform, drying the rain the kid had splashed on me during his arrest. My bangs were hopelessly frizzy, but I combed the rest of my hair out and re-braided it. I even smoothed on a touch of toffee-tinted lipstick since I didn't have to worry about my helmet smudging it today.

When I returned to my desk, I found Trey sitting at my computer, typing on my keyboard and manipulating my mouse. He looked up when I stepped up to the table. "You weren't kidding about your system. This is pathetic."

"Told ya."

He clicked a few more buttons. "It should run a little faster now. I defragged it for you."

"I have no idea what you just said," I replied, "but thanks. Faster is always better."

A sly grin spread his lips. "Is it?"

CHAPTER ELEVEN

HOT LUNCH

Ten minutes later, we made our way across the black and white checkered floor of Lorene's and slid into a red vinyl booth. A boney middle-aged waitress with menus in one hand and a lit cigarette in the other passed by and tossed two greasy menus onto the table without saying a word to us. That's the kind of service you get when a business has no real competition.

Trey picked up a menu and opened it. "What's good here?"

"Everything." What Lorene's lacked in atmosphere and service, it made up for in deliciousness. There wasn't a single diet dish on the menu, nothing heart-healthy, nothing low-calorie or gluten-free. Lorene used only real butter, real cream, and real mayonnaise, which explained why most of her customers were real close to having a coronary.

I didn't need to look at a menu. I'd eaten here hundreds of times over the years and had the entire thing memorized. I sat back against the booth and closed my eyes, the all-too-familiar post-bust shakes trying to kick in. I tightened all my muscles to try to keep them under control. When I opened my eyes, I found Trey watching me.

"You all right?"

"Will be once I get some French fries." *And a lobotomy.*

We made small talk while waiting for the waitress to take our order. Trey told me he'd graduated ten years ago from Texas Tech University with a master's degree in computer science and gone to work for a high-tech company in Silicon Valley. "I'm on a medical leave from my job right now."

My gaze roamed over him, looking for open sores, hair loss, any signs of disease.

"It's not me," Trey said. "It's my dad."

Guess I'd been a bit too obvious checking him out.

Before Trey could elaborate, the waitress stepped up to the booth to take our orders. "The usual?" she asked me.

"Yup."

"Peach cobbler?"

"Not today, thanks." The last time I'd stepped on the scale it registered well on the backside of one-fifty, and most of that one-fifty was on my backside. Even with my large-boned build and oversized breasts, that was pushing it. Better get some of this weight off, in case I had to chase down a stupid teenager again.

Trey ordered a burger with onion rings and a Coke. After the waitress left, we returned to our conversation.

"My dad had a minor stroke last month," Trey said. "I came home to help out until he recovers."

His words revealed three important things. One, like me, he was close to his family. Two, he still considered Hockerville home even after a decade living out of state. And three, he'd only be around temporarily. *Just my luck. I finally meet a cute, smart, funny guy and he'll be taking off soon.* Fate was toying with me yet again.

Then again, maybe it wasn't such a bad thing he'd be leaving. I could have a fling with Trey, then move on to the Ninja rider once Trey left town. Double my pleasure. No harm in that, right?

We talked for a few minutes about his family. Trey had an older sister who lived in Dallas and was busy with a family of her own. Just the segue I needed to find out more about his situation. Most people our age came with baggage. I was okay with that as long as the baggage was a small carry-on and not a deluxe five-piece hard-sided set.

"What about you?" I asked. "Ever been married?"

Trey shook his head. "Between my job and my God-awful commute, I don't have much time to date. I've gone out with a few of the women from work, but it was more for convenience than any real connection. What about you?"

"Married my college sweetheart. Spent eight years together in Dallas before we realized we wanted different things out of life. Got an amicable divorce and moved back home."

"Kids?"

"No." *Thank goodness.* I didn't need any more guilt than I already had. "Got a dog, though."

"What kind?"

"Great Pyrenees."

"Cool."

I pointed at his badge. "Tell me about TreyTech."

He shrugged. "I got bored sitting around my parents' house so I figured I'd do some contract work. Upgrading software, installing wireless networks, that kind of thing. Maybe develop some websites while I'm in town."

The guy clearly knew his way around computers. The most technologically challenging thing I knew how to do was download music to my phone. "We can use a guy like you around here." Normally, computer techs were sent out from Dallas to take care of any major technical problems in the area and they charged a premium for the travel time. "How long you here for?"

"'Nother month or so."

We made small talk for a few minutes and I steered the conversation into a direction where I could ask about the driver of the Ninja. Since Trey was from Hockerville, he just might know the guy. "I've seen a new motorcycle in the area recently. A yellow and black Ninja ZX-14. Any idea who the bike might belong to?"

Trey's gray eyes narrowed, looking pointedly into mine. "Why are you asking?"

A hot blush rushed up my neck to my freckled cheeks. I looked down at the table, pulled the salt shaker toward me, and twirled it between my fingers. Anything to avoid his pointed gaze. "Just curious. It's a killer bike."

I could feel his eyes still on me. "Sure there isn't more to it?"

Am I that obvious? I forced myself to look at him. "What if there is?" After all, it wasn't like Trey planned to stick around long term.

Trey sat back in the booth, stretching one arm along the top. "Yeah, I know the guy who owns it."

My heart somersaulted in my chest. "What can you tell me about him?"

"I could tell you plenty." That mischievous smile crept across his face again. "But I'm not going to."

"Why not?"

"Because you're the most interesting woman I've met in years. Why would I screw that up?"

Me? Interesting? Suddenly, knowing who rode the Ninja seemed much less urgent.

Trey cocked his head. "This has already been my most exciting date ever. Never had one before that involved a wrestling match and handcuffs."

"That's just for starters."

He raised a brow. "I like the sound of that."

I began to think all kinds of exciting things could happen with Trey. Fun things. Enjoyable things. *Naked, warm, sexy things . .* .

The waitress plopped our food and drinks down on the table, along with a bottle of ketchup which, in my current state of mind, I'd describe as half full. She headed back to the kitchen without a word.

Trey picked up his thick burger, took a huge bite, and closed his eyes in ecstasy. "Man, this is good."

"Told ya." I snitched an onion ring off his plate and popped it into my mouth. He opened his eyes just in time to catch my act of thievery but didn't seem to mind. *Another point in his favor.*

Over lunch, our conversation took an intellectual turn, and we found ourselves discussing the economics of the real estate markets in Texas and California, the pros and cons of the death penalty, the relative merits of western culture and our focus on technological advancement versus eastern philosophy that focused on achieving inner peace.

Trey listened intently when I spoke, seemingly interested in what I thought, what I had to say. In technological terms, we'd achieved connectivity, at least on a mental level. Maybe once we knew each other better we'd achieve it on a physical level, too. I was in dire need of some good lovin'.

After lunch, I drove Trey back to the elementary school and pulled up to the red-painted curb, leaving the engine idling. The storm had finally blown over, though a few puddles remained along the cracked, uneven walkway.

"Thanks for lunch," I said.

"Any time." He opened the door, climbed out onto the sidewalk, and bent down so he could make eye contact with me. "What're you doing this weekend?"

I'd probably do the same thing I did every weekend, watch *Wonder Woman* re-runs on DVD with Bluebonnet while folding laundry. I shrugged. "Nothing special."

"Good. Then I'm claiming your Friday night."

"What do you have in mind?"

"Something adventurous involving a small electronic device."

I shot him my *hell no* look. "I don't swing that way, Trey."

"It's not what you think. Trust me. It'll be fun."

His expression was so hopeful, how could I say no? Besides, I could use a diversion. *Desperately.* "Just know that if you don't show me a really good time, I'll beat the tar out of you with my nightstick."

"Is that a threat or a promise?" He flashed a seductive grin.

I jotted my address down on the citation pad, ripped the page off, and handed it to him.

He took the paper. "Is seven good?"

"Yup."

He closed the door to the cruiser and I watched as he strode up the sidewalk to the doors, looking trim and energetic. He was attractive for a computer geek. Heck, he was attractive, period. I wondered if the Ninja rider was as cute as Trey. *Only time will tell.*

CHAPTER TWELVE

NO NANCY DREW HERE

Tires squealed behind me and I checked the rearview mirror to see Tiffany Tindall's red Spyder careening into the school parking lot. Tiffany began to pull into the handicapped spot again, but she apparently noticed the cruiser sitting at the curb and yanked the steering wheel back. She drove past me and eased into a spot at the end of the lot. She climbed out, pushed a button on her keychain remote to lock the doors, and teetered toward the front doors on her heels. I rolled down the cruiser's passenger window, waiting for her.

"Slow it down, Tiffy," I called as she passed by, her cell phone once again glued to the side of her face. She acted as if she didn't hear me.

Somebody needs to teach that girl some manners. And that somebody just might be me.

***

Late that afternoon, a loud rumble outside the station caught my attention. This one didn't come from the sky, it came from the delivery truck pulling into the lot. Eric hopped down from the driver's seat, rolled up the back door of the truck, and retrieved a large box from the cargo bay. The bell jingled as he came in the door. I met him at the counter.

"Hey, Eric. You remember delivering a package to a house on Renfro Road yesterday afternoon?"

Eric set the box on the floor and pulled his handheld electronic device from his pocket. He punched some buttons with the stylus. "Let's see here. 612 Renfro. Yeah. Left a package there at 3:57 PM."

"Who was the package addressed to?"

He jabbed more buttons. "Someone named Logan Mott."

The last name sounded vaguely familiar.

"Who was it from?"

Eric consulted the screen. "Barneys New York."

"Really?" Someone sure had splurged. Chet had once shopped there when he was on a business trip in Manhattan, came home with a pair of shoes that cost more than my wedding dress.

Eric cut me some side eye. "Is there a problem?"

I'd been in law enforcement long enough to know you provided information on a need-to-know basis only. For all I knew, Eric could be involved in something fishy. Then again, I could be making a mountain out of a molehill and someone in Barney's mail order department could have simply screwed up the address. I shrugged. "I thought the house was empty, but I must be mistaken. Thanks."

I headed back to my booth, leaving Selena and Eric to chat. I logged into my computer to search the DMV driver's license records for a Logan Mott in Jacksburg. No Logan came up, but the listings showed a Hank Mott and a Rhonda Mott, both at 108-B Purdy Court. A married couple, most likely. Maybe they were related to Logan and could get me some contact information. *What the heck. I've got nothing better to do.*

I grabbed the keys to the cruiser and waved good-bye to Selena. "I'll be out for a bit."

Five minutes later I pulled to the curb in front of the Motts' half of a small, rectangular duplex. The house was white with green trim, decently kept for a rental, but not the type of place you'd expect a Barney's New York shopper to live in. On the covered porch sat a pink bicycle with training wheels and a white basket adorned with plastic daisies. A green garden hose coiled in the corner like a harmless garden snake.

A silver mini-van pulled into the court and stopped beside my patrol car. The side door slid open and a small, light-haired girl wearing a red rain slicker and carrying a ballerina lunchbox hopped down. She set her lunchbox on the ground and used both of her tiny hands on the handle to pull the door closed. She retrieved her lunchbox and headed straight inside the Mott's half of the duplex. In Dallas, gated communities were all the rage. In Jacksburg, nobody locked their doors.

The mini-van circled the cul-de-sac and headed back onto the main road. The rain was again in mist mode, so I left my mangled umbrella in the car and made my way up the narrow sidewalk to the green-painted door. I rang the bell and a few seconds later heard muffled sounds from inside. In case someone was looking out, I smiled a friendly smile at the peephole.

The door opened to reveal a thirtyish woman, also light haired. She wore yellow latex gloves, and held a sponge in one hand and a green can of Comet in the other. She was still in her pajamas, the sure sign of a stay-at-home mom.

"Hi, there." I stuck out my hand. "Captain Muckleroy, Jacksburg PD."

She stuck the Comet into the crook of her arm, pulled off her right glove, and shook my hand. "Something I can do for you, Captain?"

"I'm looking for someone named Logan Mott."

"Logan?" The woman's face scrunched up in confusion. "What do you want with her?"

Again, need-to-know basis only. "I'd prefer to discuss the matter directly with Miss Mott. Can you give me a phone number and address?"

The woman's scrunched-up face got even scrunchier. "Logan lives here."

"Is she home now?"

"Yeah." The woman stepped back to allow me into the house. She poked her head down a narrow hallway off the foyer. "Logan? Come here a minute, hon."

The sound of a door slamming and padding feet came up the hall. The little girl from the bus stepped into the foyer and looked up at her mother expectantly.

The woman put her bare hand on the girl's shoulder and turned the girl to face me. "This is my daughter, Logan."

Huh? I smiled down at the girl before looking back up at her mother. "There must be some mistake. I'm looking for a Logan Mott who placed a mail order from Barneys New York."

The little girl's brows drew together. "Do what?"

"We're the only Motts in Jacksburg," the woman said. "My husband's got family over in Jefferson, but this here's the only Logan in the family." She ruffled her little girl's hair.

"Is it possible someone ordered a gift for Logan from Barneys?"

The girl's face brightened at the thought of a gift, but her mother shook her head. "Not likely. She doesn't have a birthday coming up. I've never heard of Barneys, neither. We mostly shop at the Walmart over in Hockerville."

The situation made absolutely no sense. I had no idea what to make of it. But instinct told me this woman and her child were innocent of any wrongdoing.

"Sorry to have bothered you ma'am. I must have gotten some bad information. But in case something turns up, can I get your phone number?"

"Of course."

As she rattled off the number, I entered it into my cell phone contacts list. I reached into my breast pocket and retrieved a brown Tootsie Roll Pop, handing it to Logan after her mother gave me a nod of approval. I'd learned back in Dallas that carrying a lollipop was just as important as carrying a gun, and far more useful when it came to calming a terrified child. I'd handed out more Tootsie Roll Pops to more frightened children than I cared to remember. *Trick or treat. Say bye to Daddy, he'll be back in five-to-ten.*

I returned to the cruiser and sat in the front seat with the engine off, trying to process the available information. Had someone at Barney's made a mistake? Had someone at the delivery service made a mistake? If the little girl in the duplex was the only Logan Mott in town, who had picked up the package addressed to her that was left at the house on Renfro?

I finally decided that since I appeared to be the only one worrying about the box, maybe I should stop worrying about it. Weird stuff just happens sometimes.

So does good stuff. The good stuff was that I had a date Friday, with a high-tech hunk. What better excuse to stop by Savannah's and borrow something cute to wear?

**

Savannah had been my best friend since forever. She used to be two sizes smaller than me, but after squeezing out three boys in six years she'd expanded and now matched me inch-for-inch, pound-for-pound. Bad news for her as she lamented her lost figure, good news for me as it doubled my wardrobe.

I pulled into the driveway of Savannah's house, a red brick one-story tract home in a small suburb, if you could call it that considering there wasn't much "urb" in Jacksburg. Our downtown consisted of two square blocks of strip center retail stores and single-story office complexes, with the three-story credit union building, Jacksburg's sole skyscraper, in the center.

I parked the car, turned on my flashing lights, and stood in the open door of the cruiser. I got on the PA system. "This is a fashion emergency. Come out with a cute blouse in your hand and no one gets hurt."

Savannah's front door burst open and her boys, ranging in age from five to eleven, poured into the front yard, all bruises and Band-Aids and gap-toothed grins. Savannah trailed behind them, still wearing her work clothes, a basic black dress and flats, carrying a stained floral dish towel.

Zane ran in circles around the car, apparently re-energized after the nap he'd taken at school today. Eight-year old Dylan chimed in with "this car is lit," while eleven-year-old Braden described the cruiser as "cool as shit."

Savannah twirled the towel into a tight loop and snapped it at Braden's butt. "Watch your mouth."

By then the neighbors had begun to peek out their windows, so I turned off the lights before rumors could begin to fly. The boys wailed with disappointment.

I scooped up Zane, lifted his lime green T-shirt, and put my mouth to his bare stomach, blowing with all my might and treating him to a good old-fashioned belly blaster. He thrashed in my arms, giggling with glee. I set him down and stretched out my arms toward the other boys, fingers waggling. "Who's next?"

They squealed and ran off into the yard.

Savannah leaned against the front fender of the cruiser, arms crossed over her chest. "Fashion emergency, huh? What's up?"

"I've got a date Friday night."

Her hazel eyes bugged under brown bangs overdue for a trim. "A date? Boy howdy, girl, it's about time." She grabbed me by the arm and pulled me into the house. A variety of smells greeted me. Spaghetti sauce from the pot bubbling on the stove. Laundry detergent from the load sloshing in the utility closet at the back of the kitchen. Stinky boys' feet from, well, her stinky boys. Those stinky boys followed us into the house.

Savannah called back over her shoulder as we headed through the living room. "Don't you boys bother me and Marnie unless somebody's bleeding. Who knows when Marnie will get a date again."

"Gee, thanks."

Savannah dragged me down the hall to the bedroom she and her husband, Craig, shared. She pulled me into the cluttered room and locked the door behind us. Kicking off her shoes, she flung herself onto her unmade bed, her legs crooked up behind her, just like she'd done back when we were girls. "So, tell me all about him. Is he cute? Is he sexy? Does he have a good job?"

I sat down on the edge of the rumpled periwinkle blue bedspread and gave her the rundown on Trey, telling her all I knew, which wasn't much. *Cute? Yes. Sexy? Hell, yeah. Good job? Freelancing here, employed regularly in the tech industry in California.*

Savannah turned onto her side, her head propped up on her elbow. "All I got to say is I'm glad you finally have someone to think about other than that mystery man with the Ninja. I'm sick and tired of hearing about him."

I stuck my tongue out at her. "You're just jealous because you're an old married woman and all your romantic fantasies are over." Old friends can say things like that to each other because we both knew it was absolute bullshit. Savannah was living my dream— a sweet husband, a handful of rambunctious children, a home of her own.

Savannah rolled off the bed, stepped into her closet, and began to rifle through her clothes. "Where are y'all going?"

"I don't know. He said it would involve an electronic gadget. That's all I know."

She peeked her head out of the closet. "Electronic gadgetry, huh? I've got just the thing." She pulled a skimpy black lace teddy from a hanger, put a finger in the stretchy crotch, and slingshot the thing into my lap.

"It's not that kind of electronic gadget. I've already confirmed." I picked the teddy up by the thin shoulder straps and swung it over my head like a lasso, sending it sailing back to her.

She snatched the flying lace out of the air. "Too bad." She resumed her search.

"Remember," I said, "it's got to have long sleeves." My Wonder Woman bracelets could only do so much and didn't fully conceal the jagged, tell-tale scar on my wrist. I hadn't worn short sleeves in public since the day I'd acquired it. People might see it and jump to conclusions or, worse yet, ask questions I didn't want to answer.

After showing me at least a dozen potential outfits, she

eventually convinced me to wear a pink satin ruffled blouse, far more girlie than my standard fare, but maybe it was time to try something different. She pushed the hanger into my hand.

"The tags are still on it," I said.

She rolled her eyes. "I don't know why I even bought the thing. Craig and I never go anywhere. We never have the time or energy to go out and, even if we did, we don't have the money to go anywhere special. Every time we turn around one of the boys needs new shoes. You wouldn't believe how fast their feet grow."

I decided I'd wear jeans with the blouse. No sense going all out. Trey wouldn't be around for long and, even though it was my first date in a year, I didn't want to look like I was trying too hard. Back in my college dating days I'd discovered the ironic truth that the less special you treated a man, the more special he thought you were. Guess it's reverse psychology. Or maybe *perverse* psychology. But that's the game of love. Anyone crazy enough to join in had to play by the rules.

CHAPTER THIRTEEN

THE ONLY DIFFERENCE BETWEEN
MEN AND BOYS
IS THE PRICE OF THEIR TOYS

The next three days were drizzly and dreary, with no sign of the Ninja. Despite the weather, my spirits were bright with that pre-date high. I could hardly wait to see Trey again. I cruised by the elementary school several times, but hadn't been lucky enough to catch him on his way in or out. Good thing, probably. Didn't want to appear desperate.

When I arrived home from work on Friday, I found Dad in the kitchen, mopping huge muddy paw prints off the floor. I glanced out the back window, noting fresh holes under the scrubby cedar tree. Looked like Bluebonnet had been having some fun in the rain-soaked yard. Uncle Angus was perched on the countertop, drinking a Shiner Bock. He tipped his bottle at me in greeting.

Dad plunked the mop into the bucket of soapy water and leaned on the mop handle. "Angus and I were thinkin' of heading out to the Chuck Wagon for chicken-fried steak. Want to come along?"

"Thanks, but I can't. I've got plans."

I never had plans. Which is why Dad tilted his head, waiting for details.

"It's a date," I explained.

"Now, honey," he teased, "you know you're supposed to bring the boy to meet me before I'll allow him to take you out."

The last boy I'd brought home to meet Dad was Chet. "You'll like this one. He works in computers. He's a really good bowler, too."

"A bowler, huh? Guess he's all right then."

Bluebonnet and I ate leftover tuna casserole for dinner, then I took a shower and prepared for my date, wearing a pair of plain tan flats with the ruffled shirt and jeans, hoping they'd be suitable for whatever we'd be doing. Trey arrived promptly at seven, wearing his hiking boots, faded Levi's, and an untucked light-blue cotton shirt with the sleeves rolled up to just below the elbow. He looked sporty and adventurous.

Dad and Angus followed me to the door and the three men introduced themselves. Trey's gaze went from Dad's long braid to mine. It's not often a father and daughter wear the same hairstyle. To Trey's credit, he seemed unfazed by my dad's appearance. Good thing, too. I came from a long line of blue-blooded biker stock and made no apologies for my heritage.

Bluebonnet wandered in from the kitchen to see who was stopping by. Trey crouched down, getting face-to-muzzle with her. "Hello, there." He ran a hand down her neck and scratched under her chin. She wagged her tail and licked his cheek, a good omen. Bluebonnet was an excellent judge of character.

We bade Dad, uncle, and dog goodbye. The storm had finally broken and we made our way through the soft, early evening sunlight to the car, a bronze Lincoln sedan. Not exactly what I'd expect a single guy in his early thirties to drive, but maybe he'd borrowed it from his parents. A sizzle ran up my spine as Trey put his hand on my back to help me into the passenger side.

The seats were soft and cushy. "Comfortable car," I said as Trey slid into the driver's seat.

"It's my mom's," Trey said. "I took the first flight out after my dad's stroke. My car's back in California."

I put my hand on his arm when he stuck the keys in the ignition. "Before we go any further, show me that electronic device. I want to know what I'm getting myself into here."

Chuckling, Trey reached over my legs and into the glove box, pulling out a bright yellow device about the size of a cell phone. He held it up.

"What is it?" I asked.

"GPS." He pressed a button on the gadget and the small screen lit up.

"We planning on getting lost?"

"Nope. We're going geocaching."

"Geo-whatting?"

"Caching. It's a cross between a high-tech scavenger hunt and orienteering."

Wow. This guy is a total nerd. So how come I felt the urge to throw him into the backseat and have my way with him right there in the driveway?

Trey went on to explain that unknown people all over the world, identified only by secret code names, planted caches in hidden spots, noting the locations on websites so others could attempt to locate them. Geocaching sounded different, fun, adventurous even.

He handed the GPS to me and I looked it over. "I can't imagine there'd be many of these caches around Jacksburg." The citizens of Jacksburg resisted innovation, partly out of respect for tradition, partly due to the expense of electronics. Heck, the scoreboard on the high school football field was still changed by hand.

"Surprise," Trey said, handing me a computer printout. "There's three caches within a six-mile radius of Jacksburg."

I looked at the printout. On the list were coordinates for three caches denoted with odd names. *Kickin' It Old School. Nut Job. Tower of Power.* "What do these names mean?"

"They're hints," Trey said. "They usually give a clue where the cache is hidden. The GPS is only good to within ten feet or so." He took the device back from me and situated it on the seat between us where we both could see it. "'Kickin' It' is the closest one, so let's try that first. Watch the screen and tell me where to go."

I pointed the the road heading northeast. "That way."

We spent the next few minutes working our way to the first location. We pulled onto the road by Jacksburg High and the readout counted down the distance to the cache. Three-hundred feet. Two-fifty. Two-hundred feet.

"We're almost there." Trey turned into the high school parking lot and pulled into a spot at the back by the gym. We climbed out of the car and went the rest of the way on foot, the GPS guiding us, ending up at the gate to the football stadium.

"Kickin' it," Trey said, his face thoughtful. He looked around for a few seconds, then his eyes brightened. "Got it."

I followed him across the field to the end zone, the grass on the field still damp and soft thanks to the day's rain. The air smelled fresh, felt cool against my face. Trey stopped at the metal goal post, his gaze moving upward. "There it is." He reached up to a small cylindrical plastic container attached by a magnet to the horizontal pole of the goal post. He opened the container and pulled out a narrow, tightly wound strip of paper.

I craned my neck to see. "What's that?"

"A log." Trey explained that when a cache is found, the finder records his or her code name on a log contained in the cache. He pulled a pen out of his back pocket, smoothed the log out on his thigh, and signed his name to it. When he handed the log and pen to me, I twirled my finger in the air, motioning for him to turn around. He put his back to me and I held the log against his shoulder, using it as a solid surface to write on, fighting the urge to run my hand over the lean, hard muscle. I noticed Trey had referred to himself as "Computer Geek." I identified myself as "Wonder Woman." My eyes scanned the signatures on the list. Among them were "Rowdy Redneck," "Cowpoke," and "The Jacksburg Jackass." I had several nominees for the last appellation.

I handed the pen and log back to Trey. "This is fun." Not the typical first date, but I was beginning to think Trey was anything but typical.

Trey toggled a switch on the GPS. "'Tower of Power' is the closest cache to here. Four point two miles south. Let's try that one next."

Fifteen minutes later, we stood under a towering transformer, an occasional *zzt-zzt* of stray electricity punctuating the otherwise quiet evening. A ten-foot chain link fence topped with loops of barbed wire surrounded the structure. The gate was chained and padlocked. We followed the fence, looking for anything that could be a cache.

Having been trained to search for discarded weapons and drugs hurled from moving vehicles, I'd developed a keen eye. I spotted a clear plastic milk jug tucked at the base of a wild bush nearby. At first glance it appeared to be trash, but then I noticed it contained something. I crouched down and pulled it out from under the bush. "Could this be it?" I shook the jug and it rattled loudly.

"Sometimes people leave prizes for the others who find their cache."

I took off the red plastic cap and we peeked inside. At the top of the jug was another rolled-up paper log. Underneath the log were dozens of colorful glass marbles, the kind kids used to collect and trade back in the day. "Hold out your hands."

Trey cupped his hands and I poured a handful of marbles into them. I fingered though, picking out a glass cat's eye streaked through with yellow and black, the Ninja's colors. Trey chose a solid red one. He poured the rest back into the milk carton, bending down to retrieve the few that fell to the grass. We signed the log and returned the jug to its spot under the bush.

Geocaching was a bit pointless, perhaps, but it beat the hell out of a stuffy dinner at the country club, my ex's idea of good time. I liked the adventure of not knowing where our quest would take us next, of working with Trey, combining his technical savvy with my street skills to track down the treasure, solve the mystery. With our complementary skills, we made a great team.

Trey punched a couple of buttons on the GPS. "Now for 'Nut Job.'"

We hopped back into the Lincoln. I checked the device and pointed out the side window. "That way." We headed southwest as far as we could, took a short detour due west, then went southwest again on a narrow county road, past fields with dried-out cotton plants, a once-dry stock pond now brimming with the day's rain, and a scattered herd of Holstein cattle.

Consulting the GPS, I noted we were still on course, two point three miles from our destination. I directed Trey down a shortcut, a long-forgotten fire road that ran between a horse paddock and a cornfield. I was enjoying Trey's company, thinking how I wouldn't mind spending more time with him, when I remembered our time would be limited, why he'd come home. "How's your dad doing?"

"Really well," Trey said. "The doctors are amazed at how quickly he's recovering."

I looked out the window so Trey wouldn't see my disappointed expression. Selfish of me, I know, to hope his father's recovery would be prolonged. I didn't want Trey's father to suffer, but I'd already had more fun with Trey tonight than I'd had in the entire year I'd been back in Jacksburg. I'd like a little more time with him before he returned to his job in California.

With night now approaching, the sky morphed into a pastel tie-dye of pink and purple, the clouds having been blown to the east, now dropping their rain on the Piney Woods of east Texas and the casinos just across the state border in Shreveport.

The GPS counted the distance down to zero. Trey pulled the car to the shoulder and we looked around at the dusky, barren landscape around us.

"Nut Job," Trey murmured, thinking aloud. "What could that mean?"

I looked about at the grass, the caliche, the trees. Two scrubby mesquites. A gnarled live oak. And a tall pecan. "Bingo."

Trey followed me over to the tree and we searched around the base. *Nothing.* Not even fresh dirt indicating the cache might be buried. Our eyes traveled up to the lower branches. Nothing hung from a lower branch or perched in a forked limb near the trunk.

The night had grown too dark for us to see further up into the tree with any clarity. Trey pulled a small flashlight from his pants pocket. He stepped up next to me, so close his arm brushed against mine, setting my nerves on edge. He shined the light up into the tree. At first we saw nothing, but as he slowly scanned the beam around, our eyes caught something square lodged in a V in the upper branches.

"They didn't make it easy on us, that's for sure." Trey handed me the flashlight, still warm from his hand. I kept the beam steady on the cache while Trey jumped up, grabbing a lower branch with each hand, pulling himself into the tree, his shoulder muscles and biceps flexing visibly through the fabric of his shirt. I imagined what it would feel like to be enveloped in those arms, held closely to his chest.

The limbs shook under Trey's weight, sending a bombardment of pecans to the ground below him. I stepped back to avoid the barrage of nuts.

"Sorry about that!" he called down to me.

Trey perched halfway up the tree, looking at the branches above him, considering his options. The branches higher up were smaller and could be too thin to support his weight.

"Careful up there," I warned.

"Okay, Mom."

"Smart ass."

Trey grinned down at me before cautiously picked his way higher. "Got it." He tucked the white plastic box under his left arm and eased his way back down the tree, stopping to sit on a lower branch, one leg curved around the trunk of the tree for support, the other dangling down.

I looked up at him. "Impressive. You part chimpanzee or something?"

Trey swung his free leg. "Rock climber. Go whenever I can. I'm planning on climbing El Capitan in Yosemite next summer."

"So you're a thrill-seeker?"

"I suppose you could say that."

CRACK! The branch on which Trey was sitting gave way and he tumbled out of the tree, dropping the box and grabbing at the lower branches in an attempt to break his fall. He fell forward, right at me. There was no time to get out of the way.

Hwump! The air left my lungs in an instant rush as my back hit the soft, wet dirt. Next thing I knew, I was lying on my back with Trey on top of me. *And I had no complaints whatsoever.*

Trey's face was only inches from mine, and his lips looked soft, warm, undeniably kissable.

"You okay, Marnie?"

Other than having the wind knocked out of me, I was fine. "Yeah," I said once I managed to catch my breath. "But if this is your idea of a come on, you might want to think again."

He chuckled and pushed himself back, crouching over me now, straddling my legs, his thighs mere inches above mine. I looked up, straight into his silver-flecked eyes. He gazed back at me, making no further move to get up.

I want this guy. I want him bad. And I want him now, right here in the mud and gravel and grit. But I wasn't exactly a sex-on-the-first-date kind of girl. At least I hadn't been the last time I was on the dating circuit more than a decade ago. "You gonna let me up?"

He ignored my question, continuing to stare into my eyes. "There's something incredibly sexy about a woman who can take a hit like that."

I shrugged my shoulders in the dirt, no doubt doing a number on the brand-new blouse Savannah had given me. "What can I say? I'm built tough."

His lips pulled into his now-familiar cockeyed grin. His gaze strayed from my eyes to my lips, up the round curve of my freckled cheek, and back to my eyes, taking in my features, appraising. The grin and the look in his eyes softened, telling me he liked what he saw, a strong woman, a street-wise woman, a woman who could handle anything life threw at her. *Well, almost anything.*

He angled his head slightly and I stopped breathing again. I knew that look.

He's going to kiss me.

CHAPTER FOURTEEN

A LITTLE LESS CONVERSATION, A LITTLE MORE ACTION

Trey lowered his lips to mine. My eyes drifted closed and I lost myself in the kiss. He kissed me again, letting his lips linger this time, barely touching mine, a feather-light kiss that left me feeling all airy on the inside and wanting more.

When Trey pulled back, I opened my eyes. He gazed at me a moment more, then stood, reaching a hand down to help me up. It took everything in me not to pull him down onto the ground with me. Once I was vertical again, I walked over to the base of the tree where I'd dropped the flashlight and picked it up.

Trey retrieved the cache, removing the red rubber band holding the white plastic box closed, then pried open the lid and peered inside. He pulled out the paper log and handed it to me, then stuck his hand back into the jar. When he pulled his hand out, he held a couple of pecans, still in their shells, painted to look like people.

I shined the flashlight on them for a better look. One had tiny denim pants, a red shirt, and a smiling face, with a tiny scrap of bandana glued to his head, like a biker's do-rag. The other wore a pink-and-white polka dot skirt, a pink top, and had three strands of yellow yarn glued to her head for hair. Both had tiny pieces of cardboard glued to the bottom, made to resemble shoes, which would allow the nuts to stand on their own.

"I've heard of pet rocks," Trey said, "but not pet nuts."

Only in Jacksburg.

Facing me, Trey set the box on the ground and held up the nut people, one in each hand. "Which one do you want?"

I took the male nut. "He's kind of cute."

Trey faked a jealous pout. "I might have to crack him."

"Don't worry. You're cute, too."

"You think so?"

I gave him a coy smile. "Maybe."

"Cute enough to let me kiss you again?"
When I responded with a nod, he leaned in and gave me another kiss, this one a little more forceful, a little more fun, a little more *please-don't-ever-stop-I-need-this-like-I-need-air.*

When he pulled back, I opened my eyes and again fought the urge to grab him, throw him to the ground, and rip his pants off. A woman has needs and mine hadn't been met in over a year. Trey's kisses had reignited those needs something fierce.

We signed the log and Trey placed it back in the jar. After securing the lid, he tucked the cache into a forked limb in easy reach from the ground. No sense in someone breaking their neck for a pet pecan.

Trey draped an arm lightly around my shoulders. "Coffee?"

"Heck, yeah."

We climbed back into the Lincoln, propped our pecan people on the dashboard where we could keep an eye on them and make sure they didn't get into trouble, and headed toward Hockerville. We made small talk on the way. He wanted to know more about me, so I told him about my days as a criminal justice major at Sam Houston State University in Huntsville. The college town was home to the state penitentiary, as well as the prison museum that housed "Old Sparky," the infamous electric chair that sent hundreds of inmates into the great hereafter with a final, hair-raising jolt. During my senior year of college, I'd served a stint as a docent at the museum to earn some extra spending money, having the perverse privilege of explaining Old Sparky's workings to bloodthirsty tourists wanting all the sick, twisted details of the executions and the horrific crimes committed by those put to death. People were fascinated by violence, until it happened to them or someone they love. Then they fought to understand it, to stop it. *Futile endeavors, both of them.*

I glanced over at Trey. "What kind of computer stuff do you do out in California?"

"I program for a company that makes computer and video games."

No wonder he'd been so good at all the video games at the bowling alley. "Work on any games I might know?"

Trey turned off the highway and onto the road that led into Hockerville's town square. "I started out working on educational software for kids, the kind with math games, word games, stuff like that, then I moved on to more creative stuff. I did some of the programming for Bonzai Surf Bonanza, Demolition Derby, Mall-a-Palooza, Fel—"

"Mall-a-Palooza? That the one where you fight with other women over clothing and purses and jewelry and stuff?"

"That's it."

"I've played that." Selena was hooked on it, and often dragged me into a game with her. Cops have to kill time somehow when people aren't trying to kill each other. "That game is hilarious.

I got into a fight with a grandma over a hot pink thong. She wrestled it out of my hands and ran off wearing the thing." The graphics on the game were fantastic. You could see every wrinkle on her saggy white rear.

Trey chuckled. "I can't take any credit for the concept. A woman in marketing came up with the idea after a weekend trip to the outlet stores in Gilroy. But I did most of the programming on the game, even snuck in a couple of cheats. Next time you play it, try running in circles around the rounder rack. The prices go down each time you complete a revolution."

Too bad the real mall didn't work that way. "Sounds like a fun job."

Trey's eyes gleamed with boyish glee. "It's a freaking blast. I basically get paid to play all day. I can't imagine doing anything else."

Okay, so video games aren't essential to life, but they are part of the fun that makes life worth living, that helps us endure the daily grind. I'd been a huge Centipede fan myself when I was younger, dropping so many quarters into the machine at the Grab-N-Go that I'd single-handedly financed Chip Sweeney's bass boat. But the violent video games, the disturbing ones that portrayed brutal crimes as amusement, were another matter entirely. The worst offender was Felony Frenzy, a sadistic and horrifying game in which the player could assume the role of a pimp, a crazed drug addict, or a gangster, and terrorize innocent people, rape prostitutes, slay cops in unbelievably brutal ways. *Sick, disgusting stuff.*

I glanced over at Trey. "I'm glad to hear you work on the mild games. Whoever works on those really twisted, violent ones should be taken out to the woods and shot."

He arched a dark brow. "Wouldn't that be ironic?"

I had to admit my logic was warped. "Guess so. But the parents who buy that crap for their kids must be crazy."

Trey shot me a pointed look. "It's just make believe, cops and robbers played on a screen instead of in the backyard. Playing an animated game isn't going to turn an otherwise normal, law-abiding kid into a dangerous psychopath."

"'Course not. I just don't like the games that glorify violence. I've seen the real thing up close and personal and it's anything but entertaining."

No, there was nothing amusing about searching on your hands and knees through shag carpet, trying to help a bruised and bloody woman find her front teeth after her husband has given her an extreme makeover with the fireplace poker. Nothing fun at all in trying to console the teenaged victim of a sexual assault, her innocence stolen from her at what was supposed to be a fun, summertime pool party. Nothing enjoyable in breaking up yet another gang fight, mere boys intent on killing each other, engaging in all-out wars over worthless turf littered with garbage and covered in graffiti.

Trey turned away, looking out his window into the dark night. By putting down certain segments of his occupation, I'd probably indirectly insulted him. But I couldn't help feeling the way I did, and I certainly hadn't meant to attack him personally.

After a few seconds, he turned back with a smile, letting me know any unintended slight was forgiven. "You know, you're like a character from a video game. Tough. Heroic. *Sexy*."

My heart fluttered. I might not be a character in a video game, but Trey sure knew how to play me. "Yup, that's me. Lara Croft, Tomb Raider." Minus the waistline. Mine melded with my bust and hips.

We entered Hockerville's historic district and drove past the Magnolia Manor, a bed and breakfast housed in a sprawling Victorian. The house was painted a soft sage green, trimmed in pale yellow, and surrounded by a stand of towering magnolia trees with caladiums and white vinca surrounding their trunks. "Beautiful house," I thought aloud.

"Ever stayed there?"

I shook my head. "Nope. Went to a bridal shower there once." No sense telling him the shower had been for me, hosted by Savannah just a few weeks before my wedding. The house was full of ornate antiques, faded portraits of former owners of the manor, and gaudy old-fashioned floral wallpaper. I absolutely loved it.

A few blocks farther, Trey eased the car into a parking space in front of the Java Joint, a coffee house situated in an upscale white stone strip center that also contained a day spa and a wine shop, neither of which would have been successful in Jacksburg.

The smell of roasting beans, vanilla, and whipped cream taunted our olfactory senses as we walked in the door. I ordered a white chocolate latte, while Trey decided on a frozen coffee drink. We shared a huge slice of caramel-drizzled cheesecake from the bakery case. So much for watching my weight.

We sat at a small round table on the sidewalk in front of the coffee shop, enjoying the cool evening. The night was totally dark by then, the previous night's clouds replaced by a thin sliver of moon, bright stars, and the far-off pulsating flash of the red warning light atop the water tower east of town.

We talked more over our drinks, and I learned that Trey had graduated from high school a year before me. We shared many of the same memories. The time a crop duster crashed into the Hockerville water tower, the plane's landing gear catching on the support beams, the plane hanging upside down while its pilot miraculously escaped unharmed. The time an oil tanker overturned on the highway, the only major artery into Hockerville, forcing the road to be closed for two days straight. An opportunistic farmer created an unofficial detour through his property, charging drivers three bucks apiece to cross his back forty. The time at the Ruger County science fair when a homemade robot went berserk and burst into flame, igniting the cardboard display. The smoke had activated the sprinkler system and flooded the VFW hall. That was the last time the veterans offered to host the event.

"That poor kid," I said, thinking back.

"What a dork, huh? Those Coke-bottle glasses, knobby knees, superhero underwear."

Superhero underwear? "Did you have gym with that kid or something?"

"Not exactly."

It hit me. "That kid was *you*?"

He offered a sheepish grin. "Guess I got some wires crossed or something. But they still let me keep my first-place ribbon."

As we talked, Trey and I discovered we had a surprising number of things in common despite the obvious disparities in our career paths and lifestyles. We both liked goofy, mindless movies, the more hopelessly ridiculous the better. We both avoided social media. It's not that we didn't care about the world around us, it's just that we'd already formed our beliefs and felt no need to listen to opinionated people complain incessantly about the current state of affairs. Our online entertainment go-to was funny cat and dog videos on YouTube. And we both loved the capellini Roma at Marangelli's, a popular Italian restaurant in downtown Dallas.

Trey pushed the plate of cheesecake toward me so I could have the last bite. "I want to see you again tomorrow."

Another date? So soon? Didn't that break all the rules of dating? But, what the heck. *The rules don't apply to mere flings anyway, right?* "Okay."

Knowing our relationship couldn't go anywhere took the pressure off, allowing me to relax and simply have a good time, exactly what I needed at this point in my life. Heck, why not pack in as much fun as I could before Trey returned to California? It's not like I'd do something foolish and fall helplessly in love with the guy.

***

We debated the relative merits of Wonder Woman versus Flash Gordon as we drove back into Jacksburg, past the baseball fields with their sagging wooden bleachers, past the DQHQ where Bernie could be seen through the glass sitting at the counter gluing another model, past the brightly-lit Laundromat where a woman wearing a pink bathrobe and slippers stood in front of an open dryer folding blue bath towels and placing them in a white plastic laundry basket. *Laundry on a Friday night?* Guess I wasn't the most pathetic woman in Jacksburg after all.

Trey turned down the road to my house, pulled into the driveway, and parked beside Dad's battered Cherokee, eyeing the I GRIND STUMPS logo. His mouth spread in a naughty grin. "Please tell me that's your SUV."

"Nope. Sorry to disappoint you. And your stump."

The porch light was on, but otherwise the house was dark. Dad had apparently gone to bed already, his belly full of the Chuck Wagon's chicken-fried steak and mashed potatoes. Taking my hand in his, Trey walked me to the front porch. The moths flitted around the bright bulb while aimless June bugs thudded against the window glass and dropped, stunned, to the porch.

We stopped at the door and I looked up at Trey. "Thanks. I had a good time."

"Good? Is that all? Because I had a *great* time." He entwined his fingers in mine and stepped toward me.

My heart screamed "weee!" inside my chest as his gaze went to my lips. No doubt about it, he was going to kiss me again.

He looked up at the porch light blazing above us. Dropping my hands, he opened the front door and stuck his arm inside, feeling around for the light switch. When he found it, he flipped off the light, the darkness now giving us privacy. "That's better."

He softly closed the door and stepped back over to me. Easing a hand around the back of my neck, he gently pulled me to him, our lips touching softly. *Yum.* He stepped closer to me, closing the space between us, his chest pressed to mine.

When he slipped his warm tongue into my mouth it was all I could do to remain standing. After a few luscious seconds, he took his mouth from mine. His hand grasped my braid behind me and pulled downward on it until my head tilted back, exposing my throat, giving his mouth access to my bare neck. His actions were gentle enough not to offend, but forceful enough to let me know he wanted me just as bad as I wanted him.

He encircled my waist with his other arm, easing kisses under my chin, under my ear, down the slope to where my shoulder began. Pretty hot for a first date. But then again, I hadn't had a first date in a dozen years, not since my first date with Chet. Very likely things had changed since then. Besides, it wasn't like we were naïve college kids. We were adults who'd been around the block a few times, who knew what we wanted, whom we wanted.

And right now, I wanted Trey.

Trey's kisses got me so hot and bothered I wouldn't have been surprised to see steam seep out of the zipper of my jeans. But with my father sleeping in his bedroom just twenty feet away, it wasn't like things could go anywhere at that moment. Finally, and with great reluctance, I pushed him away. "Good night, Trey."

He threw his head back and groaned. Clearly he'd become hot and bothered, too. He pulled me to him one last time for a brief closer kiss.

I flipped the porch light back on as I shut the front door

behind me. Standing in the front hallway, I could hear my heart beat so loud in the silent house I was sure it would wake Dad and Bluebonnet.

For the first time in days, I fell asleep thinking of something other than the mysterious man who drove the Ninja ZX-14. Instead, I thought about Trey. He was proving to be an unexpectedly effective distraction. Being with him tonight had made my loneliness, my boredom, my lingering guilt all seem to fade away.

The next few weeks could be really fun, just as long as Fate didn't find out about him. If she did, that skank would find a way to ruin things for me, as usual. I issued warnings to motorists all day long, but tonight I issued one to myself. *Be careful, Marnie. You're going down a dangerous road.*

CHAPTER FIFTEEN

LICENSE AND REGISTRATION, PLEASE

On Saturday, Trey and I drove two hours west to a state park in Mineral Wells. The park encompassed not only a sizeable lake, but also a rocky bluff known as Penitentiary Hollow, a popular rock climbing destination.

Trey looked sporty and daring decked out in his climbing gear, his tools in a black vinyl pouch around his waist. The guy was sharp, but he definitely had a spirited side, too. He fitted me in a nylon harness, having to adjust the upper straps to accommodate my generous proportions. He gave the straps a tug to test them, then used the strap to pull me to him for a kiss.

"That was sneaky," I said when he released me.

"You learned your lesson, then," he said. "You've got to stay on your toes."

Connected by ropes, we inched our way up the face of what Trey considered a relatively shallow canyon but what to me might as well have been Mount Everest. But I'd made it through the police academy, right? Even if that was nine years and twenty pounds ago. Besides, Wonder Woman wouldn't balk at a challenge and neither would I.

The air was cool, an early glimpse of the fall that waited

around the corner, but the rock face was warm, having absorbed the sun's heat. An occasional breeze blew through the canyon, flowing across our backs, carrying with it the faint scents of exposed earth and cedar. A lone buzzard circled overhead, probably hoping we'd plunge to our deaths and provide him a fresh and easy lunch.

After half an hour clinging to the side of the cliff, sweating, grunting, and maneuvering, painstakingly working our way up the forty feet or so of vertical face, we reached the top. Trey had instructed me along the way, providing pointers. He probably could have made it to the top in mere minutes if I hadn't been slowing him down, but he was nice enough not to say so.

I scrambled over the edge and stood on the rim next to him, victorious fists in the air. He held up both palms for a two-handed high five. I obliged, my shout of "I did it!" echoing off the opposing cliff wall. He grabbed me in a bear hug, smiling down at me.

He looked tough and rugged, a smudge of dirt across his forehead, a bit of leaf in his hair. The guy challenged me, mentally and physically, showing me just how strong and capable I could be, making me feel alive again. And, in return, he seemed intrigued by my ready willingness to take on challenges. My heart exploded in a burst of colorful confetti. *I like this guy. I mean REALLY like this guy.* I was pretty sure he really liked me, too.

I gave him a loud, appreciative smooch. "So, where's the trail back to the bottom?"

Trey stepped to the edge of the ravine and pointed down. "That way."

I take back everything I just said about challenges. Going up was one thing, but looking over the edge at the sheer drop filled me with sheer terror. I forced my lungs to breathe and my lips to smile. "Okay. Let's do it."

Trey gave me another quick lesson, then we rappelled back down into the gulch.

"Woo hoo!" The brief sense of freefalling was an absolute rush. I could see why Trey was hooked on this sport.

We repeated the process, moving on to climb other parts of the cliff. By the end of the day, every muscle in my body ached and every joint throbbed, but it was worth each and every spasm to enjoy the luscious kisses Trey left me with that evening.

***

Trey and I Facetimed for two full hours Sunday evening, engaging in idle chatter, the kind of conversation you have when you have nothing much to say but simply want to spend time with the person on the other end of the line. I fell asleep that night with only Trey on my mind.

With the light of Monday morning, though, things were more clear. *Trey is a temporary diversion only*, I reminded myself, nobody I should let myself get too worked up about. In a matter of weeks he'd be long gone, nothing more than a pleasant memory. No sense putting all my eggs in one basket, especially if that basket would soon be catching a 747 back to California.

I drove to headquarters and checked in with Selena, happy to find out that Lucas Glick had managed to go the entire weekend without causing trouble. Maybe the guy had thought about what I'd said and was trying to get his act together. I hoped so.

With the roads now dry, the Ninja would likely be out again. If I saw the bike today, I'd pull the rider over even if he hadn't committed a violation. I could always make up some bullshit about a similar bike having been reported stolen or claim to be performing a routine insurance check.

I parked my motorcycle behind the welcome sign at a quarter after eight and pulled out my phone. *First things first. Can't wait for a hot biker without proper music.* I tuned up some music appropriate for the occasion, Golden Earring's "Radar Love."

Before I could plug in the radar gun, a red blur blasted past me, tires squealing as the open convertible turned onto Main, the blond hair of the driver trailing in the wind.

Tiffany Tindall, at it again. That spoiled brat seemed to think the laws didn't apply to her. Time to give the girl a reality check. Today she'd be getting a ticket.

I turned on my lights and took off after her. Luckily for me, Tiffany was stuck at the traffic light at Main and McDougal.

I pulled up behind her. She had her rearview mirror turned toward the driver's seat and was looking into it, applying a coat of magenta lipstick that perfectly matched her silky long-sleeved blouse. She didn't notice the flashing lights behind her. *What a self-absorbed twit.*

At point-blank range, the sound of the siren would just about burst your eardrums. Luckily for me, my helmet served as a noise barrier. Sure, I could've just called out to Tiffany. After all, she was only ten feet in front of me with the top down on her car. *But what fun would that be?* I flipped on the siren. *Heh-heh.*

WOO-WOO-WOO!

Tiffany's mouth gaped in an all-out shriek and her arms reflexively flung outward. The tube of lipstick flew out of her hand and into the street, promptly pulverized by the knobby wheels of a flatbed truck heading in the opposite direction. Tiffany covered her diamond-studded ears with her hands and whipped her head around, skewering me a death glare.

I jerked my thumb to the right, directing her to pull over, and turned off the siren. She floored the gas pedal and roared into the parking lot of the Dollar Depot, her tires squealing as she slammed on her brakes.

After parking my bike, I stepped up next to her. She'd

stopped the car, but left her engine running. "Turn off your engine and show me your license and registration."

She made no move to follow any of my instructions. "What are you pulling me over for? I didn't do anything wrong."

"You were speeding."

"Prove it. Show me the readout on your radar."

I hadn't used the gun, but Miss Fancy-britches didn't need to know that. "Cleared it already. Now turn off your car and show me your license and registration."

"No radar readout?" She smirked and gunned her engine as if to emphasize her words. "Our attorneys will have a field day with that."

Threatening me with lawyers? Not a smart thing to do. "Turn off your car and give me your license and registration. I'm not going to ask you again, Miss Tindall."

Tiffany rolled her eyes but turned the engine off. "Don't you have something better to do?"

"You mean like hunt down an armed robber? Or a rapist? Or a serial killer?"

"Exactly."

I shook my head. "Nope. You're by far the most dangerous person we've got here in—" I bent down and looked into her eyes— "*Bumfuck.*"

Tiffany's eyes blazed, but she seemed to sense I had the upper hand, at least for the moment. She reached over to open her glove box, taking her sweet time rifling through the papers inside. She handed me her registration, followed by a dog-eared Nordstrom's ad. "Here you go. You might want to check out the sale in the plus-size department."

The bitch was trying to goad me into doing something impulsive and stupid. It wasn't going to work. I may be a bit thick around the middle, but I'm also thick-skinned. Had to be to survive as a cop. Besides, I'd been called worse. Femi-Nazi. Pussy. Even the C word a couple of times. I'd discovered that a healthy dose of pepper spray put a quick end to potty mouth. Still, I could give as good as I could take. "As long as we're on the subject of shopping, you might want to pick up some Clorox at the Piggly Wiggly." I gestured at her mouth. "A little bleach should take care of that mustache problem."

Tiffany's eyes squeezed into an eat-shit-and-die glower. "Let's get this over with. I've got places to be." She grabbed her black Prada bag off the passenger seat and plopped it onto her lap. She reached inside, yanked out her coordinated wallet and flung it open, sending a cascade of credit cards onto her lap, the passenger seat, and the floorboards.

"Dammit!" Tiffany frantically grabbed at the cards, scooping them into her open purse. She must've had at least ten cards, including several Visas, a couple of MasterCards, and even a Discover. *What the heck does one woman need with so many credit cards?* Then again, coming from a moneyed family, maybe it was to be expected.

Two sharp beeps sounded from the street to my left. The Ninja drove by, its driver in black ankle boots and yellow and black leathers, his gloved hand up in greeting. My bones felt like they'd turned into noodles and I had to put a hand on the hood of Tiffany's car to steady myself. He was probably just acknowledging me as a fellow biker, after all a friendly wave was a rule of biker etiquette, but a part of me hoped the greeting was more personal. I watched him drive off down Main, realizing I'd been too shocked to wave back.

"Do you want my license or not?" Tiffany impatiently waved her license between two fingers sporting a fresh French manicure.

When I reached for the card, she let the license fall from her fingers to the parking lot at my feet.

"Oops." She shrugged and flashed an insincere smile. "Clumsy me. Guess you'll have to pick it up."

I picked up Tiffany's license, noting that she looked a bit different in the photo. I held the license up next to her glaring face.

Busted.

She'd obviously had a nose job since the photo was taken. I also noted that the color of eyes indicated on her license was hazel. She must wear colored contacts, too. The only thing real about this girl was that she was a real bitch.

I noted two offenses on the ticket, the first for for driving 65 in a 30 miles-per-hour zone and the second for reckless driving. She had me feeling generous. I held the small clipboard and a ballpoint pen out to her. She took the clipboard, but refused the plastic pen, pulling an insanely pricey Montblanc from her purse instead. She didn't bother to read the citation, just signed it, left-handed, with an exaggerated flourish. I took the clipboard back and looked down at her signature. Her handwriting slanted to the left and the T's were pointy, the top line angling down on each side of the vertical one, resembling a sharp arrow. Instead of dotting the I's in her first and last names she'd made fierce slashes.

Just for kicks, I added another charge to the citation, then tore the top copy off the ticket pad and handed it to her. She snatched it out of my hand. I removed her license from my clipboard and held it out to her. As she reached for it, I dropped it to the asphalt. "Oops." I shrugged. "Looks like I'm clumsy, too." My smile, unlike her earlier one, was sincere.

Tiffany shot me a look so hard and edgy I could've shaved my legs with it. I turned and walked back to my motorcycle, slid the citation pad in the saddle bag, and climbed onto the bike. I started the motor and rolled to the lot's exit, waiting for the oncoming traffic to pass so I could pull onto Main. The reflection in my side mirror showed Tiffany yanking her visor down to inspect her upper lip in her vanity mirror. Looked like my mustache comment had gotten to her. *Heh-heh.*

I headed down Main in the direction the Ninja had gone moments before, hoping I could catch him. At first I didn't see the bike, then a pickup truck turned off the road in front of me and there he was, three blocks ahead, driving past the Laundromat. My heart spun and sparked in my chest like a police cruiser's flashing light.

This is it. In a matter of seconds, I'd finally learn the identity of the Ninja rider.

I cranked my right wrist back to give the bike more gas. The engine had just kicked in when a school bus lumbered onto Main from a side street, cutting me off. *Gah! Where do they get these bus drivers?*

I slammed on my brakes, leaving a short skid mark on the road behind me. I eased over to the left to try to pass, but an SUV sat in the center turn lane waiting to turn into Burger Doodle, blocking my way. *Dang, dang, dang!*

I sucked bus exhaust for four blocks, ignoring the teenaged boys in the back windows, the two on the left pulling their noses up into pig snouts with their index fingers, one on the right mooning me with his fuzz-covered butt. Finally, the bus took a right turn and got out of my way.

The Ninja was five blocks ahead now, only a geriatric Dodge Dynasty with oxidized powder blue paint separating me from my dream man. Once I maneuvered around the sedan, I'd be home free. I was on the car's bumper when it began to shudder and sputter, slowing to a crawl.

"Un-freakin'-believable!" I hissed. Frustration flared inside me, like a blow torch in my gut.

We neared the end of Main and the center turn lane petered out. I couldn't pass on the right because the Dynasty would likely be pulling over to the curb at any moment. An eighteen-wheeler headed toward me in the oncoming lane. I wasn't about to take on the truck. I was stuck.

Finally, the driver of the Dodge eased his way over to the right shoulder. I probably should have stopped to help the driver, but it was his own damn fault if he ran out of gas. I zipped past the car to find the Ninja sailing through the intersection and the traffic light hanging over it cycling to red. I slammed on my brakes again and stopped for the light. As the cross traffic began to move, the taillight of the Ninja grew faint in the distance until it disappeared entirely around a tree-lined curve in the road.

He's not getting away this time.

I turned on my flashing lights and siren. Hey, if this wasn't an emergency, I didn't know what was. A green van and a silver hatchback screeched to stops halfway through the intersection. I maneuvered around them, gunning my engine once I'd cleared the cross street. Leaning forward to reduce wind resistance, I made it to the curve in eight seconds flat. My eyes locked on the road in front of me. I could see a full half mile ahead, but there was no Ninja. *Gaaaaah!* He must've turned off Main. *But where?*

Lights flashing and siren wailing, I circled through the parking lot of a shoe store. A toddler on the sidewalk yanked her hand from her mother's grasp and put her fists over her ears to block out the siren's earsplitting wail. *Sorry, kiddo.*

I headed back in the direction from which I'd come, racing up and down all of the cross streets, but the yellow and black bike was nowhere in sight. I turned off my lights and siren and banged my fist on the gas tank in front of me. *Fate, you're a frickin' bitch.*

CHAPTER SIXTEEN

CHECKING THE MAIL

I spent the next hour slowly cruising the streets of Jacksburg, but it was as if the Ninja and its rider had simply evaporated. Eventually, I gave up my futile search and headed back out to the highway to wait for more unsuspecting prey.

A few cars went by and I clocked them with the radar gun. Fifty-six miles per hour. Fifty-three. Fifty-five. All law-abiding citizens. *Where's a speeder when you need one?* At least the darn radar gun was working today.

An olive-green seventies model Charger came over the rise doing fifteen miles over the limit. *Milton Broesh, speeding again.* I must've written the guy a five tickets over the last year, four of them on this very stretch of highway. Didn't he ever learn?

As he approached, I turned on my engine and started the lights flashing. I was poised to follow after Broesh when another car came over the rise behind him, a silver Toyota Camry weaving back and forth across the center yellow stripe. The car veered onto the shoulder and off into the grass, kicking up gravel and dust, before swerving back onto the road again. *Larry Langley. Must've found Betty's latest hiding place for his car keys.*

It was Broesh's lucky day. I couldn't be two places at once, so I'd have to let him slide. I shook a finger at him as he drove past.

He shook a finger at me, too, but it wasn't the same finger. I'd have to let that slide for the moment, too.

I slid the radar gun into its sheath and squeezed the talk button on my shoulder-mounted radio. "Selena, call Betty Langley. Larry's out again."

I flipped on my lights and siren, though with as much macular degeneration and hearing loss as Larry Langley had suffered, he wasn't likely to notice either one. If nothing else, my lights and siren would warn other drivers to keep their distance.

I followed Larry for a mile with no luck. He continued to swerve side to side. Praying he wouldn't veer into me, I pulled up next to the driver's window and tried to wave Larry over. He wore a rumpled undershirt and a dopey expression. His white hair was wild, sticking out all over the place as if he'd just climbed out of bed. He stared straight ahead as he drove. I waved again, gesturing for him to pull over. Larry glanced over at me, his eyes sleepy.

I turned the siren off, beeped my horn, and hollered as loud as my lungs would allow. "Larry! Pull over!"

Larry nodded to me then rolled onto the shoulder, into the grass, and—*ping!*—straight over mile marker 192, flattening the metal sign to the ground. He rolled on another hundred feet before coming to a stop in a large mud bog leftover from last week's storm. *Ugh.* I'd just oiled my boots.

I parked my bike behind him and stepped up to the window as gingerly as I could, but my boots sunk in the muck anyway. I tapped on the window. Larry sat behind the wheel, his head lolled forward, eyes closed, fast asleep now. I tried the door but it was locked. I banged on the window with my fist. After a few seconds, Larry turned foggy eyes on me.

I made a circular motion with my hand. "Unroll the window, Larry."

It took him a full minute to find the button and roll the automatic window down in short jerks, an inch or two at a time, as he jabbed a crooked, arthritic finger at the control on the door panel.

When he finally got the window down, I put my forearms on the ledge and leaned in. "Larry you can't just—*holy crap!*"

I jumped back. Larry had an erection the size of the San Jacinto Monument sticking straight out of the front hole of his pale blue boxers. At the police academy, we'd been trained how to handle suspects wielding knives and guns, but there was nothing in the training manual about how to deal with a septuagenarian sporting a boner. I decided to wait this one out and let his wife figure out what to do. I retrieved his keys from the ignition, pulled my feet out of the mud sucking at them, and walked back to my bike. I sat side-saddle on the motorcycle, waiting, while Larry napped at the wheel.

A few minutes later, Betty Langley pulled up behind us in a *Brady Bunch*-era wood-paneled station wagon. She climbed out of her car, carefully picking her way through the mud in her tennis shoes toward the Toyota's open window. She stuck a hand through the window and shook her husband's shoulder. "Larry?" When he didn't respond, she stepped closer. "Larry? Larry? Oh, good Lord!" Betty jumped back, too.

She came to stand next to me on the shoulder. Her eyes darted around even though it was clear we were the only people for miles. She lowered her voice to a whisper. "Sorry about this, Marnie. Larry took a Viagra this morning but I wasn't in the mood. I slipped a sleeping pill in his decaf, hoping he'd leave me alone and take a nap."

With or without a sleeping pill in his system, Larry Langley shouldn't be driving. In fact, Chief Moreno had confiscated Larry's license months ago after Larry plowed into the Chief's wife, putting a major dent in both her bumper and her social life. Luckily, no one had been injured. Mrs. Moreno was pretty ticked off, though. Thanks to Larry playing bumper cars with her, she'd spilled Diet Coke all over her dress. She'd been forced to return home to change, arriving late for the Jacksburg Red Hat Society's monthly meeting at the VFW hall. All of Sally Brewer's homemade oatmeal raisin cookies had been devoured by the time Mrs. Moreno had arrived and she'd had to make do with store-brought shortbread. *Tragic.*

I stood, putting a sympathetic hand on the woman's shoulder. "Betty, you've got to sell Larry's car. As long as it's around, he'll want to drive it. If I catch him out again, I'll have to impound it."

Betty glanced over at her dozing husband, her face growing tight as if she were finally acknowledging to herself he was no longer the virile young man she'd married years ago. She turned to me, her voice soft. "I'll put an ad in the paper today." She stepped to the car door. "Could you help me get him into the station wagon?"

"Sure."

Betty tried twice to pull Larry's underpants over his erection, but both times it popped right back out the hole. She pulled a Texas map from the glove box, unfolded it, and wrapped it around him like a skirt, tucking the edges into the waistband of Larry's underwear. The odd topography indicated an unexpected mountain near Lampasas. Luckily for us, Larry was a spare fellow, not too difficult for two women to wrangle. I kept my eyes locked straight ahead, not daring to look down as we dragged him to the station wagon. Between the two of us, Betty and I managed to finagle him into the backseat. Betty strapped him in.

"I'll send our son for Larry's car," Betty said.

I took Betty's hand and looked into her sad eyes. "I'm sorry, Betty."

"Me, too, Marnie." She squeezed my hand. "But we've had a lot of good years, had three kids together, seven grandchildren. Even went to Hawaii once. What more could a woman want?"

What more, indeed. I could only hope to be so lucky someday. Oddly enough, when I considered my future, the family I might have, my first thought went to Trey.

Uh-oh. I wasn't falling for Trey, was I? Chasing down that killer last week had been dangerous, but falling for Trey was far riskier. A Kevlar vest can stop a bullet, but it can't protect a heart from being broken.

***

Later that morning, Selena contacted me on the radio about a reported burglary. After a brief investigation, I determined the stolen wind chimes were in the possession of the victim's next-door neighbor, who'd had more than enough *dinging* and *donging* interrupting her soap operas. After a few minutes of boisterous negotiation, it was agreed the chimes would be retired to the garage and replaced by a hummingbird feeder. *Bloodshed averted.*

On my drive back to the office, I crossed over Renfro. On a whim, I circled back around and turned down the street. I parked at the old Parker place and climbed off my bike to take a look around.

There were no boxes on the porch today, though there were several sets of muddy footprints. Someone had been sneaking around the place. I peeked in the few windows that weren't boarded up. A years-old calendar turned to December hung on the kitchen wall and a broom leaned in a corner next to the fireplace in the living room. There was nothing else in the house. No evidence of a squatter.

When I went in to the backyard, however, I noticed the padlock for Parker's dilapidated tool shed lay on the ground and the hardware on the door was bent. I opened the double doors to the shed to find a rotting wood floor littered with beer cans, the butts of two joints, and a foil condom wrapper. Looked like the shed was being used for private parties, most likely by high school kids. Maybe whoever had been hanging out back here was the one who'd placed the order from Barneys that was delivered to the house.

Mental note: Instruct the night shift officers to make regular stops by the property, see if they can nab anyone loitering about.

I climbed onto my bike and prepared to drive off when I thought of one more place to check. I backed up to the dented mailbox, the victim of a round of mailbox baseball, its red flag hanging down like a flaccid pecker. The thought made me shudder, thinking back on Larry Langley's morning wood. I reached into the box and pulled out the items crammed inside. A grocery store circular. A solicitation from an insurance company addressed simply to "resident." A bill from a cable company addressed to Mr. Parker with "Past Due" stamped in red ink on the envelope. *Good luck collecting on that one.* I was surprised they hadn't given up by now.

The final item was a MasterCard bill addressed to someone named Taylor Heidenheimer. I checked the address to ensure it hadn't been mis-delivered. *Nope. 612 Renfro.* This was the place.

I tore open the bill. The statement showed charges totaling over two grand in the last month. The merchants included Lord & Taylor, Neiman Marcus, and Saks Fifth Avenue. The situation was getting weirder by the minute. *Something is going on, but what?* I was a street cop, not a detective. Heck, I'd never even been able to solve the simple crimes in those *Encyclopedia Brown* children's books. *Maybe I should call the sheriff's department and let them investigate.* They had better resources than the Jacksbug PD. They could figure out what, if anything, was going on.

I slipped the bill into my saddle bag and headed off.

CHAPTER SEVENTEEN

GOOSED

As I rode, I radioed Selena. "Sel, do me a favor. Check the DMV records and see if there's a Taylor Heidenheimer listed in Jacksburg."

"Hang on."

I waited a few seconds before Selena came back. "No Taylor. There's a Martin Heidenheimer on Rural Route thirty-two and a Sherman Heidenheimer in an apartment on Newberry."

She gave me the addresses for both men and I jotted them down. Newberry was closer so I tried that address first. Nobody was home at the apartment. I stopped by the management office to find a young woman with curly red hair sitting at a desk, flipping through last month's *Cosmo*. Read that issue myself, learned the top ten sex tricks men love. Now I was just waiting for someone to try them out on. Maybe Trey would benefit from my recent literary education.

The woman glanced up as I stepped into the office. "Lookin' for an apartment? We got a one-bedroom just opened up. Overlooks the pool. Bit of a roach problem, but we got a guy coming to spray this afternoon."

"No, thanks. Actually, I'm looking for Taylor Heidenheimer. I think he or she might live here. Apartment 6B?"

She shook her head. "We got a Sherman Heidenheimer in 6B, but he lives alone."

"You sure about that?"

Still sitting, she used her bare feet to roll her chair over to a two-drawer beige metal file cabinet. She pulled the drawer open, pried a file out of the tightly packed space, and handed me a copy of a lease.

I thumbed through the document. Sherman M. Heidenheimer was the only tenant listed. The unit was a four-hundred square foot efficiency apartment, barely big enough for one person, let alone two.

I handed the lease back to her. "Sorry to have bothered you. I think I'm barking up the wrong tree."

"No problem."

Since I'd struck out at the apartments, I headed for Martin Heidenheimer's place. His property consisted of six acres, give or take, surrounded by white pipe fence. The metal gate was locked. No cars were in the driveway.

In what was likely a violation of federal postal regulations, I opened the mailbox and pulled out a stack of envelopes. All but one were addressed to Martin Heidenheimer. The only other piece of mail was a JCPenney ad addressed to Cynthia Heidenheimer. Nothing addressed to a Taylor. I shoved the mail back in the box and closed it, sitting back on my bike to think.

I felt like I was on a wild goose chase, except I wasn't even sure there was a wild goose. Was I so desperate for something interesting to happen that I was creating crimes in my mind? Or was I simply losing my mind, becoming paranoid like that psychologist had warned me might happen with the PTSD? If that were the case, my days as a cop could be numbered.

I forced the thought from my mind, started up my bike, and drove off.

***

First thing I did back at the office was call Martin Heidenheimer's phone number and leave a message on the machine asking him to get in touch with me. I spent the better part of the afternoon wiping down my boots and using a nail file to pry the dried mud out of the grooves on the soles.

Later that afternoon, the non-emergency phone line rang and Selena picked it up. "Jacksburg Police. How can I help you?" She listened, then covered the mouthpiece with the palm of her hand. "It's someone named Martin Heidenheimer. Says he's returning your call. Want to take it?"

I nodded and grabbed my receiver once the call was transferred. After identifying myself, I asked Martin if someone named Taylor lived at his residence.

"Yes, ma'am. We have a Taylor here."

Bingo!

I pulled a pen out of the chipped coffee mug on my desk and scrambled to find a pad of paper among the junk on my desk. Unable to find one, I settled for taking notes on the cover of my Harley-Davidson catalog. "I'd like to speak with Taylor, please."

"Is there some trouble?"

"That's what I'm trying to find out."

He paused a moment. "Hang on just a second."

After some muffled noises, a young girl's voice came over the phone. "Hi. Thith ith Taylor."

"How old are you, Taylor?"

"Thixth."

I wrote the number six on the catalog.

"You missing some teeth, sweetie?"

"Bofe of my fwont teef."

I sucked at detective work, but at least I'd put those clues together. "Can I talk to your daddy again?"

"Thure."

When Martin Heidenheimer came back on the line, I explained that I'd found a credit card bill in Taylor's name at the old Parker residence.

"What does it mean?" he asked.

"I don't know exactly. Could be identity theft, could be some kind of mistake." I took some information from him, including Taylor's date of birth and social security number. "I'll see if I can get to the bottom of this."

"Thanks, Captain Muckleroy. Let me know what you find out."

"Will do."

I looked down at the catalog, noting my only clue. *Six-years old.* Taylor was a child. What did that tell me? *It tells me I need to find some more clues.*

I called the bank and spoke to a representative from the legal department.

"Taylor's parents will have to file an official police report," the paralegal told me. "Once you get a copy of the report to me, I can e-mail a copy of Taylor's credit card application. It will take a few days to pull the file, though."

I wasn't sure if the identify thief would have applied for multiple cards with the same bank, but it was likely. After all, if a bogus application worked once, why bother trying a different bank? "There could be a second victim. A Logan Mott."

"I'll need a police report for that offense, too."

"Thanks. I'll get reports to you ASAP."

I called Taylor's father back and contacted Logan's mother, too, asking them to come to the station to fill out a report. After, I sat back in my booth to think. I had no idea what was going on and felt totally out of my league with this. I was the best-trained officer on the Jacksburg police force and I didn't have a clue what else to do. Speaking with Chief Moreno would be pointless. He was an old-school street officer with no detective training, either. As much as I hated to do it, I had to call Sheriff Dooley.

After my call was transferred through a series of gatekeepers, Dooley finally came on the line. "Make it quick, Muckleroy. I've got a meeting with a reporter from Channel Five in three minutes."

Bully for you, jackass. "Something odd is going on here in Jacksburg and we need your department's expertise." I ran through the events of the past few days, detailed the delivery that had disappeared and the suspicious credit card bill. "It looks like some kind of fraud ring or identity theft."

Identity theft had been a hot issue when I left the force in Dallas, but the big-city department had a specially trained team to handle the cases. Identity theft hadn't been a problem in Jacksburg before. Apparently there wasn't much of a market for the identities of those with low incomes and less-than-stellar credit scores. "Do you want to take over the investigation?"

Sheriff Dooley huffed into his mouthpiece, the sound painfully magnified at my end of the line. "You've got no victim raising a ruckus. Nobody in danger. Why the hell are you wasting my time?"

Anger shot through me like an emergency flare. "All right, Sheriff Dooley." *Sheriff Do-Nothing was more like it.* "Don't need you stealing credit for another one of our busts anyway." I slammed the receiver down before he could argue with me. "Dumb ass."

With the Sheriff's department refusing to help, I was on my own. *Dang.* I had no idea what to do. But come hell or high water, I'd get to the bottom of this.

***

The Ninja passed me again on Wednesday afternoon and also on Thursday morning, but both times I was tied up with a traffic stop and couldn't get away in time to follow him. Fate was yanking my chain again. But I wouldn't let the bitch get to me. I'd force myself to be patient. It was just a matter of time before I'd get my man.

Trey picked up lunch to go and we ate at my booth at the DQHQ on Thursday. He'd brought an assortment of the video games he'd developed and loaded them on the department's computer system to keep us entertained between calls. Selena and I spent the afternoon battling each other in a new game designed to imitate roller derby.

On Friday evening, Trey took me to a movie in Hockerville, nudging me into the back row as I started down the aisle with my extra-large bucket of buttered popcorn and small Diet Coke.

"Let's sit back here," he said. "If the movie gets boring, we can make out."

We slid into two seats in the center of the row and Trey wrapped an arm around my shoulders. "Can I interest you in a Hot

Tamale?"

"Is that a euphemism or are you offering me candy?"

He smiled and rattled the red box.

I held out my palm and he shook a handful of red candies into it. I tipped my bucket toward him. "Popcorn?"

He scooped up a handful. "Watch this. I've got a very talented tongue." He proceeded to toss a series of kernels into the air, deftly catching each of them on the tip of his tongue.

The theater began to fill up and we chatted until the lights dimmed. After what seemed like an eternity of previews, the movie began, an action-packed flick with a dubious plot and an excess of exposed cleavage, most of it store bought.

The main character, a CIA operative in pursuit of terrorists, leapt from a low-flying single-engine plane, performed a triple flip in the air, and landed on his feet and unhurt in the back of a dump truck hauling sand. I whistled through my teeth. "Wow. What realism."

Trey shrugged. "What's reality done for you lately?"

He had a point. Of course his commentary was just the kind of thing you'd expect from a video game programmer who spent his workdays constructing fantasy worlds. My workdays were at the opposite end of the spectrum. *Too* real sometimes.

We ended the night sitting on the wooden swing in front of my father's house. Trey was so unassuming, so easy to talk to, I found myself letting down my guard, sharing things, intimate details about myself, my divorce, my childhood. He opened up, too, spilling embarrassing details about growing up as a nerd, about him and his other brainy friends getting hassled by the athletes at Hockerville High.

Trey paused a moment, his demeanor and tone turning serious. "Can I ask you something, Marnie?"

"That's a loaded question."

He leaned forward and turned to me, his gaze locked on mine. "What freaked you out at the bowling alley? I know it wasn't asthma."

Dang. He wasn't as gullible as I'd thought. I looked at Trey and felt my defenses weaken. The look on his face told me he wanted to know what had upset me, that he wanted to connect with me emotionally. "I'll tell you, Trey, but it's not going to be pretty."

"Didn't think it would be."

I looked down at my left wrist, at the Wonder Woman bracelet covering the scars. *Should I do this? Spill my guts to this guy I've known only a short time? What's more, could I do this? Reopen emotional wounds that hadn't truly healed but had merely scarred over, like the physical ones?*

I glanced back up at Trey. The concern in his eyes, the compassion there, told me I not only *could* but that I *should.* I'd held this inside long enough, ever since the police department psychologist started to look at me funny when I was still returning to his office weeks after the incident.

"I . . . I killed a man, Trey." Warm tears filled my eyes and spilled down my cheeks, but I didn't bother to wipe them away, knowing they were only the beginning of what was sure to be a deluge. I removed the bracelet, pulled back the cuff on my flannel shirt, and held out my wrist so he could see the physical scars. Then I showed him the scars he couldn't see, unloading all of my emotional baggage on him as if he were an emotional bellhop.

He listened, quietly and intently, as I detailed my worst days on the job. The day I'd been first on the scene of a horrific drunk driving accident, the dead driver like a human shish-ka-bob, impaled on his steering wheel. The day I'd attended a funeral for a fellow officer gunned down by drug dealers, his wife falling to pieces during the eulogy, the children old enough to understand what was going on, yet still young enough to need the father who'd been so senselessly taken from them.

Finally, I told him how I'd been dispatched to a neighborhood park after concerned mothers had reported a homeless man digging through trash cans near the playground. I'd been as calm as possible, approaching the man slowly, talking softly, displaying no weapons, but the delusional man still saw me as a threat. Before I knew what was happening, he'd pulled a knife from his pocket and attacked, slashing at the hand I'd thrown up to protect myself. Mothers were screaming, children were screaming, *I* was screaming. Before I could finish, I broke down in shoulder-shaking sobs. But the anguished look on my face told Trey the rest of the story.

Trey put a warm hand on my cheek, forcing me to look at him. "Marnie, you had no choice."

I shook my head. That wasn't the point. Internal Affairs had thoroughly investigated the shooting, interviewed dozens of witnesses, cleared me of any wrongdoing. Hell, even the ACLU hadn't been interested in the case. I did what I had to do, I knew that on a logical level. But this wasn't a logical problem. My brain had no problem working through it. It was my heart that couldn't take it, my soul that had yet to recover.

I clenched my fists in my lap and fought to control my tears of frustration. *Nobody seemed to understand. Not Chet. Not Dad. Not Savannah. And now, not even Trey.*

"Whether I had to shoot or not isn't the issue." I took a deep, ragged breath. "I killed a man, Trey. I ended a life. And I haven't made up for that."

Trey paused a moment, his face intent as he considered my words. A moment later, he encircled my clenched fists in his hands and pulled them to his chest, looking deep into my eyes as if he'd find the answers there. "You've got a karmic debt to settle. You need to even the score."

Oh, my God. He gets it. He understands.

Trey was the first person to comprehend where I was coming from, to accept that, logical or not, I couldn't be satisfied with simply knowing that what I'd done had been justified, unavoidable. I gazed back into his intelligent, compassionate eyes, and nodded. We connected emotionally in that moment like I'd never connected with anyone before. *What an incredible, powerful feeling.*

If Fate tries to take this from me, she'll be in for the fight of her life.

CHAPTER EIGHTEEN

FIRED UP

I wiped my face with my sleeve, and Trey and I moved on to more pleasant subjects, talking about everything and nothing until the wee hours of the morning, not once running out of conversation. He left only after I promised to spend the next evening with him, too. My emotional meltdown hadn't scared him off. That said a lot about him. So did the fact that he spent Saturday morning helping his mother and father around their house. He drove over to Jacksburg in the late afternoon.

Dad and Angus headed out to the backyard, fired up the grill for supper, and slapped on a rack of ribs. Beer in hand, Angus tended to the meat, brushing it lovingly with his homemade whiskey-infused barbecue sauce. Dad, Trey, and I relaxed in lawn chairs in the shade of a misshapen live oak tree, Bluebonnet lying at our feet, patiently waiting for the scraps sure to come later.

When Dad asked Trey about his work, Trey stepped over to the Lincoln, bringing out his state-of-the-art laptop and showing Dad some of the websites he'd designed while he'd been back in the area. I pulled my chair closer to look over Dad's shoulder. Trey had constructed a fantastic new website for the Jacksburg school district, complete with a holiday calendar, a list of upcoming events, and photos of key staff. An animated Jackrabbit, the mascot, hopped across the bottom of the screen. He'd created one for Lorene's, too, making it easy for people to place to-go orders online.

"Do you have a website for your tree-trimming business?" Trey asked Dad.

Dad chuckled. "I don't even have a computer. I check e-mails and search the internet on my phone."

"Want a site? It's a great way to attract clients."

Things had been a bit slow for Dad's tree-trimming business lately. Not that it really mattered. The mobile home had long since been paid off, and with me chipping in for groceries and utilities, Dad didn't have many bills. But who couldn't use a little more cash?

Dad took a sip from his beer bottle, considering. "What'll it cost me?"

"No charge for the design," Trey said. "I've got tons of clip art loaded on my computer. I can whip something up in no time and hook you up with hosting for under twenty bucks a month."

"Guess it's long past time for me to climb out of my cave and join the electronic age, huh?" Dad raised his beer in salute. "What the hell. Let's give it a go."

Trey began tapping keys on his computer, using his finger occasionally to manipulate the mouse pad, turning the screen to Dad so he could choose from a variety of standard setups.

I shooed a fly away from Bluebonnet's face and looked over at Angus. "What's the ETA on dinner?"

Angus poked the ribs with the fork, separating two of the bones, releasing a mouthwatering scent of tangy sauce. He checked the color of the meat. "Ten minutes."

I headed into the house, gathering up plastic tubs of store-bought coleslaw and potato salad from the fridge, retrieving silverware and serving spoons from the drawers. I went back outside and laid out the spread on the picnic table, making a second run to the kitchen for napkins and plates.

By that time, Trey had constructed a basic but professional website for the tree-trimming business, including an animated lumberjack with a chainsaw in the upper corner. Dad revved up one of his saws and Trey recorded the sound on his cell phone, downloading the audio file to the laptop computer while Dad took the saw back to the garage.

"Wow," I told Trey, watching the high-tech process over his shoulder. "You've got mad high-tech skills."

"I've got mad low-tech skills, too," Trey whispered, shooting me a sexy grin.

The website turned out great, the sound of the chainsaw emanating from the laptop's speakers while Dad's phone number flashed on the screen. Uncle Angus suggested Dad go with a harder-hitting motif a la *Texas Chainsaw Massacre*, but Dad ignored him.

The men bonded over the barbecue, talking sports, tools, miscellaneous guy stuff. I wouldn't have expected a techie like Trey to have much in common with blue-collar types like my dad and Angus, but he fit right in. After dinner, Dad and Angus headed out to the Watering Hole. Trey helped me take care of the dishes in the kitchen. I washed. He dried.

He nudged me with an elbow as he wiped a plate. "You make those yellow latex gloves look sexy. I'm getting turned on."

"Control yourself." I flicked suds at him and handed him another plate. I set to work on a long spoon, purposefully rubbing the sponge up and down the handle, slowly and rhythmically.

He groaned. "Tease."

I smiled and he bent down to kiss me, his kiss hotter and wetter than the dishwater my hands were resting in. I couldn't remember ever having this much fun doing the dishes.

We met up with Dad and Angus later at the Watering Hole. I was glad to see no sign of Lucas Glick at the bar. Hopefully he was at home drying out. Trey and I danced to a few country songs, neither of us capable of more than the basic two-step taught in junior high gym class, but once the band switched to classic rock, we had the opportunity to show off our moves.

Trey was a good dancer, uninhibited and fun, making me wonder if his bold moves translated into other physical activities. With any luck, I'd soon find out. We'd already forged an emotional connection, why not go for a physical one, too? He'd brought me out of my emotional isolation, and I yearned to be close to him in every way possible.

***

Though I'd only known Trey a matter of days, I'd already grown used to having him around. I missed him on Sunday, when he was tied up with church and family obligations, his sister from Dallas driving to Hockerville for a visit. His father's recovery had stalled, and it was unclear whether this was a temporary plateau or whether this was as far as he'd get. Trey called me that afternoon and told me he'd decided to stick around a little longer, see what the doctors could sort out.

I was sorry about his father's setback, but thrilled Trey's stay had been extended, much more excited than I should have been given the circumstances. I went for a long ride on my motorcycle to try to take my mind off him, but all I succeeded in doing was acquiring a raging sunburn on my forearms, exposed in short sleeves for the first time since the incident. Still, it felt good, the air and sun on my skin. *It's been a long time since I've felt this free.*

I thought I might run into the Ninja out for a drive, too, but no such luck. I passed a number of other riders, a few of whom rode tentatively, clearly weekend bikers, yuppie posers from Dallas. But who could blame them for wanting a fun escape from their regimented lives? Heck, even Chet had liked to hang up his silk ties and get out on my bike once in a while, collect a few bugs in his professionally whitened teeth.

Trey and I had lunch together on Monday, this time opting for tacos from the taco stand, which we ate on a bench in the city park. We repeated the routine, having lunch together virtually every day over the next week, lingering longer than we should have, far exceeding my one-hour lunch breaks.

On Wednesday, we ran into Lucas Glick at the catfish buffet, and decided to share a table and a basket of hush puppies in the crowded restaurant.

Trey eyed Lucas over the table. "I saw your eagle on the freezer wall at the station. It was damn good."

Is that a blush on Lucas's cheeks? Clearly he wasn't used to receiving compliments.

"You should put that talent to work for you," Trey said. "Ever thought of doing graphic design work? I could use someone to create custom graphics and logos for the websites I design."

A look of shock registered on Glick's face, as if he'd never received encouragement before and didn't know how to respond to it. "I don't know nothin' about that kind of thing."

Trey waved his hand dismissively and fished another hush puppy out of the red plastic basket. "It's easy. You interview the client to get a feel for what type of design they're looking for, then you create some options for them. I could show you how to use an electronic drawing pad, and you could e-mail your work to me. If you're interested, I've got extra equipment I could lend you. That kind of work pays pretty well." Trey handed Glick one of his TreyTech business cards. "Let me know. My cell number and e-mail address are on there."

Lucas gave a quick nod and slid the card into the back pocket of his jeans. I might have been mistaken, but I think I saw a small gleam of hope in his eyes.

CHAPTER NINETEEN

BIKER BLING

Mid-morning on Friday, Eric pulled his delivery truck into the parking lot of the police headquarters and came inside with a long box. I met him at the counter, hoping to hit him up for further information about deliveries to the Parker house on Renfro. I was still waiting on copies of the credit card applications filled out in Logan Mott's and Taylor Heidenheimer's names. I'd forwarded the police reports to the bank as instructed, but the legal department didn't seem to be in a hurry to get the applications to me. Given the pervasiveness of identity theft, they were probably inundated with such requests.

Eric held the box out to me. "This one's for you, Marnie."

"Really? I wasn't expecting a package." I took the heavy box from him and looked at the return address. Harley Davidson. I hadn't ordered anything, though I had been thinking about treating myself to those cool pipes from the catalog for Christmas. Probably Dad had ordered something and shipped it to my office where someone would be available to sign for it. Bluebonnet would have been the only one at home to accept delivery and a paw print wasn't likely an acceptable substitute for a signature. But it was odd that my father hadn't told me a package would be coming.

Eric held out his electronic tracking device. I set the box on the floor and signed on the bottom line.

When I was done, I handed it back to him. "Any deliveries to 612 Renfro lately?"

He jabbed at the gizmo, pulling up some information. "Had another delivery to a Logan Mott there two days ago." He held out the device so I could verify the information on the screen.

What does it mean? What's happening here?

Eric turned his attention to Selena, and the two began chatting. I might not be able to solve the mystery of the suspicious deliveries to Renfro, but I could at least solve the mystery of what was in the box Eric had given me. I returned to my booth and used the tiny pocketknife from my keychain to slice open one end. I pulled back the flaps and eased the contents onto my desk.

It was bling, biker style. Chrome pipes so bright and shiny they reflected every last freckle on my face as I gazed at them. The very pipes I'd been wanting. The ones I'd circled in the catalog still lying open on the corner of my tabletop.

I checked the paperwork. Trey had placed the order, paying a hefty premium for expedited delivery. He must have noticed the catalog on my desk while I booked the juvenile who tried to rob the Grab-N-Go.

A warm blush flooded my cheeks, even though nobody was looking. Trey had spent a small fortune on the pipes. Sure, high-tech jobs paid well, but still, this was an extremely generous gift, not the kind of thing a guy bought for someone he wasn't really into. In video game terms, he'd advanced our relationship to the next level. Trey would be in for some extra lovin' the next time I saw him.

As I went to discard the box, a tinkle inside caught my attention. I reached my arm down inside the long box to find a small shiny object, wrapped in bubble wrap, lodged in the end of the box. Carefully removing the wrap, I found a small gold bell adorned with a police shield.

My heart burst into a flurry of white doves in my chest. Trey wanted me safe, wanted to protect me. No matter how strong and capable I considered myself, no matter how strong and capable he considered me, knowing he cared enough to give me this symbol of affection was, well, totally kick ass. I went straight out to my bike to attach it.

**

Later that afternoon, I was out on patrol with my new bell shining brightly on the foot peg. I decided to check on the Parker house, see if the packages for Logan Mott were still around. I headed over to Renfro, parked my bike, and took a look around. I noticed nothing unusual, no suspicious items in the mail, no packages on the porch. Someone had picked up the boxes Eric had delivered there two days ago. *But who?*

As I climbed back onto my bike to leave, I spotted Tiffany's red convertible heading up the street toward me, top down as usual. She'd racked up another speeding ticket this week, seemingly unconcerned, sure that daddy's lawyers would take care of it, make them all go away. When Andre had clocked her at twenty over the limit and pulled her over, she'd had the nerve to poke fun at the broken lights on his cruiser, saying she should perform a citizen's arrest for his equipment violation.

But what was she doing on Renfro? The road didn't lead to the highway and there wasn't much else in town that would interest a spoiled daddy's girl like her. She wasn't exactly the type who'd get excited by the day-old donuts sold for half price at the bakery thrift shop down the street.

Tiffany wore dark sunglasses, so it was hard to tell where she was looking as she headed toward me, but her head seemed to swivel just a tad in my direction. The scowl on her pink glossy lips was undeniable, but since a haughty frown seemed to be her natural expression, it was hard to say if it meant anything.

I pulled my bike crossways across the road in front of her, forcing her to stop. She slammed on her brakes and came to a stop just a couple feet from me. "Well, well," she spat. "If it isn't the Dyke of Haazard."

I wasn't about to let this bitch get to me. I let go of my handlebars and sat back as if I had all the time in the world. "What are you doing in this part of town?"

"Taking the scenic route," she said. "After all, who wouldn't enjoy such a beautiful view?" She gestured around at the rundown houses, a sarcastic smirk on her face. When I continued to sit there, head cocked, waiting for a real answer, she finally rolled her eyes and huffed. "If you must know, there's work being done on Main and traffic is backed up. I was just trying to find another way out of this Godforsaken hellhole."

I shrugged. *One woman's hellhole is another woman's home sweet home.*

I'd forced Tiffany to stop, given her a little hassle, and that satisfied me for now. I took hold of my handlebars and eased my bike back into the other lane. "Enjoy your tour." I waved her on with my gloved hand.

After she passed me, I checked my side mirror. She held her hand up by her shoulder, her French-tipped middle finger sticking straight up in salute. That was no way to treat a civil servant. *Perhaps I'm not quite done putting her in her place yet.* I pulled my phone from my belt and held it up to select proper music for harassing a disrespectful debutante. The Rolling Stones "Bitch" seemed a perfect choice.

I U-turned, caught up with Tiffany, and followed her car for a few blocks, toying with her, not turning on my lights or siren but weaving back and forth behind her, coming close then backing off, like a cat playing with a bleach-blond mouse. She seemed to be driving aimlessly through town, making random turns and backtracking, no apparent destination in mind. Finally, she turned down Main, heading toward the highway back to Dallas. Just before she turned onto the road, she took off her sunglasses, turned, and shot me a glare so icy it could have reversed global warming.

I put two fingers to my eyes then pointed them at her, sign language for "I'm watching you." With that, I gunned my engine and turned to head in the opposite direction.

CHAPTER TWENTY

THE CHET HITS THE FAN

I spotted no work being done on Main, no traffic backup. Guess it had cleared quickly. At five o'clock, I headed out to my Harley. I stopped by the dry cleaners on my way home to pick up my Wonder Woman costume for my upcoming performance at the Jackrabbit Jamboree. I hoped the skimpy thing still fit. I'd been practicing my act for weeks, even added a new stunt to the grand finale. I'd give Gretchen the Yodeling Doberman a run for her dog biscuits.

Back at home, I showered, shaved, and washed my hair, even taking a curling iron to the ends to give my straight hair a touch of curl. I applied a layer of lip gloss and double-dipped the mascara, accentuating my eyes with a chocolate-brown outline. *Tiffany Tindall isn't the only one who knows how to handle a stick of eyeliner.*

Why I was putting in more than the usual effort, I didn't know. Trey would be gone shortly and I'd probably never see him again. It's not like our relationship was going anywhere. But something about him had me feeling upbeat and attractive, made me want to make the most of myself. I'd learned by now that a relationship was only fifty percent about the guy and how you felt about him. The other fifty-percent was about who you were when you were with him, how he made you feel about yourself. And when I was with Trey, I felt strong, smart, and beautiful.

I slipped into a gauzy scarlet-red dress, sliding my feet into a pair of canvas wedges, the only pair of shoes I currently owned with even the slightest bit of heel. I'd ditched the heels I'd worn to the dinner with Tindall and his wife the instant Chet and I had arrived home that long-ago evening. Standing in front of the mirror, I tried to evaluate myself objectively. The lightweight fabric of the dress took some of the bulk off my stocky frame, and the red lacy bra just visible through the layers of sheer fabric added a sexy touch, enough to grab Trey's attention without looking slutty.

Trey showed up wearing navy pants and a striped cotton shirt, looking well-groomed yet casual. We bade goodbye to Dad and headed out the door. Trey put a hand on my back as he helped me into the Lincoln, his touch light through the fabric, his fingertips leaving warm pinpoints of sensation on my spine, making me want to feel those fingers on other sensitive parts of my body. No guy had ever had such an effect on me, had gotten my juices flowing as easily as Trey did. *Not even Chet.*

After he climbed in the driver's side, he looked over at me, his eyes running from the top of my head down to my toes. "Somebody better contact internal affairs 'cause we've got a major case of police beautality here."

I groaned at his lame joke but, truth be told, I was totally flattered. He leaned toward me and gave me a kiss. A hot one. Total power surge. He didn't skimp on the tongue, and the way his hand gripped the hair at the nape of my neck had me wondering what he'd be like if we connected physically. I had a feeling this computer programmer had a hard drive and plenty of RAM, and would know just which keys to push to effectively navigate my system. A moment later, Trey broke the kiss—*damn him!*—leaving me with all my applications running. Looked like I'd have to wait until later for further input.

As we headed down the highway toward Dallas, my overheated circuits beginning to cool, I glanced over at him. "I got the pipes and the bell."

He signaled to change lanes, then glanced back at me, eyebrows raised. "And?"

"And if you're trying to get in my pants, you're well on your way. But it'll take a fringed jacket and new mirrors to get you there. I've got the item numbers written down for you."

He faked a jaw drop. "My charm won't be enough?"

I met his gaze and smiled. "We'll see." All teasing aside now, I put a hand on his forearm and gave it a grateful squeeze. "It was very sweet and generous. Thanks, Trey."

"You're welcome. I figured a hero like you deserved a reward."

"Hero?"

"Hell, yeah. You single-handedly nabbed that armed robber at the Grab-N-Go."

"You mean the kid with the toy gun that you tackled in the parking lot?"

"Okay, if not for that, then for taking out that hit man who shot at you earlier in the week."

How did Trey know about Fulton? The news reports, both on TV and in the papers, had given Sheriff Dooley and his department all the credit. "Where did you hear about that?"

"Same place I found the catalog with the pipes. There was an incident report on your desk. I read it while I was waiting for you to book that boy."

"Nosey."

He shrugged. "I prefer to call it curious."

Trey's explanation made sense. But I still didn't consider myself a hero. I was just doing my job. And lately I was doing a crappy job. Something odd was going on with those deliveries to the Parker Place and for the life of me I had no idea how to handle it.

A commercial came on the radio, so I tuned to another classic rock station. Trey and I sang along with Boston's *Don't Look Back*, both of us loud and off key, neither of us caring. Chet had liked classic rock when we were dating, but a few years into our marriage he began listening to jazz and classical. The erratic jazz unnerved me and the classical songs always had me thinking Bugs Bunny and Elmer Fudd. Guess I wasn't cut out for sophisticated things.

"My dad had a good day today," Trey said. "He took a few steps without the walker."

I gave him another smile, this one forced. "That's great news." It was *terrible* news! Although I was truly happy his father was recovering, every step his father took meant Trey was one step closer to going back to California. Then my fun would be over, the fling flung.

During the long drive to Dallas, we never ran out of things to talk about. Although being with Trey was exciting, it was also comfortable. We hadn't known each other long, but he'd made me feel like I could totally be myself with him.

Despite having a reservation, we had to wait over an hour for our table. This was Dallas, after all, and what's a night out in the Big D without a little pretension? We stepped into the bar area, a dimly lit room with dark wood walls and television sets suspended from the ceiling in each corner of the room. All four sets were tuned to ESPN.

People packed the room wall to wall, but we managed to find a place to stand along the back of the bar. The sounds of noisy chatter and a duo of blenders performing a margarita-piña colada medley met our ears. Trey squeezed through the crowd and returned with a frozen Bellini for me and a draft beer for himself. I had just taken a sip of my peachy ice-cold drink when my nose detected the unmistakable scent of Hugo Boss cologne, Chet's signature scent. Fulton's, too, but that creep was still in the county jail, awaiting extradition to Illinois.

My eyes scanned the faces in the noisy crowd around us. I spotted Chet five feet away, tucked between a man who looked like an Antonio Banderas knock-off and a fair, stick-thin woman with whom he was talking. I hadn't seen Chet since we'd said good-bye on the courthouse steps a year ago. Guess I shouldn't have been surprised to run into him here. Chet was the one who'd first discovered Marangelli's and their scrumptious capellini Roma, and we'd eaten here at least once a month during our marriage.

I pulled my cell phone out of my purse, pulled up Chet's name in my contacts list, and tapped the screen to dial his number. Chet looked down when his phone vibrated and pulled it out of the front pocket of his pants. After checking the caller ID, he put the phone to one ear, holding his index finger to his other to drown out the din. "Marnie?"

"Hey, Cheddar." I'd come up with the cheesy nickname back in college. "Look to your left."

Chet turned, his eyes brightening when he spotted me, his mouth turning up in a smile that was broad, friendly, and above all, sincere. He slid his phone back into his pocket, grabbed his date's hand, and pulled her through the tight throng toward me. After he maneuvered his way over, he gave me a quick one-armed hug. "It's good to see you."

"You, too, Chet."

Chet wore shiny black tassel loafers, gray slacks, and a crisply pressed black dress shirt. His brown hair had a slight sheen to it, no doubt courtesy of some expensive hair product. His date was long-limbed and willowy, her short, light brown hair pulled into a chic, side-swept style. Her fitted black mini-dress was figure-flattering yet classy. Everything about her appearance was carefully thought out. She was everything I wasn't. And she was perfect for Chet.

The moment could have been awkward, but even though Chet and I weren't destined to spend our lives together, we shared a mutual respect that transcended time and divorce.

Chet turned to his date, putting a hand on her shoulder. "Sidney, this is Marnie, my former wife." No BS, no beating around the bush. Chet's forthrightness was a trait I'd always admired in him, the one trait that hadn't changed during his metamorphosis from country boy to city slicker.

Sidney extended her hand and I shook it, hoping I wouldn't accidentally break one of her bone-thin fingers.

Trey stepped up close behind me, his firm chest pressed possessively to my back. "I'm Trey Jones. Marnie's current love slave." Total bullshit, total spontaneity. Traits I was coming to appreciate in Trey. He didn't take life too seriously. Nobody had ever been able to make me laugh like Trey, to bring me out of a funk with his quirky sense of humor. He was Prozac in human form.

Trey stuck out his right to shake hands with Chet. Seeing the two of them face to face was a study in contrasts. Chet's fastidious, formal demeanor seemed stuffy and severe in comparison to Trey's easy-going style. After introductions were exchanged, we made small talk for a few minutes, voices raised over the din, discussing our careers (*going fine, thanks*), the Dallas Cowboys (*great season so far*), whether construction would ever be completed on Central Expressway (*'course not*). When Chet learned that Trey lived in Silicon Valley, the conversation shifted to the overpriced California real estate market.

"It's absolutely nuts out there," Trey said. "I paid four-hundred and eighty grand for a two-bedroom one-bath fixer upper, and that's after the discount they gave me when I found a bullet hole under the back window."

Chet took a sip of his white wine. "I hear a lot of homeowners out there are opting for interest-only loans. Seems a bit risky—"

"Whoa!" My hand reflexively shot up, pointing at the television set behind the men. "Check that out." I hated to interrupt, but this was important. The station had been broadcasting brief news blurbs during a commercial break and now Kent Tindall's face filled the screen, a professional photo pulled from his development company's website. The photo was followed by an action shot in which two police officers led Tindall, wearing an Armani suit and both a Rolex and handcuffs on his wrists, into the main Dallas police station.

It was impossible to hear the anchorwoman over the racket in the bar, but the closed captioning filled us in. Tindall's real estate company had gone belly up, investors claimed Tindall had embezzled millions from the corporation, and the district attorney had indicted Tindall for bribing a building inspector. Details at ten.

Between Kent Tindall's arrest and the speeding tickets Jacksburg PD had issued to Tiffany, the family's lawyers would be busy over the next few months.

The screen changed as a beer commercial came on and Chet turned back to me, shell-shocked, his eyes wide, his face white. "If the loan I brokered for Tindall ends up in foreclosure, my job could be on the line."

Chet had been so proud to land that pompous ass's business. Now it could destroy his career. I reached out and squeezed his hand. "Maybe it will all work out."

Chet tossed back the remaining wine in his glass. "I've got to do some damage control." He gave me a quick peck on the cheek. "Bye, Marn." He nodded to Trey. "Nice meeting you, Trey." He grabbed Sidney's hand and dragged her off through the crowd.

Trey watched them go, then turned to me. I'm not sure what I expected Trey to say, but it certainly wasn't, "He's uptight. He must've been a total bore in bed."

I was mid-sip and ended up snorting frozen Bellini into my nose. After a few seconds, I managed to get my coughing and sneezing under control. "He got the job done."

Trey's mouth curved in a naughty grin. "If it felt like work, Marnie, he wasn't doing it right."

I couldn't help but laugh. Trey was full of crap, but he was also full of life. Adventurous, unrestrained, unconventional. Everything Chet wasn't and perfect for me. *Funny how sometimes you don't know what you need until you find it.*

Yet, once again, Fate kicked me in the ass. I finally found a guy I liked, *a lot*, and he'd be leaving town in a matter of days. *Better make the most of them.*

CHAPTER TWENTY-ONE

BUSTED

After enjoying a delicious dinner and sharing both witty conversation and a scrumptious tiramisu for dessert, we climbed into the car to head back home. By then it was ten o'clock and the night was dark, but the illuminated Dallas skyline shined bright above us, the sparkling globe atop the Reunion Arena tower looming over us like a disco ball on steroids, sending flashes of light across the restaurant parking lot.

We eased our way out of the lot and through downtown, heading down Elm to the freeway entrance ramp. Trey glanced over at me, eyeing me with the same expression of ravenous desire I'd seen on his face earlier when the waiter had plunked his steaming bowl of pasta down in front of him. "Let's go someplace where we can be alone. I'm carbo-loaded and ready for action."

So was I. The way Trey had licked the whipped cream off his dessert spoon had made me wish I was dressed in nothing but Reddi-Wip.

Trey's parents would be at his house and Dad would be at mine, so we wouldn't be able to get any privacy at either place. I felt like I was back in high school, trying to find a secluded spot to make out. *How pathetic.* Where did teenagers go to fool around these days? Apparently some used the tool shed at the old Parker Place, but even a small-town biker chick like me was too classy for that.

Yet a roadside motel was out of the question, too. It would be too cheap, too awkward, too presumptuous. Better to let things happen more naturally, see where the night would take us.

Then it dawned on me. "Head back to Jacksburg. I know just the place."

Since I knew where all of the speed traps were between Dallas and Jacksburg, we made it back to town in record time. Following my instructions, Trey pulled onto the dead brown grass behind the vacant little league baseball fields. Dust and bugs swirled in the beams of the headlights as the car bounced over the uneven ground, past the sagging wooden bleachers, until we reached a small stand of scrubby mesquite trees that formed an irregular semi-circle, providing cover so the car shouldn't be visible from the road. A startled raccoon stared into the bright headlights for a moment, then scurried off into the brush.

Trey cut the lights, then the engine, enveloping us in darkness and silence. He turned in his seat to face me, heat in his gaze. "Something tells me you've come here before."

Sure, I'd come here before. In fact, thanks to a little extra foreplay and a ribbed-for-her-pleasure condom, I'd come here twice one night in the bed of Chet's pickup. But that was back in college, a whole lifetime ago. Still, if Trey was interested in breaking any endurance records, heck, I was game.

Trey pushed the button to roll the windows down, then climbed out, leaving the key in the ignition. He walked around to my side of the car, opened my door, and helped me out. In the dark, we climbed onto the trunk of the car, reclining side-by-side against the back window, looking up at the stars. Only our shoulders and thighs touched, exchanging body heat, the sensation more pronounced in contrast to the chilly air. The sky was clear and, with no lights to interfere, the stars shined incredibly bright, as if showing off just for us.

Trey reached over and took my hand, entwining my fingers

in his, pulling them to his lips. He slid the first joint of my pinky into his mouth and sensuously sucked on the tip, sending me reeling. He ran a kiss across my knuckles, then clutched my hand to his chest. "This would be the perfect spot to watch the Leonids next month."

"Hmmm."

He apparently misinterpreted my murmur as a question rather than realizing his minor foreplay had rendered me incapable of coherent speech. "The Leonid meteor shower. Comes every November. I bet it's spectacular out here. We could bring a blanket—"

He cut himself off, apparently realizing he'd be back in California next month. We couldn't make plans beyond the next few days, maybe two weeks, tops. Our time was quickly ticking away. *Tick. Tick. Tick.*

Trey took my hand and pulled it up to his face, rubbing it gently against his cheek. The rough feel of his dark whiskers on my skin made me crave more sensations that only his body could provide. Yet, as much as I wanted him, I didn't want to rush this moment. I wanted it to last.

We were both quiet for a few moments, the only sound the slow rhythmic chirp of the crickets in the woods around us.

Finally, Trey glanced over at me. "Seen the Ninja lately?"

The question caught me off guard. Being with Trey made me forget all about my Ninja dream man and my surprised look let Trey know it. An amused smile danced around his lips.

Better bring him down a peg or two before he got too cocky. Besides, to be honest, I felt a sudden and unexpected flare of anger, not so much at him, but at our hopeless situation. Here I was, getting all hot and bothered over Trey, and our relationship was doomed to end. "I saw the Ninja earlier this week, as a matter of fact. But he disappeared before I could catch up with him."

Trey's eyes narrowed. "You went after him?"

"Yup."

He arched a brow. "What would you have done if you'd caught him?"

Who was he to question my intentions with another man when he couldn't offer me any sort of commitment? Really, it was none of his business. And, truth be told, a small part of me wanted to make him jealous, make him think about what he'd be missing once he left. *Gah!* This simple fling was becoming complicated, my feelings bouncing all over the place like an emotional pinball.

I switched my voice to sultry mode. "I may not have caught him today but I will. And when I do, I'll pull him over, pat him down, perform a thorough strip search—"

"Body cavities, too?"

"Yuck, no!" I cringed and shuddered.

Trey chuckled, but as he and I stared at each other, the humor on his face slowly morphed into an expression of pure desire that made me forget everyone else, everything else, even the fact that I was upset about him leaving. A hot, dark look infused his eyes, offering something I had no will to refuse. Trey put his mouth to my mouth, his chest to my chest. His body felt warm, firm, and right against me. He wrapped his arms around me and I melted against him.

My body buzzed with an ever-increasing sexual energy, desire surging through me, threatening to delete all critical data in my brain. Our clothing disappeared, tossed onto the grass next to the car. The muscles of his chest were hard and lean. I bit into his shoulder, tasting his warm skin, for the first time noticing the tattoo on his left bicep, a computer with the words "Hard Drive" in block print on the monitor's screen. His laptop was booted up and ready for input. I hoped he'd have plenty of RAM and his system wouldn't crash until my drive could take no more.

I'm not one to boink and tell, so let's just say Trey and I achieved connectivity, overloading each other's circuits. I'd never felt anything as intense as the high-voltage power surge he sent through my system.

Afterward we held each other for several moments, neither of us wanting to let go just yet. When we'd recovered, Trey went offline, sliding down the trunk of the car to stand behind it. He shot me a pointed look, for once his face deadly serious. "You think the guy on the Ninja could make you feel like that?"

No, I didn't. I'd never experienced anything so pleasurable in all my life. I was beginning to think Trey was the only man whose system was fully compatible with mine. I looked away, declining to answer him, the anger returning, but my refusal to meet his eyes told him what he wanted to know. For the time being, he held an exclusive license to my software. *And my heart.*

Trey retrieved his pants and slid into them. He began to pick up the rest of our clothing and had just handed me my dress when a bright spotlight ignited behind him, locking on us, blinding me.

Busted.

Damn! I'd suggested the night officers make regular runs by the baseball fields to check for young couples making out in cars. No sense letting teens get pregnant any easier than they did already. But the officer on duty tonight, the pudgy Jared Roddy, rarely followed orders, usually opting to sit in his cruiser in the Grab-N-Go parking lot, dipping snuff and reading *Field and Stream.* He'd picked a fine night to actually do some police work. Guess Trey and I had been too distracted to hear the cruiser pull up.

I turned my head away, pulling my knees up and holding my dress to my chest to cover my bare breasts. Trey stepped directly in front of me, blocking the light behind him, hiding me from view as I fumbled to pull on my dress.

Roddy's voice came over the public address system. "Let's see your faces, kids."

Trey called over his shoulder. "We're both consenting adults, officer."

Roddy wasn't satisfied with that answer. I wouldn't have been either. The door of the cruiser slammed and I heard footsteps coming toward the car. The beam from his Maglite played around the car. "You got some young thing hiding back there?"

"No, sir. She's of age."

Roddy's footsteps stopped a few feet behind Trey. "Can't take your word for it. She's going to have to show her face."

Trey looked down at me, mouthing the word "sorry."

I was sorry we'd been caught, too, but I wasn't sorry at all that Trey and I had shared such an intense experience, such a special, intimate connection.

"Come on, hon," Roddy called to me. "Let's see ya."

There's no getting out of this. I finished dressing and slid off the trunk. I stood, arms crossed over my chest, and glared into the brilliant beam, my cheeks blazing brighter than the flashlight.

Roddy squinted into the night. "Captain Muckleroy? Is that you?"

I marched over to Roddy and slapped the flashlight out of his hand. It fell to the ground, spilling its batteries.

He hooted with laughter, laying one hand across his beer belly, the other on his thigh. "Well, hell, Marnie," he said when he got his laughter under control. "You was the last person I 'spected to find out here."

Trey stepped over, picked up the pieces of the flashlight and inserted the batteries. Roddy eyed Trey as he handed him the flashlight, probably trying to memorize Trey's features so he'd be able to describe him to his buddies at the Watering Hole next time they met up for beers.

"You say one word to anyone, Jared," I warned, "and you'll be moved to the day shift so fast you'll get whiplash."

His face sagged. Roddy didn't want to work days because day shift officers actually worked. The night shift was nothing more than a few hours of driving around town, listening to the radio, circling the bank buildings and convenience stores, keeping an eye out for suspicious activity that rarely occurred. Heck, I couldn't remember the last time a night officer had filed any kind of incident report.

Roddy raised a hand in surrender. "All right, all right. Keep your panties on." He aimed the beam of his flashlight at my red panties hanging from the Lincoln's bumper. "Oops, too late for that."

He laughed again and I spun him around by his shoulders, shoving him toward his cruiser.

Once Roddy drove off I turned back to Trey. He leaned against the side of the car, watching me. He'd put his shirt on and buttoned it, but he hadn't tucked it in. He looked rumpled, casual, and completely sexy.

He held a hand out to me and I took it. He pulled me to him, holding me to his chest, running a hand down my hair. "You ever gonna forgive me?"

"It's okay."

Getting caught with my pants down had been totally

humiliating. But it had also been totally worth it.

CHAPTER TWENTY-TWO

GETTING PERSONAL

The next few weeks flew by. September ended and October was well on its way. Trey and I spent every spare moment together, taking this fling as far as it would go. I found myself avoiding the highway, putting the Ninja on hold. For the time being, I wanted to focus only on Trey.

We went for leisurely rides on my motorcycle, Trey's arms wrapped tightly around me, his chest pressed to my back, taking a blanket along in the saddle bag and finding hidden, out-of-the-way places to make love. We rented goofy movies and ignored them while we made love on the couch at my house when Dad was out. We took another stab at rock climbing, located a small, private cave, and made love on the cold stone floor. The sex was so good I didn't mind that I had to dig pebbles out of my butt cheeks afterward.

Trey even invited me to dinner at his parents' house, a serious step for what was merely a short-term relationship. His mother and father, Frances and BJ, were wonderful people, down-to-earth and genuine. I enjoyed his mother's extra-cheesy lasagna, but felt conflicted at seeing his father getting around so well, his speech sounding normal, his right arm functioning at nearly full capacity. Thanks to the severe PTSD I'd suffered, I knew what it was like to be incapacitated. The man deserved to have his life back, and I was glad to see that happening. But his gain would be my loss.

Over lunch at the diner one Friday afternoon, Trey eyed me intently over the table and told me the news I'd been dreading. "I bought my return plane ticket. I'm leaving for California on Wednesday."

We had less than a week left together. Though I'd known this moment was coming, it nonetheless shattered my heart. "Maybe you could find a permanent job here," I blurted out, sounding as desperate as I felt. "You never know when your father might relapse." *Okay, so I was trying to guilt him into staying. Sue me.*

Trey exhaled a sharp breath. "I've looked into it, Marnie. Dallas is too far to commute, and the only tech jobs in Hockerville or Jacksburg are network administrator positions. I'd rather poke myself in the eye than fix people's computer problems all day long."

"You could keep freelancing."

He shook his head. "These contract gigs have bored me to death. It's mostly installations. There's no challenge in it, no creativity."

"What about the websites?"

"There's not enough work here to keep me busy full time. Besides, what I can charge for a site is a pittance compared to what I can earn as a programmer."

In other words, websites were below his pay grade. He'd thought through his options and none of them was workable. I'd soon be alone again.

***

Trey would be leaving in five days, but we'd get to spend the day together Saturday at the Jackrabbit Jamboree. At least I had that to look forward to.

Late Friday afternoon, Eric pulled his delivery truck into the lot and came inside empty-handed to flirt with Selena. Before he left, he stepped over to my booth. "I've got another delivery for 612 Renfro. Want to take a look?"

Another suspicious delivery. Something odd really was going on. I wasn't losing it. *Good to know.* "Absolutely."

I followed him outside to his truck. In the back were two boxes, a small one from Macy's and a large one from Bergdorf Goodman. Both were addressed to Zane Nichols, Savannah's youngest son. *Whoa.*

"Zane Nichols is my best friend's kid," I told Eric. "He doesn't live on Renfro." Besides, Savannah never shopped at Macy's or Bergdorf's. She was more of a Marshall's and T.J. Maxx kind of girl.

Eric shrugged. "Don't know what to tell you. I have to deliver them to the address on the label or I'll get in trouble with my supervisor."

"I understand." But understanding wouldn't stop me from swinging by the Parker house later to nab the packages.

I gave Eric a half-hour lead, then headed over to Renfro. The boxes addressed to Zane sat on the sagging porch of the Parker house. I gathered them up and carried the packages to my bike. The one from Bergdorf's was too big to fit in my saddle bags, but I managed to fasten it down with a bungee cord I kept handy. When I returned to the station, I called Savannah, telling her I'd bring the boxes with me on Sunday, when I'd agreed to babysit for her.

This situation was not only getting weird, it was getting personal. If someone was preying on people who were important to me, God help them. Wonder Woman does whatever it takes to defeat the bad guys, especially when they victimize people close to her.

CHAPTER TWENTY-THREE

PARTY TIME

The Saturday of the jamboree dawned unseasonably clear and cloudless, the endless blue sky meaning it would be hotter than hell by noon. I'd be outside all day in my uniform, a non-breathable polyester blend. Such was the risk of living in north Texas, with its unpredictable weather patterns, the four seasons constantly playing leapfrog with each other.

My head was already sweating in my helmet when I started my engine, leading the parade lineup out of the high school parking lot. I turned on my flashing lights and rolled down the road, followed by Andre driving the cruiser with the busted lights. With him was a part-time officer who worked weekends. Dante was supposed to be at the rear of the line-up in the other cruiser, but since the line snaked around the back of the gymnasium out of sight, I couldn't verify his presence. *Yet.* But today I'd learn if Dante and Andre really were twins, or whether I'd been had.

Behind Andre's patrol car, Chief Moreno rode next to the mayor of Jacksburg on the mayor's hay baler, the two men crowded shoulder-to-shoulder on the narrow seat. A metal bucket full of individually wrapped pink bubble gum rested on the chief's lap, both of the men tossing the candy into the crowd, eager hands yanking the treats out of the air.

Behind the mayor's tractor came the Jacksburg high school

marching band, led by a prancing drum major in a tall furry hat with a thick black strap cutting across his chin. Behind him, on the band's front row, followed six girls with flutes and one with a tiny piccolo, enthusiastic yet heat-weary in their heavy purple and red fringed uniforms. The remaining woodwinds followed, the brass not far behind, while the percussion brought up the rear, the drum line setting the pace with a *rat-a-tat-tat*. Flanking the band was the flag brigade, dressed in lighter uniforms of ruffled skirts and blouses, twirling their oversized flags. While swinging her flag over her head, a smiling redhead stepped in a long-neglected pothole and lost control of her flag, whacking a nearby saxophone with a loud *clang* but luckily missing the boy's head.

An assortment of homemade floats followed, many improvised from spare parts scrounged from garages or the flea market, pulled by pickups. Between the floats walked a group of kids from the elementary school decked out in their Halloween costumes. Zane looked adorable dressed as a miniature police officer. When he took off his hat and waved it at me, I saluted in reply.

Not exactly a Mardi Gras-caliber parade by any means, but this was a show, Jacksburg style. I weaved my way back and forth across the road to maintain my momentum while allowing those behind me to keep up. Once we reached the parade route on Main, I sped up and drove the entire route, making one last check that all crossroads were properly blocked and the road was free of traffic and obstacles that could impede the parade.

When I reached the end of the route, I squeezed my shoulder radio. "All clear."

One of the twins answered back. "All clear. Got it."

No answer from the other. *Hmm.*

"Take the lead, Andre," I radioed. I was going to find out once and for all if I really had twins on my payroll.

I made a U-turn and headed against the parade traffic, past Andre, past the marching band, past the dozen or so young girls from Tina's Tap and Twirl, dressed in pink leotards and tap shoes, twirling silver batons with pink streamers on the ends. When I was five, I'd marched in the parade myself, along with my fellow students from Tina's, my hair in long, dark braids tied with pink-and-black polka dot ribbons Mom bought especially for the occasion. I'd felt really special until the parade seemed to go on much too long, especially for a young girl who'd drank three full glasses of Tang for breakfast. I wet my pants before reaching the end. When I bawled in embarrassment, Uncle Angus'd pulled out the waistband of his jeans and poured his snow cone into his underpants to make me feel less conspicuous. I'd laughed so hard I'd wet my pants again. But once Mom had taken me home to change into dry clothes and we'd returned to the jamboree for a ride on the pony-go-round, I'd forgotten all about it.

Dad and Angus were participating in this year's parade, too, Dad's SUV decorated with purple and red streamers. Dad tooted his horn at me as I passed by and tossed me a Tootsie Roll, which I caught in my leather glove. Clearly, the Jamboree organizer was fairly lax on the qualifications for participating in the parade. Slap a few balloons on your butt and you could call yourself a float. But it wasn't like the residents of Jacksburg had much money to spare for fancy decorations. Besides, who were we going to impress? Ourselves?

I carefully eased my way past the local Boy Scout Pack, who carried the American and Texas flags. The Scout Master, a former classmate of mine, walked behind his charges. Not to be outdone, a troop of Brownies followed the boys, pulling radio flyer wagons loaded with cages containing dogs and cats available for adoption from the city pound. A drooling basset hound mix in the rear howled along with the marching band, sending up a racket. An ice cream truck followed, playing tinny ice cream music. The current selection was "Do Your Ears Hang Low?"

The grand finale was the big red fire truck #1. Why it was assigned a number when it was the only rig the town owned, who knows. But the buff firemen hanging off the sides, flexing their muscles and tipping their bright yellow hard hats at the ladies, were a big hit. The Jacksburg Jackrabbit, wearing the stifling costume that, despite repeated cleanings, still reeked from years of accumulated sweat, rode on top of the fire truck, his long ears nearly reaching the overhead wires.

The police officers normally rotated duty as the rabbit. I'd taken a turn last year. It was absolutely miserable. Not only was the suit stinky and hot, you couldn't talk to anyone all day. You could only gesture. It was a stupid rule. It's not like little kids thought the darn thing was a real bunny, anyway. And how would they remember a voice from one year to the next?

This year, Jared Roddy had won the honors of serving in the stench-suit, my punishment for him spilling the beans about finding me and Trey naked, rounding home base at the baseball fields. Despite my warnings, the jackass hadn't kept his mouth shut. I'd learned as much when Selena had greeted me the following Monday morning with, "Heard you finally got laid."

I passed the cruiser bringing up the rear. Jared Roddy and the other night officer sat in the front seat. What was Roddy doing in the cruiser? And if Roddy was in the cruiser, who the heck was in the bunny suit? And where was Dante? I squeezed my shoulder radio. "Dante. You there?"

After a few seconds, a voice came back. "This is Andre. Dante's on engine number one, in the rabbit suit."

I responded. "Roddy's supposed to be in the suit. Dante's supposed to be in the cruiser."

Andre came back. "Roddy paid him a hundred bucks to wear the thing."

Damn. With the bunny under a vow of silence, I'd never know if it was really Dante in the suit. So much for solving the mystery of the twins today. I pointed at Roddy through the windshield and fingered my gun before getting back on the radio. "You ever disobey an order again, Roddy, I'm shooting you."

He responded with a chuckle. "Understood, captain."

I circled around the cruiser and headed back up the other side of the parade. As I eased past the junior high pep squad clad, shaking both their pom-poms and their posteriors, a flash of yellow and black caught my eye. Behind one of the orange plastic barricades the Ninja pulled up, its rider stopping to watch the parade. My head jerked around in a double take and I inadvertently pulled on the handlebars. The bike tilted to the side, taking me with it. I turned my attention back to the road, put my left foot to the ground, and whipped the handlebars straight just before the bike could fall over on me. *Gah! How embarrassing!* I cranked back on the gas and zipped out of there.

Knowing the Ninja rider would be at the Jamboree gave me both a secret thrill and a knot in my gut. Trey would be coming, too, and I was looking forward to spending the day with him. He knew who rode the Ninja, but I didn't know how well Trey knew him. What if we ran into the guy? Would Trey introduce us?

Lights flashing, I returned to my place at the front of the lineup and led the parade slowly down Main, waving to the crowd who waved eagerly back, turning on my siren a time or two to show off when the marching band was between songs. The band performed a heck of a show, the highlight being a rowdy rendition of the classic "Deep in the Heart of Texas."

It didn't get any better than this. At least not in Jacksburg.

When we reached the end of Main a half hour later, the parade cut down a side street to return to the high school parking lot. Once the cruiser at the rear pulled into the lot, I got on the radio. "All officers report to your assigned stations."

En masse, the citizens of Jacksburg headed for the Jamboree grounds at the city park, myself included. As I pulled into the park, I spotted the Ninja in the designated motorcycle parking area, its driver nowhere to be seen, having disappeared into the gathering crowd. My heart spun like the cotton candy machine at the booth across the way. I parked next to the Ninja, noting the bike now bore an official State of Texas metal license plate, skillfully fabricated by inmate labor at the penitentiary in Huntsville. The owner information would be in the DMV's system now. Finally, I could identify him. Just as soon as I could get on the computer back at the station.

Then another sensation hit me, that plunging, hollow feeling you get when bottoming out on a roller coaster. Sure, I'd identify the Ninja rider. But could he be as great a guy as Trey? Would he be as right for me as Trey? Would he make me laugh? Comfort me when I needed it? Bring me to climax with nothing more than a few skillful flicks of his thumb like Trey had done last night? *I doubt it.*

I'd fallen for Trey. *Hard.* Damn me! How had I let that happen? I knew going into this that Trey would be leaving town. There was no hope, no chance whatsoever for a long-term relationship with him. I should've never let it get this far. But if I hadn't, I never would've felt this incredible connection to another human being. *Maybe that old saying is right, after all. Maybe it is better to have loved and lost.*

After securing a frozen lemonade to take my mind off my man troubles, I assumed my position near the corny dog booth. Despite the cold drink, beads of sweat rolled down my back and sides, and my feet and calves sweltered in my leather boots.

"Hot enough for you?"

I looked up to find Trey walking toward me, a paper plate in his hand. I cocked my head and looked him deliberately up and down. "Yup. Definitely hot enough for me."

A grin spread on his face. Today Trey wore his hiking boots with shorts and a T-shirt. He held out the plate, which was loaded with a powdered sugar-coated funnel cake. "Breakfast?"

I pulled off a bite, powdered sugar drizzling down onto the chest of my uniform. The fried batter melted on my tongue. "Yum."

Trey flicked a speck of powdered sugar off my collar, then tugged playfully on it, pulling me toward him for a sweet, sugary kiss. "Let's play some games."

I glanced around. My zone seemed orderly and free of potential threats other than a little girl with a gooey piece of the mayor's bubble gum stuck in her hair, howling as her mother tried to pick it out. "Why not?"

We made our way past a bounce house full of jumping, screaming children and a line of toddlers waiting at the improvised "duck pond," a bunch of yellow rubber ducks floating in a blue plastic kiddie pool. When we reached the midway, Trey slapped four tickets down on the counter for the first game, a shooting challenge involving BB guns and a precarious pyramid of empty root beers cans. Trey's three shots missed the targets entirely. Mine hit the soda cans dead center, sending them crashing to the ground in a tinny ruckus. No trick rifles here. The Rotarian manning the booth handed me a stuffed brown teddy bear.

I handed it to Trey. "Here you go, babe."

Trey cuddled the bear to his chest. "I feel so emasculated."

I winked at him. "Don't worry. I'll make you feel all man later."

He handed the bear to a passing child. "Now you're talking."

At the face painting booth, we found Savannah and a group of other moms putting their meager artistic skills to work painting red hearts and basic daisies on the faces of Jacksburg's kiddos.

"Marnie. Trey. Hey." She looked up and smiled, standing to give us both a hug. She reclaimed her seat and picked up a paintbrush. "What do y'all want? A star? A flower? A rainbow?"

Before I could answer, Trey leaned over and whispered something in Savannah's ear. She turned her face up to him and grinned. She then turned to me, yanking me down into the chair in front of her, dipping the brush in the red paint. She ran the brush over my cheek, the bristles tickling my skin.

"Quit scrunching up your face," she chastised me. "You'll mess this up."

"Can't help it. It tickles."

When she was done, she held up a hand mirror. I looked at my reflection. Although the lettering was backward, I could still read it. M + T inside a red heart.

The equation wasn't complete, however. What did Marnie plus Trey equal? Love? Sure seemed like it. If it wasn't love, it was a damn good imitation.

"Hey, Marnie."

I looked up to find Lucas Glick, dressed as usual in a pair of Wranglers, worn boots, and a faded T-shirt, this one a rock concert tee. "Hey, Lucas."

"Paint your face?" Savannah asked Lucas.

Lucas shook his head. "Stuff's too itchy."

He was right. The paint on my skin had dried out quickly in the heat and already had me scratching.

When I stood, a skinny boy of about eight took my seat. "Can you make me look like a tiger?"

Savannah tilted her head, her furrowed brow betraying her lack of confidence. "I'm not sure I'm that talented."

"Give me a shot," Lucas said.

Savannah gave up her chair and Lucas slid into it, looking over the paints and brushes, carefully deciding which ones to use. He finally chose a brush with thick, short bristles. He dipped it into the small bottle of white face paint and began to apply it to the boy's forehead. He alternated the white, two shades of orange, gray, and black. When he was finished, the boy could've starred in a Broadway performance of *Cats*.

The kid looked in the mirror. "Cool!"

Savannah took a look. "Wow, Lucas. Can you stay and help us out? Anybody gets a look at this kid's face and they're gonna come here expecting the rest of us to be able to do that."

The other moms murmured in agreement.

Lucas shrugged and looked off down the midway. "Wasn't nothing."

Is Lucas blushing again? Surely that pink tint had to be sunburn. Nope, he actually looked a bit sheepish to have his secret talent discovered.

I put my hand on his stubbly cheek and turned his face to me. "It wasn't nothing, Lucas. It was *something*."

"It was *something else*," Trey added. "By the way, Lucas, great job on those logos. The clients were impressed."

Lucas had surprised me by actually calling Trey, taking him up on his offer to design art for websites. Maybe now that his life was taking this positive turn, heading in a new direction, he'd get his mind on his future and off the bottle.

Trey and I left the face-painters to their task and made our way down the row of games, past the milk can toss, past the horse-roping game where a boy in blue jeans, pointy-toed boots, and a straw hat sent the rope sailing over the head of the wooden rocking horse, jerking back when the rope fell neatly around the horse's neck.

"Nice job, kid!" I called.

The boy turned to me and beamed, his teeth, tongue, and lips blue from snow cone syrup. *What a cutie.* My heart seized up. I wanted a blue-mouthed kid of my own, and I wanted him to have Trey's dark hair and steel-gray eyes.

I mentally slapped myself. *Why want what I can never have?*

We continued down the midway. The next game was a guess-your-weight booth. Trey began to slow, pulling on my arm.

"If you dare stop," I said, "you're dead."

"Aw, come on. I love that you've got some junk in your trunk. You're voluptuous."

I shook my head, but secretly I was flattered.

At the next booth, Trey beat me at darts, popping two balloons while I only broke one. The prize was a braided straw finger trap. Trey put his index finger in one end and slid the other end onto mine. "Finger sex."

I pulled back on my finger. It was hopelessly trapped in the straw tube.

"Uh-oh." He shot me the grin I loved. "Looks like we're stuck with each other forever."

I could think of much worse things. Divorce hadn't scared me off the idea of marriage. Chet and I had many happy years before we grew apart. I'd do it again if I met the right guy. Had I *already* met him? I watched Trey out of the corner of my eye as we walked along, the tips of our fingers touching inside the straw tube. He was fun, smart, unconventional, and adventurous, like me in many ways but with some complementary traits and opposing body parts. Just the kind of guy I wanted. Hell, just the kind of guy I *needed*.

CHAPTER TWENTY-FOUR

WET

Around noon, we took a detour back to the food booths for lunch, chowing down on roasted turkey legs and questionable coleslaw. Probably not the best thing to eat in the heat, especially when it was served lukewarm, but I'd never been one to shy away from risk and apparently neither was Trey. Dad and Angus joined us for lunch under a large oak, which provided a tiny bit of relief from the relentless sun. We tossed our trash into a garbage barrel and headed back to the midway.

Farther down we came upon the dunking booth. Inside sat a shirtless Mayor Bennett, enclosed and protected by the metal mesh, his old man boobs sagging over his pasty belly. He taunted passersby. "Who's got the *cojones* to dunk the mayor? Get back at the government! Give Uncle Sam what for!"

Trey cocked his head. "Isn't Uncle Sam the federal government?"

I shrugged. "Yeah, but taking down Uncle Sam sounds better than 'dunk the small-town part-time mayor.'"

Jacksburg's mayoral position was part-time, offering no vacation pay or benefits, which explained why only an independently wealthy guy like Otto Bennett could afford to serve in the position and why, as the only independently wealthy guy in

Jacksurg, Bennett had held the position for six consecutive terms.

I cupped my hands around my mouth. "Watch out, mayor. You're going down. I'll show you what happens when you don't give a police officer a raise."

I was only playing along, trying to increase interest, help the charities that would benefit from the ticket sales. Jacksburg was full of charity cases, so most of the money raised would stay in town, merely being transferred from one pocket to another.

Trey and I stepped up to the card table where Betty Langley sat next to the mayor's wife, both wearing purple cotton sundresses and big red floppy hats, representing the Jacksburg Red Hat Society.

"Hi, ladies." Trey handed Betty four tickets and she handed me three weatherworn baseballs, one of them pulling apart at the seams to reveal the thin, crisscrossed strings inside.

I'd just stepped into place for my first throw when a slurred voice behind me called, "Get 'im, Marnie!"

I turned to find Lucas standing off to the side, wobbling, a drunken smirk on his face. *Gah.* Should've checked his boot earlier. So much for him focusing on his art instead of the bottle. Beside me, Trey stiffened, standing a bit taller and placing himself strategically between me and Lucas in an unconscious act of chivalry. Sweet, even though I could take care of myself and, with a loaded .38 on my hip, posed more of a threat to Lucas if he chose not to behave.

I turned back around, ignoring Glick. I took aim and threw my first baseball, missing the target entirely. As a kid, I'd never been one for softball, opting instead for Powder-puff football. I was the best defensive tackle in Ruger County Powder-puff history.

The mayor put his thumbs in his ears and wagged his fingers at me good-naturedly. "Nanny-nanny boo-boo."

I threw the next ball as hard as I could, missing the target again. "This is harder than it looks."

By then, Lucas had come up close behind me.

"You cain't throw for shit." He followed his words with a whiskey-scented belch. *Charming.*

The Jackrabbit Jamboree had been an alcohol-free event ever since the year the junior high music teacher got plastered at the beer booth and took the stage singing a raunchy tune and dancing a bump and grind. Luckily, the basketball coach she was dating pulled her off the stage before she got too far, and she managed to hang on to a shred of dignity and her job.

"Captain Muckleroy," Mayor Bennett called, "you throw like a girl!"

Nothing like ridicule to motivate a person. I narrowed my eyes, took aim, and sent the third baseball directly to the metal target, where it hit home with a resounding *clang*. There was a momentary pause as the mechanical apparatus activated. The mayor dropped into the water, sending up a wave that splashed through the wire protective mesh and onto the muddy ground surrounding the booth.

"Nailed it!" Trey held up his hand and I gave him a high five.

Lucas scratched his belly, his shirt riding up to expose his skinny hip bones. "Get in that booth, Marnie, and I'll get even with you for all the times you've hauled me in."

I cast him a skeptical glance. "Sure you would, Lucas. Sure you would."

"You don't believe me?"

"No. You're drunker'n a skunk and probably couldn't hit the side of a barn."

Lucas glared back at me, his eyes narrowed. All camaraderie of the recent days was gone, the liquor coming between us, making us enemies again. We'd had a great time bowling, and I'd hoped he'd taken my advice about AA to heart. Clearly he hadn't. I felt frustrated. No, I felt *furious.*

The mayor climbed out of the booth and walked over in his bare feet, his Hawaiian print bathing suit dripping and leaving a wet trail in the dry grass behind him. He tilted his head to each side, pounding a palm on the side of his skull to force the water from his ears. "Man, that felt good."

My feet were sweating in my boots, my bra and panties were stuck to me, and wearing this cheap polyester uniform was like being trapped inside a personal sauna. Maybe I should go for a dip, after all. "What the hell, Glick. You're on."

While Trey stood aside, watching with an amused expression, I stepped up to the card table, took off my boots and socks, my shoulder-mounted radio, and my belt, laying them on the table. "Keep an eye on my gun, Betty."

"Sure thing, Marnie."

I rolled my pant legs up to my knees and climbed the three rungs of the ladder on the side of the dunking booth. Trey held the flimsy metal door open for me as I eased into the booth and took a seat on the hinged board. The seat creaked under my weight as I dipped my feet in the water.

Lucas exchanged tickets for three balls, and stepped back to the line. By this time a number of people, including both Andre and the unusually tall and buff jackrabbit, had gathered to watch. *What the heck had I been thinking?* The dunking booth was the G-rated equivalent of a wet T-shirt contest and I'd willingly volunteered. Clearly I wasn't too smart. No wonder I couldn't figure out what was going on with the credit cards and deliveries.

I glared at Lucas through the mesh screen. How was he ever

going to overcome his problems if he couldn't get his drinking under control? I was upset that he didn't seem to be trying, upset that I'd wasted my time giving a rat's ass about the guy. Upset that I *still* gave a rat's ass. I motioned to Lucas. "Come on, Glick. Show me what you got. Or are the only balls you've got the ones in your hand?" Nasty words, sure, but Lucas deserved them, the drunken bastard. How dare he make me feel sad and inept and discouraged. *Hadn't I suffered enough? Hadn't he?*

The crowd of men whooped and hollered. Lucas squinted his bloodshot eyes at me, handing two of the baseballs to Trey to hold. He put one leg in front of the other, bending his knees. He pulled his arm back and sent the ball sailing straight over the top of the booth into the safety net situated behind me.

The crowd of men guffawed and catcalled. I threw my head back and laughed, too. "If you were sober, you might've got me."

His next ball hit the front of the booth with a resounding *bam* and fell into the mud.

I continued to taunt him. "I'm going to write you a ticket for DUI! 'Dunking under the influence'!"

Glick yanked the last ball from Trey's palm and hurled it at me. His final ball went to the outside, missing the target by a good six inches.

I threw victorious fists in the air. "Can't get a woman wet, can you Glick?" It was hitting below the belt, literally and figuratively. But rage flared inside me. Lucas Glick had been nothing but pleasant just a few hours ago at the face painting booth, but then his old buddy Jack Daniels had brought him down. It made me mad. It made me sick. And it made me sad. This guy was ruining his life.

Lucas crossed his arms over his chest. "This game's rigged."

Trey handed Betty four tickets and gathered up the stray

baseballs while Lucas and the ever-increasing crowd of men watched. Trey stood at the marked line, flashing me a soft smile. He juggled the three baseballs. *Impressive.* Trey was full of surprises.

"Show off!" I cried.

He caught the balls and transferred two of them to his left hand. He tossed the one ball up a couple times with his right hand, catching it in his palm, eyeing me all the while.

I put my hands on my hips. "Now you're just teasing me."

Betty put her fingers to her lips and giggled behind them, enjoying our show. Trey's eyes locked on mine across the twenty-foot span, that dark, dangerous look flickering in them. No doubt about it. Trey was going to get me wet. *Again.* His hand pulled back, the ball went flying, and I went down into the water with a yelp and a splash. The mayor was right. The water was refreshing.

Trey stepped up to the booth and stuck a hand in to help me out. With all the water in my clothes, my weight had increased by ten pounds. I fell back and he stuck his other arm in, too, dragging me out of the booth, but not before I splashed him good. A pool of cool water formed around my feet as I stood facing Trey, our bodies just inches apart. Trey's stare moved from my face down to my chest. My eyes followed. My hard nipples pushed against the tight fabric of my uniform as if trying to break free.

Trey groaned and closed his eyes. "Marnie," he whispered. "You make me crazy."

I crossed my arms over my chest to hide my breasts. Betty stepped over and handed me a blue beach towel covered in pink flamingos to dry off with. The water had smeared the heart painted on my face and I wiped the remaining paint off with the towel, the gesture a subtle reminder that my relationship with Trey, like the paint, wasn't made to last.

By this time, a line of volunteer dunkees had formed, mostly the men who'd stopped for a peep show, now eager to cool off in the dunking booth.

I looked around for Lucas, but he'd disappeared into the crowd. I grabbed my handheld radio from the table and squeezed the talk button. "All officers keep an eye out for Lucas Glick. He's on another tear. Any trouble, haul him in. Check his boot for a flask."

The officers radioed back.

"Yes, ma'am, Cap'n," from Jared Roddy.

"Roger," from the other night officer.

"Sure thing," from Andre.

"Got that" and "Okey-Dokey" from the two guys who worked the weekend shift.

Nothing from Dante.

I perched on the edge of the table and Trey helped me pull my boots back on. Once I was dressed, we headed out for more fun. Selena walked toward us down the midway, her arms loaded with stuffed animals. Eric walked behind her, a proud look on his face. When Selena had taken my advice and played it cool with Eric, he'd stepped up, all but begging her to attend the Jamboree with him. *Heh-heh.*

At the end of the midway was a brightly striped beach umbrella under which sat Madame Beulah, a rotund woman with hair dyed jet black, a dozen or so bracelets encircling her wrists, and a curtain of flab hanging from her upper arms. Her sign read "Madame Beulah Sees All. Palm Reader. Fortune Teller. Spirit Medium."

Trey and I stepped over to the wooden cable spool that served as Madame Beulah's table. "How much?"

"Ten tickets."

Trey pulled out our dwindling supply of tickets, counted off ten, and handed them to Madame Beulah. I took a seat on the folding metal chair, the heat from the chair searing through the wet fabric of my pants, frying my thighs.

Madame Beulah leaned toward me across the table. "What can I do for you?"

From what little I knew about the occult, palm reading was fairly vague. The only spirit I might want to contact would be my mother's, and I didn't want to belittle her memory by trying to contact her in this environment. Not that I thought there was any truth to this bunk. "How about you tell my fortune?"

"All righty." Beulah put her meaty right hand on the table. She opened her palm and gestured for me to put my left hand in hers. I saw her eyes quickly dart to my ring finger, checking my marital status.

She closed her eyes and looked down at her lap. She sat that way for a minute or more, and I began to wonder if she'd fallen asleep. I glanced up at Trey. He shrugged.

Madame Beulah's head jerked up. Her neck craned toward me and she looked me pointedly in the eye, speaking in an eerie, mystical voice. "You will live in Jacksburg the rest of your life, but you will move from your current house into another one nearby. I see a messy but happy home, a sink full of dishes, the floor covered with toys. You will have two children, both girls."

Not bad so far, but for there to be two girls, didn't there have to be a man involved? I found myself looking up at Trey. Would *he* be involved? And was I actually believing this crap?

Her focus, too, shifted to Trey. "The man you love will disappoint you."

Trey chuckled, rocking back on his heels. "Well, heck. Isn't that what men do? Disappoint their women?"

Madame Beulah skewered him with her gaze, her tone no longer mystical. "This won't be the 'I forgot to pick up the milk' kind of disappointment. This will be much bigger."

Trey's smile melted into a scowl. "I paid for a fortune, not an indictment. I want my tickets back."

Madame Beulah tapped on a small placard on the spool table that read FOR ENTERTAINMENT PURPOSES ONLY. NO REFUNDS.

Trey turned and stalked away, marching through a crowd of kids breaking confetti eggs over each other's heads.

I stood to go after him, but Madame Beulah kept a tight hold on my hand, refusing to let me go. "Don't you want to hear the rest?"

"No, thanks." Frankly, I was irritated, too. Who the hell did this woman think she was? Some type of god? "I've heard enough."

I pulled my arm free and headed after Trey. Behind me I heard Madame Beulah's voice call, "Don't fret! Your story has a happy ending!"

My story might have a happy ending, but it wouldn't— *couldn't*—be a happily ever after with Trey. Given the lack of challenging tech jobs in the area, Trey had no intentions of moving back here. And I could never leave my home and move to another big city. I simply wasn't a city girl. But a part of me wanted desperately to believe it, to believe that I could somehow spend the rest of my life with Trey.

I found Trey leaning against a horse trailer by the pony ride, arms crossed over his chest.

"What a load of crap," he said. "I haven't disappointed you yet, have I?"

"Well, you only managed to give me three orgasms last night," I said, giving him a grin. "I'd been hoping for four."

His hard face cracked and he put an arm around my waist, pulling me to him. "I'll make it up to you tonight."

"Promises, promises."

CHAPTER TWENTY-FIVE

SHOWTIME

Other than Madame Beulah getting stuck inside a port-a-potty and a brief cat fight between two girls from the pep squad, one of whom whacked the other with her cardboard cotton candy stick, the remainder of the Jamboree was free of incident.

After a dinner of corn dogs, I headed over to the stage area to get ready for my performance. Trey waited outside while I changed into my Wonder Woman costume in the ladies' dressing room, a nylon dome tent not quite tall enough to stand fully upright in. As big as my rear was, it probably wasn't a good idea to be covering it in bright blue fabric adorned with white stars, but if Wonder Woman could do it, so could I. Besides, with my huge gold pointy breasts, who'd be looking at my butt anyway?

I folded my police uniform and left it in a corner of the tent. I knelt on the floor in front of a slightly warped full-length mirror propped in the corner and applied a generous coat of bright red lipstick and glued on my fake eyelashes. I pulled out my braid and brushed out my long hair, fluffing it out before sliding the gold headband with the red star in the center onto my head. I slid into a pair of knee-high panty hose, slick enough to make it easy to put on the tight red go-go boots that went with the costume.

When I emerged from the tent, Trey's eyes went wide and he shook his head, issuing a wolf whistle. "Damn, woman."

I didn't exactly have the tight bod of Linda Carter, but Trey's reaction had me feeling gorgeous and sexy. I'd had the tailor add thick shoulder straps to the strapless costume rather than risk fallout, and he'd also added some stretchy panels on the side for comfort. But overall I had to agree with Trey. I looked and felt quite sexy in my get-up.

Trey hurried off to get a front-row spot for my performance, which, by necessity, would be performed in a roped-off circle on the parking lot to the side of the stage. The entertainment coordinator, a PTA mom who took the job way too seriously, stood to the side with a clipboard checking in the acts, fretting that two girls from Tina's Tap and Twirl were AWOL and that the show was seven minutes behind schedule. *Like anyone cares.* Nobody in town had anything better to do.

Uncle Angus and Dad had driven my motorcycle to the Jamboree for me, and Uncle Angus was in the circle rubbing a rag down the shiny new pipes Trey had bought for my bike. Dad set the boom box on the ground at the back of the circle as I seated myself on my bike. He cranked the volume to maximum, his hand poised above the play button, waiting for the go-ahead from the mayor, who also served as the emcee for the evening's events.

The sole microphone was back at the stage, so the mayor used one of the Jacksburg PD's bullhorns to introduce me. "Ladies and Gentleman, boys and girls," he said in a voice that would make a circus announcer proud. "Welcome to Jacksburg's annual Jackrabbit Jamboree!"

A roar went through the crowed. We in Jacksburg looked for any good reason to be loud and boisterous. That's the kind of people we are.

"Jacksburg, Texas!" the mayor cried. "Home to the most-talented and best-looking people on God's green earth!" The crowd-pleasing banter incited another roar from the crowd. Guess we wouldn't qualify for the most-humble people.

"Our first act tonight is a woman who's performed at the Jackrabbit Jamboree for the past fifteen years straight."

Gosh, has it really been that long? I mentally calculated. Yup, I'd been doing this since I was sixteen. A few more decades and I'd be wearing Depends under my costume.

"Without further ado, I offer you motorcycle stunt woman Marnie Muckleroy, the Wonder Woman of Jacksburg!"

The crowd roared a third time and Dad pushed the stereo's play button.

As Pat Benatar's "Hit Me with Your Best Shot" blasted from the speakers, I started my engine, gunned it, and took off, circling four or five times to get my bearings. I positioned the handlebars so that the rope tied to hold them in place went taut, keeping the bike in a steady circle just inside the perimeter of the ring. Once momentum kicked in, I pulled up my left leg, putting my knee on the seat, then pulled up my right leg, crouching on the cushy leather, my right hand still grasping the handlebar and pulling back on the gas. The crowd hooted and hollered, cheering me on.

What Wonder Woman performance would be complete without the golden lasso? I pulled the yellow rope from my belt and twirled the long, silky lasso over my head as I made a couple of complete rotations around the ring. The next time I drove past Uncle Angus, I tossed the lasso to him. He grabbed it out of the air.

For my first stunt, I stuck my left arm straight out in front of me and pushed up on my right knee, sticking my left leg straight out in back of me. If not for the fact that I was on the back of a moving motorcycle, this wouldn't be much of a trick, but this crowd was hard up for entertainment and they gave it up for me, clapping their hands, whistling, and shouting, urging me on. Trey stood on the front row next to Savannah, Craig, and their boys, a broad smile on his face as he watched me cruise by.

I sat back down on the bike, riding side-saddle for a few seconds, waving to the crowd, my bracelets gleaming in the early evening sun. My next trick was to lie sideways across the bike, still holding the handlebars with my right hand, and kick my left leg up in the air. I nearly pulled an ab muscle executing that trick. Generous applause followed.

The rest of the performance consisted of a series of similar poses, the highlight of which was a new stunt in which I stood with both feet on the seat, hunched forward so I could still reach the accelerator. For the grand finale, I performed a three-second wheelie, then whipped the bike around to a screeching, instant stop in the center of the ring, cut the engine, and threw my hands in the air just as the song ended.

My ears met much more applause than I deserved, especially given that I'd performed virtually the same routine for the same crowd at the Jackrabbit Jamboree every year and my show was nothing new. But the town had come to count on me as one of the few sure things in life.

"Thank you!" I called, blowing kisses, waving with both hands, and bowing to the crowd. "Thank you!"

The crowd dispersed, a large chunk migrating en masse to the main stage where the other performances would take place. Meanwhile, I posed next to my bike for the aged photographer from the Jacksburg Weekly, spelling my name for him just as I'd done every year, too.

Dad and Uncle Angus came over, each of them giving me a hug. "Great job as usual," Dad said. "Your mom would've been proud."

I'd like to think so.

Trey emerged from the crowd and greeted Dad and Uncle Angus.

"I owe you a big thanks, Trey," Dad said, giving Trey a friendly chuck on the shoulder. "'Cause of that website you made, I landed a gig trimming trees in the right of ways for the power company. That job will keep me and Angus busy nearly year round."

"Glad to help." Trey draped an arm around my shoulders as we followed the stragglers over to the stage. He glanced down at me. "I loved your performance."

I reached up to curl my fingers in his and looked at him. "Come back next year, you can see it again."

"Count me in."

Our gazes locked for a moment.

Next year? Where would we be then? Right back where we'd started, that's where. I'd still be here in Jacksburg, writing traffic tickets, waiting for my life to begin again, still sleeping in my purple polka-dot canopy bed, still cursing Fate, still seeking those simple, yet elusive things I wanted from life. Trey would be in Silicon Valley, working on cutting-edge computer projects, writing challenging code, fighting traffic, earning big bucks, collecting high-priced high-tech gadgets. Our two worlds didn't mesh, could never mesh. *Could they?*

"I've used up most of my vacation time," Trey said, "but I'm coming home next month for Thanksgiving."

Next month sounded much better than next year, but it might as well be never. No matter how two people felt about each other, they couldn't build a meaningful relationship based on brief, intense encounters. Besides, I wanted more than that.

Trey watched my face as if trying to gauge my feelings. "My mother makes a mean pumpkin pie. You'll have to come eat with us."

I didn't respond. By then, we'd reached the edge of the

crowd at the stage. People sat on the ground, those with forethought sitting on blankets, the rest of us plopping straight down on the dried grass and weeds to watch the performers.

The frazzled young mother who was organizing the performers seemed to have calmed down some, and was herding the two wayward girls in pink leotards to the back of the stage to await their turn in the spotlight.

A man dressed in green shorts with suspenders, what the Germans called lederhosen, took the stairs to the stage. He led a muscular Doberman dressed in a plaid skirt. Gretchen's tail wasn't docked, a tribute to her owner's compassion. She wagged her tail as she first looked out at the cheering crowd, then up at her master, waiting for her cue. The man raised his hand, fingers fisted, and glanced back at the stage manager, who turned on the German folk music. After a brief stanza, he gave the signal, a circular motion with his index finger, and Gretchen began to yodel.

Owooowoo, Owoo. Gretchen tilted her black head back, nose in the air. *OwooWOOwoo, owoo.* She was precisely in time with the music, never missing a cue. *OwooWOOwoo!*

When Gretchen finished, she stood on all fours and bent down on her right front leg, curling the left under her in a canine curtsy. The crowd went wild, giving the dog a standing ovation. In addition to the applause, Gretchen's handler rewarded her with a dog treat, which she gobbled down immediately.

Even Trey was impressed. "Y'all sure know how to entertain a crowd here in Jacksburg."

"We aim to please."

Trey's hometown held an annual Hockerville Heritage Festival, an international event where those attending could participate in a wine tasting of both continental and European varietals, partake of gourmet international food such as sushi and baklava, and listen to classical musical interludes provided by string quartets, hoity-toity stuff like that. Not our style here. Frankly, I think folks in Jacksburg had a lot more fun.

The cuties from Tina's Tap and Twirl took the stage next, a handful of mothers weaving among the girls, moving each of them into their appropriate starting positions. As soon as the mothers left the stage, the music began, the classic *Babyface*. The girls twirled and tapped their hearts out, with only an occasional *thump* or *whump* as a baton was dropped or a girl slipped on her slick metal taps and landed on her bottom on the stage, the crowds cheering when she regained her baton or footing, giving her the confidence to continue.

"Just think," Trey said, "if Madame Beulah's right, you're going to have two of those little creatures sometime soon."

"Yeah, right."

He looked me in the eye, his expression serious. He, too, seemed conflicted about our future. "You want kids?"

"Of course. You?"

"Heck, yeah. They'd give me another excuse to play video games."

Applause for Tina's troupe of twirlers interrupted our exchange, and we turned our attention back to the stage. Following Tina's class were two old folks from the nursing home, dressed in denim overalls that bagged in the rear, playing dueling banjos. The duo had surprisingly agile fingers, despite their joints being bent from arthritis. Rounding out the show were a blond teenage girl who sang a sappy song of unrequited love, an adolescent boy who performed magic tricks in an ill-fitting tux two sizes too big, and a petticoat-clad square dancing group in which three women were forced to dance the men's parts due to the lack of willing male participants.

The final act was a round-bellied short-horned goat who could not only count, but multiply and divide. Once the goat left the stage, the mayor wrapped things up by thanking the performers for their stellar performances and the audience for its enthusiasm. "Stick around, folks. The street dance starts in just half an hour."

"Street dance, huh?" Trey said. "That sounds like fun. Can I hold you close, maybe let a hand slide down to your butt?"

"I'm counting on it. I just need to change." I took a few steps in the direction of the tent.

Trey grabbed my arm and pulled me back. "Leave the costume on. It's not every day I get to go on a date with a superhero."

Why not? The evening was still warm and the Wonder Woman get-up was a lot cooler than my cop uniform. I collected my clothes from the tent and stashed them in my father's Cherokee, but put on my belt with my .38, pepper spray, and mobile radio so I'd be ready if the Optimist Club ran out of fried Twinkies and a riot broke out.

The Six Pack took the stage. They were the same half dozen beer-bellied men in worn jeans, denim shirts, and cowboy hats who normally played at the Watering Hole. After making sure the guitars were in tune and performing a quick microphone check, they launched into their first song, Lynyrd Skynyrd's "Sweet Home Alabama." The crowd whooped and flooded onto the area in front of the stage, hands in the air, hips swaying, boots scooting. *No wallflowers in this crowd.*

Eric worked his way through the crowd past us, leading Selena by the hand. She smiled at me as they made their way by, and I gave her a discreet, conspiratorial wink.

Trey and I danced in the middle of the crowd. He was totally uninhibited, loose-limbed and natural, nothing like Chet, whose reserved side-to-side dance movements were barely perceptible. With Trey I felt free, shaking my head, my hair flaring out around me. I was having a blast, more fun than I could ever remember having. I loved this song. And I loved this guy.

What?!?Love?

Gah! It was true. It had snuck up on me like a pair of too-snug panties, but, yes, I did love Trey. This wasn't just a crush. I was too old for crushes, too careful. Hell, too cynical. Besides, with all the time Trey and I had spent together the past few weeks, we'd crammed a year's worth of dating into less than two months. Enough time to know whether it was the real thing.

It was.

I looked up at Trey. He caught my eye, grabbed me around the waist and pulled me to him, spinning me around and planting a kiss on me before releasing me again.

What was I going to do when he went back to California? How would I face each day knowing he was half a country away from me? My heart seized up at the thought.

Trey glanced down at me and his eyes flashed concern when he saw the pained look on my face. "Something wrong?" he shouted over the music.

I forced a smile and pointed down at my boots. "Blisters!" I fibbed.

Angus wiggled through the crowd until he was next to us, holding the hand of a thin woman with curly brown hair, big smiles on both of their faces. I questioned him with my eyes.

"This is Julie!" Angus hollered. "I met her on the internet." He gave a thumbs-up sign to Trey.

I looked up at Trey, pulling him close to speak into his ear. "What's that about?"

He bent down, cupping a hand to my ear so I could hear him

speak. "I hooked him up to an online dating site."

"That's great." Now Uncle Angus wouldn't be alone anymore. He looked happy, and I was happy for him. *Maybe Dad should set up a profile on the site, too.*

The next song was Rascal Flatts' "Life is a Highway", another southern rock staple. Savannah and Craig made their way over to us, their crew of kids hanging onto their legs. I grabbed Zane, still in his cop costume though he'd lost the hat. I scooped him up in my arms and he giggled. "I bet you never danced with Wonder Woman before, huh?"

"Let me go!" he shouted. "You'll give me cooties!"

Laughing, I set him back down.

Trey caught my eye and wagged his brows. "I'll take your cooties any day."

CHAPTER TWENTY-SIX

SMASHED

One hour and a dozen songs later, the band slowed things down, easing into Garth Brooks' long-ago hit, "The Dance." Trey reached out and grabbed my hand, pulling me to him as he stepped toward me, the two of us becoming one in a single, fluid movement.

We did a slow two-step around the dance floor, Trey carefully maneuvering me around the other couples in the crowd. His body felt warm, moist with sweat against mine, but right. *So right.* I started again to dread him leaving, but forced the thoughts from my head. *Why let thoughts of tomorrow ruin the perfect moments of today?*

I closed my eyes. Trey had his hand at the nape of my neck, his fingers tangled in my damp tresses. "Let's get out of here, Marnie," he whispered into my hair. He leaned back to look at my face.

I moaned, closing my eyes. I pointed down to my belt, loaded with my gun, nightstick, and pepper spray. "I'm still on duty, remember?"

He tossed his head back and groaned.

I glanced at my watch. "This'll be over in an hour. The crowd usually clears out pretty quick once the band stops playing."

"Good. Guess what I've got in my pocket?"

I grinned up at him. "I know what you've got in your pocket. You're pressing it against me."

"Not that." Trey glanced around, put his hand in the front pocket of his shorts, then pulled it out, his fist closed. He opened his hand and gave me a glimpse of a shiny silver key.

"What's that?"

"The key to the Lone Star Suite at Magnolia Manor."

The suite was the bed and breakfast's most elegant, most romantic room. I felt like Liesl von Trapp in *The Sound of Music* after Friedrich kissed her, fighting the urge to throw my hands in the air and squeal "Weeeee!"

Trey returned the key to his pocket. "What do you think, Wonder Woman? You can tie me up with your Golden Lasso and have your way with me."

"It depends," I said, playing hard-to-get. "What are they serving for breakfast?"

Trey nuzzled my ear. "Who cares? We're not getting out of bed 'til they drag us out."

***

The band played its final song, "The Girls All Get Prettier at Closing Time". Without the usual beer paycheck, they'd remembered all the words and notes to their songs tonight. The lead singer stepped to the mic and tipped his hat. "'Night ever'body. Drive careful now."

Bright white spotlights around the perimeter of the park came on full blast like a nuclear explosion, burning into our retinas. Trey followed me as I headed to the parking lot for traffic detail. My heart did a back flip in my chest when I noticed the yellow and black Ninja still parked at the far end of the lot next to Glick's orange tank truck. Being with Trey, I'd forgotten all about the Ninja. But the Ninja's rider was still here somewhere. My heart felt as if were being torn, wanting to give itself fully to Trey, but knowing that would be stupid and futile, still holding on to a wispy, desperate hope that the mystery man with the Ninja could offer me something more than Trey could.

The noisy crowd piled into their vehicles in the parking lot. The guy should be in the lot in the next few minutes to get his bike. Of course I wouldn't be able to approach him with Trey around, but at least I'd finally get a peek at him.

Trey gestured toward the far end of the lot where the motorcycle was parked. "The Ninja's here."

"Really?" I glanced at the bike, feigning nonchalance. "I hadn't noticed."

"Liar."

I *was* a liar, and if Trey didn't stop looking at me like that, with a look that was both accusing and sexy at the same time, sending a flare of heat between my thighs, my Wonder Woman costume would catch fire. But a man's ego was at stake here. Time for some damage control. "I bet he's not *hard wired*."

Trey's expression morphed from accusing and sexy to cocky and sexy. *Better.*

I retrieved my flashlight from the saddlebag of my police bike and quickly made my way to the exit. Andre had beat me there, standing in the middle of the road, a palm raised to halt the oncoming traffic while he waved a dozen or so cars out of the lot. Traffic jam, Jacksburg style. Of course it would be all wrapped up in mere minutes, nothing like the gridlock I'd experienced in Dallas.

I turned on my flashlight and swung it in a repeated arc, guiding the cars out of the lot, stopping a carload of teenagers and giving them the obligatory lecture about wearing their seatbelts. Trey waited on a nearby park bench, one arm draped over the back, never taking his eyes off me.

Gah! Couldn't these people move any faster? Didn't they know I had an orgasm waiting for me? "Come on folks, keep it moving, keep it moving."

My head snapped to the right when a loud engine revved up, but it turned out to be only Mayor Otto coming through on his tractor. The Ninja sat forlornly in the lot, still waiting for its rider. *Where the heck is he?* Maybe he'd caught a ride with friends to the Watering Hole and planned to come back for his bike later. Maybe he'd hooked up with some cute young thing and was off somewhere having wild, passionate sex. When I turned my attention from the Ninja back to the cars, I noticed another pissed-off look flash across Trey's face. *Damn. Should've been more subtle.*

Finally, I waved out the last occupied car, a banged-up mini-van driven by a weary white-haired granny hauling five screaming kids hopped up on snow cone syrup and cotton candy.

"Later!" Andre called as he climbed into his cruiser.

I raised a hand in good-bye to him and clicked off my flashlight. Besides my police bike, the Ninja, and Glick's truck, it was only me and Trey in the parking lot now. Trey must've left the Lincoln on one of Jacksburg's side streets. No problem. He could ride behind me on the police bike to pick up his car.

Trey walked over to me, wrapped his arms around my back, and gave me a sexy grin. "You're all mine now, Wonder Woman."

He leaned down to kiss me, warm and soft and full of unfulfilled desires. Still holding the flashlight, I wrapped my arms around his neck and pressed my body to his. *Mmm.* If I turned on the sirens and flashing lights on the police bike, we could be at the

Magnolia Manor in ten minutes flat.

A scuffling sound behind us interrupted the moment. Lucas staggered into the parking lot, totally shit-faced now.

I dropped my arms from Trey's shoulders. "Duty calls. Wait here." I headed across the lot. "Lucas!"

The guy was in no condition to drive. He didn't seem to hear me and stepped up beside his truck, fumbling with the key fob.

"Lucas!" I hollered again. "Stop right there!"

He dropped his keys. "Aw, shit." He bent to pick them up, lost his balance, and put out a hand to steady himself, leaning against his truck for a moment. When he went to stand, he banged his head on his side mirror with a *klunk*. "Fuck!"

He tried again to unlock the truck and was successful this go 'round. The door unlocked with an audible *click-click*. By this time, I was only twenty feet away. I turned my flashlight back on, aiming the intense beam at him. He put up a hand to shield his eyes.

"Lucas! Hold on a minute."

Ignoring me, he climbed in the truck, slammed the door and started the engine. His white reverse lights came on as I ran to the driver's side window and banged on it. "Lucas! Stop!"

He scowled at me through the window. "The fuck you want?" he mouthed.

"You are in no condition to drive!" I yelled loud enough for him to hear through the glass. "Turn off the engine and let me take you home."

He didn't bother to unroll the window, just yelled back through the grimy glass. "Back off, bitch!"

Bitch? Really? I grabbed the handle and tried to open the door of his truck, but he'd locked it.

"Damn it, Lucas! If you drive off I'm going to have to haul you in on a DUI. That's a felony. You don't want that on your record. Get out of the truck and let me take you home!"

My heart pounded in my chest like a jackhammer and hot tears welled up in my eyes. A felony would push Glick into a new category, subject him to real time in the state pen. I didn't want to see him end up like that, but I also couldn't let him out on the streets in this condition. He could kill someone.

The truck lurched back a couple feet, then stalled as his foot slipped off the clutch. I banged my fists on the hood of his truck. "Dammit, Lucas!" I cried. "Stop!"

He started the engine again and pushed the truck into gear, grinding them as he failed to fully engage the clutch. Tires screeching, he turned to the right away from me, his right front fender hitting the front tire of the Ninja parked next to him, knocking the bike to the ground. Glick's truck bounced as he rolled over the front of the bike, the tire assembly giving way with a *crunch*.

Lucas circled back past me and roared toward the parking lot exit. I ran after him in my Wonder Woman boots, my efforts to stop him futile, my screams falling on ears that refused to listen. My boots were flat-soled and provided no traction. I slipped and fell in the parking lot, skinning my knees and the palms of my hands. At the front of the lot, Trey bolted toward the truck and reached Glick as he paused at the exit, half-in half-out of the street. The mini-bus from the Jacksburg Retirement Home swerved around him in the nick of time, the furious driver at the wheel laying on the horn, frightened, wrinkled faces gaping at the windows.

Trey grabbed a cinder block that had been used to hold down a half-dozen helium balloons, now at half mast. He used the block to smash the passenger window of Glick's truck. After tossing the block aside, he hopped onto the running board, reached through the broken window, and managed to get the door unlocked and open, pulling himself into the truck.

The truck rolled farther into the road as the men scuffled in the cab. The red lights on the back of the car came on as Trey managed to set the emergency brake. A few seconds later, the lights went back out. Trey hopped out of the truck, Glick's keys in his hand.

Thank God.

Glick dove out of the passenger side of the truck, tackling Trey to the asphalt, and the two of them rolled around in the broken glass for a few seconds before Trey immobilized Glick on the ground, his arm crooked behind his back. For a computer geek, Trey was a damn good fighter.

I stomped toward the men, handing Trey my flashlight to warn oncoming traffic. He stood and backed away. "Lucas Glick you are under arrest!" I screamed, yanking off Lucas's right boot, pulling out the empty metal flask inside, and hurling it across the parking lot into the trees. "You have the right to remain silent!" Tears streamed down my face, tears for the little boy who might have grown up different if his father had stuck around, if his mother hadn't knocked him around. "Anything you say can be used against you in a court of law. You have the right—" I choked back a sob, "to an attorney. You—"

"Fuck you!" Glick yelled at me. He rolled over onto his back, threw his fists to the sky and yelled to the universe and everyone in it. "*Fuuuck yooou!*"

Lucas had tears running down his face now, too. I fell to my already-skinned knees next to him and pulled him to a sitting position, holding him to me in a tight embrace. He sobbed whiskey-scented sobs on my shoulder while I sobbed strawberry snow-cone sobs on his.

Trey backed Glick's truck out of the street and into the

parking lot, then came to stand beside us.

After a couple minutes, Lucas said, "Shit," and released me. He sat back on the asphalt, Indian style, like a child, elbows on his knees. "Shit. Shit. Shit."

I took his hands in mine and looked into his face. "Lucas, you need to get some help. You've *got* to get some help."

He looked at me with eyes full of pure grief. His voice was still slurred, but soft now. "You think I don't know that, Marnie? You know what those rehab places cost? A goddamn fortune, that's what. I ain't got money for the Betty Ford clinic." He looked down at the grease spot on the asphalt between us.

"I've got some money left over from my divorce settlement," I said. "You can have it, Lucas."

He glanced at me, then away, then back at me. "Why would you do that for me?"

I shrugged. "I guess it's 'cause I like you. When you're not drunk, that is."

Lucas snorted, then eyed me, a look of incredulity on his face as if the poor guy couldn't believe someone actually gave a crap about him. My heart felt swollen and tight, like the time I'd tried to squeeze my size sixteen butt into a size twelve pair of jeans.

He looked away again. "Got nobody to watch Tosh."

"Who's Tosh?"

"My cat."

If the guy was responsible enough to think about his cat, there was definitely hope for him. "Your cat can come stay with me for a while. Bluebonnet would love the company."

Lucas seemed to consider my proposal. "What if I say no?"

"Then I arrest you for DUI and you'll spend a few months in Huntsville, lose your septic business and your cat, maybe even your trailer."

Trey stepped up beside us. "Not to mention you'll have to fight off some guy with a thing for skinny cowboys."

I scrunched up my nose at Trey. "Yuck."

"Just trying to help you out. It would persuade me."

I turned back to Lucas. "He's right, you know. You want that?"

Lucas didn't answer.

"Sounds like a no-brainer to me," Trey said. "There's a good facility in Hockerville. My cousin's been through the program there. Sober now for four years. She's not as fun as she used to be, but at least she hasn't woken up in bed with a stranger lately."

Lucas stared up at the sky. Clearly fate hadn't singled me out to bully. Fate had been a royal bitch to him, too.

"Looks like I don't have much choice," he finally muttered. If he was trying to sound tough, he failed. His relief was clear in his voice.

I took his arm and helped him up. "Let's go."

We swept the broken glass off the seat and helped Glick into the passenger side of his truck, then walked back to the Ninja to survey the damage. The bike lay on its side like a racehorse with a broken leg, its front wheel deflated, pieces of yellow plastic littering the ground around it.

I stuck my business card between the leather seat and gas

tank where the rider would find it, making a mental note of the license plate number.

Trey stared at the mess for a few seconds. "I hope Glick has good insurance."

I snorted. "I hope he's got *any* insurance."

CHAPTER TWENTY-SEVEN

THE BEST LAID PLANS TO GET LAID . . .

Glick's truck had only two seats, so Trey drove the truck while I followed on the police bike. We swung by Glick's trailer so he could pack a few things for his stay. The hail-dented, plain white trailer had settled unevenly in the clay soil, one end a foot higher than the other, and I had to jerk on his front door several times to free it from the crooked frame.

Trey put a hand on Glick's back to prevent him from falling back down the two metal steps leading up to the front door. The inside of the trailer smelled like a typical bachelor pad, an aromatic stench of beer, stale pizza, and garbage funk. The trash can overflowed with beer cans, fast food wrappers, and whiskey bottles. A pair of enormous brown roaches scurried out from a hamburger wrapper, seeking a safer hiding place underneath the cabinets.

"Tosh? Where are ya,' buddy?" Lucas called.

A solidly-built black tomcat with long hair matted into kitty dreadlocks crawled out from under the wood-frame futon and walked over to rub on Lucas's legs.

"I try to brush him," Lucas said, "but he don't like it."

Despite the matted fur, the cat appeared healthy and well-socialized. Lucas picked up the heavy cat, almost falling over as he did. He held Tosh to his chest for a moment, looking down at him almost as if he wanted to say something to his pet. But when he glanced up at me and Trey and saw us watching, he set the cat back down on the dingy linoleum, which curled up every few feet at the seams. "Carrier's in the hall closet."

We loaded Tosh into the plastic pet carrier. Lucas went into his bedroom and returned with a round fleece cat bed and a sisal scratching post. On his second trip, he handed me a plastic box full of assorted cat toys. A peacock feather, a fishing pole type toy with a fuzzy pom-pom dangling from the end, a trio of plastic balls with bells inside.

Glick's pantry contained a veritable smorgasbord of cat delights, everything from Fancy Feast to fish-shaped treats, and we added them to the box. The five-foot carpet-covered cat tree was too big to fit into the truck, so we had to leave that behind for now. Tosh was certainly one spoiled cat.

After taking Tosh to my house, we continued on to Hockerville and dropped Lucas off at the treatment center for a six-week intensive live-in program. Trey lugged a laundry basket filled with clean socks, underwear, jeans, and T-shirts up to Glick's room. I signed a contract to pay for the treatment, making a sizable dent in my savings account balance, but what did I need the money for? I lived with my dad, had no mortgage or car payment, and only a big white dog to take care of.

I gave Lucas's hand one last squeeze before we left, the motion reactivating the pain in the raw scrapes on my palms, but I fought through it, managing to maintain a smile.

He squeezed back, then pulled me to him for a hug, whispering, "Thanks, Marnie. You're as nice as your mother."

It was the best compliment I'd ever received.

***

It was after 2:00 AM when Trey and I walked out to the parking lot of the rehab center.

I was physically and mentally exhausted. I stood next to the police bike and looked up at Trey. "Trey, I'm not sure I'm up for the Magnolia Manor." By the time we could drive back to Jacksburg for me to pack a bag and return to Hockerville, it would be at least another hour and I'd be too exhausted for a night of passion.

I could tell he was disappointed, but he said, "I understand."

I think he actually did understand. He realized I needed this, that I had to help Lucas, to eliminate my karmic debt. I could only hope that Lucas's time in rehab would make a real, lasting difference.

Since it was so late, I suggested Trey drive Glick's truck home and pick up his parent's car the following day. "No sense you making another run back and forth this late at night."

Trey nodded and gave me a soft peck on the cheek. "Let's get together tomorrow."

"I'll be at Savannah's. I'm babysitting."

"Want some company?"

"With those three boys? Heck, I want *backup*."

"You got it."

***

An hour later I lay in bed, Band-Aids on my knees and palms. Bluebonnet was draped over my legs, her head dangling over the side of my bed so she could keep a watchful eye on Tosh. The cat made his way around my room, curiously sniffing everything in sight, including the boxes addressed to Zane that sat on the floor in the corner. Despite the fact that Tosh seemed to suffer a perpetual bad hair day, the cat was well-adjusted, trusting. Lucas was a much better parent than his mother or father had ever been.

I rolled onto my back and stared up at my canopy. Seemed like I'd been doing a lot of staring at my canopy lately.

A mix of emotions battled inside me. Part of me was pissed off at Lucas for ruining one of my last nights with Trey, but another part of me hoped the night would turn out to be the beginning of a new life for Lucas. I hoped he could beat his addiction to alcohol. I needed him to get well not only for himself, but also for me. I had to know that I'd helped save a life, had to even the score and get rid of these guilty feelings that had dogged me ever since that dark day in Dallas when I'd killed that man. I said a quick prayer for Lucas, asking God to give him strength.

My thoughts then turned to Trey. Trey had gone along tonight, never once questioning my motives. He seemed to understand me intuitively, instinctively, as if we'd known each other much longer than we actually had. Trey was clever, a good listener, and he made me laugh, bringing a lightness to my life, which had felt too heavy for too long. He made me feel like a desirable woman again, even with those extra pounds packed into my Wonder Woman costume, testing its seams. He wasn't a bad dancer, either. What more could I want in a man?

I could want him to stick around. That's what.

***

I might have fallen asleep last night dreaming of Trey, but when I woke to the stark sunlight Sunday morning, things were more clear. Trey was a great guy, but I'd stupidly let myself fall way too hard for him. No doubt I'd pay for that. He was leaving in three days. Sure, he'd be back every few months to visit his family, but at this point in my life I wasn't in the market for a part-time, now-and-then, no-strings-attached relationship. I wanted a full-time, always-and-forever ball and chain.

Time for me to face reality and acknowledge once and for all what my relationship with Trey was, a brief distraction in an otherwise routine and lonely existence. But at least he would help me keep Savannah's wild and crazy boys under control today.

Normally, I went to church with Dad and Uncle Angus on Sunday mornings. We attended the non-denominational service offered at the VFW Hall, not only because the preacher didn't get bogged down with rules and restrictions, but also because the church offered an 11:30 service, the latest service in town, allowing us to sleep in, *praise the Lord.* I'd begged off this morning. At least I'd be doing some of God's work, helping my fellow man. Surely He'd forgive me for missing church under these circumstances.

I took a quick shower, braided my still-wet hair, and slid into my favorite pair of Levi's, a flannel shirt, and my ankle-high black biker boots. As soon as Dad and I finished breakfast, I decided to make a quick run by the DQHQ, to see if the Ninja's owner had called about his crushed motorcycle. Surely the poor guy would have found his bike by now.

Dad and I headed outside with the two boxes I'd retrieved from the Parker House, the ones from Macy's and Bergdorf's addressed to Savannah's son, Zane. In the dirt driveway, Dad helped me strap the boxes to the back of my bike. After giving Dad a quick peck on the cheek, I pulled the faceplate down on the daisy helmet and cranked the bike's engine.

Minutes later, I pulled under the rickety carport at the police station. At the front counter sat Linda, the weekend dispatcher, a tall fiftyish woman whose once-blond curls had faded to a pale ivory. She was reading the business section of the Dallas Sunday paper. The front page bore a color photo of Kent Tindall and a headline that read *How the Mighty Have Fallen.* Tindall's arrest was still big news, the district attorney having uncovered further financial shenanigans over the past few weeks.

She glanced up from the paper as I came in the door. "'Mornin' captain."

"'Mornin', Linda. Any calls come in for me?"

She shook her head.

Damn. Hadn't the Ninja rider discovered his damaged bike yet? Maybe he'd partied all night at the Watering Hole and was still sleeping off his night of debauchery somewhere, maybe at the house of some woman he'd met at the bar.

Linda put the business section down and fingered through the rest of the paper until she found the Piggly Wiggly ad, which she spread out on the counter in front of her. "What're you doing here on a Sunday?"

"Thought I'd come in and catch up on some paperwork." *Thought I'd come in and catch me a man was more like it.* Since the Ninja guy hadn't called in, I'd have to track him down through his newly issued license plate number. I tried to convince myself I wasn't actually stalking the guy, that I was doing him a favor, locating him for official police purposes.

Linda flipped the glossy page. "Toilet paper's on sale. Two-for-one."

Didn't take much to get people excited in this town.

"I'll keep that in mind." I poured myself a mug of coffee, added vanilla creamer, then headed back to my booth and booted up my computer. The decrepit thing seemed to take forever. Maybe if I poured some coffee into the hard drive the machine would wake up and get moving.

My hand was poised on the mouse, index finger hovering over the button, waiting. When the screen finally came to life, I clicked on the link to the state motor vehicle records and, at a speed that would make my high school typing teacher proud, input the Ninja's license plate number. The computer made a whirring sound for a couple seconds, then emitted a beep.

There it was. The identity of my mystery man.

Bartholomew Edmund Jonasili.

Really? I hadn't expected such an old-fashioned name. I'd anticipated something tough, rugged, and sexy, like Mitch or Derek or Axel. Certainly not *Bartholomew Edmund.* I looked up to plead with the heavens. *Please, Lord, don't let him be some octogenarian hiding his wrinkly gonads under a cool leather jumpsuit.* But no, he couldn't be. I'd seen him at the pumps at the Grab-N-Go and he'd had dark hair. Of course anyone could dye their hair. Chet had taught me that. But my quick glimpse hadn't left me with the impression that the Ninja's rider was old.

I looked back at the screen. Maybe the guy went by Bart or Eddie. Either of those names would do. But what about that surname, Jonasili? What was it, Italian? French? Greek? I didn't have a clue. I'd never heard it before.

I realized then that his driver's license record could give me his age and a photo. I backed out of the vehicle registration file, clicked on the icon for driver's license records, and typed in his name. The computer whirred for several seconds, then emitted an odd crackling noise as if it were about to short-circuit. I shot the screen a death glare and hissed, "Don't fail me now, you sorry piece of crap!"

"You say something, Marnie?" Linda called from across the room.

"Just cursing the computer!" I called back. "Stupid thing's acting up again."

I took a sip of my coffee and closed my eyes. The computer stopped whirring and beeped. *The moment of truth.* Time to come face-to-face with my mystery man. Well, at least face-to-photo.

I took a deep breath, opened my eyes, and checked the

screen. *No match.*

How could Bartholomew Edmund Jonasili have a motorcycle registered in his name but no driver's license? It made no sense. I must have misspelled the name. That had to be the reason no match was found.

I backed up to the input screen and checked my spelling. *Nope.* I'd spelled it exactly as it showed up on the registration records. I typed the name in again anyway. Still no match. I tried various misspellings of the name, just in case the data entry clerk at the DMV had flubbed up. Still no match.

"What the hell?" I banged my fist on the red Formica.

Fate, that nasty bitch, was taunting me, dangling two men in front of me like juicy, sexy carrots, then yanking them out of my grasp, keeping them just out of reach.

I flopped back into the booth. I sat there for a minute, fighting the urge to take my .38 and blast the useless piece of silicon and plastic sitting in front of me to smithereens. Instead, I paged back to the vehicle registration records to get the address in Hockerville for Bart. Big Bad Bart. Bad Boy Bart. I could always drive by his house and hope to catch a glimpse of him, or knock on the door and pretend to be selling tickets to the policeman's ball. Of course we didn't hold a ball, but that was beside the point.

As the machine attempted to access the registration records again, the screen flickered. "No! Not now!"

The screen flared bluish-white, then fell pitch black. The machine sat in silence. The system had crashed.

"Gah!" I bitch-slapped the monitor and it rotated a few inches on the base. I banged my forehead once on the edge of the tabletop, then left it there, staring down at the scratched tile floor. I could call the sheriff's department, ask them to run the search for me on their state-of-the-art computers, but I wasn't in the mood to be razzed about our crappy equipment. I had a full to-do list for the day and didn't have time to hang around until the irritable machine decided to cooperate again.

I marched to the dispatch desk and grabbed the dog-eared Ruger County phone book from under the counter. I opened it on the countertop and flipped pages aside until I got to the J's. I ran my finger down the listings. "Jonasili, Jonasili," I mumbled. There was one Jonah, two Jonases, and then the listings moved on to Jones, one of which was BJ and Frances, Trey's parents. *Just my luck.* The Ninja's owner either didn't have a landline, or he had an unlisted number. *Gah, gah, gah!*

Maybe this was Fate's way of telling me to focus on one guy at a time. *But maybe Fate should give me a break and go screw with someone else for a change.*

I turned to Linda. "You ever heard of anyone in Hockerville with the last name of Jonasili?"

She looked thoughtful for a moment, then shook her head. "No. Why?"

"His motorcycle was damaged at the park last night. I'm trying to track him down. I left my card at the scene. If he calls, you can give him my personal cell number."

"Sure thing, Marnie."

I slammed the phone book closed and shoved it back under the counter. "Computer's crashed again. Call the sheriff's department if you need to run anything."

"Okey dokey."

I grabbed my purse from my desk-booth and headed back out the door.

CHAPTER TWENTY-EIGHT

A DAY OF REST? NOT QUITE

I ducked into the Piggly Wiggly, emerging from the store twenty minutes later with two plastic bags full of cleaning supplies. After packing them in the black leather saddle bags on my bike, I snapped my helmet back on, slid my hands back into my gloves and aimed for the trailer park.

As I passed Jacksburg City Park, I did a double take. A bright red flatbed truck from a local towing service sat in the lot. A stocky bald man in gray coveralls bent over next to it, wrestling with the shattered remains of the Ninja.

I made an illegal U-turn, my braid whipping around and whacking me in the left boob. I drove slowly into the lot, glancing around for the owner of the bike. Besides the tow truck operator, there was no one in sight.

I pulled up behind the man and cut my engine. The guy looked up at me. We recognized each other from previous accident scenes. He nodded to me.

I looked down at the mangled motorcycle. "That bike's in sad shape."

"You ain't kidding." He picked up a chunk of ragged yellow fiberglass, what was once the wheel cover.

"Where's the owner of the bike?" I asked.

He shrugged. "He called this morning and asked us to haul it to a motorcycle repair outfit in Dallas. Said there's an extra hundred in it for me if I'd make it my first priority. Must be in a hurry to get it fixed."

If I had a bike like that, I'd be in a hurry to get it back up and running, too. Luckily, since only the front end was damaged, the repairs shouldn't take more than a day or two.

No point in sticking around if Bad Bart isn't here. "See ya." I raised a gloved hand, started my engine and drove off.

***

Lucas's key slid easily into the lock on his front door, but with the frame sitting cockeyed it took three hard shoves to the darn thing open. I made a mental note to look into what it would cost to get the trailer leveled. All these mental notes were seriously crowding my mental bulletin board.

When I stepped inside, the same stench from the night before met my nose. I dropped my grocery store bags on the floor and set about opening all the windows to air the place out. After unbuttoning my cuffs and rolling up the sleeves on my flannel shirt, I got down to business. *So much for Sunday being a day of rest.*

For the next two hours, I ignored the complaints from my sore, scraped palms and scrubbed, swept, sprayed, scoured, and squeegeed. I chiseled months-old cereal debris off the scratched stainless steel kitchen sink. I polished Lucas's particle-board bookcase, wiping off a layer of accumulated dust so thick I wouldn't have been surprised to find dinosaur fossils at the bottom. After a ten-minute battle with bleach and a long-handled scrub brush, the circle of black mildew in the toilet gave up the fight. I hauled the trash out to the curb, taking the two beers from the fridge with it, replacing them with a fresh box of baking soda.

In the bedroom, I found a sketchpad and a box of charcoal pencils on the plastic milk crate that served as his night table. A half dozen crumpled balls of sketch paper lay on the floor next to the mattress. I opened the sketchpad to find a series of drawings, three of Tosh in various poses, two of farm landscapes, and a final one of a woman in jeans and a floral-print peasant blouse, her thick dark hair hanging down to her waist, a smattering of freckles scattered across her face. The woman looked like me except for the slight gap between her front teeth. Dad had scrimped to afford my braces.

It's Mom.

Lucas had an incredible knack for detail and a fantastic memory. He'd captured her perfectly. The almost imperceptible dimple on her left cheek, the shaggy bangs brushed to the side, her unique expression, simultaneously daring and warm. I tore the sheet from the sketchbook, rolled it up, and slid it into one of the plastic grocery sacks to take with me later.

The trailer didn't exactly gleam when I was done. The fixtures and furniture were too old and scarred to give off any sparkle. But it smelled much better and at least appeared tidy. My last task was to gather up the dirty clothes strewn about the trailer, along with the bedding, and stuff it all into a garbage bag to take with me for washing.

***

When I pulled into Savannah's driveway, the sheer white curtain at the front window was pulled back by a tiny hand and Zane's smiling face appeared in the window. His mouth formed the words, "Aunt Marnie's here!" He waved frantically before dropping the curtain back in place.

Before I could even get my helmet off, he was in the driveway, dressed in hand-me-down footed pajamas covered in fabric pills, holes in the knees, a smear of peanut butter on his pink cheek. He ran in crazy circles around my bike.

When he got dizzy he grabbed me around the thigh, hugging my leg, partly in affection, partly to keep from falling.

I pulled off my helmet with one hand and put the other on his back. "Hey there, Zaniac."

After clipping my helmet to the bike, I lifted the little guy up by the armpits and plastered kisses on his cheeks. He giggled and squirmed in my arms. I put him down and he ran full tilt back into the house, straight through the door he'd left wide open. I unstrapped the boxes and garbage bag of laundry from my motorcycle and lugged them into the house, dropping the bag in the foyer and tucking the boxes under my arm.

Savannah and Craig's oldest son, Braden, lay on his back on the couch, legs draped over the arm as he watched *SpongeBob SquarePants*. Dylan was on the floor, assembling pieces of a plastic racetrack into an elaborate curlicue formation, no plain old figure eight for him.

"Hey, dudes," I called.

Braden jutted out his chin by way of greeting and Dylan said "Hey," without looking up from the track. They treated me like nothing special, like family. *I like that.*

Savannah's voice came from the bedroom down the hall. "Back here, Marn."

Zane hopped two-footed down the hall ahead of me into his parents' bedroom, leaping onto the rumpled comforter on the unmade bed. I set the boxes on the floor and flopped onto the bed next to him, tickling him until he grabbed the covers and rolled, concealing himself in a cocoon of sheets.

Savannah stood in front of the dresser in a calf-length green linen dress. She tilted her head to each side as she put on a pair of gold hoop earrings, then righted her head and fluffed out her hair with her fingers.

I eyed her in the mirror. "You look gorgeous."

She looked down and grabbed the roll of excess flesh on her belly with both hands. "Ugh. Look at this. I'm going to have to suck in my gut all day." She inhaled sharply and turned to the side to check out her abs in the mirror. "That's better," she gasped, struggling to hold in her stomach and breath.

"At least you can blame your fat on your babies. I've only got cookies to blame for mine." I climbed off the bed, picked up the boxes from Bergdorf's and Macy's, and set them on the wide pine dresser. "These are the boxes I told you about, the ones that were delivered to the Parker place on Renfro."

Savannah stepped over to look at the labels and frowned. "They're addressed to Zane, all right."

"Want to see what's in them?"

"Why not?" She pulled a pair of nail scissors out of a drawer and handed them to me.

I cut through the strapping tape with the tiny scissors and pulled the boxes open. Zane hopped down from the bed, reached his little hands into one of the boxes and tossed handfuls of Styrofoam peanuts into the air, the white foam drifting to the floor around us as if we were in a snow globe. Savannah turned the smaller box over and dumped out the contents while I pulled items out of the bigger box.

We spread the merchandise out on the dresser to take a look. A pair of midnight blue Dior sling-backs, women's size seven. A soft pink cashmere sweater, size small. A pair of Prada sunglasses with a fancy case. Five pairs of teeny silk panties in assorted pastel colors. Two black lace push-up bras, size 32A. A pair of men's burgundy silk boxers.

"That's some fancy stuff," Savannah said. "Not exactly the kind of thing people wear around here."

Women in Jacksburg primarily opted for utility rather than style, dressing in jeans, T-shirts, and tennis shoes. I couldn't think of a single guy in town who'd wear silk boxers, either. I also couldn't decide for certain whether the contents of the boxes indicated that the thief was male or female. Although most of the items in the boxes were intended for a woman's use, the fact that there was so much lingerie could mean the thief was buying things for a wife or girlfriend. Besides, the thief had chosen to steal the identities of a Logan, a Taylor, and a Zane. Zane was clearly a male name, while the names Logan and Taylor could go either way.

"What's all that?" Zane asked, standing in front of the dresser, his eyes roaming over the items we'd spread there.

"It's your new wardrobe." Savannah and I grabbed Zane, who wiggled and giggled while we dressed him up in the clothes. By the time we'd finished with him, Savannah and I were giggling ourselves.

Braden walked in to see what all the fuss was about, took one look at his baby brother in the lace bra, and did an about-face, marching out of the room.

While Savannah freed Zane from the bra in which he'd somehow hopelessly tangled himself, I perused the paperwork that came with the merchandise. Both receipts indicated the purchases had been paid for by a credit card issued in the name of Zane Nichols. The last four digits of the card number were listed as 7653. I looked over at Zane. "You got a credit card, kiddo?"

"Do I got a whattie what?"

Savannah ruffled his hair. "You *are* a whattie what." She took the papers from my hand and looked them over, her face scrunching up in concern. "What's going on, Marnie?"

"Looks like an identity theft situation to me." I'd heard through law enforcement sources that identity thieves sometimes preyed on children. With no negative credit records and nobody checking their credit histories on a regular basis, kids made easy targets. "I'll see if I can get some information on the credit card application and any other purchases. Maybe that'll shed some light on the situation."

If this was an identity theft situation, who was behind it? Could it be those teenage girls who'd been eyeing Eric at the Parker house? They had been petite, so the clothes would likely be their size, but I had a hard time believing girls so young would know how to pull off a stunt like this. Then again, maybe the younger generation would know how to use technology to their advantage. Or maybe whoever had been partying in Parker's shed was behind this. But despite having stopped by several times, neither I nor any of the other officers had caught anyone there. Besides, smoking pot and teen sex was one thing, identity theft was another.

I made a mental note to bounce my thoughts off Trey later, see if he had any ideas. With his technological know-how, maybe he could help me figure this thing out.

Savannah and I packed the items carefully back into the boxes to be returned to the store. Whoever ordered the stuff had girlie-girl taste, and no way could Savannah or I ever fit our watermelons into a 32A. I hadn't worn a bra that small since I was eight years old.

Savannah glanced at her watch. "We need to get going." She picked a round decorative pillow off the bed and hurled it at the closed bathroom door. They are called throw pillows, after all. "Craig, get your butt out here. The wedding starts in twenty minutes."

Craig came out of the bathroom wearing a white dress shirt with a striped tie, dress socks, and a saggy pair of underpants.

I whistled. "Ooh, baby."

He turned around and shook his butt at me in a pathetic imitation of a Chippendale's dancer. I pulled his pants off the headboard where they were draped and held them out to him. "Who's getting married?"

Craig took the pants from me and slid one leg, then the other into his pants. "My cousin."

"Didn't your cousin get married last summer?"

"That was another cousin."

Craig came from one of the largest families in the county. He'd been related in one way or another to a quarter of the kids in our graduating class. He'd had to check with his parents before asking a girl out to make sure they weren't related.

"Trey's coming over to babysit with me," I told them.

"Good," Craig said. "With these boys you'll need reinforcements."

Savannah tossed me a roll of wedding wrap, a roll of scotch tape, and a box of Corningware embossed with a grapevine motif. "I forgot to get a bow. Oh, well."

I set about wrapping the box for her while she added a final coat of lipstick and slid her feet into a pair of low-heeled pumps. When I finished, I handed her the wrapped box and picked up Zane from the bed.

Savannah and Craig rushed to the door. I followed, carrying Zane piggyback style.

"There's leftover meatloaf in the fridge," Savannah called over her shoulder as they stepped outside.

"Yucky!" Zane hollered after his mother.

"That goes for me, too," I said. "Yuck." If her meatloaf was as bad as I remembered on the first go-round, it would be twice as bad re-warmed.

Savannah walked to their pickup, stopping at the truck's door. "Order a pizza then."

"Hooray!" Zane let go of me to throw a hand in the air.

Just after Savannah and Craig backed out in their pickup, Trey pulled into the driveway in Glick's tank truck, a garbage bag duct-taped over the broken passenger window. My eyes met Trey's through the windshield and my insides turned to pudding. I'd never met a guy who had quite this effect on me, and I had only three more days with him. *Waah.*

He climbed out of the truck, walked up, and planted a big, loud kiss on me, making lots of slurping sounds for Zane's benefit.

"Eww!" shrieked Zane, pushing off me until I put him down. Still shrieking, he ran off into the house.

Trey pulled me to him for a real kiss this time. Warm and wild, no slurping. *Just the way I like it.*

Trey had brought an old Nintendo 64 gaming system and erector set from his closet at his parent's house. We spent the afternoon goofing off with the boys, playing Space Invaders, Star Fox, and Mario Party. The games and graphics seemed archaic and simplistic compared to the modern gaming systems, but the boys had a blast. While Braden and Dylan played each other on Trey's vintage system, he sorted through the stack of games they had for their own gaming console.

Braden glanced over at him. "I wanted to get Felony Frenzy, but Mom wouldn't let us. She said Marnie would have a cow."

Felony Frenzy was perverse, offensive, and horrifically

brutal, allowing the players to steal at will, torture innocent victims, and kill cops in a variety of horrifically disturbing ways. It was rated M for Mature, but it might as well be for Monster.

I corrected Braden. "I wouldn't have had *a* cow, I would've had an entire herd of cows. War games are one thing, but you boys don't need to be playing something that sick and twisted. *Nobody* does."

Trey glanced my way. "Studies show that violent video games don't make people more violent, you know."

"That's not the point!" I snapped. "The point is that gratuitous street violence should never be presented as light entertainment. It's anything but."

"Uh-oh," Zane said. "You made Marnie mad."

Trey cut a sideways glance my way. "That's okay. I can make her happy again later."

"Gross," Braden said, the only one old enough to understand the innuendo.

Trey and I shared a laugh, our minor disagreement immediately forgotten.

When they tired of the games, Trey and the boys designed and built a crane that actually functioned and could lift a rock-hard week-old glazed donut Zane found under the couch.

I applauded their success. "I'm impressed."

I was indeed impressed, and by more than Trey's mechanical abilities. He was great with the boys, answering their endless stream of questions, explaining how the various pieces functioned, giving them a mini engineering lesson. He didn't even get angry when Braden accidentally broke one of the pieces.

While the boys built more contraptions, I washed, dried, and folded Lucas's laundry, including his bedding. Hopefully, the guy would come home from rehab clean and sober. He might as well come home to a clean house and clean clothes, too.

I phoned in a pizza order, and we ate dinner on paper plates at the backyard picnic table, partly because it was a beautiful fall evening, partly so I could simply hose off the mess when the boys were finished.

After Trey polished off his first slice, I plopped another piece of deep-dish on his plate. "Can I pick your brain about something?"

"Pick away." He scarfed down the pizza while I detailed the recent events. "The first package was sent to a little girl named Logan Mott and—"

"I know Logan," Zane interrupted with his mouth full of half-chewed cheese pizza. "She's in my class at school."

"That's nice, sugar," I said, "but it's bad manners to interrupt, okay?"

"Okay."

I turned my attention back to Trey. "Then I found a credit card bill in the Parkers' mailbox addressed to a little girl named Taylor Heidenheimer—"

Zane interrupted again. "She's in my class at school, too."

I pointed a finger at him. "What did I ask you just a minute ago?"

He cocked his head and looked up in thought. "Not to 'rupt you?"

"Exactly. So why did you do it again?"

"'Cause I'm a kid and I don't listen good." He gave me a big grin coated in pizza sauce.

Who could get mad at such a cute face? I chucked him affectionately on the chin.

Trey finished chewing and sat back in his chair. "The identity thief could be someone who has access to the kids' records, like someone who works at a pediatrician's office or children's dentist."

"But they'd need the kids' social security numbers to open credit card accounts. I don't think a doctor's or dentist's office would have that information. Not for the kids, anyway. They'd probably just have the parents' social security numbers since they're the ones responsible for the bills."

"True." He looked up in thought for a moment, then looked back at me. "Someone may have gone phishing."

"Fishing?"

"Phishing," he repeated. "Spelled with a PH. It means using the internet to get information from people. Sometimes identity thieves phish for information by sending bogus e-mails to people. They pretend to be a bank or the IRS or a creditor, and they ask for social security numbers, account numbers, stuff like that."

"But kids in kindergarten don't have e-mail accounts."

"Maybe the identity thief contacted the parents for the information. They could have pretended to be from the doctor's office or social services. Maybe they said they needed the information for insurance purposes."

"It's certainly possible."

Zane cut into our conversation again. "Taylor pulled Logan's hair at recess on Friday and made her cry. But I gave Logan cuts in line for the slide and that made her happy again."

I ran a hand down his back. "That was sweet of you, honey."

At eight-thirty, I wrangled the boys into bed. I read the younger two a couple of bedtime stories, listened to their prayers, and tucked them in with a big noisy kiss on the forehead. Afterward, Trey and I engaged in a wrangling session of our own on the couch. But we kept our kisses quiet so we wouldn't wake the boys.

The day have given me a glimpse of what life could be with Trey, if only he were staying. My heart ached with a sense of loss at what would never be. *Why does love have to be so complicated?*

CHAPTER TWENTY-NINE

GET IT WHILE IT'S HOT

Savannah and Craig arrived home at nine-thirty. Craig's tie was off, his shirt was buttoned wrong, and Savannah's dress was wrinkled.

I crossed my arms over my chest. "You did it in the pickup, didn't you?"

"Hell, yeah," Craig admitted shamelessly. "Hard to get any when you've got a kid climbing into your bed every night."

Savannah gave me a hug. "Thanks so much for babysitting, Marn."

"Happy to do it."

Trey and I headed out to the driveway, Trey carrying Lucas's now-clean laundry. Trey dropped the bag on the floor of the tank truck, then gestured at Craig's pickup. "What say you and me go for it, too?"

I glanced at Savannah's next-door neighbor, who was rolling a trash can out to the curb, and shook my head.

"Aw, come on. Anyone sees the truck rocking, they'll assume it's Savannah and Craig."

"No. Not here."

"But somewhere." Trey's face became serious as he turned to me and grabbed my hand, entwining his fingers with mine. "We've only got two more days together, Marnie."

I looked into Trey's eyes. There was desire there, sure, but there was something else, something *more*. Trey wanted to make a physical connection, but it was clear he felt our emotional connection, too. And, like me, he seemed to sense the connection was about to be lost, like a cell phone signal in a tunnel, and that we needed to make the most of what little time we had left.

Trey raised my hand to his mouth, gently kissing my knuckles, then slipping a finger into his warm, wet mouth, sending a zing of desire to every erogenous zone on my body with his signature foreplay move. He gave my finger a flick with his tongue and offered me a grin that said he knew the effect he had on me. This guy was just as adept at the game of love as he was at video games.

"Dad's home, so we can't go to my house," I thought out loud. Lucas Glick's place was out of the question. I'd seen his mattress. It was stained and concave in the center. *No thanks.* An idea came to me a second later and I snapped my fingers. "I know just the place."

We climbed into the truck and Trey started the engine. "Where to?"

"The station. Bernie doesn't come in until ten. I'll let the evening dispatcher off early."

Trey raced to the station, exceeding the speed limit by at least fifteen miles per hour the entire way, but with Roddy on duty, he wasn't likely to be caught. Roddy was probably sitting in the parking lot of the Grab-N-Go, eating potato chips and reading the latest issue of *Sports Illustrated* while pretending to be doing surveillance.

We pulled into the DQHQ and parked under the carport. I hopped down from the truck and Trey followed me inside. Linda sat at the counter, clipping coupons from a stack of women's magazines.

I introduced Trey to Linda. "Trey's a computer whiz. He's going to take a look at the system."

"I am?"

I shot Trey a look that said *shut-up-and-play-along*, then turned back to Linda. "It's going to take an hour or two for him to get the computers up and running. Since I'll be stuck here anyway, I'd be glad to cover the phones if you want to head out early."

"Will I still get paid?"

"Of course."

Linda smirked. She clearly realized I was desperate to find a place with some privacy, but she had the sense to benefit from my lack of options and was willing to let me get on with a conjugal visit in the freezer cell. "Thanks, Captain." She grabbed her coupons, stuffed them into her oversized purse, and was out the door in a heartbeat.

I stepped up to the glass as the door swung shut and turned the deadbolt, locking myself and Trey inside. I shut off all the lights but a small desk lamp on the service counter next to the phone and grabbed a fresh set of sheets and a blanket from the cabinet.

Trey came up behind me, nuzzled my neck, and swept me up in his arms. It would've been more romantic if he hadn't grunted with the effort, but I'd take what I could get. He carried me into the freezer and set me down in the middle of the small room, the dim lamplight glinting off the stainless steel walls which gave off faint, warped reflections, like funhouse mirrors.

Trey glanced at our reflections on the wall. "This'll be kinky."

I pushed the door almost closed, leaving it open only a crack to ensure I could hear the phone if someone called in with an emergency. We had our own emergency going on in the station, a crime of passion to commit. As fast as we could, we freed ourselves from our clothing, both of us leaving our socks on to save time. Rather than risk falling off the top bunk and breaking our necks or cramming ourselves into the narrow bottom bunk, we yanked the thin mattresses off both bunks and tossed them side by side on the floor. I quickly spread the clean sheets and blanket over them.

Trey was booted up and ready. I was logged on and prepared for input. We wasted no time with foreplay.

The first time we made love was frantic and rough, a much-needed release. The second time we paced ourselves, taking more time, giving each other more attention. The third time was a fun, lazy bonus, with as many laughs as moans.

Exhausted, we lay in silence for a few moments. My head was pressed to Trey's chest, listening to his heartbeat as it eventually recovered and slowed back to normal. His body felt warm against mine, the hair on his legs tickling my thigh as I draped it over him. I wished the freezer could freeze time, keeping us in this moment forever so that Wednesday would never come, so Trey would never leave.

After a few minutes of bliss, I glanced at my watch. *Dang.* "Bernie'll be here soon. We better get our clothes on."

I finished dressing before Trey and stepped out of the freezer, leaving him behind to put the rest of his clothes on. I was putting on a fresh pot of coffee for Bernie when the emergency line rang.

I darted to the front counter and grabbed the receiver. "Jacksburg PD. What's your emergency?"

"I fell," came a man's voice.

"Are you hurt? Do you need an ambulance?"

"No. I'm not hurt. In fact, I feel great. I fell *in love*."

Trey. I groaned though my heart pumped like there was no tomorrow. "That's so corny."

He chuckled into his cell phone, and I could hear his laugh both through the receiver and through the cracked door behind me. "It may be corny, Marnie, but it's true. A man only lies about being in love if he's trying to get into a woman's pants. I've already gotten in your pants three times tonight so you know I'm being honest."

I held the phone, unable to speak or move, unable to emotionally deal with the fact that his words simultaneously brought me intense joy and immense grief. Footsteps sounded behind me and Trey stepped around the front of the counter, sitting down on one of the counter stools, his cell phone still held to his ear.

"Well?" he asked through the phone. "Do you love me, too?"

Slowly, I set the receiver down, my eyes brimming with tears. I blinked them back so he'd be more than a mere blur in front of me. "What if I do love you, Trey? What good will it do us? You're leaving in three days."

When I turned away, he stood, setting his phone on the counter, grabbing my shoulders and forcing me to face him.

"So you do love me, then?"

The tear that escaped and ran down my cheek gave him my answer. Of course I loved him. Completely. Absolutely. *Desperately.*

"Come out to San Jose," he pleaded. "See what it's like out there. You might like California."

"I belong *here*, Trey." I'd forsaken my family and friends to move to Dallas with Chet, and I'd ended up lonely in a city of three million people who constantly seemed to be moving a hundred miles an hour. I couldn't live like that again.

I blinked back the tears. "Why don't you come back here? You've told me you like Hockerville. You still call it home."

Trey dropped his hands from my shoulders. "You know I can't find a decent job here."

"You've had plenty to do," I reminded him, even though we'd already been through this before. "Working at the school, putting together that website for the Chamber of Commerce—"

"That's easy stuff, Marnie. I'd go out of my mind if that's all I did. I didn't spend four years in college and another getting my masters in computer science just to upgrade systems. I need to be on the cutting edge. I need something challenging. Silicon Valley is where all of that is happening."

"You told me the traffic out there is a nightmare. You told me that the price of real estate is outrageous." My voice rose in volume and pitch, sounding as frantic and distraught as I felt. "You said—"

"All of that is true, Marnie. But it doesn't change the fact that I have a great job out there, a job I really like."

We stared intently into each other's eyes as if each of us were trying to will the other into submission. Clearly we'd reached an impasse. There was no point in further discussion. For both of us, happiness was not only a function of the people in our lives, but of purpose, of place. We were both mature enough to know that love alone isn't everything, isn't sufficient by itself. Love could lead to resentment and regret, love could backfire if it required too many sacrifices by one person or the other.

I took a deep breath and closed my eyes for a moment, forcing myself to mentally switch gears. "I don't want to spend what little time we have left arguing." I opened my eyes and looked at Trey. "As long as you're here, would you mind actually taking a look at our computer system? It crashed when I was in here earlier today."

Trey cocked his head. "What were you doing in here on a Sunday?"

Uh-oh. I couldn't tell him I'd been researching the Ninja's owner. I used the excuse I had handy, the same one I'd given Linda earlier. "Catching up on paperwork."

Trey followed me over to my booth. He slid onto the bench and I slid in next to him. He leaned down to push the button on the tower under the booth. The machine emitted a loud whirring noise, the screen giving off an occasional flicker. Trey angled his head as he listened. "That doesn't sound good."

Trey listened for a few more seconds, then climbed under the table, wrestled the case out from beneath the booth, and set it on the tabletop, the back of the unit facing him. He spent a few seconds examining the case. "Got a screwdriver?"

I went to look in the department's junk bin stashed behind the counter at the dispatch desk. After searching through miscellaneous office supplies and tools, I found a small flathead screwdriver and took it to Trey.

He removed the computer's back panel and gently pulled out the machine's guts, boards with chips and circuits and wires. He played around with them for a bit, then rendered his diagnosis. "Your power supply's going out."

Despite the power supply problem, Trey managed to get my computer up and running and, before I knew what he was doing, he'd backtracked into the searches I'd run that morning. The Ninja's vehicle registration record popped up on the screen, showing the owner as Bartholomew Edmund Jonasili.

Trey stared at the name for a few seconds, his face contorted in confusion, then it morphed into anger. He turned to me. "I'm not even gone yet and you were checking up on the motorcycle guy?"

There was no denying it. I nodded. But I also fibbed. "He hasn't contacted the station yet. I need to track him down, see if he wants to file a report. Insurance companies usually ask for a copy of the police report."

"If he wanted to file a report, he would've contacted you." Lightning flashed in his eyes. "Here I am like an idiot telling you I love you, and meanwhile you're trying to hook up with someone else? Has our relationship just been a game to you?"

I shook my head. "No, Trey! It's not like that at all."

He crossed his arms over his chest. "Then how about you tell me what it is like, Marnie."

I paused, looking down at my lap. When I looked up, tears were running down my cheeks, tears I didn't bother to fight or wipe away. "It's going to kill me when you leave, Trey. I . . . I don't know how I'm going to get through it. If you and I can't be together, I need some hope for . . . *something*."

Trey's face softened and we sat in silence for a few seconds, both of us trying to come to terms with our hopeless situation, our conflicting emotions.

Finally, Trey gave a frustrated sigh. "Might as well check out the other units while I'm here." I stood to let him out of the booth, and he spent a few minutes booting up each of the other computers and checking our server, scribbling notes on a yellow sticky-note pad as he went along.

I perched on Dante's booth while he jotted some notes, glancing down at his illegible chicken scratch on the notepad. "What's that say, *venus*?"

"*Virus.* You need new virus protection software. The one you've got installed is way out of date."

"Everything we've got is out of date."

Trey went online and submitted an order to a computer supply company, opting for express shipping. He consulted the screen. "The part should be here Wednesday morning by ten. The virus software can be downloaded from the internet. I can install them for you before I leave for the airport."

Wednesday. It would be the last time I'd see Trey before he went back to California. And it was coming much too soon.

CHAPTER THIRTY

POOR PENMANSHIP

When I greeted Selena at the station Monday morning, she gestured toward the cell behind her. "What are the mattresses doing on the floor?"

Oops. Trey and I had forgotten to put them back on the bunks after last night's sexual tri-fecta. "Janitor must've cleaned back there." *That would be the day.* The lazy guy only cleaned the cell once a month. But with as little as we paid him, I wasn't about to complain. "I'll take care of it."

After returning the mattresses to the bunks, I slid into my booth. I supposed I could have looked up the Ninja's registration and obtained the address for Bartholomew Jonasili, but there'd be time for that after Trey left. Instead, I called the bank that had issued the the card to Taylor Heidenheimer, whose application I was still waiting on, along with Logan Mott's. When I told them I had a possible third fraudulent application, they escalated my call, transferring me to a supervisor who agreed to get the applications and statements e-mailed to me ASAP. The bank staff may not give a rat's ass about Taylor, Logan, or Zane, but they cared about their bottom line and didn't want to end up with a bunch of uncollectible accounts. I didn't know whether the applications would yield any useful information but at least it was a place to start.

After completing the call to the bank, I headed out on the

police bike to keep an eye on motorists. Tiffany passed me, heading the opposite direction as I went down Main. Radar indicated she was eleven miles over the speed limit, but I decided to cut her some slack under the circumstances. Despite all the crap she'd given me, I pitied her. It must be hard to find out your father was a lying, cheating son-of-a-bitch. With daddy now in jail, she'd probably be cut off, have to take out a student loan and—*God forbid!*—transfer to a public university.

It was a slow morning, only two speeders, one expired registration, and one seatbelt violation. Around noon, I grabbed some takeout at the Burger Doodle drive-thru and returned to the station. I settled in at my booth with my burger and logged into my computer, fighting the urge to shout "hooray!" when the waning power supply cooperated and the machine booted up. After logging in, I pulled up my e-mails. In my inbox sat a response from the bank's legal department with multiple attachments.

I took a big bite of my burger and chewed while I read the e-mail. *Attached are the documents you requested. We have been unable to reach these customers at the phone number provided on their applications. We have frozen each account pending verification of the cardholder's identity.*

Good. Maybe the frozen accounts would slow down the identity thief.

I pulled up the attachments. The first was a credit card application in the name of Logan Mott. The second was an application in the name of Taylor Heidenheimer. The third was an application in Zane's name. To my surprise, all three forms were handwritten. That fact seemed unusual given that many financial transactions were handled online now and the proverbial "paper trail" was a nearly outdated concept from the pre-digital world. These days, most trails were electronic. The statements, which were also attached, showed several purchases made on each card from upscale department stores. No restaurants, gas stations, or grocery stores were listed. The identity thief evidently only used the cards for online shopping and hadn't attempted to use a card in person. Smart strategy. A security camera at a bricks and mortar location could have easily recorded images of the thief and any vehicle the thief might have been driving.

After clicking my mouse to print out the documents, I rounded them up from the printer and carried them back to my desk, laying the applications side-by-side on the tabletop for comparison. The children's names were printed in small blocks across the top of the forms. On all three forms, the box in which the applicant was to identify themselves as a Ms., Mrs., or Mr. were left blank, probably on purpose. The home address listed on each of the forms was 612 Renfro, the Parker place. The social security numbers for each of the kids matched the ones the parents had provided. So far, nothing I'd read was unexpected or useful.

My eyes moved to the bottom of the pages. The signature lines contained a left-slanted signature. The T in Taylor was pointed, the cross line angled down on both sides of the vertical line, making the letter look like an arrow. The I's in Heidenheimer and Nichols were punctuated with angled slashes rather than dots. The small T's in Mott were likewise crossed with angled slashes.

My pulse picked up speed. *I think I've seen this handwriting before. But where? When?*

I racked my brain, closing my eyes to think, but I came up empty. Could the guilty party be someone I knew? Someone from church? An old high school classmate who'd signed my yearbook? One of the many residents who'd come by the station to pay a traffic fine? A server who'd taken my order on a notepad? A client of Dad's who'd paid him by check?

So much for brain power. The only handwriting I could remember with any clarity was Trey's, and his illegible chicken scratch looked nothing like this.

The same phone number was listed on all of the applications. The 214 prefix told me the phone had been purchased in the Dallas area. Not a surprise. Given the lack of retail options in the area, many locals drove to Dallas to shop. I logged into a reverse phone number lookup website and typed the number in, but the search yielded only the name of a prepaid cell phone provider. There was no way to pinpoint who had purchased the device. Thanks to prepaid cell phones, criminals could communicate without their calls being traced since law enforcement had difficulty linking the phone numbers to the guilty parties.

"Selena," I called. "Can I borrow your cell phone?"

She looked up from her computer, where she was playing Mall-a-Palooza, having worked her way up from the Level One Clearance Rack to the Level Ten Trunk Show. "Something wrong with the phone on your desk?"

"I don't want Jacksburg PD or my name coming up on recipient's caller ID." No sense letting the identity thief know the cops were closing in, and allow the thief to cover his or her tracks. Of course the identify thief was probably already wondering where the orders that had been delivered earlier in the week had gone, but maybe the thief would think someone else had stolen them from the Parkers' porch.

Selena walked over to my desk and handed me her phone before returning to her station behind the front counter. I dialed the number on the application. The line rang thirty-two times before I finally gave up and disconnected. I glanced back at the application. The same number that had been listed as the personal phone number for the applicants was also listed as their work phone number. Their alleged employer was "Made-Up Manufacturing, Inc.," a fictitious business if ever I'd heard of one. A quick internet search told me that my suspicions were correct. There was no such business.

I'd hit another wall. I was trained as a street cop, not a detective. I wasn't Nancy Drew or Miss Marple or Jessica Fletcher. I was in over my head on this case.

I carried the cell phone and credit card applications over to Selena. I blocked the number I'd dialed on Selena's phone in case whoever owned the phone tried to return the call. I also made sure Selena had her voicemail programmed to offer only the default automated greeting, so that the person wouldn't be able to identify her if they did call back.

I handed her the phone, and laid the printouts on the counter in front of her. "You recognize this handwriting?"

She eyed the forms for a moment, then shook her head. "Nope. Should I?"

"Not necessarily."

I showed the applications to Dante, too, who'd come in to retrieve a citation pad. "What do you think?"

He looked the papers up and down. "I think we're out of our league."

No kidding. "The only thing I know is that the thief is left-handed." I pointed to the signature. "See how the letters slant to the left?"

Dante cocked his head. "Couldn't the person who filled that out fake the handwriting, too?"

He had a point. But still, the writing was familiar and the fact that both were signed similarly told me this was the identity thief's real handwriting.

I didn't want to do it, but I was at a loss and I had to protect the kids of Jacksburg. I telephoned Sheriff Dooley, again waiting through a series of transfers before he came on the line. I told him about the handwritten applications and the additional boxes that had been delivered.

"I told you not to waste my time with this bullshit, Captain Muckleroy. Those kids are gonna end up with lousy credit anyway. Nobody worth a shit ever grew up in Jacksburg."

My blood boiled in my veins. *Damn snob.* "Let's say it was one of your precious kids over there in Hockerville. What would you do next?"

"In that case, I'd put an undercover man on watch at the Parker place."

The Jacksburg PD wasn't a busy department, but we ran lean and couldn't spare an officer to sit and watch the place all day. Besides, everyone in town knew the few Jacksburg cops by sight. Even in plain clothes we'd be easily identified. The thief wouldn't stop at the house with one of us in the area.

I thanked the sheriff, even though he'd offered me nothing of use. He hung up without another word.

I had no idea what to do next. But when in doubt, Google. I ran a search with the term "identity theft." Dozens of sites came up and I scrolled through them, skipping the ones that marketed credit repair services, perusing those that explained how thieves obtained personal data on their victims. Several mentioned the term Trey had used, *phishing,* and noted that identity thieves often hit up people for information through bogus e-mails purporting to be sent by financial institutions or government offices.

One site noted that the thief is often a family member, friend, or co-worker with easy access to the victim's personal information. That theory didn't seem to apply in this case. Three kids in one town as small as Jacksburg weren't all likely to have a criminal relative. Their friends would be more interested in their Hot Wheels or Barbie dolls than their social security numbers. The children's work consisted of learning the alphabet and gluing macaroni to construction paper, so they didn't have co-workers with access to their data.

Each of the sites recommended the victims file a police report, which the parents had done. *Like that's going to help in Jacksburg.* All the kids of Jacksburg had was me, and I was out of ideas.

***

On my way home from work, I stopped by the Heidenheimers', the Motts', and Savannah's, showing everyone the credit card applications. None of them recognized the handwriting and none had ever heard of Made-Up Manufacturing. When I arrived home, I consulted Dad and Uncle Angus, but the result was the same. Neither recognized the handwriting. Neither had heard of Made-Up Manufacturing.

At 7:00, Trey arrived at my dad's dressed in worn jeans, ratty high-top sneakers that were once white but had since faded to a sickly gray, and a sweatshirt that read HOCKERVILLE HIGH COMPUTER CLUB.

"Had to dig deep in the drawer to find this one." Trey put his arms out and turned side to side as if modeling for me. "No sense getting dolled up to service a septic tank."

I put a hand on Trey's shoulder and stood on tiptoe to give him a kiss, probably one of the last I'd ever lay on him. "Thanks for helping out."

I couldn't believe I was actually looking forward to the disgusting task that lay ahead. Of course, my enthusiasm was only because I'd get to spend more time with Trey, time that was rapidly ticking away. I'd asked him, Dad, and Angus to help me take care of Lucas's clients while he was in rehab. All three had agreed without a second's hesitation.

Dad followed us outside. Lucas's truck was in the driveway where Trey had parked it the night before after our evening of romance in the freezer cell. I'd given him a ride home on my bike, enjoying the feel of him pressed against my back. It had felt so warm, so right. Sad that I'd likely never feel it again.

Dad drove the tank truck with Trey in the passenger seat.

Uncle Angus and I followed on his Kawasaki. According to Lucas's records, today's job was the Barrington estate. The Barringtons were old money, oil money, Texas royalty. Their estate consisted of a five-thousand square foot plantation-style home on twenty or so acres set back off a county road. Though the acreage straddled the Jacksburg and Hockerville city limits, the Barringtons had chosen to build the house in the northwestern portion of the property to ensure themselves a more prestigious Hockerville address.

After we'd checked in at the house, telling Mr. Barrington the little white lie that Lucas Glick had a family emergency and had hired us to assist, we made our way into the backyard with the truck, camp lanterns, and flashlights to set about our dirty deed, removing the effluent of the affluent.

I pulled my cell phone from my pocket and called Lucas for instructions. He said he'd just finished a group therapy session.

"How was it?" I asked.

He was quiet for a moment. "It was some sad shit, Marnie. These people are really screwed up."

I wasn't sure what to say to that. Lucas was the most screwed-up person I knew. At least they were all in the right place to turn their lives around. "We're at the Barringtons. Where do we start?"

"First thing you gotta do is put on gloves and a mask. There's a box under the passenger seat."

Still holding the phone in one hand, I pulled the box out from under the truck's seat with the other, tossing gloves and white masks to the men.

"What now?" I said into the phone.

"Locate the manhole," he said. "It's under the mesquite tree."

"Locate the manhole," I called. "Under the mesquite."

Trey scanned the ground with his flashlight.

"Found it!" Angus called.

Lucas walked me through the process, and I called out orders to the men. While they wrangled to connect the hose, I took a few steps back toward the house where I could speak with Lucas without noise interference.

"How're you doing, Lucas?"

He said nothing for a moment, only his shallow breaths audible through the phone. "It's tough here, Marnie," he said, finally. "I can't remember the last time I went a whole day without a drink, and I'm going on day two now. I got the shakes. Bad."

"Give it time, Lucas. You can do this."

"I got to, Marnie. I can't keep going on the way I was."

We were both quiet for a moment.

"How's Tosh?" he asked.

"Rotten cat. He's chewed up my houseplants, slept on my clean towels, and coughed up a hairball on my pillow."

Lucas chuckled. "You're not fooling me."

Busted. Despite Tosh's faults, the cat was affectionate and entertaining. I enjoyed having the sweet critter around. He'd even let me shave his matted hair.

After Lucas walked us through the rest of the process, we wrapped up our call. "Stay strong, Lucas," I said.

"I'll try, Marnie. I'll try."

***

After returning to my house and showering, Trey and I sat on the porch swing, cuddling under a heavy crocheted afghan my mother had made years ago. The two of us talked about everything and nothing at all, comfortable talk, the talk of people who belong together. Trey had his arm around me, occasionally running his thumb down my upper arm, each time sending a thrill through me. I'd give anything to make love to him again, but I wasn't about to have sex here, not with my dad in the house. Besides, this was nice, too, just being with Trey, being close in a non-physical way.

Eventually I couldn't fight the yawns anymore and I checked my watch. Ten after midnight. I gathered the blanket around myself and stood. "We've both got to work in the morning. We better get to bed."

Trey grinned. "Sounds good to me."

"You in your bed, me in mine."

"Damn."

"We still on for lunch?" I asked.

"Of course."

Trey and I engaged in a long, lingering kiss at the door, both of us knowing we needed to get some sleep, neither of us wanting to be apart. It was pure bliss. And pure torture.

Trey took a step back and looked me in the eye. "I love you, Marnie."

My heart writhed in my chest. "I love you, too, Trey. Dang it."

He wrapped his arms around me, pulled me to him, and for a

moment we clung to each other like our lives depended on it. In a way, maybe they did.

CHAPTER THIRTY-ONE

HACKING

At 8:00 Tuesday morning, I sat on my motorcycle behind the Welcome to Jacksburg sign, listening to the Ramones' "Baby, I Love You." The morning was cool and windy, an occasional dirt devil spinning over the adjacent, now-barren cornfields.

I heard it approach. The distinctive drone of a high-performance motorcycle engine. The Ninja. *Wow.* The bike had been fixed in record time.

Heart pounding like a sledgehammer, I raised my radar gun and aimed it at the crest of the hill. The bike topped the rise doing sixty-seven. Technically two miles over the limit, but not so fast that I'd normally pull someone over and ticket them for it. I stared at the readout and slowly lowered the gun, watching as the motorcycle continued to head toward me. Warm tears formed in my eyes.

I don't want this guy. I want Trey. But I couldn't have him. Not forever, anyway.

I bowed my head and closed my eyes, trying to squeeze back the tears. When the Ninja passed by, the rider beeped his horn at me. *Beep-beep!* I didn't even bother to look up.

The engine noise faded, then grew louder again, as the bike made an illegal U-turn across the grass median and drove back toward me again from the other direction. The racing of the engine told me he was clearly exceeding the speed limit now, probably by at least twenty miles per hour at that point, but with tears pooling in my goggles, I couldn't see straight. I was in no condition to chase this guy down. Besides, the way he was taunting me could mean trouble. I wasn't in the mood for another chase.

He zipped behind me on the northbound lanes, beeping his horn again and pulling another illegal U-turn across the grass fifty yards north of me. I was in all-out sobs by then, my chest heaving, the bell attached to my motorcycle, the one Trey had given me, tinkling as the bike shook.

Tires screeching, the motorcycle headed toward me again. The rider weaved back and forth across the lanes without signaling, clearly trying to entice me to chase him. He slowed to a stop just across the highway from me, only two lanes of asphalt separating us. He sat there, revving his engine, watching me. With the helmet's dark face plate closed, I couldn't tell anything about him. But I didn't want to know anything about him anymore. Trey was the only man I wanted.

I could've written the Ninja's rider several hundred dollars' worth of tickets for speeding, the illegal U-turns, exhibition of acceleration, and illegal lane changes, but I just couldn't do it. Not now. Maybe not ever.

Choking back my sobs, I started my engine, pulled my bike around in a half circle, and headed back to Jacksburg. In my side mirror I noticed the rider lift his face plate to watch me go, but by then I was too far away to make out any of his facial features even if I'd wanted to.

***

When I returned to the station, I left my helmet and goggles on until I reached the ladies' room. I grabbed a stack of paper hand towels to blot the tears from my face. I punched the button for the hot air dryer and held the helmet under it for several minutes to dry the damp lining, soaked with my tears.

I emerged from the bathroom to find Chief Moreno standing at the front counter chatting with Selena, a Red Vine protruding from his mouth, a mug of steaming coffee in his hand.

I grabbed the credit card applications off my desk and took them to the chief. "Any chance you recognize this handwriting?"

After setting his coffee mug on the counter, he took the applications in one hand and grabbed the end of the Red Vine with the other. He bit off a chunk and chewed as he looked them over. He swallowed. "Sorry, Marnie. Doesn't look familiar at all." He handed them back to me and bit off another piece of licorice. "Write many tickets this morning?"

I shook my head. "Not a single one."

"Better get busy," the chief said. "No tickets, no Christmas bonuses this year."

I gave him a mock salute. "Yes, sir. I'll see that every driver who goes through town gets a citation."

"That's my girl."

***

A couple of hours later, I headed to Jacksburg Elementary to meet Trey for our lunch date. I racked my brain on the way over. *Where had I seen that signature?* Being unable to pinpoint the source of the handwriting was giving me a fit. The knowledge was in my brain's memory somewhere if I could only access the file.

Maybe hypnosis could free up the information. Maybe I should consult Madame Beulah again. *Nah, she'd been wrong about Trey.* She'd said he'd disappoint me, and he hadn't. Especially not in the sack. *Heh-heh.*

I pulled into the parking lot of the old brick schoolhouse and parked my bike. I didn't see the Lincoln, but Trey had probably parked in the visitor lot out back.

As I looked at the building, it hit me. On Sunday, when Trey and I had been talking about the identity theft problem, Zane had interrupted us several times, telling me that each of the other victims were students in his class. The school was potentially the unifying factor. *Why haven't I thought of this before?* Some detective I was. More like a *duh*-tective.

A spicy, beefy smell greeted me as I came through the door, making my stomach growl. Sloppy Joes again. *Yum.* After I checked in with Gwennie in the office, she gestured toward the workroom behind her. "Trey said you'd be coming by. He's back there."

I circled around the counter and stepped into the workroom. The space housed a large, noisy copier, a laminating machine, and the server for the school's computer network. Finished with his work, Trey stood at the counter, sliding a set of small tools into a black vinyl pouch. One of the single teachers, a thin brown-haired girl in her early twenties, was chatting up Trey. A dart of jealously made a bulls-eye in my heart.

I stopped just inside the doorway. "Hey, there."

Trey looked up from his tools and smiled. "Hey, Marnie. Ready for lunch?"

The teacher slid me an irritated look. Couldn't really blame her. I'd hit on Trey, too, if I wasn't already nailing him.

Leaning back against the door jamb, I told Trey about the epiphany I'd experienced in the parking lot. "All of the victims are in the same kindergarten class here. That fact could be significant."

"Want me to run a computer search on the school's system?" Trey asked. "See who's accessed the kids' personal records?"

"A search warrant would be required for that," I thought aloud. "Unless we had permission from school administration."

I glanced over at Gwennie, who'd wandered in to make copies. I stepped over to the machine. "Gwennie, got a favor to ask you."

She laid a notice of a head lice infestation on the glass, punched keys to order up four hundred copies, and closed the copier's lid, turning to me. "Anything for you, Miss Muckleroy. What is it?"

Once I'd explained the situation, she frowned. "If someone's taking advantage of these kids on my watch, I want to know about it." She gestured around the room. "You got my permission to look at anything you want to, Marnie."

"Thanks, Gwennie."

We returned to the front office, where Trey sat down at Gwennie's computer. He spent a few seconds navigating through the system to the children's personal files. "How far back should I go?"

"Start with the week before school started," I suggested. "Since all of the victims are in kindergarten, they would have registered for school in August." I remember Savannah blubbering about her youngest baby starting school, how quickly he'd grown up.

Trey ran a report and I grabbed it as it came off the printer. Eight people had accessed all three of the kids' files. The principal, the vice principal, the school nurse, Gwennie, Mrs. Nelson, Trey, the attendance clerk, and Tiffany Tindall.

The first five people on the list were unlikely suspects, having been employed by the school for years with no problems. Next on the list was Trey. Technically, he could be a suspect. The problems had cropped up about the same time he'd begun working on the school's computer system. But Trey was, well, *Trey*. He made a butt-load of money working for that software company back in

Silicon Valley. What incentive would he have to steal kids' identities? Besides, he'd made extensive updates to the school's network and had probably accessed every file on the system.

The tiny office of Arthur Silsby, the attendance clerk, sat to the side of the reception area. Arthur sat at a beige metal desk on one of those oversized rubber balls. He stared at his computer screen, typing information into the system. Suddenly, he erupted in a sputtering cough, pulled an inhaler from his breast pocket, and took a quick puff. *Kshhh.*

Arthur wasn't getting rich keeping track of the students' tardies and absences, but I couldn't imagine a guy like him stealing the kids' identities, much less having a girlfriend to order all that frou-frou stuff for. Then again, he was short and small-boned for a guy and could easily fit into those silk panties and bra. Still, I wasn't about to perform a strip search on him to find out if he was a secret cross-dresser.

With the other potential perpetrators eliminated, that left only Tiffany. It was likely she'd accessed the files as part of her duties assisting Mrs. Nelson. The rich bitch wouldn't have any reason to steal kids' identities when she had a dozen credit cards of her own. Heck, she'd had so many, they'd fallen out of her wallet when I'd pulled her over and asked to see her driver's license. She'd had to scramble to gather them all up.

Wait a minute . . .

CHAPTER THIRTY-TWO

MADAME BEULAH WAS RIGHT

My eyes snapped wide open. "Gah!"

What an idiot I was. The clues had been right in front of me all the time. All those credit cards. Tiffany driving by the Parker House when she had no business on Renfro Road. The handwriting, too. Now I remembered where I'd seen it—on Tiffany's speeding citation. The I's in Tiffany's signature had been topped with the same fierce slashes that appeared on the credit card applications. With her daddy gone bust, Tiffany had to finance her lifestyle somehow. She'd likely known his financial and legal woes were coming long before her father had been arrested.

Busted.

I sat the report on the desk next to Trey and pointed to Tiffany's name. "It's her."

"The college girl who acts like she owns the place?"

"You know Tiffany?"

Trey snorted. "She tore me a new one last week because the system crashed and she couldn't get online to check her emails. She's a royal bi—."

"A-hem." Gwennie gestured with her head toward a young Latino boy standing at the front counter, only his eyes and the top of his head visible over the countertop. Gwennie pulled a ruler out of a pencil cup on the counter and brandished it at me and Trey. "Y'all ain't too old to get your hands slapped, you know." Having properly chastised us, she turned to help the boy.

I pulled a rolling chair up next to Trey and sat. "So Tiffy got in a snit when she couldn't check her e-mails? Maybe there's some incriminating evidence in them. I'd probably need a warrant to look at them, though."

Having finished with the boy, Gwennie turned to us. "All the employees are warned not to use the school computers for personal purposes. They sign a form agreeing that the administration can access anything they do online. Would that be good enough?"

"Sure would," I said. After all, if someone was wrongfully stealing the students' private information, this was not only a police matter, but a school matter, too.

Gwennie gave us a nod. "Have at it, then."

Trey worked the keyboard and mouse, performing his magic, and the next thing I knew we were into Tiffany's e-mail account. We scrolled through the messages and learned she was at risk for failing Children's Literature 101 and had a sorority mixer with the boys of Beta Theta Pi Friday night, the theme being Bahama Beach Bash. Unfortunately, we found no smoking gun, though she'd mentioned in an e-mail to one of her sorority sisters that she'd scored the perfect outfit for the mixer. Maybe the outfit was one she'd ordered with a fraudulent credit card.

The communication was the closest thing we had to evidence. I printed out the e-mail, though any halfway competent defense attorney could poke all kinds of holes in it.

I stepped up next to Gwennie. "I'd like to speak to Tiffany Tindall. Could you page her to the office?"

Before Gwennie could answer, Arthur's high-pitched voice squeaked from his office. "Tiffany isn't here today. She called in sick." He took another puff from his inhaler. *Kshhh.*

Looked like I'd have to wait until tomorrow to approach Tiffany. At least the pending bust would give me something to think about other than Trey leaving, though I wasn't sure anything short of a nuclear bomb or the second coming of Christ could take my mind off that. It felt as if my heart were in a chokehold from which it would never break free. I looked at Trey and bit my lip to keep from crying.

"Lorene's?" Trey asked.

"It's sloppy Joe day in the cafeteria."

Trey made a disgusted face. "Remember the chocolate pudding? The hair net?"

"That was twenty years ago. Get over it."

He cocked his head. "They serve 'em with tater tots here like they do in Hockerville?"

"Tots *and* baked beans."

"The Jacksburg lunch ladies treat you right. Let's do it."

We made our way into the cafeteria and took places in line behind a fourth-grade class. When we reached the serving area, I took an orange plastic tray for myself, handing another to Trey. We slid our trays along the metal rails. One of the lunch ladies slopped a heaping pile of ground meat and sauce onto a bun, another added the tots, and a third spooned up beans. She handed the divided plates to us over the top of the sneeze guard.

Trey rubbed his belly. "This looks delicious. Thanks."

The woman shot Trey a skeptical look. Maybe she knew something about the food we didn't.

We continued down to the end of the line, grabbed a couple of pints of chocolate milk, and paid for our meal. We settled across from each other at the end of one of the long cafeteria tables, both of us digging in the instant our butts hit the seats.

"How was your morning?" Trey asked between huge, gooey bites of sloppy Joe. "See anyone interesting out on the highway?"

A hot blush rushed up my neck to my face. I'm not sure why. It's not like he could read my mind and know I'd seen the Ninja. Besides, I had no real interest in the Ninja rider anymore. He couldn't possibly be as funny, smart, and fun-to-be-with as Trey. Trey had ruined me for other men, damn him.

I shook my head and looked down at my plate, poking at the pile of tater tots with my fork. I could feel Trey's gaze lock on the top of my head like the point of a laser beam. I jabbed my fork into the tater tots and dipped them in ketchup.

"No one at all?" he asked. "No murderers? No octogenarians with big ol' boners? No marijuana farmers?" He paused a moment. *"No Ninja?"*

I looked up, a bit surprised he'd mention the Ninja after he'd been so angry Sunday when he'd discovered the computer searches I'd run. My eyes locked on Trey's. "I saw no one of any significance to me."

We sat for a moment, staring into each other's eyes, an invisible connection between us. Trey and I were meant for each other, right for each other. Why did fate—*that sick, twisted bitch*—keep toying with me like this? Why did she make it impossible for me to be with the man I loved?

My appetite gone, I set my fork down on my plate.

Trey put down his half-eaten sandwich and looked down, too. When he looked up again, his face was dead serious. "Marnie," he said softly, "I've got to come clean with you."

"Come clean? What do you mean?" The tense, guilty look on his face caused nausea to form in my stomach.

He hesitated a moment, looking away before looking back at me again. His shoulders slumped. "God, I don't want to tell you this."

My skin felt prickly and raw, as if I'd shaved over goose bumps. His anguished expression told me that whatever he had to come clean about wouldn't be good, and it wouldn't be insignificant, either. I took a deep breath. "Shoot."

Trey reached across the table for my hand, but instinctively I pulled it back. Hurt flashed across his face, and he pulled his hand back, too. He leaned toward me, his voice low. "My boss called this morning. The company's planning a sequel to *Felony Frenzy*. They want me to head the project."

My entire body went numb, as if Novocain had flooded in my bloodstream. I stared at Trey. My voice cracked as I forced it out through a throat constricted in fear and rage. "You told him no, right?"

Trey paused a moment, then slowly shook his head. "Marnie, I was one of the programmers for the original *Felony Frenzy*. It wasn't my concept, but I'm the fastest programmer they've got so I was asked to work on it. This time, they'd want me to lead the team. It would mean a big raise and—"

"But you're already making good money, more than you could possibly need. You told me so yourself." My voice sounded pleading, desperate. But I *was* desperate. Desperate to believe this was not happening, desperate to believe the man I'd fallen for was not a greedy, lying bastard in disguise.

"It's not really about the money." Trey's tone turned defensive. "This is a huge, cutting-edge project, Marnie. A career maker. The kind any computer geek would give his left nut to work on."

I stared across the table. "Keep your nuts. Work on another project. Maybe another educational game. Or even one of those war games. But not *Felony Frenzy*, Trey. Anything but that." My entire body felt tight, brittle, every muscle tensed, waiting for his response.

"No other project has the level of funding the company's putting into *Felony Frenzy 2*. This is the company's primary focus. My chance to lead something huge."

I could only stare at him, wondering how the man sitting across from me could be the same man who had held me in his arms and comforted me while I bawled like a baby, the same man I'd confided in about the shooting that had sent me into a downward spiral. The same man whom I'd opened myself up to completely, emotionally and physically, believing he'd done the same. I could forgive him for working on the first game, but if he could work on the sequel now, after getting to know and purportedly love me, what did that say about him? About us?

Trey clenched his jaw, a vein in his neck standing out as he looked at me. "I'm sorry for what you've been through, Marnie. It was awful. But that was real. This isn't. *Felony Frenzy* is just a game. It's mindless entertainment."

Torturing innocent people and killing cops was just a game? Mindless entertainment? It was so much more to me. And he, of all people, should know that.

I wouldn't—*couldn't*—allow myself to love a man who would be involved in such a disgusting, worthless endeavor, who promoted senseless brutality and violent crime as trivial amusements. Everything Trey had meant to me, everything we'd shared the past two months, suddenly felt cheap, meaningless, and fake. Simulated, like a video game in which you can role-play for a while then walk away from with no real consequences.

I was working so hard to fight back the onslaught of emotion in me that I couldn't speak. I'd loved the man I thought Trey was. And now I found out he wasn't that man at all. I felt so betrayed, so cheated.

Trey's hands clenched into fists atop the table. "The company's giving the project a huge budget. We'll be able to develop graphics like the video game world has never seen before. Very realistic, lifelike stuff."

Finally, I found my voice again. "Realistic, lifelike stuff, huh?"

He nodded.

I put my hands, palms-down on the table and stood, leaning toward him, my face only inches from his. "Be sure that when you show a cop getting his head blown open to use lots of maroon. When that much blood is in one place at one time, it isn't red. And they may call the brain 'gray matter,' but it's really more of a putty color, so get that right when you program someone's head exploding."

My voice had grown loud and risen an octave, causing a hush in the room as all of the tiny heads turned to watch us. "And if you want it to be realistic, make sure you include a funeral scene with devastated children who will never see their father or mother again, kids who run out of tears before they're done crying, grief-stricken spouses left with bills they can't pay because the police department couldn't afford to provide good life insurance. And make sure you include a cop who has nightmares for years after being forced to shoot a homeless man!"

I felt an ironic urge to slap Trey across the face and, though the bastard deserved it, I wasn't about to do it in front of a roomful of school children. I grabbed my plastic tray off the table, dumped the remains of my lunch in a garbage can, and slid the tray onto the counter for the dishwasher.

I stormed out of the cafeteria, past the gaping students, down the hall, and out the front door, hot, salty tears burning my eyes, blurring my vision. The last two months had been a joke. A twisted joke. To Trey, crime and violence were just a game. To me they were anything but. With such polar opposite views, we'd never make it as a couple, even if we could somehow overcome our other problems.

Trey was on my heels, calling my name, grabbing at my arm, but I shrugged him off and didn't turn around. There was nothing left to say. If he could do this, work on Felony Frenzy 2, what we had was over. *Case closed.*

I jumped onto my motorcycle without bothering to don my helmet or goggles, and roared out of the parking lot, tires screeching.

***

When I arrived home after work, Dad met me at the door. His gaze stopped on my puffy, pink eyes. "Trey's called the landline a half dozen times looking for you. He sounded upset. You two have an argument?"

I nodded. Trey had called both my cell phone and the station several times, too. Selena had radioed me repeatedly all afternoon until I finally told her to tell him it was over and that I never wanted to speak to him again.

I pushed past Dad into the house. "We're through."

I sat on the bench in the entryway and yanked off my boots. I kicked them across the linoleum and burst into angry, anguished tears all over again. Dad sat on the bench beside me, putting his arm around my shoulders. I sobbed for a good ten minutes. Bluebonnet wandered up and licked my hand, and Tosh hopped onto my lap and began kneading my uniform pants with his sharp claws, the pain letting me know that I was still very much alive even though I felt like I'd died inside.

How could I have been so stupid to let myself fall for that bastard?

CHAPTER THIRTY-THREE

THE DEVIL STEALS PRADA

The following morning, I woke early after a fitful night's sleep. Trey had called again after I arrived home, but I refused to speak to him.

"I think it's best you leave her be," Dad had told him.

I'd gone to bed early, curled up in a ball under my purple polka-dot bedspread, shivering uncontrollably even though it wasn't the least bit cold. My eyes were red-rimmed and swollen, my face blotchy. I applied some concealer under my eyes in a vain attempt to mask my pain.

The power supply and virus protection software arrived at the station, but I had Selena call Trey to tell him we'd made other arrangements for the installation. For all I cared anymore, he could head straight out of town and out of my life forever. I was glad he was flying out that afternoon. *The sooner the better.*

Cueing up Pat Benatar's "Heartbreaker" on my phone, I climbed onto the police bike and drove to Jacksburg elementary. Thank goodness Trey had wrapped up his business at the school the day before and wasn't there. If I saw the jerk, I'd probably beat him to death with my baton.

I stationed myself in the back of Mrs. Nelson's classroom,

where I planned to confront Tiffany as soon as she arrived. She was fifteen minutes late already.

The bell rang and we all stood to say the pledge of allegiance. Tiffany breezed in at half past eight, a large Starbuck's cup in her hand.

"You're late again," Mrs. Nelson said.

"Sorry." Tiffany offered the teacher an insincere smile. "Traffic."

Like there was such a thing in Jacksburg.

"Good morning, Tiffany." I stepped forward from the back row of desks.

Tiffany spun to face me, her mouth gaping in surprise, alarm flashing in her eyes.

I motioned to the door. "We need to talk."

"Oh. Okay."

We stepped out into the hall.

Tiffany took a sip from her cup and winced. "This is cold. Let's talk in the teacher's lounge."

"Suit yourself."

We walked across the hall to the lounge, a small room furnished with a flimsy card table and a couple of metal folding chairs. The room smelled of microwave popcorn and overcooked Lean Cuisine.

Tiffany removed the plastic lid from her coffee cup, stuck it in the microwave, and punched a few buttons. *Beep-beep-beep.* The oven kicked on.

She crossed her arms over her chest and leaned back against the countertop. "What did you want to talk to me about?"

She was trying to play innocent, but her pupils were dilated with fear. That fact gave me no small dose of satisfaction.

I got straight to the point. "Someone's been preying on the kids in this town."

"Preying on the kids?" Tiffany pursed her glossy lips. "Like a pervert, you mean?"

"Nuh-uh." I shook my head. "This predator isn't into that kind of thing. She's into Prada and Jimmy Choo." I gave her a meaningful up and down glance, from her spike heels to her diamond-stud earrings.

Her freshly waxed brows drew together. "I have no idea what you're talking about."

"I think you do."

The microwave beeped to indicate her coffee was ready. Just as she was about to snag the cup, I grabbed her wrist firmly. "Let me get that for you."

I'd noticed Tiffany had nuked the drink for a full minute, much longer than was necessary, and I wasn't about to take a scalding latte to the face. I removed the cup from the microwave with my left hand and held out my right for the plastic lid. She grudgingly handed it to me and I secured it to the top of the cup, handing it to her. "Careful now, that's mighty hot."

She glared at me and put her hand out as if reaching for the cup. Instead, she slapped my hand aside, sending the cup out of my hand to smash against the wall, sending a spray of coffee all over the room and the floor. Tiffany grabbed a folding chair from the card table and hurled it at me with surprising force for a woman with stick-thin arms. The only thing I could do was throw up my arms and duck. The chair struck my arms and chest, knocking me backward. It fell to the floor with a loud clatter.

Tiffany ran from the room. I took off after her but slipped on the hot coffee, falling to my hands and knees. I scrabbled on the wet floor, trying to regain my footing.

I got to my feet and ran after her. She'd gained quite a lead and was already at the far end of the long hallway. She glanced back at me, skidded to a stop, and grabbed at the red fire alarm on the wall, yanking the lever down until the alarm sounded. She may be a bimbo, but that was a damn smart move.

She darted around the corner, into the hallway that led to the front doors and escape. I rounded the corner after her only to find myself in a flood of small children pouring out in weaving lines from their classrooms, hurried along by teachers with worried looks on their faces, knowing this was not a drill, having received no advanced warning.

I ran after Tiffany, dodging children as best I could, eventually tripping over a tiny girl in pigtails, knocking the poor kid to the scuffed tile floor. I grabbed the girl by her arms and helped her to her feet. "Sorry, sweetie."

The tot burst into tears but I had no time to console her at the moment, not with Tiffany getting away.

Tiffany barreled out of the front doors, ahead of the milling crowd. By the time I'd made it out the doors and maneuvered around the lines of children marching across the front sidewalk, Tiffany was hopping into her car.

White reverse lights glowed as she zoomed backwards out of the parking spot without checking her mirrors, narrowly missing a line of second-graders crossing the parking lot.

She floored the gas pedal and screeched out of the parking

lot, leaving parallel tread marks on the asphalt and me cursing in her wake. She swerved around a group of children now in the crosswalk, the teacher grabbing a couple of kids by the back of their shirts and yanking them out of Tiffany's way before they became road kill.

Tiffany careened around the corner, cutting the wheel too close and taking out a half-dead holly bush. She dragged it along under her car, a trail of brown, pointy leaves in her wake as she accelerated down the residential street.

I ran to the police bike. After jamming the helmet on my head and fastening the strap, I cranked the engine, yanked the bike around, and took a short cut, roaring over the grass and bouncing down the curb, siren screaming, lights flashing. I cranked the gas, took the corner at warp speed, and was on Tiffany in an instant. The quick acceleration and maneuverability of the bike were definitely an advantage.

Despite my lights and siren, Tiffany made no move to pull over. A block down she took another corner far too fast, swerving first into the curb and then into the opposite lane, almost colliding head-on with an oncoming yellow and black motorcycle.

The Ninja.

The Ninja veered into a yard, the rider braking fast to avoid slamming into a tree, the rider setting the bike down and sliding sideways across the lawn, sending up a cloud of dirt and dead grass. The bike and rider skidded to a stop worthy of a stunt man. I stopped and hollered, "You, okay?"

The rider gave me a thumbs up and waved me off, letting me know he wasn't critically injured. I took off again after Tiffany.

I realized then that my pursuit of Tiffany would only encourage her to drive recklessly, putting innocent people at risk, so I ceased my pursuit through town, turning off my sirens, but leaving the flashing lights on. There was only one way out of town, the highway, so I knew I could intercept Tiffany there.

I radioed the other officers. "Dante! Andre! Backup! Now!"

Only one of them responded. "What's up?"

"Remember that bitch I told you about? Works at the school?"

"Yeah?"

"She's evading arrest. Heading to the highway. Red Mitsubishi Spyder, vanity license plate reads 'Tiffy T.'"

"I'm up north," the voice radioed back. "But I'll get there as soon as I can."

I cut through the back parking lot of the Dollar Depot, weaving to avoid the potholes and cardboard boxes littering the alleyway. I took a sharp right onto a side street and zigzagged down another alley behind Lorene's.

Hoping to cut Tiffany off, I took a final turn onto a private dirt road that led through a cow pasture to the highway. Through the dust I caught a glimpse of yellow and black in my side mirror. *What the hell?*

I turned my head to look. The Ninja was a hundred yards behind me. *Damn!* The last thing I needed was someone else in the mix, complicating things. Even if it was my dream man.

Just as the dirt road gave way to a cattle guard, Tiffany blew past on the highway. I bounced across the metal pipes and onto the shoulder, turning the siren back on now that we were safely out of town.

I radioed Selena. "Any reports of damage or injuries?"

"She took out two mailboxes and a garbage can, but no injuries."

Thank goodness.

A male voice came on the radio, Dante or Andre. "I'm turning from county road eighty-six onto the highway."

Good news. The county road was only two miles behind me. At least backup was close now.

Another three miles and we'd leave the Jacksburg city limits. Since we were in hot pursuit we could still chase Tiffany down, but Sheriff Dooley would no doubt want to haul Tiffany's ass in himself, take credit for what was sure to be a high-profile bust given her social status and the recent arrest of her father.

I have to nab her before she gets out of town. I'd solved this case with no help from the county. *This bust is mine!*

I pulled up next to Tiffany's car and waved her over with my arm, but she swerved at me, forcing me onto the grass median. After bouncing across the uneven ground, I recovered and drove back onto the asphalt directly behind Tiffany, quickly checking my mirrors. The Ninja was a quarter mile back, riding the shoulder. A Jacksburg PD cruiser was gaining on us. *Thank God.* There wasn't much I could do in a motorcycle. But Dante or Andre could force her off the road.

I looked up just in time to see Tiffany's red brake lights come on, tires smoking as she jammed the brake to the floor. There was no time for me to stop. The front of my bike slammed into her trunk and momentum carried the back of the bike up, flipping me off the seat and sending me head-over-heels over the top of Tiffany's car like a crazed performer at a monster truck rally.

Crunch! My left shoulder impacted the hood of her car at an odd angle and wrenched. I screamed in agony and terror as my ass slammed down on the front fender, my right knee sliced by the hard metal edge of her personalized license plate. I toppled forward into the road and rolled to a stop a dozen feet in front of her car.

Hot tears of pain seared my eyes. "You crazy bitch!"

I tried to push myself to a stand, but my left arm wasn't cooperating. My shoulder wasn't in the socket anymore, my arm hanging limp and useless. Blood poured through the gash sliced through my pants and knee. I looked at my mangled limbs in shock, a surge of adrenaline rushing through me, thankfully masking some of the pain.

I pushed myself into a sitting position with my right hand, scraped to shreds from sliding across the asphalt. In my haste to catch Tiffany, I hadn't had time to put my leather gloves on.

Revving her engine, Tiffany leaned forward over her steering wheel, piercing me with ocean-blue eyes pinched into a glare so sinister, so purely devoid of humanity, I knew my life was over. *She's going to run me down!* With my left shoulder and leg not working, I couldn't get out of the way.

Tiffany saw me struggling and emitted a cackle, continuing to rev her engine, taunting me, toying with me, just like Fate had done all these years.

The last thing I remembered before I died was the now cockeyed "TIFFY T" license plate barreling toward my face.

CHAPTER THIRTY-FOUR

TELL ME WHERE IT HURTS

Okay, so I didn't die. But with the excruciating pain in my leg and shoulder, I almost wished I had.

I opened my eyes to see an IV drip hanging on a stand over me, the tube leading to a vein on the back of my right hand where the needle was taped. My left hand felt warm and I turned to see the top of my dad's gray head bowed, my fingers gently sandwiched between his rough, calloused hands.

"Dad?" I managed to squeeze out.

His head shot up, his expression changing in an instant from grief to joy. "Marnie!"

He dropped my hand and started to grab me around the neck in a hug, impeded by the cast running from my left wrist all the way up to my shoulder. My left leg felt heavy and I looked down to see that it, too, was in an ankle-to-thigh cast. I was more plaster than person.

I reached over with my right hand and dad took it in his. I didn't have the heart to tell him that the motion hurt like hell, activating the still-raw scrapes on my palm.

"About time you woke up." Uncle Angus stood from a chair

in the corner of the tiny curtained space, his face as pink and swollen as Dad's, his forced casual tone fooling no one.

Dad held my hand to his cheek for a long moment, then gently let go. "How are you feeling, honey?"

"Never better."

He shook his head and emitted a strained chuckle. "That's my girl."

A nurse pulled aside the curtain at the end of my bed and stepped into the space. "Good evening, Captain Muckleroy."

"Evening?" Last I'd known, it had been morning.

I learned the doctors had kept me in a medically induced coma for two days while they performed X-rays, cat scans, MRIs, and generally poked and prodded me all over for injuries.

"Was Tiffany Tindall caught?" I asked.

Dad nodded. "After you flipped the bike Andre stopped to tend to you, but some guy on a Ninja cycle followed her, jumped from his bike into her convertible when she floored the pedal, and forced the wheel to keep her from running you over. He restrained her until the ambulance picked you up and Andre could take her off his hands. He drove off afterward before anyone could speak to him."

Oh, my God. The Ninja rider could've gotten himself killed. What kind of guy pulls a stunt like that for a total stranger? Risks his life to save someone he doesn't even know?

Bartholomew Edmund Jonasili was definitely a hero.

Dad and Uncle Angus stood as the white-headed doctor toddled in a few minutes later. The man perched on the end of my bed, giving my foot a friendly squeeze. "You were lucky, young lady. No head injuries, no internal injuries. But you've got a dislocated shoulder, a broken arm, and a broken leg. The break in your leg wasn't clean and will cause you some pain for a while, but you should be back on the road harassing motorists in two to three months." The doctor shot me a wink and a smile.

"Thanks, Doc."

After the physician left, Dad turned his chair to face me more directly, sat down again, and leaned in. "Lucas Glick called to check on you. He saw the report on the news. Trey came by the hospital, but the doctors wouldn't let him in to see you since he's not family. He's phoned me a dozen times for updates."

I harrumphed.

Dad stared intently at me. "The guy's a wreck, Marn. You should talk to him."

I shook my head, wincing with the pain it caused in my shoulder. "I don't want to talk to Trey, Dad. It's over."

Hell, it was over the minute it started. Regardless of the recent developments, with me unable to leave Jacksburg and Trey unable to find suitable work in the area, the relationship had been doomed from the start. His plans to work on *Felony Frenzy 2* had only sealed the deal, made the break cleaner, in fact. Besides, he'd left on Wednesday. By now he'd be back in California, programming sadistic pimps to beat the crap out of the poor prostitutes who sold their bodies for them.

While I'd slept, my father and uncle clearly hadn't. The bags under their eyes told me they were exhausted. "Go home, you two," I told them. "Get some rest."

"You sure you'll be okay without me?" Dad asked.

"The nurses can take care of anything I need."

"All righty, then."

Dad and Uncle Angus gave me a kiss on the cheek and left, leaving me the TV remote and my phone, which miraculously had not been damaged in the incident. I cued up Culture Club's "Do You Really Want to Hurt Me?" Alone with my music and my thoughts, I realized that no matter how bad my shoulder and leg felt, the physical pain Tiffany Tindall inflicted on me was nothing compared to the pain Trey had caused. He hadn't merely disappointed me as Madame Beulah predicted, he'd devastated me. His betrayal hurt worse than any of my broken bones. Tiffany had broken my body, but Trey had broken my soul.

When the song ended, I thumbed through my phone, looking for suitable self-pity music, eventually settling on "Love Stinks" by the J. Geils Band.

Yup. Love stinks.

***

The following morning, two orderlies arrived to move me out of intensive care and into a regular room for my final night's stay. The doctors wanted to keep an eye on me one more day as a precaution. The good news was that I'd be going home tomorrow. The bad news was they'd lowered the potency of my morphine drip. It hadn't only numbed my battered body, it had also helped to numb my battered heart.

A knock sounded at the door and I looked up to see two big, bald, brown and identical men in the doorway. Andre and Dante. *So there are two of them, after all.* With the identity theft case concluded, that made two mysteries solved. One of them carried a huge bouquet of yellow roses, the other a box of pecan fudge.

They greeted me in unison. "Hey, Captain."

The guys took seats on either side of the bed and filled me in on the latest police action. With Lucas Glick in rehab, not much had been going on the past few days. Andre had clocked a donkey doing eighteen miles an hour on the highway, taking a kick to the groin when he'd tried to stop the escaped beast. Dante had pulled Sheriff Dooley over in his personal vehicle and issued him a citation for expired registration. When the sheriff had argued, Dante had told him that no one's above the law.

I got a good laugh out of that one. "Wish I could've been there to see it."

The two of them stood. "We should get back out there," Andre said. "You get better quick, okay?"

Shortly after the twins left, a nurse came into the room, bringing me a lunch of colorless baked chicken in congealed gravy, plastic-looking green beans, and blue Jell-O that must've been sitting around a while because it had long since lost its jiggle. But after two days on IV fluids only, I was ravenous, inhaling the tasteless glop on my plate in record time.

I had just dipped into the gelatin when a shadow appeared in the doorway. I glanced up and froze. *Trey.* He must've sneaked past the nurse's station while they were busy delivering meals.

His face bore a dark three-day growth of stubble, which might have looked incredibly sexy if I hadn't been so enraged, so hurt. His eyes were sad, pained, his shoulders sagging as if he bore the weight of a tremendous unseen burden. His shirt and jeans were wrinkled, looking like he'd slept in them.

I didn't give him a chance to speak. I pointed at the door with my good arm. "Get out."

He stepped into the room. "Marnie, please listen to me."

This was unfair. With my leg in a cast clear up to my thigh, an IV drip in my arm, and a catheter shoved into my girl parts, I couldn't exactly get up and walk away. I didn't want to talk to him again. *Ever.* There was nothing more to say. I glared at him. "Get.

The hell. Out!"

Trey walked to the foot of my bed, a pleading look in his eyes. "Marnie—"

"Go!" I screamed.

He paused a moment before shaking his head.

Damn him! If the bastard wasn't going to leave, then he was going to get an earful. I struggled to sit up in the bed, grimacing against the pain. I threw back the covers, exposing my mangled leg and arm, the casts, the bandages covering my abrasions, the line of stitches across my right knee.

"Take a good look, Trey! This is real life cops and robbers." I wrapped a hand around the metal stand for my IV drip and shook it, the clear bag of fluid swaying back and forth. "I've got pain-killers dripping into me, an arm that's fractured in four places, and a shattered leg. There's a four-inch metal screw holding my thigh together. The doctors say with a lot of luck I might come out of this with only a slight limp. Does this look like entertainment to you? Does this look like fun?"

He flinched, but his eyes never left my face.

"This has been an absolute joyride for my father and Uncle Angus, too, wondering if I'd make it through, if I'd come out okay." By this time my voice had risen to an all-out shriek. "Dealing with the bills and the insurance company will be a regular laugh riot. Woo-hoo! What a great game! Fifty points for me!"

Trey opened his mouth to speak but there was nothing he could say that I had any interest in hearing.

"Game over, Trey!" I grabbed the plastic bowl of Jell-O off my tray and flung it at him with every ounce of energy I could muster.

Trey didn't even duck, taking the bowl full-force to the forehead as if it were some sort of penance. The blue gelatin stuck in his hair, a cube of it sliding down the side of his face, dropping off his chin to his shirt, sliding down until it disappeared into his breast pocket.

Trey stared at me for a long, silent moment and, despite my best attempts to hold back my emotions, I burst into angry, frustrated sobs, my fists clenched at my sides. He turned to go, glancing back one last time with a face so full of shame I felt a tinge of shame myself for making him feel that way. But it wasn't like he didn't deserve it.

He took one last look at me. "I'm sorry, Marnie," he said softly. "I am so, so sorry."

He walked out of my room. And out of my life.

I grabbed the white cord draped across my blanket and pushed the call button on the end. Seconds later the nurse stuck her head in the door.

"More blue Jell-O," I sobbed, tears running down my cheeks. "Please."

CHAPTER THIRTY-FIVE

ALL OUT OF LOVE

I spent the next six weeks on disability leave. Dad drove me out to the rehab hospital a few times to visit with Lucas, pushing me in a wheelchair since it was difficult for me to manage crutches with my left arm in a cast. Lucas was doing well, had overcome the shakes and even met a woman who was also going through the program, the two of them encouraging each other to stay strong, to take life one day at a time. No doubt Lucas would come out of rehab stronger, smarter, and sober. I'd come out of my ordeal, too. Stronger, smarter, and still alone.

The day Lucas completed rehab and swung by our house to pick up Tosh, his eyes bore a look I'd never seen in them before. A hint of hope, the bold glint of determination, that shiny spark of life.

"You look good, Lucas," I told him.

He smiled. "I feel good, too."

As we stood in my front hallway, Lucas cradled his cat in his arms, scratching Tosh affectionately under the chin. "Missed ya, buddy."

A loud, rhythmic purr was Tosh's reply.

Lucas turned grateful eyes on me. "Thanks, Marnie. If it

wasn't for you . . ." He choked up, unable to finish his sentence. But he didn't need to.

I put a hand on his arm and squeezed. "It's what friends do."

He packed up Tosh's bed, food, and toys. I watched from the window as he drove away in his tank truck, sparkling from a fresh wash and wax courtesy of Dad and Angus. They'd even had the broken passenger window replaced.

An enormous sense of relief and fulfillment flowed through me. I may have lost in the game of love with Trey, but my karmic score was even now. I couldn't change the fact that I'd ended a life, but I had no doubt now that I'd saved one, too.

***

Trey hadn't tried to contact me since that day in the hospital when I'd gone Jackson Pollock on him and splattered him with blue Jell-O. No doubt he was back in Silicon Valley, working fourteen-hour days to crank out *Felony Frenzy 2* as quickly as possible, our relationship now a vague memory, amounting to nothing more to him than a few romps in the hay.

How could I have been so fooled? I'd actually believed the guy cared about me, loved me. What an idiot I was. The guy had just wanted to get in my pants. And I'd let him. Then again, he had put on a convincing act. And at least he'd given me some long-overdue kick-ass orgasms.

The orthopedist removed my casts with instructions for me to follow up if my mobility didn't improve in a few days. After a month of sponge baths, I felt beyond ripe. The first thing I did when I returned from the doctor's office was take a long, hot shower. I wore out the razor blade combating the thick, coarse hair that had cropped up under the cast, making me look like a female Chewbacca. *Yuck.* I stood under the spray until the last drop of hot water ran out.

The following morning, the skin on my left arm and leg was still pale and soft, but it looked a little less pasty. I took another hot, heavenly shower, scrubbing every inch of my skin with my loofah, as if trying to erase the broken person I was and release a new me. Afterward, I sat on the edge of my bed and slid into a pair of my navy-blue police uniform pants. A searing pain rocketed down my leg as I bent my knee, but I fought through it. I had to get back to work, had to get out of this house, had to get busy and get my mind off Trey.

It would be my first day back at work since Tiffany had tried to kill me. Even though my body wasn't yet back to one hundred percent—the doctors said it might never be—I was looking forward to cruising the streets. Sitting on my butt watching endless episodes of *Family Feud* had proven pretty damn boring. I'd even grown tired of my *Wonder Woman* DVDs.

Bluebonnet had done her best to keep me company, had seemed to sense my loneliness, licking my hand incessantly. I'd had way too much time to think about Trey, how he'd made me laugh, how he'd made me think, how he'd made me feel alive again. How he'd taken all that away, ripped my heart to shreds, and left without ever looking back. *That sorry son-of-a-bitch.*

I stood and shoved my .38 into the holster at my waist, tossing my head defiantly. Why was I moping over a sack of shit like Trey Jones? Even if he had the skills to put a zip in my drive, a woman can't live on orgasms alone. I'd be damned if I'd waste another second thinking about some computer geek whose personal ethics needed major reprogramming.

When I finished dressing, I headed out of the house, Bluebonnet on my heels. I gave her a kiss on the head and ruffled her ears. While she settled on her blanket on the porch, I walked to the garage, taking deep breaths. The cool fall air bore a faint scent of hay, the last cutting of the season.

I stopped next to my motorcycle and ran a hand lovingly along the seat. I'd missed her, missed the therapy the bike provided, the tranquility of meandering down country roads, taking in the scenery, the sun on my face, my troubles forgotten, if only for a while.

Having been neglected the past few weeks, she rode a little rough at first, but she eventually worked the kinks out and we sailed down the road. The fresh fall breeze caressed my exposed cheeks as I rode, but it was nothing compared to Trey's touch.

I rounded the bend by the tall transformer where Trey's electronic GPS gizmo had led us during our high-tech scavenger hunt on our first date. I refused to let my mind linger there, forcing myself to make a mental grocery list instead. *Dog food, bread, coffee* . . . Shortly thereafter I rolled past Lorene's, where Trey and I had our first meal and several others together, Trey performing discreet acts of erotica with the onion rings for my amusement. The guy had an offbeat sense of humor, one of the things I love—make that *loved*—about him.

Unwittingly, I slowed as I passed the baseball field where we'd first made love on the trunk of his parents' Lincoln, sorely testing the shocks as we gave ourselves to each other with a rough, unrestrained, wholly satisfying passion I hadn't known I was capable of and certainly hadn't expected from a computer nerd like him. *Damn.* It had been six weeks since I'd last seen the guy, and he was still on my mind. *Will I ever be able to stop thinking about Trey?*

As I turned into town, an eighteen-wheeler came down Main, heading toward me from the opposite direction, spewing dark smoke as it struggled to gain momentum with its heavy load. For a split second I debated pulling into its path and putting a quick end to my misery, but that wouldn't be fair to the trucker, my dad, or myself. I'd have to get through this somehow. If it's true that time heals all wounds, I should feel better by the year 3862.

I parked at the DQHQ in my usual spot, shaking out my leg as I climbed off the bike. The darn thing still felt stiff. Chief Moreno looked up from the morning paper as I stepped into the station. As usual, a Red Vine dangled from one corner of his mouth, a Marlboro from the other.

The chief stood and walked toward me. "How you feeling, Captain?"

"Never better." An out-and-out lie, but what good would it do to tell him that my leg felt rigid and shaky, my muscles had atrophied, and I'd lost the will to live?

Chief Moreno put a hand on my shoulder and gave it an encouraging pat. I forced a smile. He returned to his paper and I headed to my booth.

Selena appeared at my side with a powdered donut and a mug of coffee flavored with hazelnut creamer, giving me the royal treatment. "Glad you're back, Marnie. I've missed our girl talk."

I took the donut and mug from her. "I should break a bone or two more often." I took a big swig of coffee. *Mmm.* I looked up at Selena. "How're things with Eric?"

Selena grinned and tossed her hair sassily. "He asked me to be exclusive."

"Sounds like true love."

She giggled and opened her mouth as if to say something else but looked at my face and seemed to think better of it. No doubt she'd heard about me and Trey breaking up, and no doubt the still-raw pain was evident in my eyes. Too bad I'd long since run out of Vicodin, though the painkillers did little to stop the ache of a broken heart.

I'd expected a mountain of paperwork to be stacked in my inbox, but Chief Moreno and the other officers had pitched in while I was gone. The box contained only a few items none of the men wanted to deal with, including a proposal from a vending machine distributor who wanted to place a feminine products dispenser in the station's ladies room.

At the bottom of the box was an eight-by-ten glossy photo of Tiffany Tindall, her mug shot. The bright orange jumpsuit did nothing for her sallow complexion, making her look like a bleach-blond sweet potato. Her eyes were their natural hazel, the tinted contacts seized by the booking officers to be returned when, and *if*, she was released from custody. With her daddy also under indictment and in bankruptcy, she'd have a hard time making bail. *Heh-heh.*

Some smart ass, probably Dante or Andre, had written "With all my love, XO, Tiffany" in black Sharpie across the bottom corner of the photo. I tacked the picture on the bulletin board next to my booth for all the world, or at least all in the Jacksburg Police station, to see.

In mere minutes, the paperwork was caught up. I grabbed my goggles and helmet, waved goodbye to Selena, and headed out on the police bike. I wanted to thank the Ninja rider for saving my life, but his number hadn't been listed in the phone book and, even if it had been, a phone call seemed an inadequate, impersonal way to express my gratitude. If not for him, Tiffany would have killed me. I planned to go to his house in person, that evening, right after my shift. I'd finally meet Bartholomew Edmund Jonasili, my mystery man, face to face.

I wondered how old he'd be, what he'd look like, how his voice would sound. I had no idea what to expect as far as those things go. What kind of man would risk his life for a woman he doesn't even know? One who was chivalrous, brave and selfless, that's what kind of man. One who, unlike Trey, knew right from wrong and was willing to risk his life to protect those values. Those facts told me all I needed to know. Even if nothing romantic developed between us, we'd share a bond for the rest of our lives.

But what if something romantic developed? He seemed like a knight in leather armor, riding a yellow and black 140-horsepower steed, a helmet for a crown. My stomach twisted in excitement and anticipation. I visualized him leaping from the motorcycle into

Tiffany's open convertible, prying her clenched, manicured hands off the steering wheel, forcing the wheel to prevent the car from running me over. I thought of him disappearing down the highway, refusing to claim his rightful spot in the limelight. Nervous as I was, I could hardly wait until the workday ended.

CHAPTER THIRTY-SIX

GIRL FINALLY MEETS BOY

I drove to my usual hiding spot behind the WELCOME TO JACKSBURG sign. Some do-gooders, probably the Boy Scouts or the high school Key Club, had painted over the graffiti. Some teens over in Hockerville were probably already plotting to deface the sign again. It was an ongoing battle, but at least it gave the bored kids something to do other than drugs or petty thievery.

After settling in behind the sign and cutting my engine, I debated what to dial up on my phone now that I was back at work. Loverboy's "Working for the Weekend?" Donna Summers' "She Works Hard for the Money?" Nah. Chumbawamba's "Tubthumping?" Yeah, that was it. Like the lyrics said, Tiffany Tindall could knock me down, but I'd get up again. That bitch would never keep me down.

Just as the song's slow prelude began, the far-off drone of a high-performance motorcycle engine drifted up the two-lane highway on the cool late November breeze, the volume and pitch escalating as the bike grew closer.

He's coming.

I leaned forward to peer through the oleander bush.

A moment later, the shiny yellow and black Ninja popped up

over the hill, the noise from its powerful engine now a full-blown primal scream, its rider hunched forward over the sport bike. My heart spun madly in my chest and my body broke out in an icy sweat. I wanted to roll forward onto the shoulder where he could see me, but my legs refused to move. The guy had saved my life and here I was, too awestruck to wave him down. *What a chickenshit.*

The bike bore down on my hiding spot and then he was right on me. He passed me and his helmet turned as he did a double take. The bike's brake lights flashed, then held. The Ninja slowed, pulled over onto the shoulder, and made a U-turn.

He was heading back, straight toward me. *What should I do?* My mind went blank, my stomach somersaulted inside me, and my skin felt as if fire ants were swarming all over me. All I could do was stare.

The Ninja's rider slowed as he approached me, rolling onto the shoulder and across the dead, dry grass, coming to a stop a mere five feet from me, his engine idling. He faced me for a full minute, his face still obscured by the tinted faceplate of his helmet, only a vague outline of his jaw line visible.

I sat there stupefied, saying nothing, doing nothing. *Gah! I must look like an idiot.* The guy saved my life and I can't even work up a few words of gratitude? Finally, I managed a small symbol of thanks. I gave him the same sign of approval he'd given me after Fulton's bust. A thumbs-up sign followed by a victorious fist in the air.

He nodded once and sat still for a few more seconds, watching me. Then he gunned his engine, maneuvered in three tight circles around my bike, and took off, tires squealing, wheels kicking up a spray of dust and brown grass. Clearly he wanted me to pursue him. *This time he won't get away.*

I started my engine, pulled onto the highway, and raced after him, my breathing fast and loud inside my helmet. Siren wailing, lights flashing, I cranked the accelerator back and began to gain on him.

He swerved back and forth across the lanes, blatantly taunting me before slowing down and pulling to the side. He rolled to a stop and I pulled up perpendicular in front of him, blocking his escape. I cut my engine. With shaking hands, I unsnapped my helmet and pulled it off, shaking my head and swiping at the bangs stuck to my forehead. I set my helmet on my thigh, pushed my dark goggles up onto my head, and stared him straight in the eye—or at least where his eyes would be behind the faceplate.

I stuck out a hand. "Driver's license, please."

After removing his right glove, he reached his hand into the back zipper pocket of his leather jumpsuit and retrieved his wallet. He rifled through it, taking his sweet time, torturing me with his slow movements. Finally, he pulled the card out and handed it to me.

I took it from him, inhaled a deep breath, and looked down. Trey's face looked up at me from the card. *How can this be?* There had to be some mistake. I looked up.

Trey flipped his faceplate up so I could see his eyes, eyes that bore into mine with a shameless intensity. With sorrow. With regret. And with love.

I could hardly believe it. Trey and the Ninja rider were one and the same. It couldn't be, could it?

Thinking back, it all made sense. Trey said he knew who owned the Ninja but refused to give me a name. Trey worked fairly regular hours and the Ninja rider came through town on a consistent basis. Trey's spiky hairstyle was the result of fingers run through his short dark hair in an attempt to fight helmet head. Trey had complained about the ungodly traffic in Silicon Valley, his time-consuming commute, noting how motorcycles could use the carpool lane and shorten the time spent sitting in gridlock.

But the registration records had showed the bike as belonging to Bartholomew Edmund Jonasili.

My eyes snapped to the name on the license. It read Bartholomew Edmund Jones *III*. No doubt the clerk at the DMV had been unable to read Trey's chicken scratch handwriting, mistaking his "e" for an "a" and the three hash marks after his name for the letters i-l-i.

My mind reeled. I didn't know what to think, what to feel. Should I be devastated my man of mystery was a guy I already knew, one who'd proven to be so right, and then so wrong, for me? But, my God, Trey had saved my life! I should be thrilled that Trey had risked his life for me, proven his love beyond any doubt. *But does that fix everything?* I wished it did, but it didn't. He still lived half a continent away, devoting his life to glorify the very things I fought each day. Crime and violence.

Still staring down at the license, I heard the sound of Trey unsnapping the chin strap on his helmet. He reached out, cupping his hand under my chin, softly turning my head to look up at him.

Our eyes met and locked. Tears welled in mine and I blinked to hold them back.

After clearing my throat, I managed to croak out a few words. "What are you doing here?"

He dropped his hand. "Your father told me you'd returned to work."

"He did?"

Trey nodded. "I've called him every day to check on your recovery."

Dad hadn't said a thing about it.

Trey seemed to read my mind. "I asked him not to tell you. I needed some time to make things right."

"Make things right? How?"

"I quit my job, Marnie."

"You did?" A tear escaped and slid down my cheek.

Trey wiped the tear away with a warm, rough thumb. "You were right. What I was doing was wrong." He paused a moment. "I want you to respect me, Marnie. To respect what I do. Just like I respect you and what you do."

Conflicting emotional data flooded my system. Elation. Relief. Frustration. My circuits froze, experiencing a major emotional glitch. Trey may have quit that particular job, but he'd made it clear that Silicon Valley was the only place to be for someone who wanted to work on cutting edge technology. What was there for him in Hockerville or Jacksburg? He may not be working on *Felony Frenzy 2*, but he'd find a job with another high-tech firm in California and be gone again in a few days or weeks. Nothing had changed. I was right back where I started. *Alone.*

"Are you job hunting now?" I asked.

He shook his head.

"But you said you quit your job."

He shifted on his seat. "When I told my boss why I was quitting, that I didn't want to work on a violent project and that I wanted to move back to Texas to be with you, he said he didn't want to lose me. Code can be written anywhere and transmitted over the internet. I'm going to telecommute from here. I'll have to travel out to California for meetings, but it will only be for a few days each month."

It took a moment for my brain to process the information, but once it did I couldn't help myself. I squealed like a schoolgirl, my fists clasped to my chest with relief and joy. "That's fantastic! What will you be working on?"

Trey grinned. "I pitched a game idea to them. An E-rated game starring a female motorcycle cop with a long auburn braid and a bunch of sexy freckles."

I ducked my chin. "Does she have a big butt?"

He chuckled. "She has a womanly figure, but the focus of the game is on her policing skills."

"Do the good guys always win?"

"Every time."

Happy tears pooled in my eyes as I climbed off my bike and Trey climbed off his. We grabbed each other in a hug so tight we both had to gasp for air. It felt so good, so right, to be back in his arms. I belonged in those arms, and he belonged in mine. My smile grew so wide my lips hurt.

I had someone who loved me. And I had someone to love. I wasn't alone anymore. I released Trey, reached down, and took the cuffs from my belt, snapping one on Trey's wrist, the other on my own.

He grinned. "Kinky."

"Kinky, nothing. You're busted."

"What's the charge?"

"Theft," I said. "You've stolen my heart." Corny, yeah, but what the heck. I could give as good as him.

Trey wrapped his free hand around the back of my neck, drawing me to him for a warm, deep kiss. After a few seconds, he ended the kiss and pulled his head back to look into my eyes. "I plead guilty as charged." He reached into another pocket and pulled out a ring box. My heart seemed to stop as he opened it to reveal a brilliant diamond ring. "Any chance you'll give me a life sentence?"

My heart soared with joy. "Yes!" I cried through a fresh set of tears.

Trey slipped the ring on my finger and gave me another kiss.

Fate had tired of toying with me, had a change of heart, decided to make up for all her bullying by giving me a smart, funny, sexy man to share my life with. *Maybe fate isn't such a bitch after all.*

*** *The End* ***

Dear Reader,

I hope you enjoyed *Busted* as much as I enjoyed writing it for you!

What did you think of this book? Posting reviews online are a great way to share your thoughts with fellow readers and help each other find stories best suited to your individual tastes.

Be the first to hear about upcoming releases, special discounts, and subscriber-only perks by signing up for my newsletter at my website.

Find me online at www.DianeKelly.com and on my author page on Facebook. I'd love to connect with you on Twitter and Instagram, too! Look for me at @dianekellybooks.

I love to Skype with book clubs! Contact me via my website if you'd like to arrange a virtual visit with your group.

See below for a list of my other books, then read on for fun excerpts.

Happy reading! See you in the next story.

Diane

OTHER BOOKS BY DIANE KELLY

If you enjoyed *Busted*, you'll like these other books, too!

The Busted Series:

> Busted
> Another Big Bust (coming May 15, 2020)

The House Flipper Mystery Series:

> Dead as a Door Knocker
> Dead in the Doorway

The Paw Enforcement Mystery Series:

> Paw Enforcement
> Paw and Order
> Laying Down the Paw
> Against the Paw
> Above the Paw
> Enforcing the Paw
> The Long Paw of the Law
> Paw of the Jungle
> Bending the Paw

The Tara Holloway Death & Taxes series:

Death, Taxes, and a French Manicure
Death, Taxes, and a Skinny No-Whip Latte
Death, Taxes, and Extra-Hold Hairspray
Death, Taxes, and Peach Sangria
Death, Taxes, and Hot Pink Leg Warmers
Death, Taxes, and Green Tea Ice Cream
Death, Taxes, and Silver Spurs
Death, Taxes, and Cheap Sunglasses
Death, Taxes, and a Chocolate Cannoli
Death, Taxes, and a Satin Garter
Death, Taxes, and Sweet Potato Fries
Death, Taxes, and a Shotgun Wedding

Other Romances:

Love, Luck, & Little Green Men

EXCERPTS

Love, Luck, and Little Green Men - Excerpt

CHAPTER ONE - MONDAY, FEBRUARY 14TH
MIXED BOUQUETS, MIXED MESSAGES

Another Valentine's Day and here I was again. Lonely. Loveless. Lover-less.

Yep, I'm unlucky in love. Unlucky in just about everything else, too. Life tried, and time again, to kick my ass. But, you know what? Life could piss off. I, Erin Flaherty, would not go down without a fight.

***

For the third time in as many months, I sat at the counter of my shoe repair shop screwing a new tap on the heel of a men's size thirteen tap shoe. Part of me wanted to scold my son for abusing his dance shoes, but another part knew the broken tap was a sign of his passion for dance. With his enormous feet, athletic style, and unbridled enthusiasm, Riley could stomp a stage into splinters. Heck, I'd broken a tap or two myself over the years. Might as well cut the kid some slack.

My shop wasn't much to brag about, just a small foyer and stockroom with walls painted a soft sage green and dark wood floors that, judging from the multitude of scars, were likely original. Two wooden chairs flanked the front door. Not that I was ever so busy customers needed a place to sit while they waited their turn, but best to be prepared just in case, right? A brass coat tree nestled in one corner, an oval standing mirror in the other. The white Formica countertop supported an outdated but functional cash register and one of the world's last remaining black-and-white portable TV's. A full-color map of County Cork, Ireland and a poster of Saint Fin Barre's Cathedral, a County Cork historical landmark, graced the walls, giving the shop a touch of Irish kitsch.

The bells hanging from the front door tinkled and a blast of brisk winter wind blew into my shop, carrying a sweet, flowery scent with it. I looked up to see an enormous bouquet of long-stem roses, six red and six yellow, making its way inside. My heart performed a pirouette in my chest and I emitted an involuntary squeal. "Flowers? For me?"

Dumb question, really. I was the only one in the shop. But you can't blame me for being surprised. The last time anyone had given me flowers was when Riley's father had shown up in the delivery room with a tiny bouquet of carnations and an even tinier engagement ring. That was fourteen years—and what seemed like a lifetime—ago. I'd kept the flowers but refused the ring. The right choice, obviously, given the look of relief on Matthew's face when I'd handed the small velvet-covered box back to him. But who could blame him? Like me, he'd been only nineteen, much too young to deal with a new baby and a wife, though not too young to knock me up, the knucklehead. He'd promised to pull out. Never trust a guy with a hard on.

Of course it takes two to tango, and I've accepted my share of the blame. Or should I say credit? When I think of my son, of what a clever and caring kid he's turned out to be, it's impossible to consider him as a mistake.

The roses made their way toward me, bringing their lovely smell along with them, coming to rest on the countertop next to the cash register. Their courier stepped aside to reveal himself. I knew the face in an instant. Strong-jawed, with the ruddy complexion of a man who'd spent a decade toiling at the dockyards of Dublin. Dark hair worn closely cropped in a no-fuss style. Intelligent, soulful eyes under thick brows. The roguish smile that revealed an upper bicuspid chipped in a life-changing moment the tooth would never let him forget.

Brendan.

"Happy Saint Valentine's Day, Erin."

Would I ever tire of that deep Irish brogue?

Dead as a Door Knocker – Excerpt

Chapter One - Deadbeats

Whitney Whitaker

I grabbed my purse, my tool belt, and the bright yellow hardhat I'd adorned with a chain of daisy decals. I gave my cat a kiss on the head. "Bye-bye, Sawdust." Looking into his baby blue eyes, I pointed a finger at him. "Be a good boy while mommy's at work, okay?"

The cat swiped at my finger with a paw the color of pine

shavings. Given that my eyes and hair were the same shade as his, I could be taken for his mother if not for the fact that we were entirely different species. I'd adopted the furry runt after his mother, a stray, had given birth to him and two siblings in my uncle's barn. My cousins, Buck and Owen, had taken in the other two kittens, and my aunt and uncle gave the wayward mama cat a comfy home in their hilltop cabin on the Kentucky border.

After stepping outside, I turned around to lock the French doors that served as the entrance to my humble home. The place sat in my parents' backyard, on the far side of their kidney-shaped pool. In its former life, it had served as a combination pool house and garden shed. With the help of the contractors I'd befriended on my jobs, I'd converted the structure into a cozy guest house—the guest being yours truly. It had already been outfitted with a small three-quarter bath, so all we'd had to do was add a closet and kitchenette.

Furnishing a hundred and fifty square feet had been easy. There was room for only the bare essentials—a couple of bar stools at the kitchen counter, a twin bed and dresser, and a recliner that served as both a comfortable reading chair and a scratching post for Sawdust. Heaven forbid my sweet-but-spoiled cat sharpen his claws on the sisal post I'd bought him at the pet supply store. At least he enjoyed his carpet-covered cat tree. I'd positioned it by one of the windows that flanked the French doors. He passed his days on the highest perch, watching birds flitter about the birdhouses and feeders situated about the backyard.

At twenty-eight, I probably should've ventured farther from my parents' home by now. But the arrangement suited me and my parents just fine. They were constantly jetting off to Paris or Rome or some exotic locale I couldn't pronounce or find on a map if my life depended on it. Living here allowed me to keep an eye on their house and dog while they traveled, but the fact that we shared no walls gave us all some privacy. The arrangement also allowed me to sock away quite a bit of my earnings in savings. Soon, I'd be able to buy a house of my own. Not here in the Green Hills neighborhood, where real estate garnered a pretty penny. But maybe in one of the more affordable Nashville suburbs. While many young girls dreamed of beaded wedding gowns or palomino ponies, I'd dreamed of custom cabinets and and built-in bookshelves.

After locking the door, I turned to find my mother and her black-and-white Boston terrier, Yin-Yang, puttering around the backyard. Like me, Mom was blond, though she now needed the help of her hairdresser to keep the stray grays at bay. Like Yin-Yang, Mom was petite, standing only five feet three inches. Mom was still in her pink bathrobe, a steaming mug of coffee in her hand. While she helped with billing at my dad's otolaryngology practice, she normally went in late and left early. Her part-time schedule allowed her to avoid traffic, gave her time take care of things around the house and spend time with her precious pooch.

"Good morning!" I called.

My mother returned the sentiment, while Yin-Yang raised her two-tone head and replied with a cheerful *Arf-arf!* The bark scared off a trio of finches who'd been indulging in a breakfast of assorted seeds at a nearby feeder.

Mom stepped over, the dog trotting along with her, staring up at me with its adorable little bug eyes. "You're off early," Mom said, a hint of question in her voice.

No sense telling her I was on my way to an eviction. She already thought my job was beneath me. She assumed working as a property manager involved constantly dealing with deadbeats and clogged toilets. Truth be told, much of my job did involve delinquent tenants or backed-up plumbing. But there was much more to it than that. Helping landlords turn rundown real estate into attractive residences, helping hopeful tenants locate the perfect place for their particular needs, making sure everything ran smoothly for everyone involved. I considered myself to be in the homemaking business. But rather than try, for the umpteenth time, to explain myself, I simply said, "I've got a busy day."

Mom tilted her head. "Too busy to study for your real estate exam?"

I fought the urge to groan. As irritating as my mother could be, she only wanted the best for me. Problem was, we didn't agree on what the best was. Instead of starting an argument I said, "Don't worry. The test isn't for another couple of weeks. I've still got plenty of time."

"Okay," she acquiesced, the two syllables soaked in skepticism. "Have a good day, sweetie." At least those five words sounded sincere.

"You, too, Mom." I reached down and ruffled the dog's ears. "Bye, girl."

I made my way to the picket fence that enclosed the backyard and let myself out of the gate and onto the driveway. After tossing my hard hat and tool belt into the passenger seat of my red Honda CR-V, I swapped out the magnetic WHITAKER WOODWORKING sign on the door for one that read HOME & HEARTH REALTY. Yep, I wore two hats. The hard hat when moonlighting as a carpenter for my uncle, and a metaphorical second hat when working my day job as a property manager for a real estate business. This morning, I sported the metaphorical hat as I headed up Hillsboro Pike into Nashville. Fifteen minutes later, I turned onto Sweetbriar Avenue. In the driveway of the house on the corner sat a shiny midnight blue Infiniti Q70L sedan with vanity plates that read TGENTRY. My shackles rose at the sight.

Thaddeus Gentry III owned Gentry Real Estate Development, Inc. or, as I called it, GREED Incorporated. Okay, so I'd added an extra E to make the spelling work. Still, it was true. The guy was as money-hungry and ruthless as they come. He was singlehandedly responsible for the gentrification of several old Nashville neighborhoods. While gentrification wasn't necessarily a bad thing—after all it rid the city of ramshackle houses in dire need of repairs—Thad Gentry took advantage of homeowners, offering them pennies on the dollar, knowing they couldn't afford the increase in property taxes that would result as their modest neighborhoods transformed into upscale communities. He'd harass holdouts by reporting any city code violations, no matter how minor. He also formed homeowners' associations in the newly renovated neighborhoods, and ensured the HOA put pressure on the remaining original residents to bring their houses up to snuff. These unfortunate folks found they no longer felt at home and usually gave in and moved on . . . to where, who knows?

When I'd come by a week ago in a final attempt to collect from the tenants, I'd noticed a for sale sign in the yard where Thad Gentry's car was parked. The sign was gone now. *Had Gentry bought the property? Had he set his sights on the neighborhood?*

Paw Enforcement - Excerpt

Chapter One - Job Insecurity

Fort Worth Police Officer Megan Luz

My rusty-haired partner lay convulsing on the hot asphalt, his jaw clenching and his body involuntarily curling into a jittery fetal position as two probes delivered 1,500 volts of electricity to his groin. The crotch of his police-issue trousers darkened as he lost control of his bladder.

I'd never felt close to my partner in the six months we'd worked together, but at that particular moment I sensed a strong bond. The connection likely stemmed from the fact that we were indeed connected then--by the two wires leading from the Taser in my hand to my partner's twitching testicles.

\#

I didn't set out to become a hero. I decided on a career in law enforcement for three other reasons:

1) Having been a twirler in my high school's marching band, I knew how to handle a baton.

2) Other than barking short orders or rattling off Miranda rights, working as a police officer wouldn't require me to talk much.

3) I had an excess of pent-up anger. Might as well put it to good use,

right?

Of course I didn't plan to be a street cop forever. Just long enough to work my way up to detective. A lofty goal, but I knew I could do it--even if nobody else did.

I'd enjoyed my studies in criminal justice at Sam Houston State University in Hunstville, Texas, especially the courses in criminal psychology. No, I'm not some sick, twisted creep who gets off on hearing about criminals who steal, rape, and murder. I just thought that if we could figure out why criminals do bad things, maybe we could stop them, you know?

To supplement my student loans, I'd worked part-time at the gift shop in the nearby state prison museum, selling tourists such quality souvenirs as ceramic ash trays made by the prisoners or decks of cards containing prison trivia. The unit had once been home to Clyde Barrow of Bonnie and Clyde fame and was also the site of an eleven-day siege in 1974 spearheaded by heroin kingpin Fredrick Gomez Carrasco, jailed for killing a police officer. Our top-selling item was a child's time-out chair fashioned after Old Sparky, the last remaining electric chair used in Texas. Talk about cruel and unusual punishment.

TO THE CORNER, LITTLE BILLY.

NO, MOMMY, NO! ANYTHING BUT THE CHAIR!

I'd looked forward to becoming a cop, keeping the streets safe for citizens, maintaining law and order, promoting civility and justice. Such noble ideals, right?

What I hadn't counted on was that I'd be working with a force full of macho shitheads. With my uncanny luck, I'd been assigned to partner with the most macho, most shit-headed cop of all, Derek the "Big Dick" Mackey. As implied in the aforementioned reference to twitching testicles, our partnership had not ended well.

That's why I was sitting here outside the chief's office in a cheap plastic chair, chewing my thumbnail down to a painful nub, waiting to find out whether I still had a job. Evidently, Tasering your partner in the COJONES is considered not only an overreaction, but also a blatant violation of department policy, one which carried the potential penalty of dismissal from the force, not to mention a criminal assault charge.

So much for those noble ideals, huh?

I ran a finger over my upper lip, blotting the nervous sweat that had formed there. Would I be booted off the force after only six months on duty?

With the city's budget crisis, there'd been threats of cutbacks and layoffs across the board. No department would be spared. If the chief had to fire anyone, he'd surely start with the rookie with the Irish temper. If the chief canned me, what would I do? My aspirations of becoming a detective would go down the toilet. Once again I'd be Megan Luz, a.k.a. "The Loser." As you've probably guessed, my pent-up anger had a lot to do with that nickname.

I pulled my telescoping baton from my belt and flicked my wrist to extend it. SNAP! Though my police baton had a different feel from the twirling baton I'd used in high school, I'd quickly learned that with a few minor adjustments to accommodate the distinctive weight distribution I could perform many of the same tricks with it. I began to work the stick, performing a basic flat spin. The repetitive motion calmed me, helped me think. It was like a twirling metal stress ball. SWISH-SWISH-SWISH.

The chief's door opened and three men exited. All wore navy tees emblazoned with white letters spelling BOMB SQUAD stretched tight across well-developed pecs. Though the bomb squad was officially part of the Fort Worth Fire Department, the members worked closely with the police. Where there's a bomb, there's a crime, after all. Most likely these men were here to discuss safety procedures for the upcoming Concerts in the Park. After what happened at the Boston marathon, extra precautions were warranted for large public events.

The guy in front, a blond with a military-style haircut, cut his eyes my way. He watched me spin my baton for a moment, then dipped his head in acknowledgement when my gaze met his. He issued the standard southern salutation. "Hey."

His voice was deep with a subtle rumble, like far-off thunder warning of an oncoming storm. The guy wasn't tall, but he was broad-shouldered, muscular, and undeniably masculine. He had dark green eyes and a dimple in his chin that drew my eyes downward, over his soft, sexy mouth, and back up again.

A hot flush exploded through me. I tried to nod back at him, but my muscles seemed to have atrophied. My hand stopped moving and clutched my baton in a death grip. All I could do was watch as he and the other men continued into the hall and out of sight.

BLURGH. Acting like a frigid virgin. How humiliating!

Once the embarrassment waned, I began to wonder. Had the bomb squad guy found me attractive? Is that why he'd greeted me? Or was he simply being friendly to a fellow public servant?

My black locks were pulled back in a tight, torturous bun, a style that enabled me to look professional on the force while allowing me to retain my feminine allure after hours. There were only so many sacrifices I was willing to make for employment and my long, lustrous hair was not one of them. My freckles showed through my light makeup. Hard to feel like a tough cop if you're wearing too much foundation or more than one coat of mascara. Fortunately, I had enough natural coloring to get by with little in the way of cosmetics. I was a part Irish-American, part Mexican-American mutt, with just enough Cherokee blood to give me an instinctive urge to dance in the rain but not enough to qualify me for any college scholarships. My figure was neither thin nor voluptuous, but my healthy diet and regular exercise kept me in decent shape. It was entirely possible that the guy had been checking me out. Right?

I mentally chastised myself. CHILL, MEGAN. I hadn't had a date since I'd joined the force, but so what? I had more important things to deal with at the moment. I collapsed my baton, returned it to my belt, and took a deep breath to calm my nerves.

The chief's secretary, a middle-aged brunette wearing a poly-blend dress, sat at her desk typing a report into the computer. She had twice as much butt as chair, her thighs draping over the sides of the seat. But who could blame her? Judging from the photos on her desk, she'd squeezed out three children in rapid succession. Having grown up in a family of five kids, I knew mothers had little time to devote to themselves when their kids were young and constantly needed mommy to feed them, clean up their messes, and bandage their various boo-boos. She wore no jewelry, no makeup, and no nail polish. The chief deserved credit for not hiring a younger, prettier, better accessorized woman for the job. Obviously, she'd been hired for her mad office skills. She'd handled a half dozen phone calls in the short time I'd been waiting and her fingers moved over the keyboard at such a speedy pace it was a miracle her hands didn't burst into flame. Whatever she was being paid, it wasn't enough.

The woman's phone buzzed again and she punched her intercom button. "Yessir?" She paused a moment. "I'll send her in." She hung up the phone and turned to me. "The chief is ready for you."

"Thanks." I stood on wobbly legs.

WOULD THE CHIEF TAKE MY BADGE TODAY? WAS MY CAREER IN LAW ENFORCEMENT OVER?

Death, Taxes, and a French Manicure - Excerpt

Chapter One - Some People Just Need Shooting

When I was nine, I formed a Silly Putty pecker for my Ken doll, knowing he'd have no chance of fulfilling Barbie's needs given the permanent state of erectile dysfunction with which the toy designers at Mattel had cursed him. I knew a little more about sex than most girls, what with growing up in the country and all. The first time I saw our neighbor's Black Angus bull mount an unsuspecting heifer, my two older brothers explained it all to me.

"He's getting him some," they'd said.

"Some what?" I'd asked.

"Nookie."

We watched through the barbed wire fence until the strange ordeal was over. Frankly, the process looked somewhat uncomfortable for the cow, who continued to chew her cud throughout the entire encounter. But when the bull dismounted, nuzzled her chin, and wandered away, I swore I saw a smile on that cow's face and a look of quiet contentment in her eyes. She was in love.

I'd been in search of that same feeling for myself ever since.

My partner and I had spent the afternoon huddled at a cluttered desk in the back office of an auto parts store perusing the owner's financial records, searching for evidence of tax fraud. Yeah, you got me. I work for the IRS. Not exactly the kind of career that makes a person popular at cocktail parties. But those brave enough to get to know me learn I'm actually a nice person, fun even, and they have nothing to fear. I have better things to do than nickel and dime taxpayers whose worst crime was inflating the value of the Glen Campbell albums they donated to Goodwill.

"I'll be right back, Tara." My partner smoothed the front of his starched white button-down as he stood from the folding chair. Eddie Bardin was tall, lean, and African-American, but having been raised in the upper-middle-class, predominately white Dallas suburbs, he had a hard time connecting to his roots. He'd had nothing to overcome, unless you counted his affinity for Phil Collins' music, Heineken beer, and khaki chinos, tastes which he had yet to conquer. Eddie was more L.L. Bean than L.L. Cool J.

I nodded to Eddie and tucked an errant strand of my chestnut hair behind my ear. Turning back to the spreadsheet in front of me, I flicked aside the greasy burger and onion ring wrappers the store's owner, Jack Battaglia, had left on the desk after lunch. I couldn't make heads or tails out of the numbers on the page. Battaglia didn't know jack about keeping books and, judging from his puny salaries account, he'd been too cheap to hire a professional.

A few seconds after Eddie left the room, the door to the office banged open. Battaglia loomed in the doorway, his husky body filling the narrow space. He wore a look of purpose and his store's trademark bright green jumpsuit, the cheerful color at odds with the open box cutter clutched in his furry-knuckled fist.

"Hey!" Instinctively, I leapt from my seat, the metal chair falling over behind me and clanging to the floor.

Battaglia lunged at me. My heart whirled in my chest. There was no time to pull my gun. The best I could do was throw out my right arm to deflect his attempt to plunge the blade into my jugular. The sharp blade slid across my forearm, just above my wrist, but with so much adrenaline rocketing through my system, I felt no immediate pain. If not for the blood seeping through the sleeve of my navy nylon raid jacket, I wouldn't have even known I'd been cut. Underneath was my favorite pink silk blouse, a coup of a find on the clearance rack at Neiman Marcus Last Call, now sliced open, the blood-soaked material gaping to reveal a short but deep gash.

My jaw clamped tighter than a chastity belt on a pubescent princess. This jerk was going down.

My block had knocked him to the side. Taking advantage of our relative positioning, I threw a roundhouse kick to Battaglia's stomach, my steel-toed cherry-red Doc Martens sinking into his soft paunch. The shoes were the perfect combination of utility and style, another great find at a two-for-one sale at the Galleria.

The kick didn't take the beer-bellied bastard out of commission, but at least it sent him backwards a few feet, putting a little more distance between us. A look of surprise flashed across Battaglia's face as he stumbled backward. He clearly hadn't expected a skinny, five-foot-two-inch bookish woman to put up such a fierce fight.

Neener-neener.

About the Author

Diane Kelly is a former assistant state attorney general and tax advisor who spent much of her career fighting, or inadvertently working for, white-collar criminals. When she realized her experiences made great fodder for novels, her fingers hit the keyboard and thus began her Death & Taxes white-collar crime series. A proud graduate of her hometown's Citizens Police Academy, Diane is also the author of the Paw Enforcement K-9 series and the Busted motorcycle cop series. Her other series include the House Flipper cozy mystery series. She also writes romance and light contemporary fantasy stories. You can find Diane online at www.dianekelly.com, on her author page on Facebook, and on Twitter and Instagram at @DianeKellyBooks.

Made in the USA
Coppell, TX
30 June 2020

29843775R00184